Reviews for *The Infernal*

'A magical, terrifying story, *The Infernal* will raise the hairs on any die-hard's neck ... A good choice for Poppy Z. Brite fans, or for those hell-bent on scaring the pants off their family and friends ... Read it with the lights on' *Weekend Books*

'A richly bloody fantasy of necromancy, romantic and spiritual possession, sex and murder-most-mutilatory ... A real page-turner' *Sydney Morning Herald*

'Move over Poppy Z. Brite ... Wilkins has produced a book that will make your skin crawl and your hair stand on end' *Herald Sun*

'Has enough witchcraft, murder and erotic obsession to melt the coldest Tim Tam ... Off-beat but sharp barbs ... make it required reading for head-bangers' *The Morning Bulletin*

'Talented Wilkins seems at home in any century' *Australian Women's Forum*

'Horror novels written with intelligence and devotion are rare. *The Infernal* is one of those books ... For me, the pages never stopped turning' *Severed Head*

D0550273

Kim Wilkins was born in London and grew up by the sea north of Brisbane. She wrote her first book in coloured crayon – a five-page illustrated road safety guide – at the age of five, and was asked to read it out at her school assembly. She loved the attention so much that she has been trying to repeat the experience ever since, trading in her coloured crayons along the way.

Kim has worked with equal success as a typist and as a bass player for the noise band, The Vampigs, who broke up before they released their first album. She has obsessions with occult philosophy, Renaissance literature, demonology, mythology, Gothic novels and underground music which inspire her writing. She has a first-class honours degree in English Literature from the University of Queensland, and plans to continue post graduate studies in the UK. She lives in leafy St Lucia with a musician named Mirko and a small black cat named Polly.

The Infernal is her first novel and won the 1997 Aurealis awards for best horror novel and best fantasy novel in Australia.

THE
INFERNAL

Kim Wilkins

ORIEL

First published in Great Britain in 1999 by
Oriel
An imprint of Orion Books Ltd
Orion House, 5 Upper St Martin's Lane,
London WC2H 9EA

A CIP catalogue record for this book
is available from the British Library

ISBN 0 75282 167 9

Printed and bound in Great Britain
by Clays Ltd, St Ives plc

If you would like to write to Kim Wilkins,
her e-mail address is:
Kimwilkins@mailbox.uq.edu.au

More information about Kim and her work
can be found on her website:
http://student.uq.edu/au/~333289/infernal.htm

Dedicated to the memory of Lyall Wilkins,
who would have been impossibly proud.

ACKNOWLEDGEMENTS

First and foremost, my eternal gratitude to Graeme Hague, without whom *et cetera, et cetera*. Thanks to Elaine, Ian, Spinner and the rest of my family—in which company I include the Ruckelses; thanks also to Cousin Em and co.—Kate Morton, Tiffany Patterson, Jo and Heidi; to Selwa and Linda for believing in me; to the friends and cyber-buddies who have endured my mood swings with good grace; to the staff and students of the UQ English Department who were so supportive—especially Lloyd Davis, Elizabeth Moores and the Medieval Snorries; and many blessings to Stella in the stars, to whom I owe so much. Huge sobbing protestations of undying thanks to Janine for reading more of my writing than any human being should ever have to. Finally, for unswerving encouragement, for still calling me 'sweetie' when I am acting like a grumpy moose, and for providing the soundtrack to my life, I owe so much to my partner Mirko, the most beautiful boy in the universe.

Adders and serpents, let me breathe awhile!
Ugly hell gape not! Come not, Lucifer!
I'll burn my books . . .

CHRISTOPHER MARLOWE
Doctor Faustus

PROLOGUE

Perhaps you don't really grow up until you realise that you aren't the only person whose existence counts, until you become aware that others live and breathe outside your circle of perception. It happened to me the day I heard about the first murder.

While I'd been on stage the night before, somebody had been killed in the pine forest outside of town. My imagination tends to work without consent, so the news kick-started a stubborn chain of morbid thoughts in me. I constructed a complete picture of what it would have been like, dying like that, and matched it up with what I had been doing at the time, like my band became the soundtrack for this guy's living nightmare.

More than that, the things I was doing had seemed so important and meaningful at the time, but compared to what he had to go through, we were just a pack of pretentious would-be rock stars, exploiting our negligible middle-class angst as if it were pain. I was kicking my microphone stand over; he was realising that he was about to die: shaking his head, begging, pleading, horrified, stinking of terror. I was surfing the crowd, screaming, having my hair pulled and my clothes tugged by the people underneath me; he was being lashed to a tree and maybe he was screaming too, but I was articulating a more marketable pain, his was pure and real and straight from that place in the soul that we only tap into during the blackest of dreams. And as the crowd slipped around on a thin puddle of beer and an undying teenage sense of being misunderstood, and I trashed my guitar and Brad knocked his rig over and everybody cheered because we were so clever; he was having his chest hacked open and blood and splinters of bone were everywhere and maybe, before his eyes darkened forever, he saw inside himself—and I don't mean in a spiritual sense. When did he give up hope that somehow he could get out of it? That someone would come along and call an ambulance and everything would be all right? That even though this sicko was going to take out a handful of his most vital organs it wasn't really going to change anything?

While I was just doing what I do, he was having the whole world's bad dreams.

And it seems strange to think about that day now, because that's when everything changed forever. Strange that I didn't know.

CHAPTER
ONE

Fridays sucked. I did a double shift on Friday nights back then, and the knowledge that it was a Friday morning seemed to permeate my sleep so that a part of me was sunk even before I opened my eyes.

Being in an underground band was cool, but it didn't pay much. Donning a wig and cabaret dress to croon crappy Celine Dion numbers in a downstairs bar at the Treasury Casino was not cool, but it shouldn't be hard to figure out why I did it. I liked my flat close to the city, I liked being able to eat and buy the occasional CD. I was a slave to economic rationalism as much as the next capitalist pig, so I sold out on Friday nights and Brad and I did a gig as a duo. Back then I thought that one day I might be rich and famous, and somehow the pending BMW and Beluga years cancelled out the public transport and baked beans years.

That morning I thought it was just another rotten Friday, to be endured as Fridays must, but it turned out to be more rotten than most. I rolled over, flicked the radio on and caught the tail end of a Regurgitator song before the news came on. That's when I heard:

'This morning, joggers in a plantation pine forest outside Brisbane found the mutilated body of a man tied to a tree. Police have placed the time of death at around

3

*one a.m. and are appealing for any witnesses. They are
refusing to confirm claims that the victim's heart and
eyes had been removed. The man's name has not yet been
released.'*

Just like that, then it was a story about a dog in
Germany who saved his mistress's life, and the footy
tips for the coming weekend.

At one a.m. I'd been on stage at Fire Fire, which
is where my band, 747, played every Thursday night
on account of the venue manager and my drummer
sharing a predilection for the same drugs. We were
big for a local band, gradually morphing into something smaller in a bigger pond. Brad was the eldest
of us at twenty-seven. He and I had been together in
bands for nine years, ever since I ran away from home
at fifteen to be a rock star and we did a far north
tour together in a B-grade covers band. But we never
fucked, though he wanted to badly. (Okay, we fucked
once, but I was only sixteen and I didn't know any
better. Brad had been waiting for a repeat performance ever since—he had the patience of a saint.) He
and I both played guitar and sang. Ailsa was our
fabulously fat and fucked-up gay bass player, and Jeff,
a stringy-haired creature of the night, was our
deranged drummer. We all got along fine, but it was
a business relationship.

So the four of us had been on stage when this guy
had been killed, and it made me wonder about the
way the universe works, which is something I've
always tended to worry about a great deal more than
is healthy anyway. I've always wanted to believe that
the universe is like a big spider's web that we're all
stuck in, and that when something bad is heading for
us, we might feel the tremors of it gliding up those
flimsy threads, telling us to get out of the way. But
it doesn't work like that. The trouble with a spider's

4

web is that it's too delicate, too easily destroyed by some mindless fuck with a desire to cut your eyes out of your face.

My mind was beginning to reconstruct the scene of the crime right about when the phone rang. I knew it was Karin straightaway because nobody else would dare ring me before noon. She knew I had endless patience with her, especially now: she was getting married the next day and she was brimming over with a self-consciously manic blend of excitement and terror.

'Lisa? It's me.'

'Hi, Karin, I knew it was you. It sounded like your ring.'

'Hmm.' That was one of the things I loved about Karin, the way she said 'Hmm' when she thought I was being completely unfunny or when I proposed something stupid, which was quite often. I could get along with anybody, but I was really a one-friend woman, and Karin was the friend. I hadn't always been a wild child, and Karin and I had grown up playing house together. Brad, though he liked Karin, could never figure out why we were so close. It was obvious to anybody that we were hugely different. Maybe we each made up for a lack in the other— Karin lived vicariously through my exploits, while I centred myself on her stability. She was a real sweetie, impossible not to love. I was jealous as hell that she was getting married. I wanted her all to myself for the rest of my life, but some twenty-four year old virgins do eventually find themselves forty-two year old accountants, and there's not much that possessive best friends can do about it.

'What's up?' I asked, because something had to be up—she wouldn't just ring for a chat. The responsibility of leading a topicless conversation made her profoundly uncomfortable.

'One guess. Somebody's giving me a hard time.'

'Now who could that be?'

The sarcasm was lost on her. 'Lisa, you know who I mean.'

Of course I did—Karin's mother was notorious—but I waited silently because it seemed it always fell to me to call Dana a witch.

'Okay,' Karin said finally, 'it's my mother. She's outdone herself.'

Briefly, just briefly and very guiltily, I thought to myself, 'Here we go, Karin is going to whinge about her psycho mother, and some poor guy got hacked up in the pine forest last night,' but then I squashed it because Karin had led a cardboard cutout life right up until the time she met David, and if past history was anything to go on, this would be about the most exciting thing that would ever happen to her. Her mother, Dana, had been the worst kind of totalitarian parent imaginable, literally locking Karin in her room during her teenage years to prevent her 'getting into trouble' with some boy. Needless to say, I wasn't Dana's favourite person, but I'd always been around with a cheerful obstinacy, knowing that one day Karin had to grow up and leave home. I just hadn't expected her to do it in the company of a boring old guy.

'What has she done this time?'

Next thing I had a blubbering mess on the other end of the phone as Karin sniffed and snuffled and choked on a few words that sounded like 'Germany', 'plane fare' and 'relatives'. I gathered that Dana had pulled out that hoary old chestnut, 'I brought you here from Germany to have a better life and I left my friends and family behind,' mixed in with, 'David has enough money to fly them out here but he hasn't even

6

offered', and she'd probably included a few 'ungrateful' and 'selfishes' too. If it was me, I would have ignored the old vulture, but it wasn't me, and twenty-four years of brainwashing are not subverted in the space of a six-week engagement.

I made comforting noises into the phone. Karin apologised at least a dozen times, and I just let her. I didn't get mad at Karin for her ultrasensitivity, I loved her too well. I want to stress that. Sometimes I feel as though I don't really know her now, and we certainly aren't as close. Too much has happened.

But I'm getting ahead of myself.

When I got off the phone fifteen minutes later, she had brightened up considerably. I didn't tell her about the body in the forest, and it bothered me that I had almost forgotten about it myself by the time I hung up. Maybe we indulge in mundane problems as a self-defence mechanism, so we don't all die screaming from the horror of the world.

That night I sussed Brad out about what he thought of the murder. He always had an interesting, if a little shallow, take on these things. We were getting into the car at the Treasury's loading bay, heading for the real gig at the Universal Theatre, an old 1920s picture theatre that had been converted into a 1990s seedy bar. I hated the way that murder and death close to home carried so much more weight than murder and death on the other side of the world, and I hated that murder and death were exciting things to talk about, but I brought it up anyway. You can't fight years of conditioning.

'Did you hear about that guy that was killed in the forest?'

'Yeah, grisly.'

'Doesn't it spin you out?'

'What, that it happened so close by?' We pulled into the street.

'Yes, that and . . . you know, that something like that could happen to somebody without any warning.'

Brad sniffed. 'We don't know anything about it really. Maybe the dead guy was involved in one of those weirdo cults, maybe he was a drug lord, maybe he would have done it to some twelve-year-old girl if somebody hadn't done it to him first.'

I hadn't thought about it in those terms. I watched the people crossing at the lights in front of us. A tall woman in an elegant evening gown was accompanying an obviously drunk man across the road. When they got to the other side, he threw up all over her. Brad laughed.

'So,' I said, changing the subject, 'have Numb Records called us back yet?'

'If they had, I would have told you,' he said, mildly annoyed. It had been my standard conversation opener for nearly two months.

'It's not going to happen, I just know it,' I said, slumping in my seat.

'Hang in there, Lisa. We're closer than we've ever been.'

I was so jaded by it all. Numb Records had written and asked us for a sample of our stuff after hearing that we sold a thousand CDs independently. That was seven weeks ago, and we were still waiting for an answer.

We parked in a gravel car park about a block from the Universal and walked to the gig. It was February, the dying subtropical summer was warm and close and the buildings of the city rose cool and tall around us. Brad pulled his jacket off and tied it around his waist. A couple of guys walking towards us called out

'Hey, 747,' before going on their way, smoking and laughing.

The blast of airconditioning at the Universal hit me in the face just before the cloud of cigarette smoke crawled into my lungs, hair, eyes and clothes. It momentarily took my breath away. A couple of girls at the bar waved to me and I waved back, but I didn't know who they were. Brad sidled up to one of them and said something in her ear. I walked down to the front of the room by myself. Angie, our sound guy, put a hand out to help me up onto the stage.

'Where's Brad?' he asked.

'Chatting up a charming young lady by the bar. Why?'

'There's a problem with his rig. What did he do to it last night?'

'Nothing unusual. He kicked it over during the last song but it was working fine in the encore.'

'I'd better go talk to him.' Angie jumped off the stage and lurched into the crowd. One of his legs was shorter than the other, so he always walked crooked.

I watched him go, then noticed a group of people gathered to the left of the stage, all dressed in black and holding black candles. Maybe if we were a neo-Gothic band it wouldn't have struck me as strange, but we weren't so it did. They were regulars, or frequent flyers as we called them. Ailsa grabbed me by the arm.

'Lisa, you'd better come backstage.'

'What's going on? What's with the goth squad down the front?' I asked, but Ailsa just pulled me gently past the heavy, dusty curtains to the backstage room where a harsh yellow light illuminated every squalid corner stuffed with cigarette butts and reeking with the stale smell of beer and piss.

Jeff nearly jumped on top of me in his excitement.

'Oh fuck, Lisa. You'll never guess, you'll never never never guess.'

I was used to Jeff's unnaturally up moods, but tonight he was bursting with enthusiasm; his eyes were bright as buttons and he wore a gleefully perverted smile.

Ailsa jabbed him in the ribs. 'It's nothing to be happy about, you cockhead.'

'What? Put me out of my misery,' I said, not bothering to hide my frustration. Brad came in behind me.

'The guy, the guy that got cut up in the pine forest,' Jeff said, pointing in the direction of the stage. His hands were abnormally large, and his long fingers always looked like skinny sausages. 'He was one of them. He was their friend, the ones in black. He was one of our fans.'

I opened my mouth to speak, but nothing would come out.

Brad said, 'Are you for real?'

Ailsa cut in. 'Yes, it's true. His name was Simon. You know, the redhead guy who was always in the Sonic Youth T-shirt.'

'The one with the dreadlocks?' Brad asked.

'Yeah, him.'

The whole shape of reality had changed, my body included. It was like the pit of my stomach was now somewhere around my knees. I think I said 'Fuck' a number of times. I tried to remember what he looked like but I only had a vague notion of his hair and his T-shirt, thanks to Ailsa, and not much else. I didn't take a great deal of notice of the people who came to see us. When the band first started out I tried to remember the names of every frequent flyer, but now there were too many.

'I'd better go talk to them,' Brad said. I looked up

at him, and he had strained lines around his mouth. In that perfectly cruel light, I suddenly became aware that he was now nine years older than the mental picture I always carried of him from that first day when I auditioned for his band. Now he looked like a grown-up. Especially now.

'I'll come with you,' I offered. We started out together, then Brad got sidetracked by Angie who was trying to fix his speaker cabinet, so I approached the group in black alone. I sat down on the edge of the stage and started to smile, then decided it wasn't the right thing to do and just said 'Hi' instead.

One of them, a girl of about nineteen who was obviously off her skull, put her hand on my knee and sobbed, just once but really, really loud. It was such an unexpected sound that I can still hear it now, echoing in my ears.

'I'm so sorry about Simon,' I said.

'He was supposed to meet us at Fire Fire,' said one guy, whose name I thought was Robert or maybe Rodney.

'Yeah,' said the girl, 'he rang me at nine-thirty and said "See you at 747," and that's the last we heard of him. He must have got . . . picked up on the way.'

Christ, he was on his way to see us.

'Do the police know who did it?' I asked.

'No,' said Robert or Rodney. 'We've all been up at the station today, giving statements. Somebody cut his eyes out, Lisa, and his heart. But they weren't anywhere around the body. Whoever did it took them with him.'

I wanted to scream or throw up or cry or something. 'I don't know what to say. I'm just so, so sorry.' But I was thinking, 'Why have they come out tonight? Why aren't they home in mourning?' I guess there's no fashion accessory like a dead friend.

11

'His favourite song was "Treehouse", can you dedicate it to him tonight?' the girl said.

At that point I didn't think I could go on stage at all, let alone play and sing, but I said I would anyway, then went backstage to tell the others. He had been on his way to see us.

I tried to convince the band that we should cancel but they all looked at me as though I was out of my mind, which I quite probably was at that stage. It was impossible to get into it that night and every time I felt myself slipping into my normal stage persona, the mourners would catch my eye and I'd be undone. They stood there all night, getting squashed by the smoky, sweaty crowd, but not moving, just looking up at us, their pale make-up melting in streaks into their skin. I dedicated Simon's favourite song to him, acutely aware that I wasn't really sure which one Simon was.

And that night I had The Dream. I don't know quite when The Dream had gained capital letter status. Probably about the third or fourth time I'd had it.

It took me a long time to get to sleep because my brain wouldn't turn off. Strangely, I wasn't thinking of Simon. I was thinking of anything but Simon, probably on purpose. A picture of Brad's face kept coming back to me. That line just to the side of his mouth, the realisation that he was getting older, that we were all getting older. Here was my best friend getting married like a grown-up, and me still playing rock star like a little girl. Part of me was defiant, part of me felt like the rest of the world would laugh at me, tell me to get a job and a husband. I eventually drifted off, in the early hours of the morning when the world is darkest and coldest.

Somewhere out of the dark peace of sleep, a picture started to form, and I was standing in it, but I wasn't me. I was somebody else, with a taller, thinner body and dark hair which flowed over my shoulders and onto the front of my dress. The dress was like nothing I'd ever owned or worn; it was stiff and constricting around the middle, and it fell all the way to the ground where it was getting soaked with dew. Before I had a chance to have a good look at it, I realised that there was blood all over it. That it wasn't a purple dress at all, but a blue one soaked with blood. The closer I looked, the more detail I saw. The dress was sticking to my breasts, it was so wet. I looked at my hands and they were covered in streaky gore. Then I became aware of the metallic smell of it. I could even taste it faintly in my mouth because it was in my hair and the wind was whipping the hair into my face. There was a damp, fecund smell around me, like a pile of garden rubbish after rain, and I realised that I was in a forest or a deep garden somewhere. Beside me somebody was wailing, crying so loud that she was almost screaming. The muscles in my arms were tired because I was pushing something like a wheelbarrow, and the wheel was squeaking. Squeaking over and over. My breath was harsh and laboured.

I wished she would stop it, I wished she would just stop crying because it was too late, too late. He was already dead. There he was, in the cart, with the red stain spreading over his clothes. I was filled with a sickening sense of approaching doom, and I was thinking about death, wondering what it sounded like, smelled like. Conscious that I would only hear or smell it once. The wheel squeaked over and over. I timed my footsteps to it. My breathing. Her sobs, her wails. I felt unbearably pressured, as though something inside me would explode. I tried to open my

13

mouth to scream at her, or just to scream, but my jaws were locked together, my teeth crushing against each other. I was forming a word that started with a laboured, guttural sound.

This was where I always woke up, the wheel still squeaking in my ears.

A recurring dream is always creepy, but it was twice as creepy that night after I had just found out one of our fans had been murdered by a sicko in a pine forest. I became dizzy with the reminder of my own mortality. I had to turn on the light to convince myself that the world was normal and I was in it, at least for the time being.

I got up and looked around my flat, scanning for reassuring detail. Messy. A dusty desk where my computer stood, swamped in books and magazines. Three empty mugs in different places. A sofa heaving under the weight of two weeks' worth of laundry that needed to be put away. A tiny kitchen where I now headed and, almost automatically, switched on the electric jug. Christ, I wished I would stop having that dream.

I made myself a cup of chamomile tea, slid open the door to my tiny patio and settled on the deckchair. Over the next-door neighbour's roof I could see the lights of the city, the river moving and the world breathing. I tried to breathe with it.

CHAPTER
TWO

The taxi dropped me off outside a two-storey house with immaculate gardens and pink flowers climbing up to the windows, a view over the river to die for, and a double garage that housed a brand new Japanese sports car. And all this came from adding up people's books. I was in the wrong business.

I stood outside David's house at two-fifteen p.m. Upstairs somewhere Karin was putting on a frothy white dress and preparing to link herself, till divorce did them part, to a boring accountant. Sure he had the house, the car, the ready cash, but boredom was worse than death to me. Karin was welcome to him.

My boots crunched on the gravel driveway as I made my way to the front entrance. I was wearing Doc Martens and a long floral dress. I knew Karin wouldn't mind that I wasn't formal, but her mother would. One of my chief joys in life was to annoy Dana Anders, and today would be no different. I'd even managed to show off the tattoo on my left arm to good advantage, although, truth be told, I hated the damn thing almost as much as Dana did. That's why girls shouldn't run away from home to join rock bands at fifteen. They end up scarred for life. Literally.

I hit the doorbell and waited. David opened the door and invited me in.

'Lisa. How are you?' He moved forward as if he thought he should offer me a hug or something equally intimate, then pulled back at the last moment, creating an uncomfortable space between us.

'Fine. All ready for the big event?' The banality tripped off my tongue, but for the life of me I couldn't work up an interesting comment around this guy. It was as though his dullness was contagious.

'Yes, yes. We're all ready. Karin's very excited.' He was exceptionally well spoken, which made him sound a bit toffy.

'I know, she was excited when I spoke to her yesterday.' Silence prevailed, still coloured by that queasy space he'd created between us.

'Well,' he said, 'go on up. It's the first door on your left at the top of the stairs. I won't come with you. Bad luck to see the bride and all that.'

'Sure, sure. Thanks. I'll see you . . .'

'Yes, outside. At the . . . um . . . service. I'll see you then.'

I left him there and went up the stairs. Everything was carpeted in cream. The paint smelled new and I remembered Karin telling me that David had had the place renovated when he'd first moved here, which I guess was only six weeks ago because that's when he'd met Karin and they'd fallen in love and done one of those whirlwind courtship things.

I knocked gently on the door to her room, and she called out, 'Who is it?'

'It's me.'

'Lisa?'

'No, Hermann Goering.'

'Not funny. Come in.'

She looked so pale. She was pale anyway, but the added combination of a white dress and a good dose of fright had made her positively ashen.

16

'Are you okay?' I asked, walking over and grabbing her hand.

'Yes, yes. I'm nervous as anything. I see you've got old blackie on show.'

That's what she called my tattoo. I hadn't gone for a delicate, girly butterfly, much to my eternal regret, but a band of celtic design looping around my upper arm in black ink. Brad had a matching one on his right arm. I was still mad at him for convincing me to do it, because he was older and should have known better.

'Yeah, thought I'd give Dana one last tweak before I never see her again.'

'I'll still have to see her,' Karin replied, going to the window and looking down into the garden. 'She's not here yet, thank God.'

'Has it been really bad?'

'You have no idea. She hasn't let up on me in a week. I wanted to come and stay at David's but he's been so traditional about it all. Besides, it would have been the final insult to my mother if I'd worn a white dress on my wedding day without a right to. She thinks it's bad enough that we're not getting married in a church.'

'She doesn't even go to church,' I replied, joining her at the window.

'Don't ask me to explain. She comes up with some of the strangest ideas.' She turned to face me. 'Thanks for coming.'

'As if I wouldn't. Are you sure you want to do this?'

'Don't you start.'

'I was just checking.'

'Of course I'm sure I want to do this. God, what else have I ever had or ever done?' She flopped down

17

onto the bed, her skirts puffing and frothing around her.

'I'm sorry, I was just asking. I didn't mean anything by it.'

'You're lucky, Lisa. You've had an interesting life. You ran away from home, you play in a band and you get to travel all over the place and you're probably going to be famous one day. I left school and now I do people's fingernails. I've been doing people's fingernails for seven years. After I get married, I'll probably still be doing people's fingernails. I'd never done anything spontaneous or romantic until I met David.'

'That's what I'm afraid of. That you're only doing this to rebel.'

She shook her head. 'Don't underestimate the depth of my feelings, Lisa. I really have fallen in love.'

'Well then, you've done something I haven't.' I hated that she had said that to me, because perhaps I *had* underestimated the depth of her feelings.

'I'm so nervous,' she said, grabbing my hand in her cold fingers.

'Don't worry, I'll be there.'

'You won't be there when the thing I'm most nervous about happens.'

'I did warn you to try before you buy.'

'God, I stayed a virgin this long, six weeks didn't seem too long to wait.' She looked into her lap and a flush of shyness lit up her otherwise pale face. 'Can you give me any tips?'

'Sure. Men love it when you don't wash.'

'Come on, be serious.'

I ran my hand through my hair, no more comfortable with the subject than she was. 'I don't know. He's older, he's probably a lot more traditional than any of the guys I've fucked.'

18

'He's not that old.'

'He's a million and one to me, Karin.'

'He's got a great body.'

'When did you see it?'

'I've seen him without his shirt on. He hasn't got a spare inch on him. Not like Brad with his beer gut.'

'Brad has not got a beer gut.'

'Have another look. Tuesday, when we were both at your place, I noticed he's getting a little squishy round the middle.'

Great. Brad had a beer gut as well as wrinkles. Maybe David wasn't a million and one after all, and maybe if I was going to get together with Brad I shouldn't put it off too much longer.

'Okay,' I said, 'just be enthusiastic, and don't be afraid to ask for what you like.'

She giggled. 'I can't imagine doing that.'

'Oh, you don't have to be specific. Just your "higher", "harder", "slower" stuff will do.'

'Higher, harder, slower,' she repeated, then burst out laughing.

There was a sharp knock, then a familiar needling tone faintly overlaid with the remnants of an accent reached us through the door.

'Are you going to come out and get married or what?' Dana said.

Karin's face fell. 'Oh God, oh God. I wish she'd leave me alone.'

'I'll take care of her. You take five minutes, breathe deep and think happy thoughts. I'll get her down to the garden. Just think, next time you speak to me you'll be married.'

'I think I'm going to be sick.'

I gave her a quick squeeze. 'Don't sweat it. Tomorrow morning you'll wake up in a house without Dana. You're being freed after twenty-four years. Rejoice.'

19

I left her sitting on the bed looking pensive, and greeted Dana outside the door.

'Mrs Anders, how are you?'

'Fine. Is she coming or what?'

'Yes, she's just gathering her thoughts. Let's get down to the garden.' I started down the stairs with Dana next to me.

'I suppose you're happy about all this,' she said. 'You won't have to see me any more when you visit Karin. I don't suppose I'll see *her* either; she's walked out on me after all I've done for her.'

'Mrs Anders, it's her wedding day for Christ's sake. Can't you be happy for her?'

She turned on me and held her index finger in front of my face. 'Happy for her? I brought her out here from Germany when she was four years old because I wanted her to have a better life. Her father was a boozer and a gambler, and I wanted to get her away from his influence. So I left my own family and my own friends behind. But I did it for her. This is the thanks I get. Six weeks' warning and then she deserts me without a single care for how I feel or what I'm going to do now.'

This was the point where I was supposed to say, 'With all due respect, Mrs Anders', but I was very conscious that this was probably the last time I would see the snaggle-toothed old crone. So I said: 'You're a fucking psycho. It's your personality that drives people away, not their selfishness. You probably turned Karin's poor father into a boozer. He was probably a fucking Jesuit priest before you got hold of him.'

'You little tramp,' she hissed back. 'You and your disgusting tattoo like a whore, and your filthy band, and showing your body off on stage. I know what you do.' She stormed off ahead of me, and I didn't go after her because I'd had my fun, though I would have liked to have heard what she thought I did on stage.

Dana and I hadn't always been archenemies. I can still remember her bringing Karin and me cordial and Tim Tams while we played, and at one stage I even liked her better than my own mother because she was blonde and pretty like a lady off the television. But something had happened right about when Karin had started high school and begun developing a personality of her own. Dana had disintegrated into a possessive vampire. Maybe she was afraid of being alone, I don't know. It was probably far more complex than that, and I hated her too much to be bothered with the psychology of it.

I followed Dana out to the garden and watched her take a seat at the front, pulling a tissue out of her handbag to dry her eyes. I must have come pretty close to the mark. Maybe Karin's father was a Jesuit priest. Not that Karin would know, Dana had steadfastly refused to tell her anything about him.

I sat at the back to put a good distance between Dana and me. I could still see the back of her head, her snow white hair looked like a halo with the sun shining on it. Ironic.

Shortly, somebody hit the 'play' button on a tape deck set up under the marquee and some churchy wedding-type music came on. Karin appeared from the house behind me and walked down to the front where David was standing. There was nobody to give her away. She hadn't wanted to ask Dana, and if she'd asked anybody else, Dana would probably have hanged herself to be the ultimate martyr.

The ceremony got under way, presided over by a fat lady in a shiny green dress. I was thinking up a song in my head, staring off into space. It was pretty cool, my fingers were twitching around as I felt in my lap for which strings, which frets would work best. I could hear a fly buzzing around me. The wedding seemed a very long way away, like looking through the wrong end of binoculars. The sky was so big and blue that day, a perfect day for a wedding, if you're into that kind of thing.

I think the celebrant was getting towards the vows when there was a commotion down the front. There was a gagging, choking noise, and when I glanced up I realised that Dana's blonde head wasn't where it should have been. People were standing up and moving towards the front, and Karin and David had turned around to see what was going on. I heard Karin scream, 'Mum!' and I realised what had happened. Dana was going out in grand style as the mother of the bride. I jumped up and went to the front of the crowd, and there she was, writhing on the ground, clutching her chest and making a sick, gagging sound.

Karin's boss from Becky's Beauty Bar was there, kneeling over Dana and calling, 'Get an ambulance, get an ambulance!' but I knew that would be pointless—she was obviously faking it.

'I don't need an ambulance!' Dana shrieked, sitting up and pounding her fists on her lap, 'I need a heart transplant, to replace the one she's ripped out of me.' Her face was red and puffy and she cried and cried into her clenched fists, just like a kid throwing a tantrum.

Karin burst into tears and started to sob: 'Mother, how could you? How could you?' David had his arm around her, trying to soothe her.

Becky helped Dana to her feet and led her toward the house. She was a sad shambling wreck. Now Karin had turned to David and was saying, 'How could she?'

over and over. I felt sick for her. Her one day to feel special and her mother had ruined it. I wondered guiltily how much my argument with Dana had contributed to her tantrum, then decided that she'd probably been planning it for the past six weeks.

People started to sit down again. I tried to catch Karin's eye to give her a reassuring smile, but David was turning her to the celebrant. He motioned for the woman in green to continue. I sat down and realised the song in my head had gone.

I felt bad leaving before the reception but I had a sound check to get to. I went up to Karin after the photographer had finished with her and put my arms around her, pulling her close. She rested her face on my shoulder for a moment. She was so thin, like a little bird.

'Where's your mother?'

'Becky took her home. She ruined everything, Lisa.'

'You're married, aren't you? She didn't stop you doing that.'

'I'm chained to her until the day she dies. That's if she does die. She'll probably hang on forever just to spite me.'

'Nonsense. You have no obligation to see her. You can ignore her if you want.'

'Lisa, she doesn't have anyone else.'

Obviously the twenty-four years of conditioning had been effective. I patted her shoulder. 'Sorry I can't stay.'

'No, that's fine. I know it's not your scene, but I'm quite enjoying it, being the centre of attention.'

'I thought maybe the whole party could come on down to the Black Flag and see the band after dinner.'

'Hmm. Perhaps not.'

I kissed her goodbye, then found David and shook his hand. I wanted to say more to him than just 'Congratulations'. I wanted to tell him how important it was that he gave Karin all the chances to grow that her mother had taken away from her, but I couldn't. He was too ordinary; it would have embarrassed us both.

Monday morning found me hitting the redial button on my phone thirty-eight times. There was a dream interpreter on the radio every week and I was determined to get through to her. Finally somebody answered the phone, asked me my name and told me to hold. They played the radio to me over the phone so I could hear what was going on. One guy was going into excruciating detail about a dream he had that went for hours. It was all joined together by 'and suddenly I was in', and jumped from scene to scene like an Australian soap opera. I wished he would shut up so that they would put me on. My heart was beating really hard.

I must have been on hold for half an hour before they finally got to me. The radio announcer said, 'Lisa, are you there?'

'Yeah, hi.'

'Tell us about your dream, Lisa,' said the dream interpreter.

'Okay. Well, I'm in a weird old-fashioned dress, and I know I'm me but I don't look like me. I'm all covered in blood and I'm pushing this thing like a wheelbarrow and there's a dead man in it. I'm going through this forest and there's some other girl with me, but she keeps crying and she doesn't shut up. I get really tense, like my head's going to pop off, and the wheel on the wheelbarrow squeaks and squeaks. It's really scary because I've had it about nine times, and it's so realistic it doesn't ever feel like I'm dreaming.' I was a bit concerned about the tiny note of desperation that had crawled into my voice. Perhaps I'd been ignoring the stupid dream for too long.

'God, Lisa, that's quite a dream. Nine times you say?'

'Yeah, since the beginning of the year.'

'Nine times in eight weeks? I think the universe is definitely trying to tell you something.'

'Like what?'

'I'd say it's a past-life memory. I think something happened to you in a past life and for some reason it's becoming important to you now.'

'You mean I actually did this in a past life?'

'Maybe, but not necessarily. It might be symbolic of something else. All that blood, you know. It might symbolise the dead man's life energy. I think you need to look around in your life now, at where you might be taking somebody's life energy, where you may be draining somebody. It's probably somebody you knew in this past life.'

Well, that didn't make any sense, but I wasn't about to tell her that on national radio. 'Okay,' I said, 'thanks.'

'You're welcome, Lisa. As I said, it's definitely linked to a past life. Perhaps you should explore that idea further. There are plenty of places where you can get past-life therapy.'

They switched me off and moved on to the next person. I put the phone down and realised I'd forgotten to plug the band. Brad would kill me if he ever found out.

I had actually already considered the past-life memory idea. I generally believed in nothing—the cold hard light of cynicism seemed infinitely more intelligent than risking my pride in some embarrassingly self-justifying leap of faith. However, reincarnation was a very appealing solution to an otherwise incomprehensible problem. What happens when we pass out of this existence? Is there something of us left over? Is death the end or just one stop on a continuum? I could remember all those times during my childhood when I would start to drift off to sleep then suddenly be struck by a thought that seemed terribly important, but as soon as I started to concentrate on it, it would slip down that dark corridor where thoughts never come back from and all I could remember was the sense that somehow, in this other thought, I hadn't been me, but somebody else, in another place and time. So maybe I could accept the reincarnation idea, just maybe. But it still left me wondering what to do next.

I remembered a coffee shop in town that had a sign out the front advertising tarot cards and past-life readings, and as the 485 bus down town was leaving in just under ten minutes, I grabbed my backpack and locked up. I knew if I had time to think about it I would realise it was completely stupid and not go.

Unfortunately for business, the coffee shop was on a major intersection. The sound of buses accelerating past and the continual pumping of car fumes through the front door made it less desirable to the cosmopolitan cafe culture set. When I arrived, there were only two people sipping coffee in a corner, no doubt discussing some French film they hadn't quite understood. I went up to the counter, where a handsome young man, probably a student or an actor earning some extra income, wiped his hands on his apron and greeted me with a sexy smile.

'Hi, what would you like?' he asked, almost suggestively. Maybe I was imagining the suggestive part.

'Hi. I actually want a past-life reading.'

'Oh. Hang on, I'll just buzz Laura.' He turned his back to me and picked up the phone; I waited, watching the traffic go by outside.

'She'll be out in a moment,' the young man said, turning back to me. 'Do you want a coffee while you wait?'

I'd just as soon drink rat poison as coffee, so I declined and took a seat. Shortly Laura emerged through some swinging bead doors behind the counter and I was immediately struck by her ordinariness. I'd thought a person who styled themselves as a psychic counsellor would somehow appeal to my sixth sense. She was plain, middle aged, plump, going grey and wearing a truly ugly blue suit and purple scarf. If I'd run away then, I would have saved myself fifteen bucks.

She took me through the bead doors and out through the kitchen into a tiny white room hung with dozens of dolphin pictures and pyramid pictures, and some pictures with both dolphins *and* pyramids. I decided right then that I wasn't going to tell her about my dream and give her a lead in. If she was genuine, she'd know.

'So,' she said, 'I'm Laura.'

'I'm Lisa,' I said as she sat me down at a card table. 'I want a past-life reading.'

'So Adrian said. Any particular reason?'

Ha, she was already trying to pump me for information. 'No.'

She waited a few beats, as if the silence might make me give up more than I intended. There was some crappy New Age music playing, something that a loser with too much midi equipment and no originality had put together. I was having a bad experience already.

'Well, I can see you in a long dress, Lisa,' she said out of nowhere.

I started. Was she really going to be able to tell me?

'Surrounded by books. It's the nineteenth century and you live in an old parsonage in England.'

This was getting interesting, but I was almost sure that the dress I was wearing in my dream was not Victorian. I wasn't great with history, but I thought she was out by a couple of hundred years.

'I see you writing. You have such patience.'

She kept building the picture and I listened, but didn't feel any inner point of contact with her or with what she was saying. Finally, she screwed her eyes shut and said, 'I'm coming up with a name . . .'

The suspense was killing me, not.

'Jane Eyre,' she proclaimed triumphantly, looking me in the eye.

'Are you sure you don't mean Charlotte Brontë?' I asked.

She smiled as if indulging a child. 'Lisa, we can't be who we *want* to be. I'm sure many people would be excited to find that they were a famous writer like Jane Eyre.'

I didn't know whether to tell her or not.

'I bet you love books even today,' she said. 'Am I right?'

Maybe I looked like a student and that was why she said it. I was scruffy and badly dressed and had messy long hair the brassy shade of burgundy you can only get from mixing a number of cheap dyes.

'Yeah, yeah. I love books. I've read all her books,' I said, then added, 'we read them at uni.'

She clicked her fingers. 'I knew you were a student,' she said, genuinely happy with herself that she was such a good judge of character. 'I think perhaps you should take up writing again.'

'Thanks for the advice. How much do I owe you?'

'Fifteen dollars.'

I winced as I paid her, but told myself I deserved to lose the money for doing something so pointless with somebody so ordinary.

'Bye, Jane,' she said as I left. She was on another planet.

'How did it go?' said Adrian, the cute actor/student/coffee shop attendant.

'She's full of shit,' I said. He laughed. I guessed he already knew.

Around three the next morning I made a cup of lemon tea, sat down at my desk and booted up the computer. It was the best time to surf the net, when my server wasn't clogged up with weirdos playing multi-user Dungeons and Dragons. I flicked from screen to screen, looking for a New Age or natural therapies site. The closest I found was a psychic experience bulletin board, choked with endless pages of near death experiences. I posted a request for help in exploring a past life that I had been dreaming about, left my e-mail address and signed off 'yours desperately, Lisa'.

Brad had a key to my flat, and I had a key to Brad's flat. It was just a convenience thing—we seemed to spend so much time in one place or the other, picking up CDs or various musical instruments. I wasn't surprised when he woke me the next morning by jumping on my bed.

'What time is it?' I said, trying to open my eyes.

'Ten o'clock.'

'Let me go back to sleep. I got to bed around four.'

'Too much exciting news. I can't possibly go home now.'

'Go make me a cup of tea then. Mint. It's in a green box on the bench next to the microwave.'

He went out to the kitchen. 'Christ, I don't know why you drink the stuff.'

'It's good for my nervous system,' I replied, yawning and dragging myself out of bed. I pulled on a T-shirt and a pair of shorts, went to the kitchen and sat down. Brad had brought the newspaper around and dumped it in the centre of the kitchen table. I pushed it aside and put my head down.

Brad put a cup of mint tea in front of me. 'Do you want to hear the news?'

I looked up and peered at his waist. 'Come here,' I said, pulling him towards me. I hoisted up his T-shirt and it seemed Karin was right. He was starting to get a serious set of love handles. 'Do you ever do any exercise, Brad?' I asked, poking him in the soft part of his stomach.

'That's a waste of good drinking time,' he said, pulling away and sitting down across from me.

'You could come to the gym with me.'

'Numb Records called this morning.'

'What?' That woke me up.

'Selena somebody or other, her name was. Not the guy that originally asked for our tape. He left a couple of weeks ago.'

'And? And?'

'They said they haven't forgotten us. They're just looking at their budget and deciding whether or not to finance an EP. They're only talking about it at the moment, but if they do, they'll do the distribution and everything. It'll be a proper national release.'

'Man, that is fantastic. Do you think they will?'

'She sounded really positive but, you know, let's be calm. It's a long way to fall if they decide not to.'

For once, just once, I let myself be hopeful.

'Anyway,' he said, 'there's more news. We're famous today.'

'How?'

He pushed the newspaper towards me. 'Check page seven.'

My sleep-addled brain didn't quite know what was going on, but I turned to page seven anyway. There was a large photograph of a young man who looked familiar, but before I could figure out who it was, my eye was caught by a picture of us, 747, in inset. It was a crappy amateur live shot.

'Christ! What's this about?' I mumbled, then I read the headline. DEAD MAN LOVED HIS MUSIC, SAYS MUM. I looked to the caption under the man's picture. *Victim Simon Trussworth at his nineteenth birthday party, just one week before the slaying.*

'Oh, no,' I said. The caption under our picture read, *747: victim's favourite band.* 'Great, just great, "victim's favourite band". Why couldn't we be Princess Diana's favourite band or something.'

'It's free publicity.'

'It's fucking horrible.' I scanned the article briefly. It was an emotional piece about Simon's distraught single mother. Between the comments like, 'Simon was a bit of a hell-raiser, but he was a good boy' and 'I think he experimented with drugs, but he was very smart and knew when to stop', was the invisible journalistic inference that somehow Simon's lifestyle had invited the murder. Every straight person who read it could feel safe that it wouldn't happen to them. Life could go on.

'Do you want to come out to McDonald's for breakfast?' Brad asked. 'Like a celebration.'

'Celebration?' I was appalled.

'You know, about the record company.'

'Oh,' I said. 'No, I think I'll go back to bed. Can I keep this?'

'Sure. I'll steal another one from McDonald's. Are you feeling okay?'

I shook my head. 'I don't really know how I feel. Come back this afternoon and ask me again.'

After Brad left I cut out the article and pinned it to my corkboard among the other yellowed press clippings about the band. I took a good long look at Simon's face and, yes, I could remember him vaguely, which was some comfort. I promised myself that I would never forget him, but I did just as soon as I got back into bed and closed my eyes.

CHAPTER
THREE

By Wednesday, the need to figure out my dream was becoming less urgent, and I flipped through the yellow pages under 'Hypnotists' only half-heartedly. I'd already done fifteen bucks, another ninety would break me. I knew if I went along and forked out the money, I'd just be told that I needed a couple of sessions before I got anywhere. Besides, my head was too full of imagining myself as a rock star to be overly concerned about The Dream. I expected the phone to ring any second and Brad to tell me that Numb had signed us. Of course, getting signed and becoming a rock star were two very different things, but one was a necessary pre-condition for the other. And I was allowed to daydream.

747 had a web page from which people could e-mail us and tell us they loved us or that we sucked or just leave their addresses so that I could send them our tacky newsletters and free tickets to some gigs. I put the phone book away and decided to get on with checking my e-mail for the week.

747 go off.
You guys try to sound like the Pixies and fail miserably. Give up while you are still ahead.
Fuck that horneeee singer.

> *Could you please send a signed copy of your CD to my friend in America? She knows somebody who . . .*

I cursored through the list, barely glancing at the predictably boring messages. Then I came across a long message from someone who called herself Whitewitch. She was replying to my request for help in exploring a past life. There were meditations and spells, she said, and she could work with me on them if I was willing. She sounded like a fruit loop to me, but at least she didn't propose to charge me anything. I typed in a reply, told her I was willing to try anything that didn't involve mind-altering drugs or a pact with Satan, and signed off.

There was a quiet knock at the door and then Brad let himself in. I quickly sent the message and cleared the screen. I didn't want him to know what I was up to because he'd laugh his fucking head off.

'Here,' he said, handing me a postcard. 'It was in your mail box. It's from Karin.'

'Don't read my mail,' I said, taking the postcard from him. 'Do you want to go make yourself a drink?' I motioned him away and he disappeared into the kitchen.

I flipped the postcard over:

> *I'm having a good time but looking forward to coming home. I'll be back on the eighteenth, so keep that day free to join me for a coffee, or one of your revolting health shakes. So much to tell you. New Zealand is great, but I didn't go skiing. Chickened out. Can't wait to see you. Karin.*

Brad had returned and stood beside me drinking orange juice. 'Is she having fun?' he asked.

I passed him the postcard. 'Tell me what you

think. Does it sound like she's counting down the days till her honeymoon is over?'

Brad quickly scanned the postcard. 'That might be your imagination, Lisa.'

'I'm so worried that she's done the wrong thing.'

'It's got nothing to do with you.'

I turned on him. 'Yes it has, she's my best friend.'

'Hey, you were the one who told me to tell you it's got nothing to do with you, remember?' he replied defensively. 'The week before the wedding you said that I was to remind you of it constantly.'

'Oh, yeah,' I said. 'Sorry. Anyway, you didn't come here to deliver my mail.'

'No. I came to collect you for a photo session down at the agency.'

'I hate photo sessions.'

'It's for Numb Records. They want to make sure we don't all have three heads, I guess.'

'You mean they want to make sure we're marketable.'

Brad rubbed his stubbly chin. 'Well then, we'll have to put Ailsa at the back. They'll take one look at her and ask if we're a Mamas and Papas concept show.'

'That is so unfair.'

'She's fat. I tell it like it is.'

'And what about you?' I poked him in the stomach.

'It doesn't matter with guys. Come on, Lisa. Don't you have to wash your hair or something?' He settled on the sofa in between the piles of laundry and switched on the television.

We arrived at our agency about an hour later. We were running late because Brad had wanted to watch the end of some children's drama show he had got involved in while I was in the shower. IAM, or International Artist Management, was not international, dealt with very few real artists and couldn't manage a rubber duck around a bathtub. But they were an excellent booking agency, and Clark, the guy that looked after 747, had kept us in regular work. The trouble with Clark, as with most entertainment agents, was that he was a failed muso with the personality of a used-car salesman. I could only do so much nodding and smiling in his company before I either had to run away or tell him he was a fuckwit.

We found Jeff, Ailsa and Clark in one of the side offices, sitting on a sofa with stuffing pouring out of the arms, smoking and watching amateur videos of bands.

'Hey, Brad,' Jeff said, as always oblivious of how loud his voice was, 'check out the tits on this chick.' He picked up the remote control and rewound the video until he found some footage of a blonde girl with enormous breasts, barely covered by a shiny vinyl halter top, singing badly in front of an equally bad covers band.

'Crap band, but the punters love her,' Clark offered as his expert opinion.

'I can see why,' said Brad, snatching the remote from Jeff and pausing the video at a particularly advantageous frame.

I realised I was the only person in the room not interested in the girl's breasts. 'Can we get on with it, please?'

Nothing made me more self-conscious than getting my photo taken. Try as I might, I couldn't seem to hold my mouth naturally, and I never knew what to do with my hands. To make it worse, the staff photographer was about ten years behind. He tried unsuccessfully to convince us we'd look good pouting seductively over our shoulders, while every other band in the world was staring at their shoelaces. When he had finally run out of film, he rushed off to develop the pictures so that Brad could courier them down to Numb Records the same day.

And this time we got an instant response. Two o'clock the next afternoon I had cleared a space on the sofa and was lying there reading when Brad called. 'They're flying up tomorrow to see us play live.'

'You're kidding.'

'No. They got the package and called me immediately.'

'Are we that good looking?'

'I don't know if it was that, but it might have been the press clipping.'

'What press clipping?'

'The one about the dead guy.'

I felt sick. 'Tell me you're joking.'

'I'm not joking. Handle it, Lisa. It's not our fault the guy's dead.'

'I can't believe you sent them that clipping. And I can't believe that's why they're interested in us.'

'Let's be realistic here. It just made them *more* interested. They were already on the verge.'

I was silent.

'Come on, Lisa,' Brad said. 'Where's the problem here? There's nothing wrong with what we did.'

'Then why do I feel like we're cashing in on some poor guy's grisly death?'

'Lisa, he loved the band. This way something good comes of his death. He would have wanted it that way.'

'Oh please! You aren't talking to Jeff or Ailsa here. I'm the one with brains remember?'

'Sorry. But what's done is done, Lisa. If it's any consolation, I'll tell everybody that you, high-principled woman that you are, wanted nothing to do with it.' The lazy edge of sarcasm touched his voice.

'Yeah, thanks. I'll see you Friday night then.' I hung up, half excited, half disgusted.

On Friday I checked my e-mail again and, in among the normal babble of pseudo-American jargon and self-conscious counter-culture criticism, there was another message from Whitewitch.

Dear Lisa

We'll start off slow and see how far we get. This is kind of like self-hypnosis, which means you're in control the whole time.

Find yourself a quiet space where you won't be disturbed—take the phone off the hook and make sure you're alone. Start by deep breathing; close your eyes and relax. Then picture a clock in your mind. Visualise it in close detail. When you have a clear picture, start imagining the hands are running backwards. Watch the second hand ticking anticlockwise, the other hands following.

Then, when the vision is completely lucid, say out loud on every breath, 'Time flows backwards'. Repeat it over and over. You may need four or five attempts at the whole process before you get anywhere, and even then your memories may be patchy. But if you persevere you'll eventually start to put a picture together.

Keep in touch to let me know how you're coming along.

Whitewitch

I had a giggle, but it could have been to dispel the faint chill that settled on me as I read her words. Make sure I was alone while I did it—well, that went without saying. I'd look like a complete dickhead lying on my couch muttering incantations like a deranged bag lady. I printed out her message and folded it up on the side of my desk. Perhaps this nonsense wasn't for me.

I hadn't had stage fright for nearly nine years. I was so used to being on stage, to slipping into that LisaSheehan which was all one word and somehow wasn't really me. But knowing that Selena from Numb Records was in the audience on Friday night sent me into a panic backstage at the Universal. I was sitting on a broken old chair, gnawing my fingernails and compiling a mental list of everything that could go wrong. Ailsa was stoned and Jeff was running about the cement box, yelling 'We're going to be famous' in a weird, childlike voice.

Brad stood in the doorway to the backstage room and checked out the audience.

'Is there a good crowd?' I asked him.

'Just the usual. Stop worrying.'

'Are those people in black here? I don't know if I can get into it if they're here again.'

'I saw one of them before, but he was just in his ordinary clothes. No black candles.'

'This sucks. I hate being nervous.'

'Well, stop.' Brad walked over and stood behind me, his firm, warm hands kneading my shoulders. I leaned into him. He had such a magic about him. He was all male: warm, rough, sexy.

'God, Brad, I wish you wouldn't.'

'Am I turning you on?'

'Just a bit.'

He leaned in and kissed me delicately on the ear. I pushed him off. Ailsa and Jeff laughed at us.

'Why don't you two just fuck? It's obvious you want to,' Ailsa said.

'We have,' said Brad.

'No we haven't,' I said.

'Which one of you is lying? Which one of you is lying?' Jeff chanted in the same childish singsong. He wriggled his long sausage fingers in front of my face. I told him to fuck off.

I had nothing to worry about of course. The extra adrenalin made us all play better, perform bigger. The mosh pit was dense at the front, so I threw off my guitar and jumped in for a surf. Some guy grabbed my crotch, but I got him back by kicking him in the head as I sailed over. They threw me back onto the stage and I gashed my knee on the corner of a foldback wedge. I barely felt it. There is nothing in the world like being high on adoration.

Selena introduced herself after the show. She was a hip young thing: late twenties, MBA, lots of gold jewellery and a diamond nose stud. She wouldn't commit to much, but she kept repeating that Numb was 'very impressed' with us. We were pathetic, trying so hard to be liked by her that I had to leave. They were moving beyond bourbon and starting to unwrap dainty packages of powder. Brad said he'd call me tomorrow. As I was leaving I heard Brad tell Selena I wasn't into drugs.

'Is she sure she's in the right business?' she said, downing the last of her bourbon.

Well, maybe I wasn't.

Numb Records kept us hanging and hanging. They danced around saying 'maybe' a lot, telling us they were waiting on budget estimates, telling us they were considering two other bands from interstate. My hope started to dissolve into cynicism. Unfortunately, my cynicism fitted me much more comfortably.

I was so absorbed in band business that I almost

forgot about Whitewitch's note. Then I had The Dream again.

It was a Thursday night after a gig at Fire Fire and I had nodded off in front of the television, watching infomercials. At first I was dreaming of a mincer that also purees and juliennes, still half aware that I was in front of the television in my own living room. But then there was a subtle shift, and I found myself back in the stiff, blood-soaked dress, struggling with the squeaky wheelbarrow that wanted to slip out of my gory hands, and listening to that woman wailing. Wet leaves and branches touched me, scratched me. I was going to kill her if she didn't stop, she was driving me insane. 'We have no choice,' I screamed at her. 'We have no choice.'

I snapped awake again, and the reassuring tones of the infomercial washed over me. 'If you ring now, we'll also include these fabulous recipe books.'

What did we have no choice about? And who were 'we' anyway?

I found Whitewitch's note and read through it again. I was getting close.

Nine o'clock Saturday night there was a knock at the door. I knew it was Brad come to pick me up for the evening's gig, so I called out for him to come in.

Ten seconds later there was another knock. I wondered why he didn't just let himself in as he always did. I opened the door and was just about to say, 'Did you forget your key?' when I realised that it wasn't Brad, but Jeff.

'Jeff?'

'Hi, Lisa. Hey, your flat is messy.' He said this with his customary weird grin, as if he was pleased to find out that I was a slob.

'Yeah, thanks for pointing that out. To what do I owe this pleasure?'

'I'm picking you up tonight. Can I come in?'

I let him in and pointed to the sofa. He sat down, picked up one of my bras from the pile of laundry and laughed. 'Your underwear.'

'You want a drink of something?'

'Sure, sure. Just something sweet.'

'Is orange juice okay?'

'Yeah, fine.'

I went to the kitchen to get a drink for him. 'How come you're picking me up?' I called.

'Brad's got a da-ate,' he replied.

'A date? With a female?' It was meant to sound flippant but I hated that little stab of jealousy.

'Yeah. Real serious too. He said she's beautiful and very smart. She goes to university, studies computer science or something.'

I brought him his orange juice.

'Does she have a name?'

'Umm . . . Marian? Mary? Might even by Marie. Starts with M. Are you jealous?'

I shook my head, sitting on the coffee table in front of him. 'No. I suppose he wants me to be.'

'I guess so. He said to make sure I told you she goes to university. He said you've got a thing about not having finished high school.'

'The rotten prick.'

Jeff took a sip of his orange juice and screwed up his nose. 'Got any vodka?'

'You know I don't.'

'Hmm, yes, Polly Pureheart has no vodka. That's a fucking tragedy.' He gulped his drink and handed me the empty glass.

'So how come you don't go out with Brad?' he asked. 'Ailsa and I have a bet.'

'A bet? On what?'

'Ailsa has fifty bucks reckons you'll never fuck him because you're a . . . a . . .' He screwed his eyes shut to think, then reopened them when he remembered the words. 'A candy-arsed bitch.'

'Great. And you bet otherwise?'

'Yeah, only 'cos Brad's the man who always gets the girl. Even if it's Lisa.' He leaned over and put his hand on my knee, looking up at me with puppy-dog eyes. 'Mmm, Lisa, lovely Lisa. Sure you don't want me instead of Brad?'

I brushed his hand off. 'I don't want either of you. Between you, you own the most diseased pair of dicks in the known universe.' I took his glass to the kitchen, burning up over what Ailsa had said. I knew we weren't close, but I thought at the very least I had her respect. And Brad had a new girlfriend and Jeff was a space cadet and my best friend was away being a new bride. I felt very alone.

'Let's go,' I said, pulling Jeff off the couch. 'I want to meet Brad's new sex toy.'

Marnie was her name. She was doing a further education course in word processing, not a university degree in computer science. I loosened her tongue when Brad wasn't around and she told all. She had blonde hair and big tits. She was the classic fuck-me-Brad girl, the type that he loved. I didn't like her, and I liked even less how good it made me feel that she wasn't actually smarter and prettier than me. She ended every sentence with 'you know?' and her voice rose into a nervous shriek as she warmed to her topic. Brad stood by impatiently while she told me inane stories about people in her class. I could see him set his jaw every time she did one of her rising terminals.

43

Finally he gave her ten bucks and told her to go buy some drinks.

'Don't laugh,' he said when she was gone.

'I'm not laughing.'

'I have to go out with someone—you don't want me.'

'That's right. I don't want you.'

'Do you think you'll ever want me?'

I sighed in discomfort. 'I don't know, Brad. I think I'm looking for something else.'

'If you change your mind . . .'

'I'll let you know.'

I was so down that night, feeling friendless and out of sorts, like I was standing on the outside of a whirl of excitement that excluded me because I didn't possess the same nihilistic drive the others did. My mind kept returning to The Dream, Whitewitch's note, the possibility that I needed to get my internal world sorted out to feel right in the social world again. I resolved to try Whitewitch's meditation, no matter that it was loopy. Just try it once and see if it got me anywhere, even though I knew that nothing could possibly come of it.

Trouble was, I didn't know at all.

I wanted to do it during the day. I don't think anyone ever really gets over that childhood fear of the dark, so if you're going to do something a bit spooky, it's a natural impulse to make sure it's broad daylight outside. I locked up the flat and even put the chain on the door so Brad couldn't get in if he came by. I read the instructions over and over again. My stomach was fluttering so I guess I was a little nervous or excited—perhaps my cynicism about the whole project didn't run so very deep.

44

I put all the laundry on the floor and lay down on the sofa. I closed my eyes and started drawing deep, deep breaths. It relaxed me pretty quickly. I visualised the clock just as Whitewitch said, but I kept getting distracted by the sound of traffic or the fridge suddenly humming into life. I remembered I hadn't taken the phone off the hook and my body tensed in anticipation of it ringing. I thought about getting up to fix it, but the picture in my head was getting clearer and I didn't want to lose it. The hands started backwards, first slowly, then faster and faster. I tried to block out the world, tried not to think.

'Time flows backwards,' I said. Then again on the next outward breath. An ambulance siren raced past outside and I lost my cool. I would get up, take the phone off the hook, close all the windows in spite of the heat and start again.

So I tried to sit up.

And that's when something large and dark and firm pushed on my head. I couldn't sit up, I was pinned to the sofa and I couldn't open my eyes. I was engulfed in a terrible darkness. I panicked. I could hear my arms flailing against the sofa as I tried to pull myself up, and I could hear a voice—my voice— saying something strange and guttural and incoherent over and over.

Then I was becoming undone, filling a void. It was as though I wasn't me any more, but something huge and formless, and I was expanding and expanding. There was a sound like fast rushing air, like violins out of tune, like planes crashing. Then from somewhere a voice calling, a small female voice. I couldn't make out what it was saying.

I stopped expanding and started to contract. I was being pulled backwards and headfirst down a black mine shaft, getting smaller and smaller.

The voice became louder, closer. 'Elizabeth. Elizabeth.'

The sensation of a golden pattern, diamonds on diamonds and . . .

CHAPTER
FOUR

'Elizabeth.'

Her childish voice plucked at every nerve. I turned to see her hurrying towards me, waving a handful of lace.

'Mirabel,' I said flatly, turning back to the silks I had been looking at.

'Look, it's Italian lace.' She held the lace under my nose.

'It's very nice. Are you going to buy it?'

'Yes. For some new gloves.'

'Nancy will ruin the lace trying to make gloves out of it.'

'Ah, but *you* wouldn't. You're so clever, perhaps you could make them for me.' She fluttered her long lashes, trying, in her usual fashion, to look appealing.

'I have no time for making you gloves.'

'Cross old thing. Father will buy me the lace and he'll make you do it.'

I knew Uncle Tom would do nothing of the sort, but I nodded and waved her away. 'Go on then, leave me alone.'

She turned her little nose up at me and walked off. Others found her childish exuberance and pettish manner charming. I did not.

I ran the silk through my fingers, the smooth

friction making my nerves tingle. The fair was crowded, hot. The sun gleamed off the stalls and lazed on every leaf and petal. A man in a hair shirt screamed warnings of eternal damnation from beside the exchange stall. I closed my eyes and imagined the East Indies, where the silk came from. Warm and wet. I wanted to sail there myself, the tang of the sea all around me, the world opening up before me, wider and wider, my soul expanding to fill the breach.

Ah, the desire, the desire. Always with me. My stomach contracted with anxiety, knowing that every year I got closer to death and no closer to fulfilment. I wanted to throw off this world and dance with the stars. But because I was a woman I was doomed to wither slowly in this body, to be nothing but an empty shell shuffling through a meaningless existence.

'How far away are you?' said a voice at my side. I opened my eyes and turned to see a man beautifully dressed in a blue doublet with black sleeves. He had a small dark beard and compelling grey eyes. He seemed to be standing terribly close.

'On a boat to the East Indies,' I replied.

'Why the East Indies?'

'The silks.' I held up some red silk. 'I was trying to imagine where they came from.'

He took the silk from my hand and closed his eyes. 'Mmm. Hot and moist, the chatter of a million voices, the sky broad and blue, the sun huge and brilliant, the smell of exotic blooms and spices.'

'You've been?'

'Yes. Last year.'

I hung my head and tried to swallow down the envy that was my lot.

'What's your name?' he said.

'Elizabeth.'

'Would you like to walk with me, Elizabeth?'

I looked around for Mirabel and Uncle Tom. They were nowhere in sight. I turned back to my companion. He wasn't handsome. His nose was too big, his brows too straight and heavy. But he appealed to something deeper than my sight. Deeper and lower. I gave him my hand.

We left the site of the fair and began to wander slowly down the main street of the village. In a soft voice he told me about being away at sea: the tiny cabin he had to sleep in, the sounds and smells of the ocean, the terrifying storms he had endured, and all about sailing east into the heart of the fertile world.

We were leaving the village and walking into the forest. The deeper we went, the more bewitching his voice became. I felt as if I were sleeping with my eyes open, dreaming while standing up. Out of the sun the temperature dropped dramatically, and we found ourselves under a dark oak tree, its cool branches spread above us.

I knew he would make love to me there. He pushed me onto the ground and his hands were up my petticoats and down the front of my bodice. The ground smelled damp, but with my eyes closed I could imagine we were somewhere else, under a fanning tropical palm in the Indies perhaps. It was strange, but as that thought slipped through my mind, I could hear the ocean beating at my feet. My lover was hard and bold and lush. His lips were all over my face, he breathed my name over and over again like a spell.

Which, of course, it was.

Mirabel, Uncle Tom and I stepped out of the coach at Prestonvale very late that evening. Servants rushed about us like ants, taking our new purchases from the coach into the house: silk and rugs and spices, bronze statuettes and elaborate clocks from Switzerland. Once a year we went to the fair, and each year our house became more and more full of extravagant trinkets.

As Mirabel headed toward the house, Uncle Tom helped me down and gave my hand a squeeze. 'Did you have a good day?'

'Yes, thank you.'

'Was Mirabel too much trouble?'

'To be honest, Uncle Tom, I didn't see her for much of the day.'

'I know she can be a trial.' He smiled at me, and his warm soft eyes crinkled up at the corners. He was getting older, greyer and more soft at heart every year.

I wound my arms about his neck. 'You are such a dear.'

He stroked my hair. 'Ah, Elizabeth. Sometimes I wish you were my daughter.'

'I think of you as a father.'

'You're all my joy and all my solace,' he said softly, squeezing me tight.

'Not to mention your financial manager.'

'Yes, yes. That too.' We stood apart and he gave me that smile again. In that smile I could remember my mother, his sister, who had died while I was still a child. My father had been lost at sea before I was born. Uncle Tom had been the only parent I had ever really known.

A dark figure approached us. It was one of the village women, wrapped in a grey cloak. She tugged at my sleeve. 'Lady Elizabeth, could I have a word in private?'

I looked to Uncle Tom as though I didn't know what this was all about, although I suspected I did.

He drew his brows together and was about to dismiss the woman, but I raised my hand.

'No, it's fine, Uncle Tom. You go inside. I'll be along shortly.'

As he turned to leave, the woman drew me aside. 'It's my sister,' she said. 'She's taken very poorly. She can't keep any food down and she's shivering and pale. We're afraid we've lost her this time.'

I looked behind me. Uncle Tom had disappeared into the house. A page was fetching the remaining packages from the carriage. I asked him to go to my room and bring out my writing case, which he did quickly and dutifully. I took the case from him and nodded towards the house.

'Tell Sir Thomas that I've gone into the village to translate a letter. I should be back within the hour.'

He bowed and hurried off.

I turned to the woman. 'What is your name?'

'Maryanne Roberts, ma'am. And my sister is Elizabeth, just like you. But we call her Bessie.'

We began walking towards the village, past the tall stone gateposts of Prestonvale. 'Named after the Queen like me, I take it?'

'Yes, ma'am. Our beloved Queen. This new Scottish fellow could never replace her.'

I hardly felt the need to discuss politics with a village woman, so I fell silent beside her as we trod the dusty path towards her home. She eventually guided me into a side alley. 'It's over there, ma'am.'

We headed over to a small house with a lantern burning in the window. Inside, I was immediately aware of the fatty smell of cooking meat. An elderly woman in a chair by the fire look up as I came in. The house contained only one room, and in a filthy bed in the corner lay another woman, pale and sweating, her bedclothes stinking of vomit. I approached her with my leather case and sat on the edge of the bed. She found my hand.

'Lady Elizabeth, it's so good of you to come.' Her hand was burning hot. I massaged her fingers. Mary-anne and the older woman came to stand close by.

'It's fine, Bessie. Do you have a cough?'

'No, no. But I'm so cold.'

I leaned over, pulled back the bedclothes and placed my ear against her chest. 'Breathe in deeply.'

She did so. There were no rattling noises from her chest, which was promising.

I placed the covers over her again. 'Don't try to eat anything between now and tomorrow morning.' The key to the leather case was on a chain around my neck. I took it off and unlocked my 'writing case', which Uncle Tom thought was full of books, paper, pens and ink. It was to preserve him more than to preserve me. As the local Justice of the Peace, he was responsible for trying witches at the petty sessions. I owed it to him never to turn up there, accused of dabbling where I shouldn't. Not that I considered what I did witchcraft, though more suspicious folk than I would certainly see it that way. I considered myself skilled in herbal medicine and healing spells, a cunning-woman as they called me in the village, but with a far more privileged and educated background than most. In a way, it was Uncle Tom's encourage-ment that had started me. He had brought me the book on herbs and flowers that had piqued my inter-est. Now I kept a well-stocked garden in my window box, and periodically threw Rosemary, the cook, out of the kitchen to make my medicines.

I held a small bottle of foul-smelling liquid up to Bessie's lips. 'Here, try to drink this.'

She took a sip, then turned her head away and wrinkled her nose.

'Please try,' I said.

She drew a deep breath and drank some more. I took the bottle away and leaned over her, my lips nearly touching her forehead, my hand stroking her hair. She stank violently, but I stayed close, and almost against her skin I whispered the words, repeated them slowly so that they would sink from my lips straight into her mind, where the real healing would take place. They stood about astonished, the unfamiliar Latin like a secret, mysterious language to them—to me it was the most perfect of languages. I closed my eyes and let the words fall from my lips, taking comfort in their roundness, slipping into the dark with them, almost wishing never to return. Finally I heard her breath drawing deep and regular, and I sat up.

Maryanne helped me to my feet. 'Thank you so much, ma'am.'

'If she's no better in the morning, she'll have to be bled. Don't give her any food until she asks for it.' I collected my case.

'We must repay you, we must,' said the older woman, who I assumed was Bessie's mother.

'Your silence is the only payment I request.' And then I did something that I always did, I touched each of them on the shoulder and said, '*Tace*', Latin for 'keep quiet'. It was nothing more than a parlour trick, but of course they believed they'd been put under an enchantment. It was the easiest way to ensure their silence, to keep them scared of me. And yes, I did enjoy being considered with awe.

I wandered home through the shadowy street, enjoying the solitude and the sounds of the soft darkness. Night-time always seemed to match my mood, and while my frustration didn't abate in the moonlight, at least it felt as though it fitted somewhere in the grand scheme. My mind licentiously replayed the afternoon's dalliance under the oak tree, vividly and in full colour. I felt neither guilt nor fear. No guilt, because I did it often—it was one way I could transcend the mundanity of my existence. No fear, because other women's curse was my blessing: I was blissfully barren. During my brief, ill-fated marriage, my dear husband, Christopher, had fathered four bastard children throughout our village, but my stomach had remained conspicuously flat. He died without a legitimate heir. And just as well, because I had no patience for small, selfish people. That was why Mirabel annoyed me so.

Uncle Tom was still in the parlour, waiting up for me.

'If I were you, Elizabeth, I'd tell those village people to leave you alone.'

'It's fine, Uncle Tom. I like to be able to help.'

'What did they need you for?'

'They had a letter from a relative in France. I translated it for them and wrote their reply.' I sat next to him on the floor and put my head in his lap. He was wearing a silk housecoat and the material was cool against my cheek.

'My clever girl.' He stroked my hair.

'I'd go mad if I couldn't be of use somehow. There's never enough for me to do.'

'You need to take up a hobby. Mirabel has taken up embroidery, though she's not very good at it yet. Perhaps you could join her.'

I groaned. 'I can't think of anything worse. Mindless work with mindless chatter for company.'

'What would you like to do?'

I closed my eyes and breathed, and I could smell the ocean air again, as I had this afternoon. 'I'd like to sail to the Orient. I'd like to explore new lands and discover new things, and bring back gold and silver for you. I'd like to write poetry and publish it in books. I'd like to go to a university and discuss the classics with others like me.'

He kept stroking my hair. He didn't need to say anything, because I knew as well as he that none of these things were possible.

'I should have been born a male,' I said.

'Perhaps you should have. However, it's too late now.'

We sat in silence for a while. Finally he said: 'Would you like to marry again? I could find somebody.'

'Somebody who'll take a barren wife? Hardly.'

'There's my friend Joseph. He's just lost his wife and he already has five sons, so I'm sure he won't want any more.'

'Uncle Tom, he's older than you are. I'm twenty-seven. I deserve someone young and handsome.'

'That you do.'

'Besides, I don't want to marry again. I'm happy here, managing the estate for you.' Poor Uncle Tom was completely bewildered by figures and taxes and exchange rates. His second wife had died around the same time as my husband, so I had returned to live with him and taken over management of the books.

'Ah, but that can't go on forever. I'll eventually need to find a decent husband for Mirabel, someone who can capably manage the estate when I'm gone. Someone who can look after you both. Then it will be his job to watch the finances.'

'And I will be left with nothing, my brain will shrivel up and die and I'll sit senseless in the attic waiting for Rosemary to bring me soup and bread, which I'll spill all over myself like a simple.' I hadn't meant to sound quite so bitter.

'Do you want me to send for something new for you to read?'

This was Uncle Tom's solution to my frequent bouts of frustration and, while it never solved anything, it was always a welcome gesture. 'Yes, please. I'd like to learn Italian. Could you get me some Italian books and perhaps a grammar guide?'

'Consider it done.'

'Why don't you arrange for Mirabel to marry Joseph?' I said slyly.

'That's not very fair. You just finished telling me how old he is, and Mirabel is only nineteen.'

'But it's different with her. She's immature, she needs somebody mature and stable.'

He chuckled. 'I'm not going to punish Mirabel for you with an unpleasant husband. But I suppose I should be thinking about her marriage.'

'Already? She's so young.'

'Elizabeth, I don't know how much longer I'll be around.'

'Don't say that,' I said, looking up into his eyes. 'Please don't say that.'

He touched my cheek. 'You're so clever, yet you haven't learned life's major lesson: accept what you cannot change.'

And it seemed by that I was always bound.

I was in the study the following afternoon, with the account book opened before me, but my mind somewhere beyond the mullioned windows from which the gold afternoon light streamed, when there was a light knock at the door. Rosemary entered and curtsied briefly.

'Yes, Rosemary?'

'Ma'am, I had word this morning from the village.

Bessie Roberts is well as can be and walking around this morning, where only just last night they were giving her up for dead.'

I smiled. 'Thank you for that news, Rosemary.'

'You're so clever, ma'am. I was just saying to Nancy the other day how clever you are and how lucky we are to work for you. If we get sick it's only a matter of calling you and . . .'

'That's enough, Rosemary. You know you aren't supposed to talk about it.'

'Sorry, ma'am, only, could I ask you for some advice?'

'Go ahead.'

'My brother's eldest boy is marrying in a fortnight, and the girl is . . . well, it's rumoured she's unchaste.'

I raised my eyebrows. She looked so shocked. I was briefly possessed by a perverse desire to tell her in intimate detail about the stranger I'd made love to at the fair yesterday. I fought it down. 'And?'

'Can you tell if there's some mixture, like, to make her stay faithful?'

I suppressed a laugh. 'Yes, there is. You need to make a balm from vervain, angelica and garlic for him to rub on his private parts before the consummation.'

She blushed. 'I see.'

'And boil some nettle leaves, then sprinkle the water over him.' That would cure his jealousy.

'I see. Thank you, ma'am.' She backed out of the room, pleased but afraid. The itch of power jangled my fingertips. I gained a disturbing sense of enjoyment from her fear.

I don't know if Rosemary overcame her superstition enough to try my recipe. In any case, I thought no more of weddings until Mirabel appeared at my chamber door late one night, some weeks later.

'Elizabeth,' she called. I could hear damp hiccoughing tears in her voice.

'Yes, come in.'

The door opened and I heard her footsteps tapping over towards my bed, then the hangings were drawn back and she climbed in with me, dressed in her white nightdress, her long blonde hair unbound. She used to climb into bed with me when she was very small, before I had been married, when I still had some small amount of patience with her. I grudgingly moved over and she curled into my side.

'What is it?' I asked.

'Don't be cross. The most awful thing has happened.'

I remained silent as she snuffled and sniffed next to me. She reached out a damp little hand for mine and I let her take it. I stroked her fingers with my thumb.

'I'm to be married, Elizabeth.'

'That's no tragedy. That's something to be celebrated.'

'But I don't know who it is. It's somebody Father has chosen, the son of one of his business acquaintances. He has lots of money but no title.'

'Don't worry. Christopher had a title but no money. Trust me, it's good that your husband will have money. Uncle Tom is thinking of your future.' Our future.

'I know it's good, it's just . . . I always thought I'd fall in love and then marry.'

'That's what happens to us, Mirabel,' I replied. 'Expediency thwarts our purest intentions.' Strangely I felt a connection with Mirabel for the first time.

She too wanted to rail against her fate. I allowed her to snuggle closer.

'Did you love your husband?'

'Yes. I adored Kit, but Kit didn't love me.'

'That must have been terrible.'

'It's worse than being married to someone you don't love, being married to someone who seeks his pleasure with every wench in the village.'

'Oh no, really? Did he really do that?'

I sighed. I didn't know why I was telling her this. 'Yes, but don't say anything. He had four bastard children. I'd see them around from time to time, they had his eyes and his mouth.'

'But you didn't have any children.'

'No.'

'That's very sad.'

I patted her head. 'I think it's very propitious.'

'What's propitious?'

'Lucky.'

'Oh.' Then after a while. 'You're odd, Elizabeth.'

'I should have been a man.'

'Then I could have married *you*. I should have liked that very much. You're so clever.'

I was overcome by a rare moment of tenderness for her. 'Has Nancy made you those gloves yet?'

'No. I won't let her, she'll ruin the lace.'

'Then bring it to me tomorrow. I'll make you lace gloves for your wedding.'

She brightened. 'Would you? That would be lovely.'

'Would it make you happier about marrying?'

She sighed a little, then nodded. 'I suppose if I must marry I may as well have new lace gloves. I hope he's nice, Elizabeth.'

I hoped so too, but not for her sake. Or maybe just a little for her sake.

*

Gilbert Lewis arrived late on a Thursday afternoon to meet his new bride. The entire household was in a state of chaos, readying themselves for the guest, scrubbing floor boards, laying fresh rushes and airing linen. To get away from the bustle I shut myself in the study with Uncle Tom's accounts book open in front of me. But I had a little book of my own in there, and I was earnestly writing poetry, some of which was probably very bad. I was enjoying myself nonetheless. While I wrote, I pretended that this was my house, bought from my earnings as a poet and playwright and famous actor, and this my own study where I could pen my next masterpiece. Idle dust motes floated on the beams of late afternoon sunshine. I felt warm and lazy, dreaming in my corner.

A sharp rap sounded at the door and Uncle Tom came in, while I hastily shoved my poetry book beneath the accounts.

'Still working?'

'Just checking my adding up.'

'Gilbert's here in the parlour. Come and meet him; I think you'll like him.'

I checked that my poetry book was well hidden and stood up. Uncle Tom took my hand and led me out into the hallway and through to the parlour.

'Gilbert Lewis,' he said as he thrust me into the room, 'I'd like you to meet my niece, Lady Elizabeth Moreton.'

He turned to me, and it was the man from the fair. The shock of recognition temporarily stupefied me. He put his hand out as if he'd never seen me before in his life. 'Pleased to meet you, my lady. Sir Thomas, you didn't say you had another lovely young maiden rattling about in this enormous place.'

60

'Please, just call me Tom. Elizabeth is the widow of Sir Christopher Moreton.'

I saw him looking at my clothes, noting that I wasn't wearing my widow's weeds, so I hastily explained. 'It was six years ago, sir. Life goes on.'

'It does indeed.'

'Elizabeth is invaluable to me, Gilbert,' Uncle Tom continued. 'She takes care of my accounts, manages the household, and the villagers love her.'

'Ah, a she-wit. I don't meet many of those.'

I was unbearably uncomfortable, but he seemed to be showing no signs of disquiet. I couldn't, however, force myself to relax.

'Did you have a pleasant journey, sir?' I asked stiffly, conscious that I had to say something or risk looking like an imbecile.

'Yes, and please, call me Gilbert. May I call you Elizabeth?'

I nodded, keeping my eyes fixed on his face for any signs of recognition.

'Elizabeth, do you read?'

'Only in four languages,' Uncle Tom interjected. 'English, of course, Latin, French and Greek.'

'Only a little Greek,' I said. 'Please, Uncle Tom, don't embarrass me.'

Gilbert continued. 'Have you heard of Christine de Pisan?'

'No, I don't believe I have.'

'You must read her. She too was a she-wit in her time, which was around two hundred years ago if I remember correctly. I think you'd like her work. It's in French, but that shouldn't present a problem to you.'

I looked expectantly at Uncle Tom. 'Would you like me to send for her books?' he asked.

I nodded eagerly. And how glad I was in that

second to have somebody in the house with whom I could talk about books and ideas, even if he was a man that I had given myself to without even knowing his name. But maybe he didn't remember. He wasn't acknowledging our previous meeting in any way, not even with a furtive glance from those narrow grey eyes.

'Ah, here's Mirabel,' Uncle Tom said as Mirabel finally entered the room, pale, quaking with fear and eyes ringed red with tears. 'Mirabel, I'd like you to meet Gilbert Lewis.'

'How do you do, sir?'

'Very well,' he said, and I could see him making a quick assessment of her. I thought he looked pleased, and with good cause. Mirabel was very pretty in her childish way. 'And do you read too, Mirabel?'

'No, sir,' she replied.

'Your cousin hasn't bothered to teach you?'

'No, sir. I don't wish to read.'

'Ah.' He nodded gravely, then smiled. She gave him a tentative smile in return. Then he turned his attention back to me, and there it was, a flicker of barely concealed suggestion in his eyes. I knew in that instant he was seeing me again, lying there with my skirts twisted about my waist.

'I must get back to work,' I said, squirming.

'Will you join us for supper?' he said.

'Yes, of course.' I smiled up at Uncle Tom. 'Please excuse me.'

I swept past him and back to the study, where I locked the door and spent an hour staring at the wood grain in the tabletop.

I should have known that one day one of my encounters would come back to haunt me. I'd been having them since Kit had died; the first one with a stable boy at Kit's funeral, and one at least every time

I went to London with Uncle Tom. But always with people I could be sure never to see again. Or so I thought.

And how could it be that the stranger could turn up in my house as a prospective husband for my cousin? I knew that Uncle Tom had met with many of his business associates at the fair. Had Gilbert been there with his father? Had Uncle Tom met him when he returned, spent and somewhat dusty from his tumble with me in the woods? I was mortified beyond all reason, terrified that he might possess a tongue as loose as my morals.

Somehow I endured supper, and then I didn't see Gilbert for two days. He was either locked in deep conversation with Uncle Tom or out hunting with the game team. Mirabel didn't see him either, and would only say to me that she was glad he wasn't too old, though I'm certain he was nearly twice her age.

When he did come to me, which I knew he eventually would, it was early morning. Very early, before the sun was up. There was a tap at my door and then I heard the door swing open and close softly behind him. I knew it was him even before he drew back the curtains on my bed and I could see his profile silhouetted against the moonlight.

'Gilbert?'

'Yes. It's me. Have you been expecting me?'

'Yes, I suppose. But we mustn't . . .'

'I'm not here for your body.' He sat on the edge of my bed.

'Please, please, don't tell Uncle Tom.'

'Of course I won't. Do you think he'd let me marry his daughter if he knew I'd already plumbed his niece?'

I fell silent, waiting.

'I have a stiff knee,' he said finally.

'Pardon?'

'A stiff knee. The wet weather occasionally brings it on. I was complaining about it to your cook, what's her name?'

'Rosemary,' I said, my apprehension growing.

'Yes, that's it. Rosemary said all I need do was see you and you'd give me a remedy. Only she didn't use the word "remedy", I think she called it a "spell".'

I was going to beat Rosemary within an inch of her life the next time she happened by. 'I don't know what she means by that.'

'Don't you? She said that you're quite famous throughout the village for it. Does Sir Thomas know this is why you're so popular?' I heard good-natured humour touch his voice and, although I couldn't see in the dark, I could sense him smiling. Relief burst into my veins.

'Gilbert, you know far too much about me. I can only trust that you won't say anything to my uncle.'

'No, never. So what do you recommend for my knee?'

'Black pepper oil for the joints.'

'And the spell?'

'It's just a traditional healing spell. I could show you my book.'

He breathed deeply and sank down next to me. 'Elizabeth, why do you waste your time?'

I was acutely conscious of the proximity of his body, the raw heat emanating from him and wrapping me in its folds. It was all I could do not to reach out and touch him. 'How do you mean?'

'Wasting your time with silly remedies and wives' tales. Don't you long for something more?' But before I could answer, he answered for me. 'Of course you do. I felt it when I first saw you at the fair, holding that silk and imagining you were in Asia.'

64

'What more is there?' I asked. 'What more for me anyway?'

He rolled over until he was lying half on top of me, his breath warm on my cheek. I felt his fingers close over my breast. Even through my nightgown I could feel how warm and firm his hand was. I let him kiss me, felt his warm tongue probing my mouth, felt him drinking me.

'Godhead, Elizabeth,' he murmured. 'The pursuit of godhead.'

CHAPTER
FIVE

I was going to throw up. The certainty of that queasy liquid feeling was the only solid thing I had. And if I didn't get up I was going to choke on my own vomit and die like Bon Scott and John Bonham and Jimi Hendrix. My mind lighted on the thought that Bonham died in 1980 and I felt a surge of happiness because 1980 had been and gone. I was hanging on the numbers, on the big loop of the nine and somehow the eight fitted me too, but that didn't make any sense.

If I didn't get up I was going to throw up and die on my couch.

My hands pawing at the back of the sofa, trying to haul myself up.

Quickly.

Somehow, somehow my eyes opening, forcing them open, using every muscle in my head to force them open. Open, damn you, open.

And here was my flat. I swung giddily into a sitting position. Then I vomited all over my feet.

Suddenly everything moved into sharp relief. I stared at the vomit all over my toes, some splashed onto the carpet. There was more coming.

I got up and dashed to the bathroom, where I emptied my poor retching stomach, then sat there next to the toilet, my face against the cool porcelain, my jaw shaking as if I was jabbering away in a silent language.

What the fuck had happened to me?

I knew who I was, I was Lisa Sheehan. I always had been Lisa Sheehan and I would continue to be Lisa Sheehan. I said my name over and over until it no longer made sense. LisaSheehanLisaSheehan LisaSheehan . . .

I stood, unsteady on my legs, and looked in the mirror. Yes, it was me, though I was pale and sweating. I checked my watch. It was four a.m. I had been under for twelve hours.

I stepped into the shower cubicle fully clothed and turned the cold tap on. The shock of the water started my heart, took my breath away. I hung my head and the water ran off my hair and down over my shorts and T-shirt. I knew who I was, but I also knew who she was. Elizabeth.

It hadn't been like dreaming. It hadn't been like watching a movie. It had been like living another life, unaware of the life I already had. I started crying— confusion, bewilderment, fear, oh, big big fear. Deep breaths, Lisa. Nothing to be afraid of. I looked at the tiles, the grouting between the tiles, the specks of black in the grouting. This was what reality was made of, not lace gloves and men in strange hats and adding up books in that room . . .

Something of that musty, dreamy smell came back to me and I was afraid I was going to be sucked back in time again, so I screamed. The sound sobered me up some. I turned the shower off and stepped out, stripped out of my wet clothes and went to the television. Open Learning was on. Government Studies. The Australian political system. Economic rationalism. Corporatism. The Hawke years. I watched twenty minutes of it, stupefied. I pulled some clothes out of the laundry pile and put them on, cleaned up the vomit, taking comfort in the mundanity of the task. Then I had to sit down. I was so tired, as though I hadn't slept in days. I wasn't going to go to sleep though, no way. I was afraid that I wouldn't make it back to the real world again. I sat there with my eyes open, aching with weariness. I sat through Anthropology. I sat through Astronomy. I sat through Marketing II. By the first edition news, I was fast asleep.

I surfaced when somebody knocked at the door. It was one o'clock in the afternoon, and I was relieved that I was awake in my own world, and hadn't had any more visions. I felt almost normal. The knock came again and I called out, 'Hang on'. I flicked off the television, quickly went to the bathroom tap to rinse the foul taste of daytime sleep out of my mouth, then hurried to the door. It was Karin.

'God, you look terrible,' were the first words out of her mouth.

'I didn't sleep very well.' I couldn't bring myself to tell her. It would be like acknowledging something that I didn't wish to acknowledge. Daytime was good. Daytime made last night's adventure just a little bit less scary. I grabbed her in a bear hug and squeezed her hard. 'I missed you.'

'I missed you, too.'

'Come in. Do you want a cup of something?'

'Okay.'

I led her into the kitchen and put the kettle on. She perched on the edge of the kitchen bench. All the chairs were covered in old newspapers and magazines.

'So,' I said turning back to her, 'how was it?'

She nodded slowly. 'Good, good. New Zealand was lovely. The beaches were quite nice and we went for a cruise around the islands.'

I looked at her. 'Is that all? You don't sound very enthusiastic. Aren't you supposed to be glowing with honeymoon fever?'

She sighed, lowered her eyes. Didn't reply.

'Come on, what's wrong? Don't tell me you've made a mistake.'

'No!' Her head snapped up. 'No, not at all. It's just . . . not what I expected, that's all.'

'What . . . is David weird or something? You know, in bed.'

'No . . . well, I guess I don't know, I haven't had much experience. But I'm not uncomfortable or anything. Except when I'm talking to you about it.'

'Point taken. End of interrogation,' I said, holding up my hands. 'You want honey?'

She nodded.

The kettle was whistling. I switched it off and made two cups of apple cinnamon tea and squirted some honey into them. I handed Karin hers and we went back to the lounge room. She tiptoed carefully over my underwear on the floor; I just kicked it out of the way.

She sipped her tea in silence and I looked at her profile. She was almost angelic. I'd been jealous of the way she looked forever. As long as I'd known her, I'd felt like a big moose around her. She was everything I wasn't: fair, delicate, fine-featured. She looked so pensive.

'You'll get used to being married,' I said.

She leaned into me. 'It feels so weird sharing a bed.'

'I always think it feels quite nice. You know,

waking up next to somebody. Although it's been a long time since I did that.'

'You're right. I'll get used to it. And of course, when the baby comes—'

'Hang on,' I said, interrupting her. 'What baby?'

'We didn't want to wait. We started trying on the wedding night. With a bit of luck there's already one in there.' She patted her tight little stomach.

'Jeez, Karin. You only just got your freedom, why the hell do you want a munchkin to tie you down?'

She looked taken aback, and I realised my voice had been a little too harsh. Fuck, I'd probably sounded like her mother. 'Sorry,' I said. 'But it seems like you're too young to have a baby. I mean, I never even think about that stuff and I'm your age.'

'But you're different. Stop expecting me to be you. I want to have a baby, and so does David. In fact, I think he wants it more than me.'

'Are you sure you don't mean he wants it and you're just going along with it?'

'God, you see an ulterior motive in everything.' At least she was laughing. I was being paranoid. Or possessive. Or both.

I changed the subject. 'Did you do history in high school?'

'Yes, why?'

'Do you know anything about kings and queens of England?'

'Is this leading somewhere?'

I shrugged. 'Um, yes. Was there a Scottish king after Elizabeth the First?'

'I think so. James the First was Scottish I think. Wasn't that the Stuarts? That sounds like a Scottish name.'

'Any idea when that happened?'

70

She looked amused. 'What on earth do you want to know that for?'

This was my opportunity to tell her everything: The Dream, the regression, the whole lot. But I couldn't. I was still trying to sort it out myself. Talking about it might drag me into a screaming bout of hysteria. 'Just some movie I watched. It got me curious. You know I didn't have the benefit of our fine education system like you did.'

'I think it was about the end of the sixteenth century, or maybe the early seventeenth,' she replied. 'Don't you have an encyclopedia on CD? You could look it up.'

'Maybe . . . it's not that important,' I said.

The phone rang and saved me from further explanation. It was Brad.

'Where have you been?' he asked.

'I've been right here.'

'I tried to ring all yesterday afternoon and last night. You weren't home.'

I'd been so far under I couldn't hear the phone ring. Scary. 'I was here. There must be something wrong with the phone.'

'Yeah, right. If you've got some guy, you can tell me. I can handle it, you know.'

'Did you ring me to abuse me?'

There was a short silence and then: 'No. Sorry. I actually rang because it's good news. I was so anxious to tell you yesterday I got a little testy because you weren't around. Jeff and Ailsa already know.'

My heart was lifting up and up. I knew what he was going to tell me. There could be only one piece of good news. 'What is it?'

'Numb are contracting us for an EP. National release. We start recording in four weeks.'

'Oh my God, oh my God!' I yelled into the phone.

'Hey, not so loud.'

'This is so fantastic. This is it, Brad, this is the start of something.'

'Don't get too excited. It's only one EP—they want to see how we go before they sign us up and give us heaps of dollars.'

'How can I not be excited? Oh, God, Brad, this is it! This is where it starts.'

Karin was watching me from the couch, and I guessed she had gathered what the news was because she was smiling at me indulgently.

'So do you want to come out and celebrate tonight? Dinner at that Mexican place near Ailsa's house?'

'Yes, yes, a thousand times, yes. Hang on.' I covered the mouthpiece of the phone and said to Karin, 'Are you up for a celebratory dinner tonight?'

She nodded. 'As long as you don't mind David coming.'

That's right. Her husband. Couldn't have her all to myself any more. But I was so full of love and good vibrations at that moment that I would have happily had Ted Bundy at our dinner table.

'Brad? Karin and David are coming. Are you going to invite Marnie?'

'Maybe. If I can gag her first.'

'Then she won't be able to eat.'

'No loss—she's got a fat arse anyway.'

I hated that he talked that way about other women, but I loved that he talked that way about other women. If you know what I mean.

'Whatever. How about seven o'clock?' I asked.

'Cool. See you then.'

I hung up and grabbed Karin in another bear hug. 'My life starts now,' I said. The seventeenth century seemed like a very long time ago.

*

We must have made an odd-looking party: Brad, Jeff, Ailsa and I all unkempt and dressed in op-shop clothes; Karin dressed in crisp floral and with her hair rolled into a neat bun; and David looking like a forty-two year old accountant with his round glasses perched on his nose, his silvering hair neatly combed and his clothes immaculately pressed. Despite this, we had a good celebration. Jeff took a liking to David and sat next to him all night, asking him questions about Sydney, where he had just moved from, and London, where he was born. I couldn't tell if David was enjoying the attention or suffering some kind of social hell—his face gave nothing away. I guess it was a successful evening, and I was thinking at the time that it might just about have been the most hip and exciting thing David had ever done: dinner with 747, soon-to-be-famous rock stars. Perhaps that was a little egotistical. He shook everybody's hands very sincerely when he left, while Karin gave me a hug.

'Did you have a good night?' I asked her.

'Yes. We both did. It was good for us to get out. We kind of ran out of things to talk about on the honeymoon.'

'How could you run out of things to talk about?'

'We're both very quiet. Sometimes it's hard.' She looked over at David with a weak smile. Now I was getting worried. 'Maybe we should take Jeff home with us. He seems to make conversation easily,' she said, laughing nervously.

'That's because he's off his face. Perhaps you could try that.' I gave her hand a squeeze. Then David was there, taking her other hand and pulling her gently away. They disappeared into the car park.

'Who's coming to my place for copious amounts of alcohol?' Ailsa said.

I went home alone.

If it wasn't for Brad, I think I would have felt alienated from the rest of the band. For a start I didn't drink, smoke or dabble in substances, and while they were swapping poisons I looked on mutely, feeling like the Polly Pureheart Jeff always said I was. But you couldn't blame me. My father didn't smoke, drank only socially, ate a fairly normal diet and even managed to get out for a run every so often. But he dropped dead of a heart attack two days before his forty-third birthday. Just sitting there one minute, Mum said, next minute dead on the floor. It was the most awful time of my life, and it didn't help that it was shortly after I had run away from home and I was on the road somewhere with Brad's band. Mum couldn't contact me, so I rang on Dad's birthday only to find that it was actually Dad's funeral.

So, six years later, when I collapsed on stage and ended up in hospital for a week after a heavy dose of something Jeff had dug out of his sock drawer, I swore off everything. I don't want to drop off a chair like that, dead on the floor.

At our practices over the next four weeks, Brad was all that stood between me and total alienation. He and the other two went thirds in bags of tobacco, bottles of bourbon, joints and pills. But Brad's constant desire to get into my pants meant he always acknowledged my existence at least, and sometimes took pity on me and opted out, sitting with me in the corner of our hot little practice room while I quietly ran over the songs on my guitar.

It was hard to be unhappy about this isolation,

though. In the wake of our wonderful news I found I was bubbling over with eternal forgiveness for everybody: Jeff, Ailsa, Brad, Clark, Angie, the pointy-faced woman who scowlingly took my phone money at the post office, even the guy who rang up at eight a.m. asking if I wanted to buy roof tiles. As the weeks went by, my adventure through the land of stupid clothes and arranged marriages started to seem more and more like a vivid dream. In any case, my nocturnal habits returned to normal, and I was more likely to dream about being back at school and not being able to find a toilet than about the seventeenth century. I started to think that maybe that one little trip had been all I'd needed.

But of course, the universe doesn't work that way. The universe is not orderly, reasonable or to be bargained with. The universe is chaotic, insane and very fucking frightening.

I called Karin late Sunday afternoon before I left for practice. It was also the day before we were due to start recording, and I wanted to give her my phone number at the studio.

'How long do you think your recording will take?' she asked.

'We're booked in for two weeks, and we've got six songs to put down.'

'You mustn't be very good.'

'What do you mean?'

'As far as I can figure it out, six songs times four minutes is only twenty-four minutes. What do you do with the rest of the time, make mistakes?'

I laughed. 'I won't bore you with the intricacies of multitrack recording, Karin. Just know that I'm smarter than you are.'

'I've known that for years. That's why you're going to be famous and I'm going to be a mummy.'

'Are you for real? You're pregnant?'

'I'm eight days late and I'm queasy all the time. I might go for a blood test next week.'

I hesitated. 'Am I supposed to say congratulations?'

'I guess so. Let's wait until I'm sure.'

'Well congratulations in advance. Do you want me to be its godmother?'

'I haven't thought that far ahead.' She sighed. 'I'm scared about all this.'

'Don't be. Women have babies all the time. Jeez, if your mum could do it, I'm sure you could.'

'It's not just the pregnancy-childbirth thing. It's the ongoing responsibility.'

'I'm sure you'll make a fantastic mother,' I said. 'Does Dana know?'

'Mother? God, no. I don't think I'll tell her until the day before it drops out. She rings me every day, asking me if my marriage has fallen apart yet, and assuring me that she won't take me back if it does. No, nobody knows except you. I think I'll wait until the doctor confirms it.' She yawned loudly. 'I am so tired. I haven't had a good night's sleep in a week. My hormones must be out of whack because I'm having some really horrible nightmares.'

Yeah, I thought, but I bet they're not as grisly as mine. 'Maybe you should have an afternoon nap.'

'I can't—I've got a roast in the oven. You know,' her voice dropped to a whisper, 'I don't think David likes my cooking.'

'Why's that?'

'He never says anything. He just eats and then does the washing up, and never says "that's good" or "that's bad" or anything. It's very frustrating.'

'Why don't you ask him about it?'

'I don't know. It seems like I'm fishing for compliments then. Mind you, he doesn't really say much about anything. Up until the wedding there was a lot to talk about: the ceremony, the honeymoon, all that stuff. Now it seems we've run out of conversation.'

I didn't know what to say. If it was like this after seven weeks, what was it going to be like after seven years? And 'I told you so' was not something you said to your best friend.

'You're not regretting getting married, are you?' I asked.

'No,' she said, almost too quickly. 'No, I'm very happy. There's just some adjusting to do, that's all. He really is a lovely soul, Lisa. He's romantic and considerate, and he brings me flowers every Friday afternoon after work. I think he's been living on his own so long, he just doesn't know how to make conversation.'

'Well, the baby will give you something to talk about.'

'I hope so. I really do.' Clearly she was uncomfortable with this conversation because she changed the topic. 'Hey, I looked up that stuff for you.'

'What stuff?'

'You know—Queen Elizabeth.'

'Oh, thanks.' My comfortable state of denial evaporated.

'She died in 1603 and was succeeded by James the First, who was James the Sixth of Scotland. Does that help?'

'It wasn't important. But thanks anyway.'

'David's got this amazing encyclopedia, better than that CD one you've got.'

'It came with the computer.'

'Why don't you drop by one afternoon and check out all his books. Maybe when you've finished recording. I'd love you and David to get to know each other better.'

I guess I had to make the effort some time—it was obviously important to her that I like her husband. 'Sure, why not. Give me a ring to remind me.'

'Okay, I will. I'd better go, I think I can smell something burning. Love you, Lisa.'

'Yeah, Karin, me too.'

The phone clicked. I wondered if she really was happy cooking spuds for David. Maybe some people were easily pleased.

The bathroom window in my flat didn't quite close properly, and on windy nights like that Sunday when I got home from working at the Black Flag, the wind would make a creepy, howling sound that echoed off the smooth tiles. It was nights like that I hated living alone. The trees outside my bedroom made odd shifting shadows in the moonlight and, thanks to Karin reminding me, I couldn't stop thinking about my regression. I had buried it under the excitement of the past few weeks, but now I couldn't stop myself retracing the events I had witnessed, wondering what they meant to me now, and why I was plagued with that awful dream.

Despairing of sleep and craving a nice, safe, electric light I went to my desk and e-mailed Whitewitch. The regression had made me sick, I told her, had sucked me under for twelve hours, displaced me, left a cold moth of fear in my stomach, beating its wings madly if I thought about it too much. Finally, I hit send and went back to bed. I slept with the light on.

I figured the only way to keep the anxious, creeping feeling from worming its way into me was to forget about the esoteric and mysterious by throwing myself violently into the material and the temporal. Which is exactly what I did. From the moment I arrived at the studio, I took recording very, very seriously. I wouldn't go home. I was there when the engineer—who called himself Dick, though I doubt if that was what his mother had christened him—miked up the drum kit, ran leads all over the floor like skinny snakes, sound-checked the bass, rewound the tapes, fixed a pair of rogue headphones. I was there for every knob twiddle, every button push, every fader slide. Dick got sick of me, so did Brad, so did Jeff, so did Ailsa. I slept on the couch in the dark, airconditioned control room. Everybody else went home when they weren't needed, I just stayed and stayed, displaying a manic interest in the proceedings that slowly wore everybody down.

It was three days into the recording and I was lying on the couch, trying to catch a few minutes of much needed sleep, when the phone rang. I had my T-shirt pulled up over my nose because Dick and Brad were at the desk smoking. Dick answered the phone and Brad blew smoke rings at me just to be perverse. I was headachy and starting to unravel, and on the verge of telling Brad where to stick his cigarette, when Dick held the phone out to me. 'It's for you. Some guy named David.'

Momentarily, I couldn't remember anybody I knew named David. But when I heard his voice, I realised it was Karin's husband.

'David. What's up?'

His voice had jangled edges. 'I rang your house but you weren't there. The number was programmed into the phone because, you know, I didn't realise it until I needed to contact you that I don't even know your surname and it's just one of the things I should have asked Karin about, but it's good that you left this number on your answering machine because I wouldn't have known where to find you otherwise . . .'

'David?' I tried to sound calm, he was rambling like a madman. 'Karin knew where I was, I gave her the number on Sunday night.'

'Sunday night? You spoke to her Sunday night? Have you spoken to her since? Have you spoken to her at all since Sunday night?'

'No, David, I haven't.' I was starting to get worried. According to Karin this guy was Mr Mute, but right now he was just about blowing my ear off with the kind of anxious jabbering that Jeff was capable of on a bad trip. 'What's all this about?'

Suddenly he started sobbing. 'You haven't spoken to her? You haven't heard from her or seen her?' His words coughed out one at a time. Brad was standing close, looking at me with concern. Panic must have been seeping out of all my pores. My brain felt as though it was being squeezed by a large, hot hand.

'David, what's happened? What's happened to Karin?' I could feel the pulse in my neck throbbing. I wanted to scream at him.

He sobbed again, stopped speaking and just cried loudly into the phone. I was beyond patience. 'What the fuck is it?' I yelled. 'What's happened, for Christ's sake tell me what's happened!'

I heard him take a deep breath. I heard his lungs shaking with the effort. Finally, finally, in a small voice he said, 'She's gone.'

CHAPTER
SIX

The two policemen didn't look comfortable. One was perched on the edge of the sofa next to my feet, the other was making do on a broken swivel chair which wobbled violently every time he moved. It was a day later, and they had come down to the studio to talk to me. I still hadn't been home. The current crisis pushed me even further into my work at the studio. I was in a state of complete denial: everything would be normal if I just didn't think about it.

Brad and Dick looked on from the mixing desk. I had given them exactly ten minutes' warning that the police were on their way, and they had been smoking mull at the time. They had opened all the doors to give the place a much-needed airing, and Brad had to run out to the local convenience store for a can of air freshener. Now the studio smelled of marijuana overlaid with heavy floral perfume. The police didn't seem to notice, or if they did they were ignoring it for the sake of expediency.

'Miss Sheehan, you last spoke to Mrs French on Sunday?' said the younger officer.

Mrs French. I hadn't thought of Karin in terms of her married name yet. 'Yes, that's right. Around six or seven o'clock.'

'Can you recount, in as much detail as possible, what you spoke about.'

'I rang Karin to give her the number here so she could contact me if she needed to. She said she hadn't been sleeping well and she thought it might be because she was pregnant and—'

The officers were exchanging glances. I felt something sink inside me. They hadn't known, which meant that David hadn't known. My heart overran with pity for him.

'She said she was pregnant?' the older officer repeated. He was a tubby man with a shiny red bald spot.

'She suspected that she was. She was going to have a blood test this week some time. She was eight days late with her period.' I saw the younger officer blush, but the tubby one took it in his stride.

'Was it a planned pregnancy?'

'Yes. Karin had told me previously that they had been trying since the wedding night.'

'What else did she say on Sunday night? Remember, any piece of information, no matter how small, could help.'

I pulled my bottom lip between my teeth and tried to recall what we had talked about before we got onto seventeenth century history. 'She said she was scared, you know, worried about being a good parent. Then she complained about her mother.' I glanced up. 'Have you spoken to her mother?'

They gave me a 'do you think we're idiots' look. I smiled sheepishly. 'Oh, of course,' I continued. 'Anyway, she was complaining about Dana being a psycho bitch again. Then she talked about her relationship with David and how he never says if he likes her cooking or not. That's right, and she said they haven't got anything to talk about, which I think is a real concern after seven weeks of marriage.'

Again they exchanged glances. 'What was the nature of the complaint about Mrs French's mother?' said the young officer.

'Dana had been calling to ask her if she had realised she'd made a mistake getting married, and if so that was tough because Dana wouldn't take her back. That's the kind of woman she is—all heart. Then we just talked about general stuff and she ended by inviting me over some time in the next couple of weeks.'

The police officers didn't respond, they kept scribbling. Finally, the tubby one sitting at my feet leaned forward. 'So you're telling me, Miss Sheehan, that Karin told you she was probably pregnant and not entirely comfortable about it, that she admitted that her relationship was already on shaky ground and that her mother had told her in no uncertain terms that she wouldn't take her back?'

I was frustrated because although that was what I had said, I didn't mean it to sound so negative. 'She didn't say she was unhappy. In fact, I asked her if she felt she had made a mistake getting married and she assured me she didn't.'

'But you yourself suspected that she might be feeling that way, otherwise you wouldn't have asked. Mr and Mrs French met six weeks before the wedding, is that correct?'

'Yes. But Karin wouldn't run away. If she could stay with her psychotic mother for twenty-four years, she could endure anything. A husband who hardly talked to her would be a breeze in comparison.' But as I spoke, I started to think maybe it was feasible. Her one chance at freedom hadn't worked out as she hoped, she had a new baby coming . . . No, I refused to entertain the notion. 'I'm her best friend, officer, if she was going to go anywhere she would have told me.'

'Not if she thought that somebody could trace her through you. Did you know that Mrs French withdrew two thousand dollars from four different automatic teller machines on the morning of her disappearance?'

'No, I didn't.' And now doubt seeped into my mind. Could she have done a runner? After all this time, did she have it in her?

The tubby man was handing me a card. 'If you are her best friend, Miss Sheehan, she may try to contact you. Please call this number if you hear from her. Her husband is at his wits' end.'

I looked at the card, then up at them. 'Her mother? How did she take the news?'

'She seems to think that Karin has run away. She was more angry than upset.'

I considered this for a moment. Then the older man put his notebook away and stood up.

'Now,' he said, 'do you mind if I have a look around the studio?'

I could see Brad's body snap rigid with panic.

'Why?' I asked.

He gave me a self-conscious smile. 'I play a little blues guitar. I've always wanted to be in a band, but . . . well, my job is very demanding.'

'Sure,' I said. 'Dick will show you around.'

Dick gave him a guided tour of the control room and then took him and his younger companion into the sound booths. We could see them through the glass, Dick trying hard to appear straight, pointing to things and explaining how they worked. The tubby officer was eyeing off Brad's guitar. Dick walked up to the microphone and his voice boomed through the speakers in the control room. 'Brad, is it okay if he has a go on your guitar?'

Brad nodded. The next thing we heard was bad blues guitar. The police officer had an expression of intense concentration on his face. The younger man had an expression of intense embarrassment. Brad laughed. I tried to laugh with him but my face was made of stone. He came over and sat next to me on the couch, and stroked my hair. 'You need to go home and sleep, Lisa. You look absolutely wrecked.'

I gulped back tears. 'Brad, there's a lot of weird shit happening in my life and I'm really scared.'

'It's understandable that you should feel that way. You need to rest.'

'No, it's not just the obvious stuff. There's other weird shit I haven't told you about.'

'Your mind can play tricks on you when you haven't slept.'

I lapsed into silence and closed my eyes. The physical contact was soothing. I heard the police officers emerge from the recording booth.

'Thank you very much,' the older one said. 'And Miss Sheehan, please call us if you remember anything that may help, or if Mrs French tries to contact you.'

I lay there with my eyes closed and waved my hand to indicate that I'd heard. Shortly after, they left and the room became dark again when Dick closed the door. It was growing dark in my head too. I was very tired.

'Dick,' Brad said, 'I'm going to take Lisa home. I'll be back in half an hour or so if you want to take a break.'

'Sure, man. I'll see you back here around seven o'clock then.'

'Okay.'

Brad helped me off the couch and outside to his

car. The fading daylight was still bright enough to make my eyes ache after days of darkness in the studio, and Brad's car was hot and sticky. I sat in silence until we got home and Brad walked me up the stairs and let me in.

My flat had been locked up for three days and it smelled musty and airless. Brad went around opening all the windows as I sat in a weary stupor on the couch.

'Why don't you go take a shower?' he asked.

'I'm too tired.'

'Go on. You'll feel much better.'

I dragged myself into the bathroom, but once I was in the shower I was too tired to get out. I stood there watching the water glistening in the twilight that filtered through the window. I don't know how long I would have stayed in that position had Brad not eventually knocked on the door.

'Have you drowned?' he asked.

I hadn't realised he was still here. I twisted the taps off and emerged in the living room wrapped in a towel.

'You can go,' I said.

'I want to make sure you're in bed asleep before I go anywhere.'

'Okay, okay. I'm going to get into bed right now. You can go.' I walked into my bedroom, dropped my towel and snuggled under the covers. The sheets were cool and comforting. They hugged my damp body. 'Okay, I'm in bed,' I shouted. 'Go back to the studio and do some work.'

He came to stand in the doorway to my bedroom. 'Will you be able to sleep?'

'Right now I'm thinking I might never be able to wake up.'

He moved forward and half sat, half lay on top of

my bed next to me, and began to stroke my hair as he had at the studio. 'Do you think Karin really did run away?'

'I don't know,' I replied, not really thinking about Karin, thinking about the proximity of his body. 'I just can't believe she wouldn't tell me.'

'What other explanation could there be?'

'How about kidnapped by a madman? The same guy that killed Steven?'

'You mean Simon?'

I sighed. 'Yes, Simon.' I never was good with names.

'It's not very likely, Lisa.'

I rolled over on my side so my body was parallel to his, and I studied his face. He had narrow green eyes, long eyelashes like a girl's, dark eyebrows. He needed a shave. I reached out and stroked his chin.

'Growing a beard?' I said.

'I will if you want me to. Do you think that would be sexy?'

'I always think you're sexy.'

He kissed my forehead gently and I could feel something melting and moving inside me. His lips moved down along my nose and finally he kissed my mouth. His stubble scratched my face, but his lips were warm and soft and wet. His long, tawny hair fell across my cheek. His kiss was deep and slow. I felt his warm, rough hand in my hair, but as it travelled lower and began to pull at the sheets, I stopped him.

'What are you doing to me, Lisa?' he said close to my face. 'I've got a hard-on like a fucking rail spike.'

'Brad, I'm sorry. It would make our relationship too complicated.'

'Our relationship is already complicated, if you hadn't noticed. The whole world can tell we want to fuck but we don't. So I go out with a string of bimbos and you haven't had sex in . . . how long?'

'A while.'

'It must be over a year. Have you taken a vow of celibacy?'

'I've still got my right hand, you know.'

'We're both dissatisfied with our personal lives, we both want each other, we get along great, we share the same interests . . . I don't see what the problem is here. We're made for each other.'

'I want something different.'

'What, a guy with an extra arm growing out of his forehead or something?'

'No.' I squirmed under the covers. This conversation was making me very uncomfortable. 'I'm so manic and unstable and so are you. I want a person who's gentle and calm. Somebody like my dad.'

'A bit rotten and worm-eaten, then?'

I laughed in spite of myself. 'Maybe just somebody who won't make jokes about the dead.'

'Fine, you want to go out with some pansy, you do so. But you won't stop wanting me.'

What a terrifying thought. But I was so tired, too tired to think about things like that. Too tired even to think about Karin or murder or nightmares or trips into the past. And maybe I'd made myself that tired on purpose, so I could have a proper rest. So I could sleep like the dead.

'Brad, I'm tired.'

'I'll stay here until you're asleep.'

'I won't be able to sleep with you lying there.'

'Turn over.'

I rolled onto my other side and he cuddled up behind me. I went to sleep like that, with his arms around me. I slept so deeply I didn't hear him leave.

Fourteen hours later I was paying a cab driver outside the studio. I'd slept for what seemed like years, but when I woke up, there was nothing but my thoughts to keep me company, and they weren't friendly, being so intent as they were on constructing grisly endings for Karin. So I came straight down to where I knew something was happening. Dick usually slept from three a.m. until eight, so I knew that somebody would be there.

In fact, everybody was there. The control room smelled like coffee and McDonald's breakfast bags full of greasy hash browns and bacon. Jeff was chasing Brad around inside the large recording booth in one of his manic fits. Ailsa was in my customary spot on the couch, pigging out on McDonald's. Dick had the paper spread out across the mixing desk. The soundtrack to all this was the drums and bass track for one of our songs, which was up way too loud for this time of the morning.

'Hi, everyone,' I yelled. Brad and Jeff couldn't hear me. I pulled up a chair next to Dick and asked him where we were up to.

His look said it all: oh no, she's back. 'We're just having a breakfast break and then we're going straight back into it,' he said, almost defensively.

'Okay,' I said, resting my elbows on the desk.

'Hey, check this out,' he said, flipping back to the front page of the paper. 'They found another body in the forest.'

'Yeah? What, killed the same way?'

'Yep. Tied to a tree. It had been there since early Monday morning according to this. Can you imagine the mess after four days? Jeez, I'm glad I didn't find it.'

Of course I could imagine it: the grey body, the dried blood, the gaping holes where organs should be, the sightless face covered in ants. I could imagine it too well. I shivered.

'He was only a young guy too,' Dick continued. 'Here, look, they've got a picture.'

At first I thought he meant a picture of the body, and I recoiled. But it was actually a family snap provided by the grieving mother, a picture of a whole young man with a blond ponytail, wide forehead, smiling eyes. But now I was looking at him closer, so close he became a mass of black and white dots and I had to rub my eyes. Then I refocused and hot stars of fear were bursting into my veins and I couldn't stop the torrent of emotion that was rising in me. At the same moment as the music stopped, a loud hysterical sob broke out of me and I collapsed onto the desk. Dick looked alarmed, Ailsa rushed over, and even Brad and Jeff must have noticed the movement because Brad was hurrying out of the booth as well, pushing Dick and Ailsa out of the way and grabbing me almost violently around the shoulders.

'What is it?' they were all asking.

'Look at him, look at him,' I repeated, shaking the paper and pointing like a simpleton.

Brad took the paper off me. He scrutinised it momentarily, then let it drop to the desk. 'Oh God,' he said. 'Another one.'

Now that two of our frequent flyers had bought grisly murder at the hands of a madman; now that Karin had disappeared, and now that I knew I had been some kind of mad nympho witch in a previous incarnation, I realised that life wasn't ever going to be the same again. And that made me more angry than you can imagine. Things were way beyond my control, and this should have been the happiest time of my life, the last hurdle before the big time. I felt robbed. I felt trapped, like there was this fate planned out for me that I couldn't escape or change no matter what I did. It rendered me powerless.

I was struck by a desperate need to do something, anything, to make me feel effective. So I left the studio immediately and went straight home to find the business card that the tubby police officer had given me. His name was Sergeant Pyle, and I wondered briefly if his first name was Gomer. But there's not much humour in anything when your whole world has been turned on its head, so I didn't laugh. I tried to ring, but the line was busy. I waited ten minutes and tried again—still busy. I couldn't bear sitting around in my living room doing nothing, waiting for the line to be free. Instead I caught the bus down town, and walked the five blocks to the police station.

The airconditioning in the police station was up way too high. I shivered as I stood at the counter waiting for the two receptionists to finish their conversation. I mustn't have looked like a rape victim, because they treated my arrival with a casual air.

Finally, the blonde one came up and asked if she could help me.

'I want to see Sergeant Pyle in relation to a case he's working on.'

'I'll just see if he's available. What's your name please?'

'Lisa Sheehan. It's about the disappearance of Karin French.'

She picked up a phone and dialled through to Sergeant Pyle, indicating a row of seats with her spare hand. I sat down heavily. Directly across from me was the open door to a cramped office where a young man was working. He was looking at me but quickly looked down at the papers on the desk in front of him when I glanced up. His heavy, black hair fell over his face and he pushed it away with one hand.

Sergeant Pyle emerged from behind the receptionist's area and came to sit next to me.

'Good morning, Miss Sheehan.'

'Hi. Jeez, it's cold in here.'

'Yes, we've all complained about it. They're supposed to fix it some time this week. Until then we all dress up warm.' He indicated his woollen vest, which was stretched too tightly across his belly.

'Have you heard from Karin?' he continued.

'No. But something else has happened and I need to speak to somebody. You know the body they found in the forest?'

'Yes, but that's not being handled by—'

'No, just hear me out. He was one of our fans, you know, a regular at all our gigs. So was the first guy.'

'Is that right?'

'Yes. So now I'm thinking that maybe . . .' My voice started to crack. I was being made to say aloud what I hadn't given words to yet. 'I'm thinking maybe whoever did it might have taken Karin as well.' It was no use holding it in. I was blubbering like a teenager, and I was so embarrassed because the guy in the little office had looked up again.

Sergeant Pyle called over his shoulder to the receptionist. 'Alice, put the jug on, will you?' He turned back to me. 'Would you like a coffee?'

'No, no. I don't drink coffee. I don't suppose you have any herb tea?'

'Alice, have you still got that hippy shit that Constable Foster used to drink?'

'Yes, Sarge.'

'Can you make us up a cup of that, and a coffee for me: two with moo.'

'Coming up.'

Sergeant Pyle sighed and looked at me carefully. 'Let's be rational for a moment.'

I nodded tearily.

'Your friend Karin was unhappy, although she probably expected to be very happy, being newly wed. She knew she couldn't go back to her mother, and maybe she was even too embarrassed to go to you. More importantly, people who get abducted don't withdraw money from their bank accounts first.'

'Somebody could have forced her.'

'We have a photograph taken of her at one of the ATMs. She was by herself.'

Again I nodded.

'So, we're not treating Karin's disappearance as though it were suspicious. Can you understand why?'

'I guess so. But what about the other—'

'Now, that *could* be suspicious. Are you sure that both of the murder victims were fans?'

'Absolutely. The first one, Simon, was on his way to see us the last his friends heard of him. The other guy was killed early Monday morning. Our last gig was Sunday night.'

Alice came across bearing two cups. My tea was too weak: she hadn't let it draw. I sipped it once then put it on the floor beside my feet.

Sergeant Pyle pressed his lips together and fell silent for a while. 'Again,' he said eventually, 'let's be rational. We could still be looking at an unfortunate coincidence. Drunk kids hanging around nightclubs are easy targets for all kinds of looneys. And there is absolutely no reason to believe these deaths are in any way connected with Karin. Next time I'm upstairs with the CIB guys I'll mention it and get them to contact you, but I want you to calm down and not jump to any conclusions. Okay?'

I sniffed and wiped my nose on my sleeve. 'Okay.'

He blew on his coffee, then sipped it gingerly. 'Well, Lisa, I have about a million and one things to do. You don't mind if I leave you here to finish your tea?'

I handed him the cup. 'I don't really want it. Thanks anyway.'

'Fine. Thanks for coming down.'

'No problem.'

He stood and headed back towards the reception-ist's area. I checked to see if the dark-haired man was watching, but he had his head bent over his work. I dragged myself to my feet and left.

Halfway down the block, I heard somebody call-ing, 'Excuse me'. I didn't think it was for me until the third time he said it, then I turned and noticed the young man from the police station hurrying towards me. I stopped and waited, curious. He caught up and stood next to me, shifting uncomfortably from one foot to the other.

'I'm Liam,' he said at last, extending his hand. I took it and shook it lightly. His hand was warm and firm, his nails neat and clean.

'I'm Lisa,' I said. 'Are you a police officer?'

He glanced back over his shoulder at the station, then shook his head. 'I'm working here temporarily on a juvenile crime project. It's just that I couldn't help overhearing some of your conversation with Ser-geant Pyle. About your friend.'

'Oh.' I was embarrassed; I don't like to let people see me blubber like a kid.

'Yes. I thought . . . I mean, you seemed upset and I thought . . .' He trailed off and bit his lip. Obviously he was regretting coming to speak to me. I tried to look unthreatening. He was really cute, with large, liquid brown eyes and full lips.

'Go on,' I said.

'I just thought I'd keep an ear out for you at the station. I . . . I sometimes hear what's going on. They don't tell people everything.'

'Ah. That would be great. My friend's name is Karin Anders . . . no, now it's Karin French. If you hear anything . . .'

'Yes, sure. I'll let you know.'

I looked at him closely. 'Why are you doing this for me? Won't you get in trouble?'

He shrugged. 'I don't know. You seemed so . . . I mean, you were so upset.'

It was more than that, I knew it was more than that, but I had trouble believing that such a straight looking guy could find me attractive. Honestly, in my crumpled satin skirt and old T-shirt, I must have looked like something the cat dragged in.

'Thank you.'

He was pulling a business card out of his pocket and scribbling on the back. 'This is my home address and phone number if you want to talk to me or . . . you know, if you want to ask me anything.'

I took the card from him. Liam Baker.

'Were you very close?' he asked.

'With Karin? Yes. Very close.' The shaky feeling in my chest started again, and I felt on the verge of tears.

'They said she went to four different automatic tellers and withdrew five hundred from each. That's why they think she's run away. But you don't think she's run away?'

I pressed my lips together hard, as though that could hold back the tears. 'I don't know any more,' I said quietly. 'I just want to know that she's okay.'

Then a little sob broke out of me and the hot tears sprang to my eyes. He felt in his pocket and handed me a clean white handkerchief. I was stupefied. I didn't even know a guy who *owned* a hanky, let alone one who would offer me one. I took it carefully and wiped my eyes and blew my nose.

'I'll wash it and send it back,' I said, feeling foolish.

'Don't worry. I've got plenty more.' He scratched the back of his head. 'I'd better get back.'

'Thank you so much. Here, let me give you my phone number in case you do hear anything.'

He handed me a pen and another business card, and I scribbled my number on the back.

'Thanks,' I said, handing them back. 'Do you think you could keep an ear out for any information about those two murders too?'

He looked curious. 'The bodies in the forest?'

I nodded.

'Sure. But CIB is on level five. I don't see them much.'

'Whatever. I really appreciate this.'

He stood quietly, looking at me, then nodded and said goodbye before heading back towards the station.

Too many unpleasant things were happening at once, and I couldn't help but speculate that they might all be related. I kept remembering what that phone-in psychic had said: 'The universe is definitely trying to tell you something.' Was there a warning in my dream, something related to a life lived nearly four hundred years ago?

I knew, deep down, there was only one way to find out, but I was scared to go tripping back to the

96

past again. Whitewitch had said I would be in control, but she had been wrong.

When I got home from the police station, I checked my e-mail. Whitewitch hadn't let me down. She had written 'Don't panic' in the subject line.

> . . . *You woke up, didn't you? I'll admit your reaction was extreme, but that just convinces me more that you must go back there.*
>
> *You can protect yourself by boiling some water with chopped celery leaves and parsley on top—both are well known for their purifying and grounding qualities. Allow it to cool and then drink it directly before you regress. This should help you stay anchored to the real world.*
>
> *Please, Lisa, don't stop now. It sounds as though it's far too important to ignore.*

This was ridiculous. Celery and parsley soup?

But she was right—it *was* far too important to ignore. I sat, not moving, for about twenty minutes, trying to decide. Okay, so there was probably some hundred year old rubbery celery in the bowels of my fridge, and I grew parsley on my kitchen windowsill, though it wasn't looking real healthy.

And I could always do it sitting up at the kitchen table with my head on my arms, then I wouldn't choke on my own vomit and die like a seventies rock star.

So I called the studio and told Dick to let Brad know I was taking the afternoon off. I could hear the relief in his voice. I put the chain on the door and pulled the phone out of the wall.

I got cooking.

CHAPTER
SEVEN

I didn't have the opportunity to speak to Gilbert again for nearly two months. Every evening when I climbed into my bed I died with frustration, and every morning I was reborn with hope. But he would be with Uncle Tom or with Mirabel or away on business or out hunting. The wedding was arranged and executed quickly. The night before, a tearful Mirabel crept into my bed and swore to me that she would try to love him, before falling asleep virginal at my side. The wedding was held in our own chapel, with our chaplain Master Gale presiding. Gilbert took Mirabel to London with him the next day, where he kept rooms. He had made a small fortune trading in wool and also held interests in the Eastern trade industry, hence his trips to the Orient. He was well connected, though not titled, and as all his family's property was entailed upon an older brother, Uncle Tom insisted upon his residing at Prestonvale and learning our family business so it could be passed on to any heirs Mirabel might produce. The trip to London was to collect some of his belongings. I was more jealous than you can imagine, seeing that beautiful man take Mirabel to London, she who could never appreciate him as I could. My already restless spirit hammered at my ribcage.

When I did finally see Gilbert alone, it was most unexpected. I was in the habit of walking by the river every afternoon if the weather was fine. I took a path through the woods, picking over the bracken and running my hands over the rough trees along the way. The river, which was narrow and sluggish through our estate, was full of mossy rocks, and mugwort and bog weed grew in the shallows. The trees crowded up almost to the river's edge, but Uncle Tom had had a few cleared away and occasionally fished from one of the stumps. And it was on one of those stumps that Gilbert sat as I emerged from the woods, looking at me almost as if he were expecting me.

'Elizabeth,' he said, showing no surprise at all.

My frustration had mounted to such a degree that I nearly let all the words I knew split me open and gush forward. I hurried over and knelt next to him, my skirts dragging in the boggy ground. 'Gilbert. At last, at last.'

He smiled at me in a kindly, almost fatherly way. 'Ah, but you don't want me. You only want what I can teach you.'

He was terribly appealing. I took his hand in mine. 'Sir, I couldn't have you, even if I did want you. You're married to my cousin.'

He stood up and pulled me to my feet. 'Let's walk. What do you want to know?'

We began to walk along the river's edge. 'I want to know what you meant that morning you came to my room. You said "the pursuit of godhead". What did you mean? How far have you gone?'

He drew a little breath, and I couldn't tell if it was a weary breath or the breath of a storyteller about to embark on a tale. 'You would understand if I told you that my whole life has been devoted to the gathering of knowledge. That besides knowledge there is nothing worth having in this world.'

I nodded, dividing my attention between his dramatic profile and the uneven ground below my feet.

'And I started early, gathering knowledge. My father was a scholar. I learned Latin at his knee. I read the great classics before I was eight. I studied medicine, philosophy, law at a university on the Continent. And yet I thirsted for more. I made friends at university, friends who had other acquaintances that knew things which could take me higher, further, faster than ever before.'

'What kind of things?'

'Alchemy, astrology. I immersed myself in the Hermetica, the Kabbalah, the writings of Agrippa and Paraclesus. I began to realise that I wanted to understand nature and the principles of the universe only in order to control them. That is when I started experimenting for myself.'

He fell silent for a few moments.

'I consulted ancient manuscripts bought from strange, furtive people who smelled of incense and damp earth. I went beyond the principles of the universe I'd already learned. I entered a different realm, where man was no longer the only conscious being at work, where formless essences crowded around me, whispering their arcane secrets into my ears. I was up until the blackest hours of the morning, working by dim lamplight because they wouldn't come to me unless it was dark, listening, copying down secrets, incantations, spells. I began to piece the information together. I grew tired of shadowy sprites. I wanted to go further yet, all the way into the burning light of true, pure knowledge. True, pure power. I wanted to be a god myself. I wanted to be immortal. I summoned their master.'

We had stopped. He took my hand and led me to a rocky outcrop over the river. He settled down on a large flat rock and I sat beside him, gathering my skirts around me. A little weak sunshine fell on us. The woods were very quiet.

'Who was their master?' I asked, more to fill the silence than to know, because I thought I already did know.

He turned to me and smiled. 'You'll find out soon enough. For now, I want to show you something. Close your eyes.'

I leaned into him and closed my eyes. He slipped his arm around my shoulders and touched two fingers to my temple. I breathed in the warm musky scent of him.

'Just relax,' he said.

The warmth from his fingers seemed somehow to be working its way into my brain. Far off I thought I could hear a low, rushing sound. A smell of tropical flowers engulfed me. A wash of warm blue gushed into my mind and I felt giddy with the movement. A vision came to me so clear and so beautiful that I thought briefly I was in heaven. Warmth. Sunlight. Tropical blooms. Trees hung heavy with fat fruit. The ocean, beating and beating against sand so white it dazzled me. The water was effortlessly blue, and it was as if I could see right into it, see it teeming with life. Pinks, greens, yellows. Even the air I was now breathing, which really came from the damp boggy woods, smelled of the tang of salt and was hot and wet like the kiss of the sea in the tropics. I sighed, and the sound came from very far away. The ocean was so loud, thundering onto the shore. I couldn't hear the silent woods, couldn't even comprehend how they must sound. My whole body became warm and

101

wet like the ocean, felt as though it were starting to pull apart, float away.

Then the vision was retreating, withdrawing from my mind through my temple as Gilbert gently pulled his fingers away. I tried to breathe the warm ocean air again, but all I got was the scent of damp earth. I opened my eyes. Gilbert was looking at me, his eyes seemed more focused than I had ever seen anybody's eyes before. As if he were looking at some real and unbendable truth about me that even I didn't know. I tilted my face up to kiss him, but he pulled away.

'No. There's more.' Once again he touched my temple and once again I relaxed into him and closed my eyes, expecting more divine tropical images.

But this time icy bolts shot into my head from his fingers. My first response was to pull away, but he held me firm. The vision was pale, bleak, cold. The sky was so far away, the sun a distant, blurred glimmer. Dark shapes circled above.

The vision came further into focus, solidified. The smells were like funeral smells, musty, mouldy. I could taste grit in my mouth. It was a field, tilled but empty of life. The ground was frozen, nothing could grow. But a plough had been through and it had overturned bones. Freezing and white they jutted out of the ground.

I heard a cold, passionless voice say, 'Behind you', and the vision started to reel around, as though I were turning. There were bodies on the ground. One man with blond hair like dirty straw gazed at the white sky with sightless green eyes. Small black beetles crawled in and out of his ear, suckled like infants around his nostrils and his mouth, scurried across his eyeballs. I could feel myself struggling with Gilbert, but in this vision I was powerless. A sense of hopelessness and desolation swept over me with such

102

exquisite clarity that I fell to my knees and grabbed at the sterile soil with my hands. My fingers struck a skull, grinning up at me through the dirt. I screamed somewhere far away in somebody else's body.

Suddenly the vision disappeared and I opened my eyes, gasping for breath, taking big gulps of reality. I was kneeling in the shallows with my fingers around a jutting rock. Gilbert moved his hand towards me and I recoiled in terror, thinking he would induce me into that place again.

He smiled gently and pulled me back to his side and brushed my hair out of my eyes. 'Unfortunately,' he said, 'your journey into knowledge will not always be pleasant.'

I stared at him mutely, trying to shake the horrible dead feeling that had settled on me. Perhaps I was getting in too deep with this man. Healing spells and love potions were one kind of witchery, but I had never experienced such compelling visions passed from one mind to another. The power he possessed must be immense. Through my horror ran a vein of something stronger, more solid. It was hope. Hope that I could become what he had become and forever escape this monotonous life I had been given without choice. Unpleasant? What could be more unpleasant than being eternally chained to a colourless existence, with no hope of reprieve?

'I don't care,' I said. 'I want a life of my own, to do with as I please.'

'We'll need somewhere to work. Can you help?'

'I'll do what I can. Uncle Tom would let me have any room in the house.'

He stood up and pulled me to my feet. We picked our way back over the rocks and onto the boggy ground at the edge of the river. 'I don't want a room in the house. We need something a good distance from the house. I was thinking of the gardener's cottage.'

'But Hugh and Nancy live there. They won't be happy if we move them out.'

'Their brief, pointless lives hardly make a difference to us. Do you understand that?'

I stared at my feet. 'I'll see what I can do.'

He stopped, turned me to him, looked at me carefully and smiled. 'You sound unsure of yourself, Elizabeth.' Sometimes his upper lip curled a fraction too much when he smiled, so that he almost resembled an animal baring its teeth.

'I am a little unsure. A little . . .'

'Frightened?'

'Unsettled. That vision . . .'

Without warning he pulled me violently into his arms and pressed his hard body against me. 'Ah, you feel like a woman. Not like Mirabel. She's still a child.' I could hear the desire in his voice, and moulded my body into his, turned my face up for his hot, wet kiss. 'Lie down,' he said thickly. 'I'll show you the pleasure in sorcery.'

'Lie down in the mud?'

'Yes, yes, lie down.' He gently pushed me onto my back on the ground. At first I tried to twist my neck up so my hair wouldn't get tangled in the mud, but he kissed me again and pushed me down with the force of his lips. I could feel his hand pulling at my skirts, pulling them up above my waist. I lifted my pelvis so he could clear the petticoats from underneath me. He pushed my legs apart and buried his face between them. I groaned and writhed on the slippery, cold ground.

'Close your eyes,' he said. I did so. I was back on the tropical island, and we weren't lying in the mud, but on the fine white sand. I could feel it under my hands. The hot sun was beating on us, I could feel its warm caress through my clothes. I gave myself over totally to the vision. I moved my hand through Gilbert's hair, and it was warm as though the sun had been shining on it. I began to feel the build-up of pressure in my groin, and then the hot rushing jolts of the little death beat through me and I lay still. But he didn't stop and miraculously the warm build-up started again. And again. And again. Over and over the unnatural spasms swelled into my private parts before I screamed for him to stop, thinking I would lose my mind if he continued.

He pulled his body up over the top of me, dragging mud all over my gown. He kissed me hotly with the taste of me on his rough tongue. I sucked at it gently. 'Sorcery?' I whispered.

'Yes. Sorcery. But there was some skill involved.'

I laughed softly, and his lips closed over mine, as if he wanted to capture my laughter in his mouth and swallow it.

We waded into the river, fully clothed, to wash the mud from ourselves, then headed home, freezing cold and dripping wet. Uncle Tom, sitting in the garden, believed Gilbert's story that I had fallen in the river and thanked Gilbert with embarrassing profusion for pulling me out.

'From now on when you walk by the river, Elizabeth,' he said to me, 'I want you to see if Gilbert is available to walk with you. I've always thought it unsafe, you wandering off by yourself.'

I was partly delighted and partly angered. That familiar feeling of being restricted unfairly wrapped its bands around my chest, and I merely nodded, looking at my toes.

'Go and put some dry clothes on, both of you,' Uncle Tom continued. 'I'll see you at supper.'

'But Elizabeth has something to ask you,' Gilbert said, and my head jolted up. Uncle Tom turned to me and gave me his fatherly smile. I didn't have the faintest idea what Gilbert meant.

'Go on,' Gilbert said. 'You can tell him what you told me, surely. He's your uncle.'

I stood bewildered for an instant, then the thought appeared, whole and formed in my head, that Gilbert meant me to ask for the gardener's cottage. I looked at him, wondering whether my mind had thrown up the idea spontaneously or he had put it there. His face was impassive. I had to do some quick thinking.

I looked at Uncle Tom. 'You said I needed a hobby.'

'Yes?'

'I know it sounds like a fond notion, but I've always wanted to paint.'

'Ah, painting. Do you want me to get you some art supplies?'

Gilbert interjected. 'I have some back in London that I can send for. I enjoy painting also. Elizabeth has asked me to teach her and of course I've agreed.'

Uncle Tom smiled broadly and nodded. 'Excellent. Gilbert, thank you so much. Our Elizabeth hasn't been the happiest of women these past six years. It will do her good to get away from her books.'

'We need a space, though,' I continued. 'A large space, an artist's studio.'

'You know you can have any room in the house.'

'Larger. I was hoping for the gardener's cottage.'

'Hugh's cottage?' he said.

'Hugh and Nancy are getting older. That cottage must be so cold in winter. I'm sure they'd rather stay in the house. And it's not as if Hugh gets up early and disturbs us any more. He's getting lazier and lazier as he gets older.'

'I don't know, Elizabeth. I'd hate to upset them. I think they're happy there.'

I pouted. 'I'd be even happier. Please, Uncle Tom. You know I don't ask for much.'

'You don't, you don't. And you've been so good to me.' He stroked his beard and pondered. 'What do you think, Gilbert? You and Mirabel will be in charge here one day.'

'Sir Thomas, I wouldn't presume to influence your decision. But Elizabeth is very bright and obviously very frustrated. And when I take over the financial management, she will have nothing to do. If she really is interested in painting, then I would recommend you give her the space and privacy she needs to indulge in it. If I feel after a few months that she doesn't have the talent for it, we'll close up the studio and Hugh and Nancy can move back in.'

'There's the big room on the chapel side of the house that they can have,' I said, my voice taking on the pleading tone that Mirabel used when she wanted Uncle Tom to acquiesce. 'And if you feel uncomfortable, I'll tell them myself.'

He looked slightly relieved, and I remembered that Uncle Tom liked always to be seen as the kindhearted, magnanimous master. 'All right then. All right, Elizabeth, you tell Hugh and Nancy. Gilbert, you can send for your art supplies.'

I threw my arms around Uncle Tom and kissed his cheek. He felt my back, realised how damp and cold I was, and sent me directly into the house to change.

That's how the first deception was laid. That's how I lied to my beloved uncle.

When I walked into Hugh and Nancy's cottage the

next morning, I made a mental note to air the place out as first priority. In the custom of old people, they had grown used to their own musty scent. Hardly any sun shone into their cottage as it was nestled in trees, and a damp smell was mingled with the smell of pipe smoke, stale cooking, and sickness and decay.

Nancy glanced up from her embroidery, then quickly hopped to her feet and gave me a small curtsy. Hugh was old and stiff, and was still struggling to get up when I said: 'It's all right, Hugh, stay where you are. I just wanted to have a quick word with you.'

Nancy settled down again and looked at me suspiciously. Rosemary shared all her own secrets and some of mine with Nancy. Nancy was old and superstitious, and far less likely to be enthusiastic about my dealings with the villagers. I tried a smile, and she smiled back narrowly, insincerely.

'Uncle Tom has been worried about you two, tucked away down here at the bottom of the garden. It's getting too cold for you in winter.'

'No, ma'am,' Nancy replied respectfully. 'Once we get a fire going in here, it's lovely warm. We haven't any complaints.'

I continued as if I hadn't heard. 'Uncle Tom has had a room on the chapel side of the house cleared for you. It's one of the largest in the house. You'll be able to have your meals in the kitchen with the other servants. Rosemary will cook for you. It will be far more comfortable for you both.'

Hugh shook his head sadly. 'But we love it down here, my lady. We love our little private place.'

'We're just trying to make life more pleasant for you. You'll have company up at the house.'

'We're company enough for each other,' Hugh said.

'Don't throw me in with that Rosemary,' Nancy

pleaded. 'She's hardly company—she never shuts up for an instant.'

'Please, please,' I said, 'trust me. This is for your own good. You'll settle in quickly and it will be far more cosy up at the house. I'd like you out by the end of the week.'

'And there's nothing we can do?' asked Nancy, distrust darkening her features.

'No. Nothing,' I replied.

'And what's to become of the cottage?' she asked.

'I'm turning it into an artist's studio. Mr Lewis is to teach me how to paint.'

'And that is the real reason we're being uprooted from our happy home, Hugh,' she said.

'Nancy, quiet,' Hugh said sternly.

'You're not endearing yourself to me, Nancy. Let's make this amicable,' I said.

She fought briefly with her temper. 'Ha! Whatever that means. You and your big words. You already know too much for a woman. Painting. Ha! I should tell your uncle about you and what you get up to in the village.'

Hugh reached across and clipped her around the ear. 'Nancy,' he said firmly, 'you've said too much. Please apologise to Lady Elizabeth.'

Nancy looked at me with eyes narrowed. Then she dropped her gaze to her lap. 'Forgive me, Lady Elizabeth.'

'We are both sorry, my lady,' Hugh said sincerely. 'And I hope this hasn't changed your good opinion of us.'

'You're forgiven,' I said, forcing my voice to sound even, charming. Nancy had frightened me, but I was fairly certain that she wouldn't dare tell Uncle Tom— my little commands of silence must surely appeal to her sense of superstition. But one of the first things

I would ask Gilbert to teach me would be how to silence people more effectively.

'I'll send somebody down to help you pack and move. Good day.'

I turned and left, closing the door behind me. I was momentarily haunted by the vision of Hugh sadly telling me they loved their little private place, then I stamped my foot. 'They are only servants,' I said aloud. 'Why should they have it better than I?'

But I knew that the guilt was attached to lying, not to taking what I wanted. So this was the road to deceit and evil. I was glad that my travelling companion would be Gilbert.

I supervised the cleaning of the cottage once the last of Hugh and Nancy's things had been moved out. Although we lit a roaring fire and the walls were scrubbed and new rushes and rugs brought in, the subtle mouldering smell could not be completely removed.

Mirabel came late in the afternoon, tapped lightly on the door and waited for me to greet her before she would come in. I grudgingly let her have a look around.

'Nancy's not very happy about living up at the house,' she said after she had settled on a rug in front of the fire. I sat down next to her.

'Nancy's a sour old crone. She's a servant and should be happy to have a place to live at all.'

She stared into the fire for a while, then turned to me. 'Gilbert's gone down to London.'

I hadn't known that. 'Has he? For how long?'

'He's gone to pick up his art supplies. For you.' The jealousy in her voice was painfully plain. I wondered if she knew how transparent she was.

'I'm sure he probably had other business there too.' And of course, the 'art supplies' weren't actually art supplies at all, but his books and potions. He had obviously wanted to travel with them.

She set her little jaw firmly, but she had such a doll's face that she couldn't possibly look serious. 'It's true what they say about you, isn't it? That you can do spells.'

'That's nonsense.'

'That you heal the villagers. Everybody loves you because of it.'

'I wasn't aware that everybody loved me.'

'Do you know how to make love potions? Have you used one on Gilbert? He talks about you all the time.' She slumped a little and went back to gazing at the fire.

I picked up her hand. 'I promise you, I have not put a love spell on Gilbert.' But I suspected he had put one on me. 'Gilbert's your husband. He loves you, not me.'

'When he said he was going to be down here teaching you to paint, I said I should like to learn also. He said that I was not mature enough.' She sounded like the petulant little girl again. 'Do you think I'm not mature? I'm a married lady after all.'

'Sometimes you're still like a little girl,' I said. 'Do you really want to learn to paint?'

She sighed. 'No. I only wanted to because I was jealous of you. You're clever and beautiful and mature. I'm sure you're the kind of woman he would rather have married. It's just that you don't have any property. Nobody would marry me if I weren't an heiress.'

I wasn't sure if this was false modesty or real insecurity. Either way, I felt no need to reassure her. So she sat there looking like a sad mammet, her big eyes shiny with unshed tears. I patted her hand then moved to stand up.

She grabbed my hand quickly. 'Promise me something, Elizabeth?'

I was growing impatient. 'What?'

'Promise me you won't put him under an enchantment to fall in love with you.'

'I've told you, that is all nonsense.'

'Just promise.'

'All right, I promise. Happy now?'

She nodded weakly. I continued with my duties. The next time I came into the sitting room she was gone.

It was strange how I felt about Gilbert being away. I was used to my heart skipping a little when I saw him walking in the garden with Mirabel; I was used to sneaking glances at his dramatic profile over supper. But not seeing him for days, after all that he had promised, was nearly unbearable. However, my life had been unbearable for so long that I was accustomed to it. I had a large oak desk moved into Hugh and Nancy's cottage, and I started to spend more and more time down there, reading, writing poetry, daydreaming by the fire—and those daydreams nearly always returned to Gilbert. I began to read Christine de Pisan's *Book of the City of Ladies* and I was so impressed with it, despite her primitive reliance on Catholic morality, that I embarked on my own treatise about women. Unfortunately, everything I wrote sounded bitter, and not evenheaded at all. But I was only a fledgling writer and had no doubt I would improve.

The time passed, as time does whether you want it to or not, until one afternoon we finally received word that Gilbert would be arriving home soon. Then, shortly afterwards, a long carriage full of old wooden boxes pulled up outside the cottage and a stream of pages and servants began to unload them into the sitting room. I gave strict instructions that nothing was to be opened until Gilbert returned home.

When all the boxes had been brought inside and I was by myself again, I sat on the floor next to the fire with my pens, ink and paper and continued writing, willing the hours to pass quickly. A commotion outside late in the afternoon roused me and I went to the tiny window to peer out through the trees. Another coach had arrived and Gilbert was stepping out of it, resplendent in rich red satin doublet and breeches. I expected him to go to the house first to greet his wife and Uncle Tom, but instead he came striding straight towards the cottage. I opened the door and waited for him.

He walked in, kicked the door closed behind him and gathered me into his arms. 'Elizabeth,' he whispered against my hair. I felt myself melting into him. He kissed me once, softly, then said: 'I have to go and be seen to be doing the right thing. Can you meet me here tonight?'

'What time?'

He smiled. 'Midnight is always the best hour for dabbling in mischief.'

'I'll be here at midnight then.'

Again he kissed me, deeper, slower. My hands felt his back, his shoulders. He released me suddenly. 'I'll see you at supper.' Then he was on his way back to the house.

And I realised then that I had fallen in love with him, but not how dangerous that could be.

CHAPTER
EIGHT

The grass was wet with dew and the air keen with the scent of midnight as I padded through the garden and out towards the cottage. Gilbert greeted me at the door, and I saw that he had already started to unpack the boxes. The sitting room was filled with frames, easels, oils in progress, all casting soft shadows in the lamplight.

'Real art supplies?' I asked, admiring a half-finished landscape.

'Yes. Your uncle will want to see some kind of work going on in here. We're going to set up in the smaller room at the back of the house. Here, help me with these.'

One by one, we dragged four boxes into the back room. The foliage was dense around this part of the house, and no direct sunlight would ever penetrate.

'It will be dark in here, Gilbert,' I said as we brought the last box in and made to pry off the lid. 'The trees are thick outside.'

'All the better. They don't like to come near open spaces.'

I nodded silently. My apprehension grew when he spoke of 'they' or 'them', but I fought it down. I was not a weak-livered idiot like Mirabel, afraid of my

114

own shadow. What had to be faced would be faced, with Gilbert as my guide.

We began to unpack the boxes. There were leather-bound books, some with fresh, new pages, some that were very old and filled with the kind of English spoken hundreds of years ago. Most were in Latin and Greek. One particularly large volume with thin bleached leather pages had *Liber Omnis Scientiae* embossed on the cover. I ran my finger over the letters. The book of all knowledge. Gilbert took it from me.

'This is the most important book I own,' he said.

'Why is that?'

'This is the one I'm writing.' He opened it and quickly flicked through the pages, and I could see his sprawling handwriting and strange symbols covering the vellum.

'You're writing a book?' I tried to take it from him again, but he held it back.

'No, Elizabeth. This isn't for the eyes of others. As I learn, I write it all down. You should consider doing the same thing. Commit your dark secrets to the page.' He caressed the book thoughtfully, almost lovingly. Just watching his hands move in that manner was enough to thrill me. I leaned over him and kissed his mouth.

'Back to work,' he said, stacking the book with the others at the back of a table pushed against the wall. 'Plenty of time for that later.'

Among the goods that Gilbert had brought from London were jars of thick green glass filled with murky liquids, bottles of herbs and seeds, copper dishes and a burner which he set up carefully on the table.

While unpacking the last few items, I pulled out two tall jars. At first I couldn't make out what they were filled with, but on closer inspection I realised I was looking at two containers of tiny organs.

'My God, Gilbert, what are these for?'

He patiently took them from me and stacked them on the table. 'Don't worry. They're from animals, not people.'

'But what are they for?'

He sighed and settled on the chest next to me, taking my hand. 'Do you need to know immediately?'

'Yes.'

'There is a lot of power to be captured at the moment of death.'

'You sacrificed these animals?'

He recoiled slightly, as though the words offended him. 'Sacrifice is such a crude word. I killed them, yes, in order to capture that power. Their hearts and their eyes prove useful at times.'

'I don't understand.'

'We're talking about the workings of the universe now, and I don't want to share that with you until after you have committed to joining me as an apprentice.'

'You know that I want to.'

'But you have to make a commitment.'

'Well, then, I commit myself,' I said lightly.

'You don't have to make a commitment to *me*.'

He paused. I looked at him for a clue to what he meant.

'Who then?' I asked finally.

'The dark angel. The master of spirits.'

'Satan?'

'Again, a crude name. A biblical name; he's older than the Bible. He's older than the Greek myths, so you can't call him Hades. He's older than the Egyptian legends, so you can't call him Set. He's eternally old.'

His voice had taken on that soft, captivating qual-

116

ity. I had to rouse myself to ask the question, 'Is he evil?'

'Good and evil are difficult terms to work with, Elizabeth. Don't you think it would be rather too convenient if there were good and evil in the world, rather too organised for a universe that makes so many mistakes? He's a very powerful force, and he doesn't mind sharing that power. Think of him as a channel between the energy of the universe and those who serve him, instead of as a force for evil.'

'But you called him the dark angel.'

'Dark because he's mysterious, hidden from the eyes of the world.'

I was becoming frightened. My dabblings in magic had been to do with healing and divination. Nothing that required death, nothing that required a pact with the Devil.

'I don't know if I can make that commitment,' I said quietly, looking anywhere but into his flinty eyes.

I could feel the anger radiating from him; it was so tangible and so violent that it occurred to me I might be in great danger. But he didn't touch me, didn't say anything. Finally I looked up at him. He had set his jaw hard as if that could keep the anger inside.

'I can see inside your head,' he said. 'I can see what's happening in there.' He put on a female voice, mocking me: "I only want to use my powers for good, Gilbert. Healing spells help people, I only do it because I want to be helpful." You're lying to yourself, Elizabeth. You don't care if those stupid villagers live or die, you just love the rush of power you get. You love their awe and their fearful reverence.'

'I don't want to be damned,' I said, tears welling up in my eyes.

'Who says you'll be damned?'

'But if I make a pact with Satan . . .'

'What are you talking about? Forget what you've learned from that pious fool Master Gale. There are no souls to be traded here. There is no hell for you to burn in eternally. When you die your soul lies dormant until another body is conceived that suits it. There, now I've told you too much. You can't learn more until you've made a commitment.'

'Stop talking in such veiled terms. Made a commitment, what does that mean? What commitment does he want?'

'You're worrying like an old woman. I've been through it and I'm still alive and well, aren't I? And the powers I have, Elizabeth. Don't you want them?' He reached forward to touch his fingers to my temple the way he had that day at the river, but I brushed his hand away. I remembered it very clearly, he didn't need to remind me.

'I'm afraid I'm not sure any more. I just wanted to go a little further than I've already gone,' I said. 'Can't I do this in small steps?'

'You're frightened. Your safety is more important to you than your dreams.' He paused for a moment then said, 'I've read what you've been writing, you know, your treatise.'

I was embarrassed to think that somebody as brilliant as Gilbert had passed his eyes over the crude words I had committed to paper.

'Go and get it for me,' he commanded.

'No.'

'All right, I'll get it myself.' He went to the other room and came back clutching a few sheets of paper with my writing over them. 'Would you like me to read this to you?'

'I know what it says.'

'But I don't think you *remember* what it says.

You're acting as though you don't remember. Let me see: *A Treatise Condemning the Subjugation of Women, in the Form of a Dialogue*. Ah, a worthy topic, Elizabeth. Let's see if you can take some of your own advice.

'*Cornelius: Tell me, good friend, why do you suppose it is that no women hold authority in this land?*

'*Timothy: Well, sir, that is incorrect, because until her death four years ago the greatest authority in this land was held by a woman, that being the Queen, Elizabeth, daughter of Henry the Eighth.*

'*Cornelius: Yes, the daughter of a king. Thus she came to her post through birthright, and not through wit or ambition.*

'*Timothy: I concede your point. I would be compelled to say, therefore, that women hold no authority because they desire no authority, but only desire their lot as the keepers of homes and mothers to the nation's sons.* Is that what this is about, Elizabeth? Do you only desire what Uncle Tom offers you: making gloves for Mirabel, playing the hostess to your uncle's guests?'

'He lets me manage his money,' I protested.

'And I can tell him tomorrow that I would rather do it, and that would be the end of that. Now listen, let me continue. *Cornelius: I ask why anybody could desire that lot when its only rewards are boredom, frustration and the occasional grudging thanks of men who know public life and have the means and the freedom to do exactly as they please at all times. Do you not think that awareness of the dichotomy between the two ways of life would quell any desire for the pastimes of a home-maker?*

'*Timothy: But sir, women are different. They think differently from us, and have been created only to crave security.* Ah, now we see where Elizabeth's motivation lies. Master Timothy is right, is he not? You, like all women, have been created only to crave security.'

'Gilbert, this is a little bit different from—'

'Shh. Let me continue. *Cornelius: I advance that women only* accept *security through custom, and actually crave something more. I wish to ask your opinion: in what ways are women different from men, my good friend?*

'*Timothy: Obviously they differ physically from men. They are weaker and more susceptible to emotional fluctuation.*

'*Cornelius: Let me ask, do you know of men weaker than yourself?*

'*Timothy: Yes, sir.*

'*Cornelius: And more prone to fits of depression or anger than yourself?*

'*Timothy: That I do, sir.* Lovely Socratic method, Elizabeth. I don't know why you're looking so embarrassed.

'*Cornelius: And yet you are not willing to deny them the world of men for these small differences. You are not willing to condemn them to a life of strangled fancies dreamed behind the ever-dipping embroidery needle.*' He threw the paper on the floor and crouched down next to me, his face almost touching my ear. 'Who is condemning you to this life of strangled fancies, Elizabeth? Is it me? Sir Thomas? The King? The Parliament?'

'Stop it, Gilbert.'

'Who is it, Elizabeth? Who is stopping you, right now, from achieving more power than a woman has ever known, from pushing beyond the bounds of knowledge, from commanding spirits to do your bidding, from achieving godlike status, from allying with dark forces beyond your comprehension? Who is it, Elizabeth?'

120

I resisted the urge to mutter a quick prayer, though I hadn't thought of God or heaven or sin since I was a girl, my weekly visits to the chapel having more to do with custom than faith. I shook my head mutely.

'Just answer the question,' he said, grabbing my upper arms violently.

'Me,' I said. 'It's me. I'm stopping myself.'

He released my arms and reached up to touch my face. 'Complicit in your own subjugation. What a good girl.'

And it was as if I could sense the years of frustration present in the room with us, as if they were pressing in on me. I felt keenly that all there was without Gilbert was waiting to die, the long empty years stretching before me. 'All right,' I said. 'I'll do it.'

Walking to the cottage the following night felt very similar to walking to my husband's bedroom on our wedding night. It was the same mixture of fear, excitement and unbridled desire. My husband had been a beautifully made creature, almost feminine in his lean lines and fine features. Gilbert, by comparison, was positively ugly, but he possessed something that Christopher had never had: a brilliant mind, the one quality guaranteed to arouse my desire beyond all temperance.

I let myself into the cottage. I could hear Gilbert moving about in the inner room. He had unrolled a thin feather mattress in front of the fire. I smiled to myself, thinking about making love to him there.

'I'm here, Gilbert,' I called, going to the mattress and kneeling in front of the fire.

'Good, I'll be out shortly,' he replied.

I sat back on my haunches and gazed into the

flames. Last-minute doubts crossed my mind fleetingly, but I suppressed them. Gilbert was alive and well, and he said he had done the same thing. He would be with me the whole time, so I had nothing to worry about. I just hoped there would be no pain.

Gilbert came into the room to sit beside me, and placed a small stone jar on the floor in front of us. He was completely naked. His body was warm and hard next to mine. I had to stop myself from staring at him.

'Where does your wife think you are tonight?' I asked.

'In bed next to her. She won't wake up.'

'Can you be sure?'

'Of course I can be sure. It's something you'll learn to do as well. Then you can send beautiful young men to sleep after sex and rob them.' He chuckled softly. I thought the idea had a certain appeal.

'Take your clothes off,' he said. 'It's warm enough next to the fire.'

I did as he bade and folded my clothes next to the mattress. He pushed me back slowly and lay down next to me, running his fingertips over my breasts and belly playfully. 'Elizabeth, you are so beautiful,' he said. 'Why haven't you remarried?'

'I have no desire to,' I replied.

He ran his hand over my stomach, then pressed it down gently. 'Ah, now I know. Nothing can grow in here.'

'You can tell?'

'Certainly. Give me your hand.' He took my hand and pressed it into my belly, placing his own hand over the top. 'Can you feel that?'

And I could. I could feel a barren silence, a kind of mute emptiness lying impassively beneath my fingers. He moved my hand up to my chest and pressed

122

there. Now I could feel activity, warmth, busy working organs. When he took his hand away all I could feel was my flesh and the low pulse of my heart.

'All the secrets I have to teach you,' he said. 'I'm so looking forward to it, Elizabeth, aren't you?'

'I'm a little frightened. Will you be with me?'

'I will always be with you, Elizabeth. I love you.'

I let him kiss me. 'I love you, too,' I said finally.

'I know. That's what makes it so perfect.'

He rolled away from me to open the stone jar. I saw that it contained a balm, not unlike those I had made over the last few years. He took a handful and rubbed it generously on his erect penis.

'That isn't a fidelity charm, is it?' I asked.

He laughed loudly. 'No. What need have I for your fidelity? I positively encourage licentious behaviour in you.'

'What is it then?'

'You'll see.' He put the jar aside, positioned himself over me.

'I'm scared.'

'Don't be. Open your legs.'

Just like the wedding night again. I opened my legs. He pushed my knees as far apart as he could, then entered me. But instead of moving, he remained still.

'What are you doing?'

He pushed down on my stomach, ground me hard into the mattress, thrust himself as far into me as he could, and yet remained still. Then I began to feel a burning sensation deep in my private parts. It started as a warm flush, but quickly began to spread and burn.

'Gilbert, what is it? That hurts. Stop it.'

'Just remain still,' he said.

The burning was growing, spreading, becoming

123

unbearable. 'Oh God, Gilbert, stop it.' I began to struggle, but he put one hand on my forehead and pinned me to the floor. I lay there, my entire body from the waist down on fire. It felt as though my insides were blistering and cracking. I howled in pain. A darkness began to descend on my head as I wriggled underneath Gilbert, trying to get away from the fire he had put inside me. I heard Gilbert say in a low voice, 'Take her with you', then the darkness descended and engulfed me.

I know not if what happened next was illusion or reality, or a weird hybrid of both. The burning had gone, and now I had a dry throat and couldn't swallow properly. My skin felt alive, as though it were covered in a swarm of tiny ants. I tried to move my limbs, but the most I could manage was to move my fingers at my sides. There was dirt under my hands, cool and dry. I didn't know where I was, it was very dark. I realised that the reason I couldn't move my limbs was because they were tied down, my wrists by my sides, my ankles spread apart. My eyes were adjusting to the darkness and I could see sentinel flames beside each of my ankles, but when I blinked they became short posts to which I was tied. The illusion shifted and returned, now flames, now posts. I called out for Gilbert, but there was no answer. My skin still tingled, and as I looked down at myself I thought I could see feathers sprouting from my body, but as I focused they were gone and my skin was smooth and naked. Now feathers, now skin, shifting and changing. I rolled my head back and groaned, closing my eyes. If I didn't look, it couldn't hurt me.

But I sensed through my closed eyelids a blinding flash overhead, and I opened my eyes to see what it was. High in the sky above me a ball of fire hung suspended. By its light I could see that I was in a clearing among tall pine trees, then they became towering stones, now trees, now stones. But the fireball remained constant.

As I watched, tiny flickers broke from the fireball and descended to the earth all around me, some landing on my skin and fizzling momentarily before disappearing into my flesh and plummeting into my body, their tiny white-hot points causing me to cry out in pain. Then larger flames jumped from the fire in the sky and howled down to the ground. This time, they landed all around me and formed a circle. As I looked at them, faces seemed to form out of the flames, then retreat again. They closed in on me. I was screaming and thrashing about, but unable to get away. I was sure that I was going to be burned alive, as a witch deserved.

I wanted to scream that I was sorry, that I repented, but strangely I had forgotten all words and only primitive grunting noises came out of my mouth, noises without meaning; the whole universe seemed to have lost its meaning, seemed to be beyond laws and principles, and had become something obscure and utterly, utterly chaotic. Still the flames moved closer, their faces appearing to taunt me, horrible twisted visions with tiny sharp pointed teeth, chattering then disappearing, grotesque features, eyes different sizes, different shapes, then nothing, nothing but the yellow-orange fire, coming closer and closer.

The first one touched my fingers and I jerked my hand away. Then they were on my bare feet and my ankles, moving over my arms and onto my chest, hot bright flashes swarming onto my body. A dozen with their vicious mouths were crowded over my breasts, greedily biting and sucking at them. Many others were swarming up between my legs, sending hot flashes into me, some swelling big and hard momentarily, then just as quickly becoming insubstantial again. But while I felt pain and expected to see my flesh turning black all over me, wherever they went they left my skin whole and smooth. I looked back up to the sky, focused on the fire above me, tried to block out the violation of my body by its fiery minions. I appealed to the light in the sky, with only meaning and no words to assist me. In an instant the small flames disappeared, and a hush fell on the woods that was eerie in its absoluteness.

Slowly the fireball descended. Slowly it began to take the rough shape of a man. Closer and closer until it was suspended less than a foot above my body. Somewhere inside my mouth a word like 'please' was trying to form. A hand reached out of the fire and stroked my cheek as if to reassure me. I did not burn, I felt nothing. More detail began to emerge from the blazing light: two strong male arms, a tightly muscled torso. The face remained blurred. The warmth from the light floated across my body, as it descended to the ground and kneeled before me, between my legs. It placed its forming hands on my upper thighs, dropped its forming head to my stomach and kissed my belly with such passion and tenderness that I nearly groaned in pleasure. Its face was emerging. I thought I saw two horns, then they were square animal ears, and then they were the leaves of a wreath. The nose was sometimes long and hooked, sometimes the snout of a creature, sometimes a strong line on a handsome male face. Clearer and clearer. Satan, Set, Hades. The three incarnations of the dark master that Gilbert had mentioned. There must have been more names for him, but it was feeding off my own imagination. I focused on Hades's handsome Greek face and melting brown eyes. The harder I concentrated, the less frequent the appearances of the other two creatures.

The beautiful Greek man kissed my stomach again, moved his face down. I could feel myself opening up to accept his deep kiss, but instead he trailed his mouth over my hip and down my leg, his beard scratching my soft flesh. Grasping my thigh firmly, he put his mouth over my tender skin. I sighed and relaxed into it. His hot, wet mouth sucked at my inner thigh for a few seconds. Then a blinding flash of pain shot through me as he sunk his teeth into my flesh. Just once. But the pain was unbearable, as if every nerve in my body were attached to the place he had bitten. He stood up and pulled a knife out of the air, a large curved sword, perhaps a small evil dagger—whatever it was, its sharp edge gleamed in the gloom. He lifted it over me, and once again I screamed. Only he didn't hack me with it, he hacked off the ropes that tied me to the ground. One by one he cut them, then cast the knife over his shoulder and disappeared instantly into nothing.

My body was still jangling with the pain of the bite. I barely realised that I was floating up and away from the ground. When I did, I flailed my arms and legs trying to find something solid. But still I drifted away from the earth, higher and higher. I placed a hand over the place where the man had bitten me and words seemed to be coming back to me. 'Stop the pain, stop the pain,' I cried. The pain began to retreat through my body, jaggedly dragging through my veins and nerve endings, withdrawing back into my thigh then disappearing.

As it disappeared, I had the horrible sensation that the pain had been the only thing holding me together. I could feel my left foot getting loose at the joint, then drifting off altogether. Then my right foot. I couldn't see what was happening to me, but all my joints felt as though they were loosening and coming apart; parts of my body were floating away from me. I tried to gain control of my arms, but they were going as well. First at the wrists, then at the elbows, then at the shoulders. Pieces falling off me and drifting into oblivion. Finally my head loosening at the neck, my torso floating away from me. My eyes feeling as though they were rolling hollowly in the sockets, popping out. Slowly falling to pieces and no sound coming out of my disintegrating mouth. Tiny piece of me left, little black part of me. Separating, undoing me, universe consuming me. Crumbling into blackness.

'Elizabeth.'

Gilbert was leaning over me. I could smell something bitter and I realised that it was me, sweating in terror. I was back on the feather mattress in the cottage, the fire burning cosily beside us.

'Was I. . .?'

'Dreaming? It depends on what you classify as dreaming. Something happened, didn't it? I can tell, look at your leg.'

I sat up, feeling both dazed and comforted by reality. Gilbert rolled my thigh around to show me. Where I had been bitten there was a small brown mark, slightly raised, about half an inch across.

'That appeared on your thigh about twenty minutes ago,' he said.

'I was here?'

'Your body was here. I don't know where the rest of you was. Watch this.' He poked the mark with his fingernail. I felt nothing. Numb.

'Completely impervious to pain,' he continued.

'What is it?'

He shrugged. 'I don't know what to call it. Some would say it's a witch-mark. You've been marked by the dark master.'

My heart picked up a few beats. 'Am I damned?'

He shook his head impatiently. 'I keep telling you, you can't be damned. There's nowhere for damned souls to go. Or innocent ones for that matter. They just keep revolving here around earth.'

I poked at the mark. I scratched it with my fingernail. Nothing. 'What's it for?' I asked.

'The spirits that you command need somewhere to feed. They suckle from it. It's like a nipple.'

'What do they feed on? Blood?'

'No. They take some of the power you gain for yourself. It doesn't hurt. You must trust me, Elizabeth.'

He kissed my forehead, then rose and walked back into the other room. I sat there looking at the mark on my leg, trying to regulate my breathing. He returned with a bowl of water, a cloth and a cup. He sponged the sweat off my body lovingly, kissing my face as he wet my hair and twisted it above my head in a neat knot.

'You need to sleep,' he said.

I nodded dumbly. My head was full of half-formed words and ideas. Terror was abating, bewilderment growing, excitement a barely formed impression.

'Drink this,' he said, handing me the cup. 'Wild celery and parsley. Purifies the blood, helps you sleep after the pact.'

I took the cup and sipped it slowly. He pulled me down next to him and nuzzled at my shoulder.

'Sleep now, Elizabeth. There's much excitement in store for you.'

I lay back and closed my eyes. 'I love you, Gilbert,' I said.

'I know. Now sleep.'

The dozy feeling of approaching sleep settled on me. Somewhere on my thigh I could feel something like a tugging sensation, perhaps a warm, moist little mouth feeding from me. I shivered in revulsion. 'Oh, God,' I said.

Gilbert touched my cheek. 'He can't help you now, Elizabeth.'

CHAPTER
NINE

This time I came to sitting in a puddle of my own piss. I'd forgotten that all-important last chance trip to the toilet. As my mind was off four hundred years in the past, my bladder had made an executive decision and decided to empty rather than explode. Thanks, bladder. Good to know somebody in the present was looking out for me.

I glanced at the clock above the table. This time it had been fifteen hours. I was surprised two months hadn't passed. It certainly felt that long since I had seen the inside of this flat. What had Gilbert said? 'Your body was here. I don't know where the rest of you was.'

So was he the dead man in my dream? It was hard to tell. It could have been the other man, Uncle Tom. The body was soaked so thoroughly in blood it was hard to make out features. But the woman with me had definitely been Mirabel. Blonde and childlike and crying helplessly. How the three of us ended up in the forest covered in gore was the next question. And the final mystery was what it had to do with me now.

I switched on the kettle and began cleaning up the puddle around the kitchen table. As I was rinsing out the mop, the kettle started to whistle and I reached over to switch it off.

Then froze.

In the steam rising from the kettle a face was forming, just like the faces in the fire that Elizabeth had seen. Two narrow eyes seemed to be blinking at me, a mouth stretched and twisted as though it was trying to say something. The face squirmed in the steam for a moment then shifted and disappeared. I kept watching. Closed my eyes and rubbed them. Looked again. Nothing. The kettle was screaming for me to switch it off, so I did. I'd been imagining it, right? Not unusual after what I'd just been through, surely.

I made a cup of tea then sat down to e-mail Whitewitch and ask her if hallucinations were part of the deal. And while I was at it, I mentioned the two murders, Karin's disappearance and my growing apprehension that it might all be related.

The whole thing was utterly disorienting, but not nearly so frightening as the last time and at least I wasn't nauseous. Once again I felt the need to sleep it off before I could think even remotely clearly. I got into bed, closed my eyes, tried to think happy thoughts. The record deal—I was going to be famous, that's right. Think about being famous, being loved by millions, being rich and having a big house by the ocean—real things, things that could happen in the present. Forget the past.

But I already knew I'd be going back there. No turning back now, I had to know the whole story.

'Jeez, Lisa, we've been worried about you.' Ailsa opened the door to the studio for me.

'I've been catching up on some sleep.'

'We haven't seen you for two days. Brad's spewing. We needed you yesterday.'

132

We were in the control room. I could see Brad in the large recording booth, hacking away at the guitar track for one of our songs. He hadn't seen me yet.

'I told Dick I wasn't coming in. Did you try to ring?'

'I think Brad did. And he went round, but he said you'd chained the door.'

The music stopped and Dick called through to Brad that I was here. He came into the control room scowling. 'Christ,' he said, 'first we can't get rid of you, then we can't get you in here.'

'Sorry. I was taking it easy.'

'You locked me out.'

'Well it is my flat. I can do that if I want to.'

He narrowed his eyes at me, then shrugged it off. 'I suppose you needed the break. I did your guitar track for "Morose". Do you mind?'

'No, I don't mind. Can I listen to it?'

'Sure. Dick, can you put "Morose" on again? Lisa wants to hear it.'

Dick grumbled about having to rewind the tape, but did it anyway. I sat down in the broken swivel chair in front of the desk and listened. It was magic, hearing a song that I'd written come together like that. In the studio, everything was cleaner, more definite than it was live. Dick had pulled an excellent drum sound. I marvelled at how something that had come out of my head, something intangible, had become something so big and so noisy. I smiled, a genuine, happy smile for the first time in what seemed like forever. I looked at Brad and nodded. 'Sounds great,' I said.

'We're starting vocals the day after tomorrow. We should be finished by Friday. Just in time to go back to the Treasury. Won't that be fun?' Brad loved playing cabaret music even less than I did, if that was at all possible.

'I guess we have to. My rent's due. Come on, let's get me miked up for the next song.'

Playing guitar in the studio was fun for the first twenty minutes and a bit of a drag for the next two hours as I went over and over parts, being criticised by Dick for racing or lagging or erratic dynamics. It was great to have something to do though, to be working towards something, making something happen. I felt as though I had some kind of influence on a life that had suddenly spiralled completely out of my control.

Brad took me home and I invited him up for dinner. It was rare that he would accept such an invitation because I refused to cook any meat and he was strictly a steak-and-potatoes man. He must have been as full of excitement as I was—that kind of energy loves company. He walked me up the stairs, jabbering away about how Numb were going to love us and how we were going to be big stars, while I tried to talk over the top of him, essentially saying the same thing.

I cooked some pasta while Brad cleared the piles of junk off the table and stacked them on the couch. I heard the phone ring and I called out to Brad to get it. Next thing, Brad was standing in the doorway looking at me.

'What?'

'Some guy on the phone for you. Liam somebody.'

'Liam? Oh. Can you just watch that pot and make sure it doesn't boil over?' I straightened my hair, I don't know why, just a spontaneous reaction. Brad caught the gesture and I could see his jaw tighten.

I went to the phone. 'Hello?'

'Hi, Lisa. It's Liam Baker here, from the police station. We met the other day.'

'Yeah, hi Liam.'

'You said I could call if I heard anything.'

'Yes, of course. Has something happened?'

'Oh, nothing major. I just . . . Um. A woman named Dana Anders came into the station yesterday to see Sergeant Pyle about your friend.'

'That's Karin's mother. Do you know why she came in?'

'As far as I know they called her and got her to come down. But Sergeant Pyle took her into his private office, so I guessed it might be important. She came out looking pretty upset.'

I froze. 'How upset?'

'Oh sorry, I didn't mean to panic you. I think she was angry more than anything. She had a scowl on her face and her eyes were shiny like she might have been crying.'

It didn't sound too serious. Dana was such a drama queen that the whole world would have known about it if it was really bad news. 'I wonder what that was all about. I'll have to give her a call. Thanks, Liam.'

'Well, I just hope it can be of some use to you,' he said. He sounded embarrassed. I wanted to reassure him.

'Oh, it is. I really, really appreciate it. Please, don't hesitate to call again.' I nearly added 'if you hear anything' but that wouldn't have been what I meant.

'Okay. Fine. Okay . . . um, I'll see you.'

'Sure, bye.'

I replaced the phone. Brad was watching me.

'You weren't supposed to be watching me, you were supposed to be watching the pasta,' I said, brushing past him into the kitchen.

'So, who's Liam?'

135

'I met him down at the police station.'

'Oh great, you're making gooey noises at a cop.'

I pulled the pasta off the stove and drained it. 'Number one, he's not a cop, he's a youth worker or something. Number two, I was not making gooey noises at him.'

He shoved both his hands up his T-shirt to make a mock pair of breasts, and put on a simpering female voice. 'Oh, I really appreciate you calling, Liam. Please call me again soon.'

I flicked him with a tea towel. 'I didn't say that. And I don't sound like that either.'

'And your tits aren't that big.'

'Oh, you're doing such a great job of making me want you, Bradley. I bet Liam wouldn't make fun of me.'

That got him where it hurt. 'So how did you meet him?'

'He overheard me talking to Sergeant Pyle. He felt sorry for me so he offered to tell me if he heard anything.'

'Jeez, some guys will do anything to get into a girl's pants.'

I added some pesto to the pasta and put it back on the stove. 'Yeah, like jumping on her bed when she's too tired to protest.'

'You protested eventually. How far has it gone then, this thing between you and him?'

'It hasn't "gone" anywhere. I've met him once; I've spoken to him on the phone once. The most intimate thing I did was borrow his handkerchief when I was blubbering everywhere.'

'He loaned you a hanky? What a pansy.'

'Fuck you, Brad, you're such a Renaissance man.'

'But he turns you on. I can tell.'

'He's attractive. Tall, dark, no beer gut.'

136

He ignored my pointed reference to his waist-line. 'Hanky boy turns you on. I can't believe it. If I'd known that all I had to do was loan you a hanky—'

'Oh, shut up. You're so full of it. You know I don't want you.' My voice slipped out of banter and edged into real anger.

He looked as though he was going to bite back, but he stopped himself and nodded quietly. 'Sure, you don't want me. If that's what you really believe. Let's have some dinner and cut this crap out.'

I rang Dana as soon as Brad left. She answered the phone after about twelve rings, just as I was about to give up. I realised when I heard her sharp voice that it was after ten o'clock and I'd probably got her out of bed.

'Hi, Mrs Anders. It's Lisa Sheehan here.'

'Do you have any idea what time it is?'

Her voice, her attitude, everything about her irked me, even though I knew I was in the wrong. 'I'm sorry. I lost track of time. Did I wake you?'

'Yes. This had better be important.'

'I wanted to know if you'd heard anything.'

'About Karin? No, have you?'

'No, it's just . . . somebody said you were down at the police station today and—'

'Those idiots. They dragged me down there to ask me silly questions and then told me what I knew all along: she's run off. I knew that marriage wouldn't work, but I did think she would have the decency to finish things properly.' I couldn't believe she wasn't worried about her daughter, but then again it probably fitted her paranoid world view. Here she was, abandoned, and playing it for all it was worth.

'So you don't think anything suspicious has happened to her?'

She made a snorting sound, which was probably meant to be a scornful laugh. 'Use your head, girl. She's gone off the rails. She knew that man for only six weeks before they got married; does that sound like the action of a rational person? She'll come back in a week or two, tail between her legs, asking to move back in here.'

'You'd love that, wouldn't you?' I said, my voice cracking with anger. 'You'd love to have that kind of power over her again. You're so busy playing a part in your stupid self-absorbed soap opera, it hasn't even crossed your mind that she might be in some kind of trouble or—'

The phone clicked and went dead. She had hung up on me, the bitch.

I sang all day Wednesday, then came home at about seven-thirty because I wanted to have a shower and wash my hair. Brad, Jeff, Ailsa and Dick had smoked their heads off all day, and I reeked of it. When I came out of the shower, I hit the rewind button on the answering machine, expecting the usual couple of hang-up calls. Instead, there was a call from Liam.

'Hi, Lisa. It's Liam Baker here. Um . . . I just wanted to see if you'd called Karin's mother and if everything was okay.' Short silence. 'Well, call me if you feel like it. Bye.'

I stood next to the phone, drying my hair with a towel and considering Liam. Sure I could ring him back, but I felt a sudden desire to see him. It seemed kind of lonely here at home after the noise and bustle of the studio. Besides, he was lush and I wanted to get another look at him. I could remember thick, straight black hair and dark eyes and a generous mouth, but I couldn't remember enough details to make him more than a fictional character in my head.

So instead of calling Liam, I called a cab.

The cab dropped me off halfway up a dark, empty suburban street. Uniform trees lined the footpath, all planted and pruned at the same time. And while the street was a little cold and a slight evening drizzle descended, the houses all had warm, welcoming lights on, and cooking smells filled the air. Liam's house was a small weatherboard place with a waist-high mesh fence and a large letterbox. I stood outside the gate for a few moments, wondering if Liam was married and if a very surprised Mrs Baker was going to open the door to me. Well, it would serve him right for coming on to me, if in fact that was what he was doing.

I opened the gate and walked up the path. I could hear music inside, piano music, something classical. I knocked and waited.

A few moments later, he opened the door. 'Lisa?' he said, surprised.

'Hi. Sorry for not calling first . . .'

'No, no that's fine. Come in. Are you wet? It's raining out there.'

He touched me lightly on the shoulder and led me inside. The house's cosy muted interior seemed to permeate right through to my core. I almost wept with the desire for this kind of normal life.

'Do you want me to get a towel?' he was saying as I was taking it all in—the soft surfaces, the quiet music, the warm, silent light.

'No. I'm okay. It's only drizzling a bit. This place is nice; do you own it?'

'Actually it belongs to my parents. They live inter-state and rent it to me at a ridiculously low price.'

I nodded. 'It's . . . nice.' I looked at him—he was nice too. 'I hope I haven't disturbed you.'

'No, I was just making something to eat. Have you eaten?'

I just remembered that I hadn't eaten since breakfast, and suddenly I was ravenous. I shook my head.

'I'm only making spaghetti on toast, but I can make something more substantial if you'd like to stay for dinner,' he said.

'Spaghetti on toast sounds fine.'

I followed him out to the kitchen and sat at the kitchen bench while he made dinner. 'What's this music playing?' I asked.

'Chopin. He's my favourite.'

I listened to the music for a while, just watching him quietly. He was tall and lean. He was wearing a pair of blue jeans and a striped T-shirt that was a couple of sizes too big, and no shoes. I even looked at his feet. He had little black hairs growing out of his toes. His face was angelic, almost feminine except for his dark eyes and eyebrows. Under the fluorescent light, his hair was dark brown, not black. I wanted to reach out and touch it, but I stayed where I was.

'What have you been up to all day?' he asked. 'Do you work?'

'Kind of. I'm a musician. Not this sort of music though.'

'Really? Do you play an instrument?'

'I sing and play guitar in a band called 747.'

'A rock band?'

'Yeah, I guess that's what you'd call us . . . in a generic sense. We play underground clubs and stuff like that. Today I've been in the recording studio. We've been contracted by a record company to make an EP.' God, that sounded impressive.

140

'That's pretty exciting. And you make a good living out of that?'

'No. I make a puny living out of that, and I have to sing in a cabaret duo every Friday night at the casino to pay my rent. There's no justice in the world.'

He laughed. 'Do you want to set the table? If I leave the spaghetti now I'll burn it, I always do.'

'Sure. Where is everything?'

'Knives and forks in the top drawer, tablecloth and serviettes in the third. If you want a drink of something, the glasses are in the cupboard above the sink. Just help yourself to whatever's in the fridge.'

How domestic. He cooked while I set the table. Somehow it felt different from having dinner with Brad. It felt homey, comfortable. Which was nuts because I'd known Brad for nine years and Liam for less than a week. But Brad had a destructive streak, a ruthless cynicism that prevented him from ever relaxing or accepting things without question. And it was that side of myself I sometimes wanted to be rid of, to dump the burden of judgement and scrutiny, to stop trying to be cool. Again the craving for normality swept over me. It would be so easy: give up the band, go back to school and get a proper education, find a job, get married, have babies, and every night Liam would cook while I set the table, just like TV parents. Seductive and frightening at the same time.

Liam came out with two plates of buttered toast and warm spaghetti. 'I feel so cheap giving you this for dinner,' he said, sitting down across from me.

'Don't. It's just what I feel like. I haven't eaten since breakfast.'

We started eating, and it was kind of ridiculous, us having spaghetti on toast when we had romantic designs on each other. Tinned spaghetti isn't really the food of love, and it's kind of messy to eat too.

'So, what's it like working for the police?' I asked.

'Not too bad. But I don't work for them, I work for myself. I'm a consultant.'

'Yeah? How did you get into that?'

'I have a Masters in sociology. When they advertise for contracts in the newspapers, I just submit a project outline and a tender. This is the second project like this I've done.'

'And you enjoy it?'

He shrugged. 'Yes, I guess so. It pays well and it's great working for myself. It's much more flexible and . . . well, you'd know all that. You work for yourself too.'

I nodded. 'I never thought of it like that but, yes, I guess I do.'

'I might come and see your band one night. Where do you play?'

'I don't know if you would have heard of the clubs: Fire Fire, the Black Flag, the Universal.'

'I know the Universal.'

'But I don't know if you'd like the kind of stuff we play.' I was acutely conscious of the elegant, sophisticated music he was listening to.

He smiled. 'Artistic temperament. You're being defensive.' He leaned back in his chair while I finished the last of my dinner. 'I play a bit of music too,' he said.

'Really? What instrument?'

'I play piano. Not terribly well.'

'Have you got a piano here?'

'Yes, in the spare room.'

'Will you play something for me?'

He looked uncomfortable, twisting his serviette between his hands. 'I don't know . . .'

'So who's got an artistic temperament now?'

'It's not that, it's just that if you're a professional musician . . .'

'Please. I can't even read music. Go on, play something for me.'

He considered for a minute. 'All right.' He sprang up and quickly cleared the table, then switched off the CD player. He came back and showed me through to a spare room containing a couple of unpacked crates and a piano. He switched on a lamp on top of the piano. The lampshade was apricot, and the room filled with a soft orange glow.

'Any requests?'

'Whatever you're best at.'

He opened the piano stool and rifled about among some sheet music. He found what he wanted and placed it on the piano, closing the seat. From the top of the piano he took a glasses case and perched on his nose the nerdiest glasses I have ever seen. They had thick black frames and were an extremely unflattering shape. Somehow they just added to his charm.

He put his hands on the keyboard and started playing one of the pieces we had just been listening to. At first he was nervous and made a few mistakes in the left hand, but once he got into it he played very well. And I could tell he loved what he was playing, as sad and sombre as it was. I stood by the piano watching him, watching his beautiful hands move across the keys, wishing I could read music so that I could turn the pages for him, so he didn't have to fumble at the corners and disrupt the continuity of the piece. I relaxed into the music, into the lazy, loving feeling that washed over me. When he finally finished, I had a smile on my face. He looked up through his nerdy glasses. There was a big dirty fingerprint in the corner of one of the lenses.

'That was beautiful,' I said.

'Thanks. I can't believe I played for you. I'm usually too shy.'

'Well, thanks for playing for me. I really appreciate it.'

He took his glasses off. 'Would you like a cup of coffee?'

'Actually I don't drink coffee or tea, unless you have some herbal tea?'

He shook his head. 'No, sorry.'

'But I'll sit with you while you have a coffee. You can give me a glass of water in a coffee mug and we can pretend.'

He smiled. 'Okay.'

We sat in the lounge room, Liam in a big armchair, me on the floor in front of his bookcase, pulling out books and reading the back covers. I always think there's a lot to be learned about somebody from their books. He had a little fiction, a number of books on sailing and the history of ship-building, a set of works on the great composers that looked as though it had been bought through a mail-order company, and a few biographies of successful businessmen. We made smalltalk for a while, mainly about his interests, his books. Then he fell silent, watching me as I systematically checked out his bookcase.

'Can I ask you something?' he said as I was examining a book about Bill Gates.

I looked up. 'Sure.'

'Why are you interested in the murders in the forest?'

I put the book down on the floor, shaken out of my comfortable mood. The scary universe had intruded. 'They were both fans of the band.'

144

'Are you kidding? Both the dead guys?'

I nodded. 'And because Karin disappeared about the same time . . .'

'Don't do that to yourself, Lisa. You just have to accept that sometimes bad luck comes with reinforcements.'

I thought about that. It made me feel marginally better.

'Did you speak to Karin's mother after I called?' he asked.

'Yes. She's a cold-hearted bitch. She's convinced that Karin's run away and hasn't even thought that something bad might have happened to her.'

'She may not be cold-hearted, she may just be rational.'

'Trust me, Liam, she's nuts. I've known her a long time. She's completely self-centred.' I placed the book carefully back on the shelf. A sense of *déjà vu* washed over me, like I'd placed this book on this bookshelf a million times before, stretching back into eternity. That was when it first struck me to suspect Dana. I became aware that Liam had asked me something and now expected a response. I hadn't the faintest idea what he had said.

'Can I use your phone?' I said. 'I need to call a cab home.'

He looked taken aback. 'If you want to go I'll drive you home.'

'No, I'll get a cab. I've got something to think about.'

He pointed towards the phone. 'Sure, feel free.'

I phoned a cab, and Liam waited with me at the front door for it to arrive. He was very quiet.

'Sorry I'm leaving in such a hurry,' I said.

He shrugged. 'I didn't say something to offend you, did I?'

145

'No, not at all.'

'It's just we were talking about Karin, and I didn't mean to suggest that you were being irrational . . .'

I reached up and touched his cheek lightly. 'I swear, you haven't offended me. I just remembered I have an important phone call to make.'

The cab beeped out front. I said goodbye and left him standing there by the door, no doubt wondering if he was dallying with a looney.

As the cab swept me back home through the greasy suburban streets and into the city, I thought about Dana. Who else had made it clear to the whole world that she wanted to keep Karin all to herself? Who else could make Karin withdraw money from her bank account, probably by putting her through some heavy guilt trip? Dana had always been highly strung, but the turn she'd put on at the wedding proved she was capable of losing the plot entirely.

I paid the cab driver out the front of my block of flats and went inside. I hoped it wasn't too late to ring David.

CHAPTER
TEN

Unpleasant thoughts sometimes get stuck in my head and play over and over like a broken record. On Thursday, the thought preoccupying me was the way David's voice had sounded when I'd called him the night before. I rang at ten-thirty, and hearing the phone ring at that late hour must have already made him jumpy. Then hearing my voice—he must have thought I had news one way or the other. His tone was equal terror and hope. I could *feel* his gut turning, as if mine was turning with it.

He said, 'Lisa, have you heard something?' but it came out more like one word, as if he was trying to get his question out of the way so that the news, good or bad, could follow as quickly as possible. I realised then that whatever I was going through over Karin's disappearance, what he was going through was infinitely worse. If there was foul play involved, then he had to worry about her safety. If there wasn't, then Karin had offered him the most insulting rejection known to mankind. Either way, he couldn't win. It made me very sad, and the sadness consumed me for most of the day.

I hadn't even told him that I suspected Dana. It seemed almost childish to say it aloud. I knew I'd have to screw up the courage to say it when I saw him, but for now it was enough that I had suggested getting together to go over what evidence we had, to see if we could succeed where the police had failed.

So, after another successful day recording, when everybody was happy with my vocal track and happy that I seemed to be over my manic interfering stage, I made myself a quick dinner and caught a cab to David's house.

I sat in the front with the driver. He was one of those men that refuse to acknowledge his advancing years. Despite a sizeable bald patch, his hair was long. His large, porous nose and pate were covered with a sheen of sweat, even though the airconditioning in the cab was freezing my knees through the thin cotton of my skirt. He also fancied himself a comedian and, from the moment I climbed into the car, he kept me entertained with a stream of jokes, most of which were in extreme bad taste. I smiled in all the right places, but I was staring out the window, trying to figure out how I was going to suggest to David that we approach Dana. I was afraid that he'd either accuse me of being paranoid or place all his faith in the idea and become too hopeful. I didn't want to hurt the guy any more than he had been already.

'Hey, sweetheart,' said the cab driver, 'why do they call it a wonder-bra?'

I kept my eyes on the passing scenery. 'I don't know, why?'

'Because when your boyfriend takes it off, he wonders where your tits have gone!' He burst into manic laughter.

I turned to give him a look which would express my distaste. But something happened in my head, like a shifting noise that sandpapered the inside of my skull, and I had to stifle a scream of horror when I looked at him. He was a grisly thing without skin, like one of those cutaway pictures in an anatomy book. Stringy veins pulsed and muscles bulged sickeningly as he turned the wheel of the cab. The image flashed into my head in a half second, then vanished, and the sounds and smells of the real world rushed back in.

He caught me staring at him. 'Hey, what's the matter? Have I got something on my face?' He brushed rough, cracked fingers over his chin.

Another flash, and his eyes stood out like white marbles amongst the red and pink channels and ropes of his face. I closed my eyes and bit back rising bile.

'Hey, are you okay? What's the matter?' I could feel the cab pull over and hear him unbuckle his seatbelt. He leaned towards me.

'Are you all right?'

I opened my eyes, and he was just a balding, sweaty cab driver again, with all his skin on, looking reassuringly ordinary. I realised I was having another hallucination. I concentrated on his nose, the large pores in the skin. I tried to breathe deeply. He became more definite, the other image fading completely.

'I'm sorry,' I said. 'Please, keep driving.'

'You're not going to flip out on me again, are you?'

'I don't think so. I don't know what came over me.'

He reached a hand towards me. 'Are you sure you're—'

I squealed and pulled back from his hand. It was an involuntary response: I didn't want to see the narrow cords that moved those fingers, not here in the keen air of reality.

'Okay, okay. Settle down. Jeez.' He sank back behind the wheel, accelerating into the traffic. 'I'd like to know what you're on.' It was a common accusation levelled at me, because of the way I looked. At least he stopped telling jokes. I kept my eyes closed all the way to David's house, hoping this wasn't going to become a regular thing.

David answered the door before I even had a chance to knock. He must have been watching for me.

'Hello, Lisa,' he said, a note of desperation in his voice.

'Hi.' I moved towards him, tried to give him a hug but only managed to grip his shoulder lightly and squeeze it. My pity for him nearly overran my heart and poured out of my eyes, but I restrained myself.

'Come in. We'll sit down in the living room.'

I followed him into a spacious lounge room with an unlit fireplace. I could see little touches of Karin here: a few plants, an oil sea-scape hanging on the wall, which had hung in her bedroom at Dana's. My heart tightened with the effort of staying calm. David indicated a large, soft leather lounge and I relaxed into it gratefully, still spooked by my hallucination but trying to keep it together for his sake.

David sat across from me and looked at me with his hands clasped in front of him, almost as if he were praying. The lamp next to me reflected in his round glasses. His skin was very pale and clean shaven, his eyes an unremarkable hazel.

'How well do you know Dana?' I asked.

He shook his head. 'Only what Karin has told me. I met her a couple of times before the wedding, but generally Karin wanted to keep me away from her.'

'You know she's a bitch?'

'Oh yes, Karin told me all about her. And she proved it at the wedding with that performance she gave.'

I fell silent briefly. David leaned forward. 'You said

150

you thought we could maybe figure out what happened to Karin ourselves?'

'Dana,' I said. 'I think there's a possibility she's with Dana.'

'You think she's gone home to her mother?'

I exhaled, pressed my lips together and shook my head. 'Not willingly.'

He thought about this for a moment then nodded. 'What, you think that Dana may have abducted her?'

The word seemed to stir something in my brain. *Abduction, Lisa? Really?* Perhaps I wasn't thinking straight—it was okay to imagine Dana considering kidnapping her daughter, but a different thing all together to imagine her executing the plan.

'Well, not abducting as such . . . Perhaps . . . I mean . . .'

'Of course!' He balled his hands up into fists. 'Of course, that makes sense.' He was growing agitated now. 'Karin was happy with me, Lisa. I know she was.'

I was a little disturbed by how violently he had latched onto the idea. 'Yes, she told me she was happy,' I said.

'She told you she was pregnant, too,' he said, almost accusingly.

'She said she might be. Probably.'

'She didn't tell me that.' He looked down into his lap, and I was afraid he was going to cry. I didn't know what I'd do if he did.

He looked up again. 'Of course, Dana *must* be responsible. We have to go around there and tell her that we know, tell her to—'

'David. No. We can't just go round there and accuse her of abducting her daughter.'

'What then? What did you have in mind?'

What I'd had in mind was starting to seem more

151

and more ill-considered. 'It's Thursday night. The mobile blood bank goes out until midnight. Dana is their receptionist.'

'She's working late?'

'Yes. She does every Thursday,' I said.

He stroked his chin, pondering on this. 'Do you want to go to her house while she's not there?'

'Well, my original idea was to break in. Have a look around. But now I'm not sure if—'

'No need to break in. I have Karin's keys.'

I was speechless for a moment. It was my fault David was so keen—I could hardly say no.

'Okay,' I said. 'Okay if you want to, then let's go.'

He grabbed a torch from under the kitchen sink and led me out to the car.

I felt a twinge of guilt, seeing how excited and hopeful David was as we sped through the dark streets to Dana's house. If we found no sign of Karin, not only would I look like a paranoid fruit loop, but David would have to suffer the anguish of Karin's disappearance all over again. But he wasn't capable of acting rationally. He babbled in an agitated way about how he'd known all along Karin wouldn't leave him, how he'd had nagging doubts about the calm way Dana had accepted her daughter's disappearance. He thanked me for having the courage to do this, thanked me for coming with him, thanked me for everything, repeatedly. I tried to calm him down, tell him that we didn't know anything for sure, but he was beyond the point of accepting anything fatalistically. He was suddenly a man with a mission.

After we had pulled up outside Dana's house, we sat out the front for a few moments, both of us probably thinking the same thing: could we really do this?

'You'd better park a bit further away,' I said finally, 'in case she comes home early.'

He nodded silently and reversed back about four houses. He locked the car and we walked down together. I had an anxious knot in my stomach. We paced silently and softly towards the house. I felt like a criminal, which in a way I guess I was. Trespassing on private property. I looked up at David. He looked older in the eerie light of the streetlamp, the grey in his hair more noticeable, the lines on his face thrown into sharp relief.

The only light on at Dana's place was somewhere deep inside the house. She had probably left it on accidentally. David fumbled with the keys, eventually got them in the lock, and let us in. He closed the door quietly behind us. We stood in a shaft of light coming in through the fanlight from the streetlamp outside. Our shadows were long and gaunt. I shivered slightly and moved closer to David, feeling assured by his masculine presence.

'Where do we start?' he said in a low voice.

'I guess we check through the rooms. Come on.'

I led the way into the kitchen. 'Should we turn a light on?'

'Better not, it could attract attention. Maybe her neighbours know she's supposed to be out tonight—Neighbourhood Watch or something.'

'David, if her neighbours hate her as much as everybody else does . . .'

'Still. Better to be safe.' He switched on the torch, and its beam swung around the room. Nothing, just an ordinary kitchen, still hung with the smell of cooked onions. A cockroach scuttled across the sink then disappeared under a benchtop. The fridge hummed, unaware of the two intruders.

'Nothing in here.'

'Of course,' he said. 'Would you hide somebody in the kitchen? Let's go upstairs to the bedrooms.'

I followed him back into the sitting room and up the stairs. We went first to Karin's room. The torchlight fell on a couple of old teddies grouped together on the bedspread. I could hear David choking back a sob, so I reached over and rubbed his arm lightly.

'It's okay, man. She'll be okay,' I said.

He nodded. I could see him pinching the bridge of his nose between his glasses. Then he looked up and took a deep breath. In a quiet voice he called out, 'Karin?'

No answer. We made a cursory check in the wardrobe then moved on to Dana's room. Here the scent of Dana was strongest, that choking floral perfume she wore. We checked everywhere, still nothing. I began to feel more than a little silly.

We went through the spare room and the bathroom in the same way. After we had come up empty-handed, I sat on the edge of the bath and looked up at David, standing there in front of me, paralysed with grief. Dana had left the light on in here, and it seemed strange to be looking at him in the full light, given the nature of our visit.

'She's not here, Lisa,' he said.

'I know.'

'Which means one of two things.'

'Don't say it, David. Don't torture yourself.'

'Either I couldn't protect her, or I couldn't please her. I don't know which is worse.' He hung his head, but he wasn't crying. Just staring at the bathroom floor in the bright fluorescent light, as if the answer might be written there.

A thought suddenly occurred to me. 'Wait! There's another room.'

He looked up.

'When we were kids, Dana used to let us play in the attic. Only it's not a real attic. It's a room in the ceiling, about four feet high. We had to use a ladder to get up there and, after Karin had fallen and sprained her wrist one time, Dana forbade us from going up again.' As I spoke I led him out into the hallway and down to the corner, where the access hatch to the roof was. I pointed up. 'Up there. We just need to push the hatch open and climb in.'

He stood on tiptoe and reached up, but his fingers brushed the air several centimetres below the hatch. 'I need something to stand on. Does she still have a ladder?'

'I don't know. Maybe it's in the garage.'

He nodded. 'Let's go look.' I saw him gaze forlornly at the hatch, then he backed away and we went downstairs and out the front door. I shone the torch on his hands as he tried a couple of different keys in the lock on the garage door, but none of them fitted.

'Damn,' he said at last. 'It's not on here. We can't get in.'

'Maybe we can use a chair or something.'

He shook his head. 'Not tall enough, and besides, what if Karin's here in the garage? I need to know.'

God, he looked so desperate. What a stupid, stupid notion this had been.

'Okay. Let's be calm. Maybe we can pick the lock.'

'Do you know how to pick a lock?'

'No. Damn, I feel so unprepared for all this.'

As I spoke, a car drove up the street. I realised that David and I must have looked suspicious, standing there checking out somebody's garage door with a torch. We ducked back into the shadows.

He checked his watch. 'We've still got a while before she's due home. Wait here.' He disappeared around the corner of the garage and over the waist-

155

high hedge that formed a fence to the yard. In a moment he stuck his head around the corner. 'Come on. There's a window around the back.'

He helped me over the hedge and around the back of the garage. At about head height was a small grimy window. David strained to see inside, shone his torch around.

'I see a stepladder.'

'Is the window locked?'

He gave it a shove. 'I don't think so, but it's painted shut. Here, hold this.' He handed me his torch and gave the window another shove. Something creaked.

'Did you open it?'

'Only about an inch. I'm going to try again.'

Once again he pushed, and I could see all the muscles in his back straining. This time a long loud howl came from the window as it grudgingly swung open. I stood back a couple of paces so I could see. The window was now standing out about eighty degrees from its frame.

'It's not much of an opening,' I said.

'I know. But you'll fit. You can get in and open the garage door from inside.'

'I don't know, David.'

'Please, Lisa, please.' He grasped my wrist and gave it a squeeze.

I looked up at the window. My heart began to pound. Now we really were doing something bad.

'Okay. You'll have to give me a leg-up.'

He made a step for me with his hands. I kicked off my shoes and let him help me up. It was strangely uncomfortable, our bodies being so close. I started to scramble through the window. I had my front half in, my legs being supported by David outside. I wished I had worn shorts instead of a skirt.

'Where am I going to land?' I asked.

'I'll hold your feet. Just reach down to the floor and when you think you can support yourself I'll let you go.'

I wriggled in further, scratching my belly on the windowsill. I heard something tear and realised my skirt had caught on something. I tucked it between my legs and inched my upper body down the wall and reached for the floor. The garage smelled musty and cold. My hands touched chilly, dusty concrete. I walked my hands out as far as I could and told David to let go of my feet. He did so slowly, and at first I thought I would be able to bring my legs behind me, but there wasn't enough room and I tumbled forward, grazing my forearms on the concrete.

'Ow,' I said, probably too loudly.

'Lisa, are you okay?'

I picked myself up and tried to see my wounds in the dark. I could see a bit of dark blood trickling down to my elbow.

'Yeah, I'm just grazed. I'll have to clean myself up though. It's pretty dirty in here. Pass me the torch.' I reached up and David handed the torch to me. I shone it around the garage.

'Can you see anything?' David asked. 'Is there anywhere Karin could be hidden?'

There was a dark oily patch on the floor where Dana parked her car. The corners of the garage were stuffed with old boxes, a rusty bike, empty ceramic pots and a dirty old garden hose. The stepladder stood under a shelf on the left-hand side. It had the remnants of a couple of old stickers on it that Karin and I had decorated it with as children. I kicked an old newspaper across the ground. 'No. No secret trapdoors, no hidden vaults.' Then, realising I had sounded flippant, I added: 'Sorry, David. Go round the front and I'll open up for you.'

I went to the garage door and twisted the metal handle. It creaked and opened. David was waiting on the other side.

'Can you shut that window while I grab the ladder?' he said.

I pushed the window shut. It creaked in protest but eventually gave. Then I followed David back into the house.

Once the front door was shut behind us I felt safe again. We took the ladder back up to the access hatch. It creaked as we pulled it open.

'I'll go up first,' David said. He sounded excited. I had a horrible feeling he was about to be disappointed. He climbed up the ladder and pushed on the hatch. It gave lightly.

'See?' he said. 'Must have been used recently.' I saw him disappearing into the hatch, and I climbed up after him.

'Karin?' he was saying, shining his torch around the room. I could see him scrambling along, bent almost double. I pushed myself up and onto my knees, and began to follow him on all fours.

'Karin!' he said again, sharper, more urgent. There was no answer. My heart sank. He swept his torch beam into every corner of the room. There were about half a dozen cardboard boxes stacked beside the access hatch, but nothing else except cobwebs and a chalk door and window drawn on the back wall—a legacy of Karin and I playing house about fifteen years ago. The childish, uncertain lines looked lonely up here.

David came back and sat down next to me. 'Lisa, she's not here.' He seemed to be sitting awfully close and I tried to shrink away from him without being too obvious.

'I'm sorry,' I said. Then, 'Here, hand me your torch.'

He passed his torch to me and sat in despondent silence while I pulled the first box from the top of the pile into my lap and flipped it open. It was stuffed with papers, letters, cards and photographs. I rifled through it. They were mostly old Christmas cards, copies of bills, a couple of photos of Dana and Karin. I picked one up to have a closer look. Dana was smiling proudly at the photographer, her arm around Karin's narrow shoulders.

'Nothing in here that can help us,' I said, tossing the photo back into the box.

David was still silent. I sorted through some more papers and found a letter addressed to 'Miss Karin Anders' at Dana's post office box, with an airmail sticker on it. It had been slit open, so I tipped out the letter. It was dated only three months ago.

Dear Karin
Your mother tells me you are getting married. I cannot believe my little girl has grown up so much. I hope that you can send me a photograph of you and your new husband, and I hope that he will be good to you. I have enclosed a money order to help with the wedding. I would love to hear from you one day, but I know that you are busy with your life and probably do not want to write to a silly old man like me. If you ever decide to come and visit please let me know. I will be happy to pay the aeroplane fare for you and your new husband.

Love to you, Papa.

'Christ, David, look at this.'

My voice shook him alert and he took the letter from me and read it in the torchlight.

'I don't understand. She said she didn't know anything about her father,' he said.

I flipped the envelope over. The return address was for a Mr Will Anders in Bonn, Germany. I was shaking with rage. 'Her mother *hid* this from her. Christ, she probably even cashed the money order.'

He was ploughing through the other boxes now. We found a birthday card from last year, another brief letter. A couple of photos in an envelope of a handsome, bearded man smiling at the camera, holding a newborn baby. On the back was written, 'Here is me and your new baby sister, named Claudine'.

'I just don't believe this,' I said. 'She knew nothing of this, *nothing*.'

We went back through the years, pulling out correspondence dating back to Karin's childhood, some in German, but the more recent ones in steadily improving English. When I opened a seventh birthday card, read the simple message: 'To my little girl, I hope to see you very soon', I nearly wept. How long had Dana been hiding these from her daughter? How long had Karin's poor father been thinking Karin didn't want to know him?

'God, David. This is awful. *She* is awful. What kind of a woman would do this?' I looked up and saw he was picking out cards and letters and stuffing them in the pockets of his jacket.

'What are you doing?' I asked.

'I'm going to the police, and I'm going to show them some of these letters. Lisa, this is hard evidence that she's unbalanced; the police will have to look at her more closely now. They'll find Karin, I know they will.' His voice sounded very calm and determined.

I was taken aback. 'They're going to wonder how you got this stuff. I don't know if it's wise.'

'I'll make something up. I don't care, I just want

my wife back. Here . . .' He leaned over and started poking letters into the pockets of my overshirt. I couldn't protest, I just sat there dumbly and let him, hoping it was just a desire that I take some letters that motivated him, and not a desire for a bit of illicit physical contact. When he had finished he moved back and tidied the boxes, making them look like they hadn't been tampered with.

'Where is she, Lisa?' he said finally, taking his torch back from me. He said it so quietly I almost didn't hear him at first.

'I don't know.'

He turned to me and took my hand in his. 'Don't feel bad about bringing me here. I'm glad you did.'

'I'm sorry. I shouldn't have got your hopes up.'

He squeezed my hand. 'Really, it's okay. But Lisa, you're her best friend. You must have some idea where she might go.'

'I wish I did.' A quick, warm tingle had started behind my eyes, like in the cab. I was frightened that another hallucination would overtake me so I closed my eyes. When I opened them again and focused on the back wall of the attic, I was suddenly assaulted by a vision of Karin standing in thick darkness, screaming soundlessly. She was staring at her hands in horror and they were bathed in blood. I snapped my eyes closed in terror. David leaned in, concerned.

'What's the matter?'

'I . . . I have a headache coming on.'

'We'd better get you home then.'

I opened my eyes and we were alone in the attic again. David shone the torch over towards the hatch and we clambered out of the ceiling and along the hallway. The vision of Karin seemed as though it was burnt into the back of my eyes, and the dark was spooking me in a big way.

161

The light from the bathroom fell on me as we passed, and I could see dried blood on my arms. I would have to clean up my grazes as soon as I got home.

David and I took the stepladder back outside and locked the door to the house behind us. As we stepped into the garage to replace the ladder, David shone his torch on the boxes in the corner. 'Look. There might be some more in there.'

I looked around nervously. 'Okay, we'll have a quick look, but you'll have to close the garage door. If somebody drives past they'll spot us.'

He pulled the door closed behind us and we squatted to go through the boxes. I was about to comment that it looked as though they were all empty, when the sound of an approaching car disturbed me. I jumped. David looked at me bemused. 'Relax,' he said, 'we won't be a moment and you said Dana's not due home for over an hour.'

He bent down again to clear away the few boxes on top. The engine seemed to be close and idling slowly, as if it had pulled up.

'David, that's outside.'

'There's nothing in here anyway.'

'But we can't leave through the garage door, that car is idling outside.'

Then the engine revved, and unmistakably the car pulled into the driveway.

'Shit, it's her,' I hissed. 'What the fuck do we do now?'

'Out the window,' he said in a panicky voice. 'Hurry.'

He yanked the window open and offered me his hands as a step up again, but on this occasion there was no time for a careful landing. I fell on my wounded forearms as gently as I could, suppressing a screech of pain. David threw the torch out to me and I grabbed it. I could see his hands trying to heave his body up. I thought there was no way he would fit through the window. Dana's car door slammed and I heard her jingling her keys as she came to the garage door. I watched anxiously to see if David would make it. There was a loud chime as Dana's keys hit the concrete—she had dropped them, giving him valuable seconds. He squirmed through the window. I grabbed him under the arms and pulled. For a horrible moment I thought he was stuck, but suddenly he came loose and we both fell to the ground. I landed on my back in the grass, David on top of me. I could hear Dana unlocking the garage door.

'The window,' I said softly but urgently. He jumped up and slammed it shut just as the garage door creaked open. If Dana heard anything, she gave no sign.

David ducked back down. I could barely move, I had landed so heavily, and his body had knocked the wind out of me. We heard her get back into the car and drive into the garage. It seemed an age before she locked the garage door again and we could hear her shoes clicking over the driveway and up to her front porch. Her front door creaked opened then slammed shut.

'Now run,' David said. He pushed me around the side and over the hedge, then clambered over it himself. We dashed up the street to where the car was parked. I was aching all over, and the grazes on my forearms were bleeding again. David unlocked the car door for me and I noticed the back of his pants was ripped and he was bleeding from a graze on his left buttock. I switched the torch on and pointed the beam at his wound.

'You've hurt yourself, man.'

'I thought I felt something scratch me. Is it bad?'

The torch lit up every detail, and I found myself looking at a first-class butt. His skin was very pale and smooth apart from a dark mole nestled under the well-formed curve of his buttock. A nasty purple scratch bled onto his ripped trousers. I realised with some discomfort that I was staring at my best friend's husband's arse and quickly switched off the torch. 'Yeah, it looks pretty deep.'

He found a handkerchief to press over the wound as I climbed into the car.

He let himself in, started the car and looked across solicitously. 'What about you? Are you hurt?'

'Just bruised, I think.' I took a deep breath. Not too much pain.

I saw the lights come on at Dana's house. 'This is freaking me out, can we just get out of here?'

'Sure,' he said. 'I'll take you home.'

We did a U-turn so we wouldn't have to pass Dana's house again, and then we were speeding off into the night, just like a pair of criminals.

CHAPTER
ELEVEN

We sat at my kitchen table, the letters and cards spread out before us. My arms were cleaned up and covered in yellow disinfectant. We had each tended to our own wounds, thankfully. David had disinfected the scratch on his backside and pinned up the rip in his trousers. I couldn't imagine how uncomfortable I would have been if he'd asked me to do it for him. I held the photo of Will Anders and Karin's little half-sister Claudine in my right hand, and I stared into it. I was trying to squash the thought that came to me unbidden. What if Karin died never knowing her father? But I wasn't allowed to think about death and danger and that horrible vision I'd had in the attic; I was supposed to be thinking about where else she might be. Here in the sane light of my kitchen, the idea that Dana had snatched her and stashed her somewhere seemed outer limits, but that may have been hindsight. David was hopeful that if we took the letters to the police station, they might be more interested in investigating Dana. But he had to be hopeful. I could accept that Karin might have run away, he couldn't.

'I saw the door and the window drawn on the wall in the attic,' he said. 'Did you draw that as kids?'

'Karin drew it, yes. I never could draw very well

and she was always good with shapes and sizes. We used to play house up there. Karin would always be the mummy and I was the daddy. She had this doll, most of its hair was missing and one of its eyes was permanently rolled back into its head, but she loved it. It was our baby.' And I remembered always wanting to leave our baby downstairs and Karin insisting on taking it everywhere but I didn't say that to David because, at the mention of babies, he had lapsed into a dejected silence, staring down at the tabletop. He looked like a broken man. I tossed the photo I was holding back onto the table, rose and came over to him. I crouched next to him, put my arms around him.

'David, I'm so sorry. This is my fault. I shouldn't have led you on this wild-goose chase.'

He smiled weakly. 'No, I'm glad you did. I'm glad we found this stuff.' He indicated the papers on the table with a feeble sweep of his hand.

I pulled him close. First he held his arms stiffly at his side, then he seemed to relax into the embrace and encircled my waist with his hands. I stroked his hair with my left hand, and he bowed his head onto my shoulder, like a little boy. I could feel his body shaking lightly with sobs.

'Lisa, how can I go on? How can I go on knowing that she may be in danger? How can I go on knowing that I couldn't make her happy?'

I rocked him gently, letting him get his tears out.

'She was everything to me, Lisa . . . The whole world. And the baby . . . we wanted a baby so much.' His words were choking out in gasps between sobs. I thought I would explode with pity.

'We've got to pull ourselves together,' I said, drawing away from him. 'We've got to be reasonable and logical and hopeful, and have faith that we'll find out what's happened to Karin, one way or another.'

'I'm still taking these letters down to Sergeant Pyle.'

I nodded. 'If that's what you have to do. Just don't tell him how we got them.'

The thought of action seemed to help him regain his composure. He collected the papers up and stacked them neatly. 'I'll go down first thing tomorrow morning. I'd better get out of here and let you get some sleep.'

He pushed his chair back and I showed him to the front door. He thanked me again, then reached out his hand and touched my face gently, let his hand slide down to the side of my neck, under my hair. I felt a frisson of sexual tension that made me unbearably uncomfortable, and I stepped back.

'Goodnight,' I said. 'Call me if you need me.'

He glanced down at his feet. He probably felt uncomfortable too. 'Yes. Thanks again, Lisa.'

I closed the door after him and realised guiltily that I was glad he was gone.

The Universal was packed. One of the local entertainment rags had run a feature story about 747 getting signed to Numb, and it seemed like every frequent flyer, past and present, had turned up tonight to celebrate with us. We had finished recording. Brad and I were going to be at the studio on and off for the next week or so mixing down, but the main job was out of the way and we were all high on self-love, thinking that we were the best band that had ever lived and breathed.

Brad and I got there late from our gig at the Casino, and I was still in a long-sleeved cocktail dress, though I had chucked my wig in the back of the car. We squeezed our way through the crowd and went backstage. Jeff was talking to a couple of female fans, Ailsa was tuning her bass.

'Hey, nice frock,' she said.

'Yeah, thanks. I have to get changed. Jeff, can you kick out your buddies, I don't feel like undressing in front of them.' I pulled a pair of cutoff jeans out of my backpack and wriggled them on underneath my dress. Jeff ushered the girls out and stood in the doorway talking to them. I pulled my dress off over my head and squirmed into a singlet top. Brad caught my wrist gently and turned my arm over, examining the grazes I had inflicted on myself in Dana's garage.

'Christ, what happened to you?'

'I fell over.'

'How did you fall over?'

'I slipped and fell in the driveway at home. When I was collecting the mail.'

Jeff came back in and crowded around me with Brad. 'Hey, Lisa, nice carpet burns. You been taking it from behind too hard?'

I turned to give him a withering look. 'You're foul, Jeffrey.'

'I try,' he said, then launched into a song that had 'Lisa's got carpet burn' as its main lyric.

'He's so creative,' said Ailsa, heading out towards the stage. As she did, she nearly ran into Angie coming in the other way.

'Hey, Lisa, there's some guy out here to see you, waiting up at the desk,' he said.

'Yeah? Who?'

'I think he said his name was Ian. He's got black hair, good-looking bloke.' He directed this comment at Brad, who was paying close attention.

'That would be Liam, not Ian. Jeez, what's he

168

doing here?' I turned to pick up my boots, but Brad grabbed me around the wrist again, not quite as gently this time.

'What?' I asked.

'Is this guy fucking you?'

'What kind of a question is that?'

'Is he?'

'Are you fucking Marnie?' I shot back.

His voice dropped. 'Lisa, you can't do this to me. You can't be all gooey over me and lead me on and spend all this time with me and be close to me, then expect me not to get jealous if some other guy comes along.'

Jeff had stopped singing and was listening intently. Brad sounded so serious.

'Brad. I like this guy, but at the moment we're just friends.'

'At the moment?'

'Well, I don't know what's going to happen,' I said.

'What do you *want* to happen?'

I twisted my arm away from him. 'This is ridiculous. I don't have to answer these questions. I'm going out to see Liam, and maybe we can discuss this at a later date when it's more relevant.'

I pulled on my boots and laced them up, then plunged into the bodies cramming the nightclub, fending off hugs and backslaps from drunken fans. I could see Liam standing up at the sound desk, the lamp that Angie had screwed onto the front illuminating his features from below. He hadn't seen me yet. He stood so straight, and he didn't quite fit in, although he was fairly casual in black jeans and a loose button-up shirt. Something about him just looked too classy to be here, and I felt mildly embarrassed.

I sidled up to him. 'Hi.' I had to shout over the

taped music pumping through the front-of-house speakers.

He turned to look at me and smiled. 'Hi, Lisa. I thought I'd come out and see the band. There's a lot of people here.'

'Yeah, it looks like it'll be a good night.'

He seemed to be checking out what I was wearing, then his eyes lit on my tattoo, and he looked closer. I squirmed for an instant, wished I'd remembered to cover it up before I came out. When he realised what it was, he looked surprised.

'Is that real?' he asked.

Why did I care so damn much what he thought of me? 'Um . . . yes. A legacy of my wild youth.'

'Wow.'

'What's wrong, don't you like it?'

He shook his head. 'It's not that, it's just I've never met a girl with a tattoo before.'

I laughed. 'I've never met a guy who carries a hanky before, so we're even.'

He looked momentarily embarrassed, then gave a short laugh. 'I've got some information for you,' he said.

'About Karin?'

'No, about the murders. Can we go somewhere quieter for a few minutes?'

I looked up at the stage. Ailsa was still setting up, which gave me some breathing space. She was usually slow.

'Sure, come outside.' I didn't want to take him backstage where Jeff would hang on our every word and Brad would give us the evil eye, so I led him out the front door of the Universal and into the street. There was a busker across the road from us, singing off-key versions of Rod Stewart songs. We found a bench about twenty metres up and sat down.

170

Liam turned to look at me. 'The police station's in a state of chaos at the moment. They've brought in homicide experts from all over the country to help in this case, and they've cleared a few people out of offices to make room. It's only a matter of time before I get the boot down to the Council Chambers, so I don't know how much longer I can help you. But while everything is in turmoil, they're letting their guard slip and I'm picking up some interesting information.'

'Like what?'

'They have absolutely no evidence.'

'How do you mean?'

'They found nothing at the crime scenes except the bodies. Absolutely nothing, no footprints, no fingerprints, no signs of struggle, not so much as a broken twig or a crushed leaf, no blood more than a metre from the body. The guy that's doing this must be dripping with blood, but they find *nothing*. The detective in charge is losing it—he has absolutely nothing to go on. It's like the bodies are materialising in the forest out of nowhere.'

'Out of nowhere,' I repeated softly. It gave me the creeps.

'I also got this.' He stood up and pulled a folded piece of paper out of his back pocket then sat down again. 'Someone left it on the photocopier so I took a copy myself.' He unfolded the paper as he spoke and smoothed it out in his lap. I leaned over to look.

'Is it a map?'

'Yeah, a map of the pine forest.'

'Couldn't you get in trouble for making a copy of this?'

'Very likely. But nobody's going to find out.'

I was touched. 'Thanks, man.'

He shrugged. 'It's okay. It's their fault for leaving

it out. See these dots? These mark the places where the bodies were found. These blocks are the lots of plantation timber—around half a kilometre square with unsealed access roads running between them. See, the bodies were found in adjacent lots.' He indicated the blocks with his finger.

I leaned back on the bench and closed my eyes.

'What's the matter?' he asked.

'My imagination works too well.'

'Ah, I know what you mean. The other thing I know for sure is this: with both murders, the abduction took place around four hours before the actual murder. I thought that might give you some comfort, you know, because of Karin.'

'What do you mean?' I couldn't imagine how anything he was saying could give me comfort.

'No third body has been found, and Karin disappeared three weeks ago. Whatever has happened to her, it probably wasn't what happened to the other guys.'

'Probably?'

He shrugged. 'How can I say definitely? But if I were you, I'd relax.'

I thought about it for a moment. 'Okay, so this murderer abducts his victims, kills them four hours later, after God knows what kind of preparation, then leaves the bodies in the pine forest. Just because only two have been found, doesn't mean only two have been murdered. How many kilometres of pine forest line the highway out there anyway? Sixteen? Twenty?'

'I think it's closer to sixty.'

'So, she could have been . . .' I couldn't finish the sentence.

'Lisa, he's leaving the bodies in conspicuous places. Dozens of people camp in the pine forest. People bushwalk through there, class excursions go there.

We're not talking about the depths of the Amazon.' He could see I didn't look convinced. 'I'm sorry. I told you all that stuff to make you feel better not worse.'

I tried a brave smile. 'It's all right. Show me that map again.'

He passed me the map and I stared at it, as if it could provide answers to questions I dared not even ask. It was the not knowing that gnawed at me. Sure, Karin could be hiding out interstate, renting a one-bedroom flat and pondering the meaning of life. But she could also be lashed to a tree, sightless like the others, her small, white body sagging from the trunk with only the elements for company. My heart rose up in my throat. I had to swallow it down.

'Have you ever been out there?' I asked Liam.

'Once, as a kid. We went camping.'

'What's it like?'

His brow furrowed as he called up the memories. 'Dark. Smelled strange. I don't remember much. I think I stayed in my tent a lot of the time, reading comic books.'

I folded the map and handed it back to him. 'I'd like to go out there.'

'Go camping?'

'No, now, tonight. I'd like to go out there and have a look. In the blocks around where they found the bodies.'

He looked momentarily stunned. 'What for?'

'I have to *know*, Liam. And if those bodies were in adjacent blocks, perhaps . . .'

He looked dubious. 'I'm sure the police have already checked it out.'

'Look,' I said. 'I know how crazy it sounds, but . . . I mean, it can't hurt, can it?' But there was more. With all the weird shit that had been going down in

173

my life lately, I was starting to suspect something bigger than I could understand was going on. The vision at Dana's place still haunted me. Was it possible for me to sense Karin somehow? 'I . . . we were really close,' I offered lamely. 'You just never know.'

'I don't think that sounds too crazy,' he conceded. 'Do you want me to take you?'

'Yes. If you wouldn't feel too uncomfortable about it.'

'No, not at all.'

'Do you have a torch or something in your car?'

'Yes, in my glove box. But are you sure you want to do this?'

It was a good question. What if we did find something, how was I supposed to handle that? But I had to know what happened to Karin. I had to do something. 'I don't know. It might give me some peace of mind, I guess. That would be worth the trip.'

We were interrupted by Brad shouting to me from the door of the nightclub. 'Lisa, what the fuck are you doing? We have to go on.'

I looked up. He was striding towards us.

'Settle down, I lost track of time. It's not the end of the fucking world,' I said, refusing to be bullied by his macho act, which was obviously for Liam's benefit. I turned to Liam. 'Liam, this is Bradley Harper. Brad, Liam Baker.'

'Nice to meet you, Bradley,' Liam said. He wasn't to know that Brad hated being called by his full name.

Brad nodded in response, then turned to me. 'Come on, Lisa. You've got work to do. I've already set you up.'

I pulled myself to my feet, and Liam followed us inside.

'Where's the best place to stand?' Liam asked me

as we passed the sound desk. 'Should I come down the front?'

'No, no.' I could just imagine him copping a steel-capped boot in that gorgeous face during a crowd-surfing frenzy. 'If you stand back here with Angie you'll hear everything really well. It gets a little rough down the front.'

He nodded and tucked himself back in behind the sound desk. Angie was a super-friendly guy, and the last I saw before I headed up to the stage, Liam was receiving a detailed explanation of Angie's new EQ rack.

It was our first night back at work for over a month. I had trouble fighting my way through the crowd to clamber up on stage. When Brad hit a chord to test his sound, the crowd surged forward and a huge cheer went up. I remember thinking, 'Fuck, maybe we will be stars', then Jeff was counting us in for the first song and I was feeling for the first chords. All the studio practice had made us very tight and the music cracked along like a series of neatly controlled explosions. I actually forgot all my woes and worries for a while. It was the best feeling in the world being up there that night, knowing all those people had come to see us and hear the songs that Brad and I had written. It was one of the most successful gigs we ever played; it's still permanently etched on my memory. That was 747 at its peak.

When we had finished and I was kneeling down to pull the gaff tape off my leads, a young guy with long black hair heaved himself up on stage and squatted next to me.

'What kind of system are you running?' he asked, obviously a music buff. I didn't want to talk to him, I wanted to get out into the crowd and find Liam, see what he thought of the band.

'A Marshall JMP-1 pre-amp and a Mossvalve power amp into a Laney cab,' I replied, not meeting his eyes. Making eye contact was the fatal move with hangers-on—they took it as a sign that a bond had been formed.

He was already walking over to where my guitar was propped up by the speaker. 'And is this the real thing or a copy?' he asked.

'The real thing.'

'Wow, a Les Paul Junior. How long have you had it?'

'About four years.'

'Mind if I have a go?'

Frustrated, I swore under my breath and moved to stand next to him. I showed him how to adjust the signal on my pre-amp and he began to thrash away at a meaningless series of power chords that looked as though they would bruise the neck of my guitar. I glanced back to the sound desk to see what Liam was doing, and was surprised to see Brad standing there talking to him. Even more surprised that they were both smiling and laughing, like they were sharing a joke. I desperately wanted to get away from this guy.

'Look,' I said, 'I don't mean to be rude, but I've got someone waiting for me . . .'

'Are these the right chords for "Treehouse"?' he asked me, ignoring what I'd said.

I shook my head and moved his fingers down two frets. 'G minor 7, that's it. Leave your pinky out of it, it's getting in the way.'

Again he thrashed away, playing some semblance of one of our songs. I had to be flattered. I threw a glance back to Liam and Brad. Now Brad was leaning close and Liam was listening carefully, nodding his head seriously. Brad had been acting like such a prick

176

lately, I had no idea what notions he'd be putting into Liam's head. I turned back to my new friend, closed my hand over the neck of the guitar to shut him up.

'I've got to go. Maybe next time I'll show you how to play another song, okay?'

He nodded reasonably. 'I'll take you up on that.'

He went on his way, and I quickly unplugged all my gear and rolled the leads up. Then I headed down to the sound desk.

'All ready to go, Angie,' I said.

'Good girl. The Black Flag tomorrow night?' he asked.

'Yep, we go on at eleven, but the band before us wants to use Jeff's kit so I guess you'll have to be there around nine-thirty.' Out of the corner of my eye I was watching Liam and Brad, leaning their heads together like new-found best friends. I left Angie to finish packing up his desk and stood anxiously next to them, waiting for them to finish their conversation.

When I saw an appropriate break, I leaned forward. 'Liam, do you want to go now?'

Brad turned and gave me a sharp look. 'Is Liam giving you a lift home?'

I didn't want to tell Brad where we were really going so I just nodded and tugged at Liam's arm.

'Is that okay with you?' Liam asked Brad.

Brad gave a magnanimous wave of his hand. 'Sure. I don't mind.'

'It's got nothing to do with him,' I said to Liam softly. He looked uncertain.

'See ya, Brad,' I said, turning Liam towards the door.

'Yeah, bye Lisa. Bye, Liam. We might see you tomorrow night?'

'Um . . . I don't know. Maybe,' Liam answered, allowing himself to be led away.

We headed into the fresh air of the street and towards the car park.

'So,' I said, 'what did you think of the band?'

'You sounded great. It was pretty loud though.'

'Maybe you should have worn earplugs.'

He shrugged. 'Maybe. It's not the kind of music I usually listen to, but I really enjoyed the show. But don't you get hurt, flinging yourself around like that?'

I winced as I remembered at one point surfing into the crowd and having the graze on my left arm scratched open again. I think I bled on a few people before I was thrown back on stage. I must have violated about a dozen public health codes.

'I did hurt myself tonight, but I don't usually. I never notice it anyway. I'm having too much fun,' I said.

'It was pretty violent down the front. Has anybody ever been injured?'

'We've had two murdered, remember?' I replied, immediately regretting the sharp edge to my voice. 'Sorry, didn't mean to sound like a bitch.'

He shrugged it off. 'You didn't sound like a bitch. You sounded like a person under stress, which I guess you are. Brad told me you haven't been yourself lately.'

We had arrived at his car, a late model Toyota. I waited until we were both inside and Liam was backing out of the car park before I responded. 'What else did Brad tell you? You seemed to be getting pretty chummy at one stage.'

Liam turned the car into the street. 'He was just telling me stuff about the band, and about your drummer—is it Jeff?'

'Yeah, Jeff.'

'Just band stories I guess.'

'Nothing bad about me?' I asked.

'No, not really.'

'It's just . . . don't believe everything Brad tells you. He has a hidden agenda.'

He was distracted briefly as he took the turnoff and drove onto the freeway. Then he settled in at a comfortable hundred and twenty kilometres an hour and we were on our way to the pine forest. His car smelled thickly of new upholstery and it hummed along in silence, the coloured lights on the dashboard dimly illuminating our faces.

'How long have you and Brad been together?' he asked.

I settled back into my seat, stretched my feet out. It was about a half-hour drive from the city to the forest. 'Nine years. Since I was fifteen. I was a teenage runaway, did he tell you that?'

'No.'

'I hated school and I hated my mother, still do. But I loved music and I had been learning guitar off this guy who lived next door to us at the time. He knew Brad and introduced us. Brad was looking for a girl singer for a dumb covers band he was putting together. I told him I was eighteen, but he must have known. There's a world of difference between a fifteen year old and an eighteen year old.'

'So you ran away to join the band?'

I nodded, then realised he couldn't see me. 'Yep. I joined the band, we played a couple of gigs in the city, then we got offered a tour all along the coast up to Cairns and back. Of course my parents wouldn't let me go, so I just took off. I didn't come back for nine months. When I did my dad was dead, my mother had collected his life insurance, sold the house and pissed off to Europe to spend the proceeds.'

'Have you seen her since?'

'Oh yeah. She's got a place on the beach that she stays in periodically. But she's hitched up with some

179

guy and they're doing a caravan tour of the country at the moment. I see her at Christmas and on my birthday and sometimes in between if I need money.'

The suburbs were disappearing behind us, and we were moving past new estates under construction, roadhouses and market gardens. 'Do you know how to get to where we're going?' I asked.

'I've got a fair idea. It's just finding the right access road. The lot numbers should be marked somewhere, so we shouldn't have too much trouble.'

He lapsed into silence. I watched out the window, anxious about our trip to the forest but trying to shove it down and be a brave girl.

Shortly Liam said, 'Nine years is a long time for a relationship to last.'

I turned back to him, wondered momentarily what he was talking about then realised he meant Brad. 'Well, we're used to each other I guess.'

'You must really love each other.'

'Love each other? God no, it's not that kind of relationship. We're not, like, *together*. We're business partners. And close friends I guess, but he's not my boyfriend.'

I was watching his face. He looked surprised. I started to get suspicious. 'What did Brad tell you?'

'Um . . . now I think of it, he didn't really tell me anything. I guess he just inferred it.'

I gave a short laugh, and I guess I was flattered. 'Brad's a good friend, but I've been turning him down as long as I've known him. I think he may have been trying to scare you off.'

And that comment led into a whole other conversation that neither of us probably wanted to have yet. Scare Liam off from what? Why would Brad be jealous? Was there a relationship developing here? Silence seemed more comfortable. I was lulled by the hum of the car, by his presence. I could still feel an unsettling gnawing in my stomach, but I focused on Liam and squashed all the nasty feelings. I looked across at his profile, his eyes concentrating in front of him, his dark hair, his wrists, his hands firmly clasping the steering wheel. I felt something warm shift inside me and I wanted to touch him so bad that I thought I'd explode with the feeling. But before I could reach out my hand he interrupted my train of thought.

'This is the turnoff,' he said. 'Are you sure you still want to do this? I mean, you've considered it properly?'

'Yes. Are you scared?'

He gave a short laugh. 'Let's just say I don't know what I'm doing here.'

'I still want to go.'

'Then I'm coming with you.'

CHAPTER
TWELVE

Bad idea. That's what I thought as we parked on a dirt access road and Liam killed the headlights. We were plunged into pitch darkness. Liam opened the glove box, and I willed the tiny soft light in there to get bigger, brighter.

'Shit. It's so dark.'

Liam looked at me as he grabbed his torch. 'Afraid of the dark?'

'I didn't think I was, but I guess I didn't know what dark was before. You know, I grew up in the healthy glow of streetlights.'

'Never been camping?'

'I've never liked being that far from running water.'

He flicked the torch on and slammed the glove box shut. 'Come on.'

We got out of the car. I untied the shirt that was hanging around my waist and pulled it on. I wanted to grab Liam's hand, but it's always hard to make the first move like that. Even in those circumstances it was hard. So I walked close beside him, my eyes locked onto the torch beam as we moved into the forest.

Plantation forests are not good places to be if you've been hallucinating. The rows and rows of trees, gliding off seemingly into orderly infinity, loomed forebodingly in the grey gloom. Every time Liam's torch beam lit upon one, shadows would deepen behind it, around it, giving the impression of something moving. It took me a while to adjust.

'You can see so many more stars out here, away from the city lights,' Liam was saying.

I looked up at the sky. He was right. 'Oh no, now we're going to start talking about the meaning of life, like everybody does when they start counting stars,' I said.

'We don't have to if you don't want to. But doesn't it make you wonder? Doesn't it make you think about how small and insignificant we are?'

'I don't need to look at the sky to make me think about that. I think about it while I'm cleaning the toilet.' I looked at him and laughed. 'Especially when I'm cleaning the toilet.'

He stopped for a moment and pulled the map out of his pocket. He inspected it in the torchlight. 'Damn. I think we're in the wrong lot. I had the map upside-down. This is the lot where the first body was found.'

'Can we go there? Have a look?' I felt a need to pay my respects to Simon. I was starting to suspect it was partly my fault he was dead; if he hadn't been on his way to see us, perhaps he would have lived to down another six-pack.

'Yeah. If you want. It's about three hundred metres in.'

'How will we know we're there? X marks the spot?'

'There'll be police tape everywhere. How's your sense of direction?'

'It's up there with my camping skills. You lead the way.'

We moved forward. The silence of the forest contrasted starkly with the mental noise in my head: what the hell was I doing? Being here seemed more and more ill-considered the further we pushed into the depths of blackness. I stayed as close to Liam as I could.

But then I began to wonder whether I was safe with him. Could he protect me . . . from what I didn't ask myself. For a full thirty seconds I wondered if it was possible that Liam could be the killer; after all, he had the map, the information, and the tenacity to bring me out here. My heart raced in my chest, then slowed down as I realised how ridiculously paranoid I was being. Liam was here because he fancied his chances with me, which I had always suspected anyway. Reassured of this, I groped for his hand and held onto it tightly.

In the distance, Liam's torch beam was picking up a reflective silver line. 'That's the police line,' he said. 'We're nearly at murder site number one.'

'We must be crazy,' I said.

He gave my hand a squeeze. 'Just relax. The dark is spooking you out. There's nothing to be afraid of.'

'How about a psycho serial killer?'

'He doesn't pick them up in the forest. He brings them here for . . . Look, let's not think about that any more.' He picked up his pace and soon we were standing on the safe side of a police line that marked out a space about ten metres square. The trees standing indifferently in the marked area looked the same as the other pines in the forest. We stood and stared. Liam shone his torch this way and that.

'Nothing,' he said. 'Nothing at all.'

'Nothing at all,' I repeated, staring at the tree in the centre of the square. Something was happening inside my head. The silent forest was suddenly filled with a humming, as though I had tuned into the soundtrack of life itself. I wasn't even aware of what was happening to me, but suddenly it seemed the most natural thing in the world that I could see . . .

Blood. Everywhere. Splattered everywhere, rivers of it and a man, Simon . . . Ah yes, I remembered him now. He'd tried to grab my breast once when I'd been standing at the bar with Brad. I'd slapped his knuckles and he'd grinned and kissed them. The scene replayed in my head. Kissing his own freckled knuckles. Fine ginger hair on his fingers; I could see them so close, as though through a microscope: the pores that the hairs grew out of, and his mouth, wide and dry, puckering up to kiss the knuckles that I had slapped. But now those hands were by his sides, loose, limp, a trickle of blood running past those gingery hairs, between the knuckles, over the light freckles. The blood coming from a massive, agonising wound in his chest, so black with blood that it was like looking into the mouth of hell. Black holes where his eyes were, those eyes that had tried to flirt with me even after I'd slapped him, told him to fuck off.

By now I knew a hallucination when I saw one. I squeezed my eyes tight and opened them again, and of course the body was gone, but even now, with cool reality caressing my face, I could see blood. So much blood.

How had they missed it? It was everywhere, dark maroon staining the grass, the weeds, the bark, trailing off into the forest. I grabbed the torch from Liam and pointed it at the tree trunks, at the bracken on the ground. God, the stuff was everywhere. And the bracken was disturbed, kicked up, scuffed through to the fertile dirt beneath.

'What is it, Lisa, what's the matter?' Liam was asking.

'The blood,' I said. 'The mess, how could they miss it?'

'What blood?'

'It's everywhere.' My eyes lit on a small white splinter glinting up from the bracken. 'Bone.' Then, no, it wasn't. It wasn't anything but . . . and the ground was undisturbed. And the blood was not there.

'Christ!' I said. My desperation terrified me.

Liam put an arm around me. 'Are you going to faint?'

I angrily pulled away from him and handed back the torch. 'No. I'm fucking hallucinating. I'm fucking . . . hallucinating.' I bit back tears. 'Sorry to yell. I've had a bad couple of days.'

'Imagination working overtime?'

'Perhaps.' Perhaps something more sinister. 'Can we . . . ?'

'Get away from here?'

'Yes. Let's just go into the other lot, where we said we'd start. If I freak out, just slap me or something. I promise I won't be angry.'

We crossed into the opposite lot, tramping through the bracken and fighting off insects attracted to the torch beam. We found nothing, of course. No Karin, no blood and bone. I maintained my death grip on Liam's hand as we walked back out to the access road. I was aware that this unscheduled bush-walk had become nothing but an opportunity to make a fool of myself in front of him. I was having trouble understanding how I'd got myself into this situation, how the temporary insanity of desperation had brought me this far.

'This is dumb,' I said. 'I think I've cured myself of this notion. I want to go home.'

'If you're sure,' he said.

I shrugged helplessly. 'I'm freaking out and I want to get out of here.'

He opened the map and shone his torch on it. 'If we go a couple of hundred metres into the next lot we'll be at the old sawmill.'

'Sawmill?'

'Yeah, I remember playing there with my big brother on one of our camping trips. We found some used condoms. I didn't know what they were and Mark made fun of me. It's been closed for years, since before I was born, according to my folks. There's nothing there any more, just a big old condemned shed.'

Again the rushing feeling in my head. I fought it down, and found that by concentrating I could make it go away.

'Do you want to go and have a look?' he asked.

'I don't know why, but yes.' The sense that it was important overwhelmed me. Then I remembered how wrong I was about Karin being at Dana's place. 'But I'm probably being paranoid. I'm not . . . I haven't been thinking straight the last couple of days . . . weeks. I'll understand if you don't want to.'

'No, I'm enjoying myself. It's a beautiful, fresh night. It's like getting back to nature.' He began to move forward again. 'Besides, it's completely understandable that you haven't been thinking straight lately, a lot has happened to you.'

'Yeah, and you don't even know the half of it.'

'Do you want to talk to me about the other half?'

For a moment I actually thought I would; just for a moment I thought it was a sane thing to tell him about my regressions. Then I realised I didn't want him to think I was a total looney, that I'd probably ruined my chances with him anyway, so I just said:

'No, I don't want to talk about it at this stage. Just trust me, my life has been getting pretty weird.'

Once again we plunged into the forest. No matter how far we walked, the scenery didn't change and it felt as though we hadn't got anywhere at all. It was like walking on an alien planet, where earth's natural laws didn't apply. On and on we walked in silence, until the first glimpse of the old sawmill. Only then could we measure our progress.

What was left of the sawmill sat in a yard that had been cleared of pine trees, but had now overgrown with native bush. A huge concrete slab with weeds and rusted wire springing from the cracks was crumbling into the ground. Pieces of the foundations of long-dead buildings jutted out here and there. One large shed stood impassively in the middle of the riot of vegetation and industrial remains. We shuffled past the tea trees and spiky bushes. The door to the shed sagged off its hinges and we went inside.

The first thing I noticed was the proliferation of spiders' webs. We nearly walked straight into one, but Liam pulled me up in time. The spider glittered silver, undisturbed by our intrusion. One narrow strip of floor was cement, and a staircase on either side rose up to two enclosed wooden platforms. We climbed the stairs and the floorboards creaked underneath our feet as we walked the length of the shed.

'You actually found used condoms here?' I asked.

'Yeah, my brother Mark was making a collection of them until Mum found out and flipped.'

'I just can't imagine anybody wanting to fuck in a place like this. Would you want to fuck in a place like this?'

He was suddenly tongue-tied, spitting out a couple of consonants but unable to get any vowels to follow.

I had to laugh. 'Don't worry,' I said. 'It's not an offer, just a hypothetical.'

'You're so frank,' he said finally. There was no hint as to whether this description was meant to be a criticism or a compliment, so I was caught between embarrassment and self-conscious pleasure.

My legs were tired and my feet were squeezed too tight in my boots for all this walking, so I sat down on the edge of the platform. Liam sat next to me. I placed my hands on the wood beside me. It felt warm.

'Strange,' I said.

'What?'

'The floor feels warm.'

'I can't feel it.'

Then I seemed to feel a low-level vibration. I was aware that my senses were going into shock again, so I took a deep breath and closed my eyes. I was filling up with an overwhelming sense of Karin's presence. I kept my eyes closed, took long, slow deep breaths. It was as if every nerve in my body was tuned to a radio station that was playing Karin's vibrations. I groped for Liam's hand. 'She's not here, is she?'

'No. Why?'

'I'm strung out. I don't want to hallucinate visions of her. It would be too . . . painful.' I remembered the unsettling vision I'd had in Dana's attic.

'Is something the matter?'

'I want to go home,' I replied, opening my eyes. 'I want to go back to civilisation. This place is fucking with my head.'

'You've got to trust your intuition, Lisa. Go with your gut. If you want to stay . . .'

'There's nothing here. We can both see that. I'm just overwrought.' I looked at him. 'Have you ever taken a bad trip?'

He shook his head.

'You can imagine all sorts of shit. That's what this feels like.' I stood up and stretched my legs. 'Let's go somewhere with bright lights.'

We ended up in a roadhouse twenty minutes further up the highway, squinting under the harsh fluorescent light and buying midnight snacks at three a.m. Liam bought coffee and a hot dog; I bought apple juice and salad sandwiches. We settled in a couple of orange plastic seats bolted across from each other with only a white laminex table to separate us. I opened my sandwiches. There was too much butter on them. I vainly tried to scrape some off with the flat end of Liam's coffee spoon. He smiled at me and I melted a little.

'Feeling any better?' he asked.

'I'm feeling glad to be out of the woods, if that's what you mean, but I don't know if I feel any better for having gone there in the first place.' I took a sip of my apple juice. It was freezing cold and made my teeth ache. I was struck by a deep sense of not knowing what to do next. I looked at Liam. I wanted to say something, to fill the silent space with sparkling conversation.

'So . . .' I said.

'So?' He smiled at me again, and his eyes crinkled up at the corners. I wanted to ask him how old he was, but it seemed rude. I felt uncomfortable and excited at the same time. It seemed I was suddenly fifteen again, with a crush on the guitarist in my band. And yet, in some ways, it was not like that at all.

We finished our midnight snack in silence. I wished I knew what he was thinking.

'We'd better head back, hey?' he said eventually.

Again I couldn't think of anything to say to extend our stay in this, the most romantic of roadside diners, so I nodded and we made to leave. I realised that I was falling for him.

The glass sliding doors opened for us and we were once again in the fresh night, the bright diner behind us.

'I just have to make a pit stop,' I said, indicating the cool dark brick of the ladies' toilet block.

'Sure, I'll wait here.'

While I was washing my hands, I examined myself in the dim mirror. I looked pale, but then I always looked pale. I breathed into my hand to see if I had bad breath—all I could smell was the soap I had just washed my hands with. I gripped the sides of the stainless steel basin and glared at myself. 'You're a grown woman,' I said. 'Just handle it.'

He was sitting on an outdoor picnic table, with his feet resting on the seat. His knees were a little bit apart. I was overwhelmed by a desire to kiss him.

I walked up and stood in front of him. He didn't move and we looked at each other for a minute. The tension was tangible. I was not imagining this. I pushed his feet apart and knelt between them, pressed my body against his and kissed his neck. I could feel his pulse quicken. His skin was very smooth. His hand touched my hair. He said 'Lisa' softly.

I pushed my face close to his. Our lips were almost touching, our breath embracing. Most promising of moments. He moved forward and kissed me, slowly and deeply, surprising me because I thought he would be more tentative.

When he drew away I made a little sighing noise. 'I think my brain just melted,' I said.

He laughed and kissed me again. I was turning to warm mush. Then a set of headlights swept over us as some late-night revellers pulled into the picnic spot. They hooted at us and Liam broke the kiss and shook his head.

'Time to go home,' he said.

The kiss had broken the silence and we talked all the way back. We talked about Karin, about the band, about his childhood camping trips, his job, my parents, his parents, family pets both past and present, then the philosophical ramblings of people who stay up too late. After God, the meaning of life, the universal truths, we managed to get onto death.

'Do you believe in reincarnation?' I asked, treading carefully.

'I don't know,' he said. 'A lot of religions believe in it.'

'Have you ever felt . . . you know . . . ever *remembered* something?'

He considered it for a while. 'I once had this really vivid dream where I was a woman. It was World War II and I was looking through the rubble of some bombed houses for my children . . .' He trailed off then gave a nervous laugh. 'Now you think I'm nuts,' he said.

'No, not at all.'

'Anyway, it was probably just a dream. I must have seen something on television.'

I let it lapse. We were back in the city now, heading towards my place. I was thinking about kissing him again. I was thinking about other things I'd like to do to him, but I wasn't sure how to broach the subject.

We drove down by the river and I told him how to get to my place. Soon we were idling out front. I took a deep breath and turned to him. 'Would you like to come up?'

'Ah . . . it's pretty late. I'd better get some sleep.'

'You could sleep here.'

He looked at his hands on the steering wheel. I could see him catch his lower lip between his teeth. Then he said: 'Not now. Maybe next time.'

I told myself not to take it personally and leaned across to kiss him. Once again he explored my mouth with passion. I pressed my body as close as I could against his. His hands lingered over my breasts lightly, then pulled away.

'Are you sure you don't want to come up?' I said.

'I don't know what to say, Lisa. It just doesn't feel right at the moment. Sorry.'

I shrugged. 'Okay. Well, give me a call or something.'

'Would you like to go somewhere on Sunday? To the morning markets?'

'Call me Sunday morning.' I looked into his face. 'Goodnight.'

He pecked me on the cheek. 'Goodnight, Lisa.'

My flat seemed very empty. The fridge hummed in the dark and the digital clock on the microwave blinked coldly—it was after four a.m. I unlaced my boots and kicked them off, then reached over to play back my answering machine messages. Hang-up calls. Brad: 'Lisa, I ran into Gerard from the Black Flag and he's cancelled tomorrow night. And by the way, where are you?' Another hang-up call, probably Brad again. And another. Then his voice again: 'Lisa, I'm worried about you. Can you call and let me know you're okay? It's three-thirty a.m. I'm still up watching *Rage*. Is hanky boy with you? Ring me.'

I picked up the phone and dialled. He answered on the third ring.

'I'm home,' I said.

'Where were you? I was worried.'

'I was with Liam.'

Silence. No—*angry* silence.

'Is that why you rang? To check up on me?' I said.

'No, no. Just that tomorrow night's gig—well, tonight's gig technically—has been cancelled.'

'You could have called tomorrow.'

'Okay, so I wanted to check that you got home safely. I mean, you don't know anything about that guy.'

'His name's Liam. Not "that guy". Not "hanky boy". Come on, Brad, don't make this hard on both of us.'

'I'm sorry, Lisa. But I just get burned up when I see you with someone else. I'm truly sorry.'

It was unlike Brad to sound so penitent, so sensitive, so I forgave him. 'It's okay. I get a little jealous sometimes too.'

'Just . . . don't fall in love with him, okay? I couldn't handle that.'

I thought it would soon be too late for that. 'I'm just taking one day at a time, Brad. I guess I'll see you Monday morning down at the studio then?'

'Okay.' Then: 'Did you fuck him?'

'No, not that it's any of your business. We went for a drive.'

'Will you tell me if you do fuck him?'

'No.'

'Will you tell me if he's got a bigger dick than me?'

I laughed. 'No.'

'Good. Because I'd really hate to know that.'

I couldn't sleep. My brain was full. I came back to the living room and flicked on the computer, hoping for a reply from Whitewitch. She hadn't let me down.

194

. . . You aren't thinking straight. You started the regressions for help with a dream, not for help solving murders and disappearances. If these things are related, you will find out soon enough. Trust the universe to give you all the information you need to learn this lesson.

Hallucinations are sometimes the side-effect of an altered state of consciousness. You've opened up a window in your mind, which sometimes doesn't close properly when you come out of the regressions. Remember, you're in control, you can always make it go away.

Do not be disturbed by what happens in your past life, it is over and done with and you cannot change history. Try to relax and enjoy the ride. Forget the murders, that's what the police force is for. Do not worry about your friend, and tune into what the universe has to tell you. Please, let me know how you go.

Tune into what the universe had to tell me. She made it sound so simple. And the weird thing was that I had started feeling I *wanted* to go back there, to find out what happened to Elizabeth and Gilbert.

I turned the computer off and paced my lounge room, thinking. Whitewitch was suggesting that all these weird things happening at once needed to be disconnected and dealt with separately. In her new-agey way, perhaps she was right. Perhaps if I could believe in reincarnation, I could believe in a message from the universe, God, whatever you wanted to call it. I could believe that if I chilled out and got to the bottom of the unresolved situation I'd inherited from Elizabeth, the rest would just fall into place.

And it sure as hell beat doing nothing and feeling helpless.

I secured my flat, put my head on my arms and said Whitewitch's mantra. Within seconds, the cool velvet hush of centuries engulfed me. I was rushing through a soft tunnel and every sound in the universe filled my ears.

CHAPTER
THIRTEEN

We were on our way to London, Gilbert, Mirabel and I. We were in a closed carriage and the motion had been making Mirabel sick since two miles from Prestonvale's main gates. It was six hours later, and we had stopped eight times so that she could throw up outside. I knew that she was with child, but I wasn't sure if I knew because of common sense or intuition. I was mildly jealous that she was carrying Gilbert's child in that belly, then reminded myself that a child was not something I had ever desired.

She drove me mad with her constant complaining. 'I don't know why I had to come with you to stupid London, Gilbert,' she said. 'I don't see why I couldn't have stayed at home with Father. I am so sick.' And she glowered at me, no doubt wondering what I was doing there too. But Gilbert had insisted to Uncle Tom that Mirabel needed a companion, not the least because of her current condition. A condition Mirabel had not realised she suffered from yet, poor little innocent. She had squeezed herself into a whalebone body and farthingale under her dress this morning, wondering aloud why it seemed tighter than usual. I, who usually wore padded petticoats rather than the ridiculous cartwheel farthingale, suggested she do the same. She had not, calling me unfashionable and saying she would not have all the fine ladies of London laughing at her.

We pulled into an inn on the thoroughfare at supper time. It was bustling with activity. A couple of servants came out to help us with our bags and showed us to our beautifully furnished rooms on the second floor. It was glorious to stretch my legs after being cooped up in the carriage all day, and glorious to think that I would soon be away from Mirabel. But that wasn't to be. I saw Gilbert talking in an undertone to one of the porters, and then he strode across to us.

'You and Elizabeth will share one room,' he said, touching Mirabel's cheek. 'I will be coming to bed much later and I don't want to disturb you.'

Mirabel just nodded wearily and settled herself neatly on the side of the bed. 'Will you help me off with my dress, Elizabeth?'

I looked desperately from Mirabel to Gilbert. He smiled lightly. 'Something the matter, Elizabeth?'

'Where are you going?' I asked.

'There's a world of men out there. I'll have supper sent up to your room.'

I leaned close to him. 'This is so unfair,' I hissed.

'You'll have your time. I have something planned for London.'

'What are you whispering about?' Mirabel squeaked from the bed. 'Are you keeping secrets from me?'

Gilbert's eyes flicked over to Mirabel, then back to me. 'I think you should tell her why she's been so sick. She hasn't worked it out for herself yet.'

I nodded then turned back to Mirabel. 'Come, cousin. Let's sit down together and have a little talk. Gilbert is going off to do some business.'

I heard the chamber door close behind him, and I helped Mirabel out of her dress and stiff underwear.

'I don't feel well, Elizabeth,' she said, her voice taking on that petulant little girl tone that I hated so much. I gritted my teeth. She lay back on the bed in her linen smock. 'I don't think I want supper.'

I settled next to her and looked into her face. 'Do you know why you're sick?'

'I expect it's the journey.'

'Have you noticed anything else that might have contributed to an illness?'

She looked at me, puzzled. 'This isn't one of your healing spells, is it? Because I want you to know that I don't want anything to do with—'

'Shh,' I said. 'That's nonsense. Here, let me touch your stomach.' I laid a hand flat against her belly.

'What are you doing, Elizabeth?'

I could feel the life in her belly. Like a low humming, like a sense of unlimited potential, all the promise in the world. I was overcome with such awe that I felt tears spring to my eyes.

'What is it?' Mirabel said, panic edging into her voice.

'It's all right, Mirabel,' I said, 'lie still.'

I pressed just a little firmer and closed my eyes, took a deep breath. Something about my calm attitude seemed to relax Mirabel. I felt her muscles untensing beneath my hand. 'Ah, it's so beautiful,' I said, feeling again that huge hope. I knew, without knowing how, that the child would be a girl. I opened my eyes and bent down to kiss Mirabel's face.

'You're with child, cousin. You're going to have a little girl of your own.'

She made a little 'o' with her mouth, and a tiny popping noise sounded in her throat.

'What's the matter?'

'How can that be?' she said.

'Surely you know how,' I replied.

'Yes. No. I mean, I *know* how babies come, but I don't know how I could be having one. Gilbert doesn't . . . We haven't . . .' She blushed deep red. I was beginning to feel uncomfortable, although I couldn't say why.

'Are you saying that you haven't consummated your marriage?' I asked.

She looked at me speechless, fat tears springing onto her cheeks.

'It's all right, Mirabel. You can tell me.'

'Oh, please. Don't tell Gilbert I've said anything. I should hate for him to be cross.'

'I won't tell him. Haven't you made love?'

A small voice answered. 'No. Not . . . not as a man and a woman are supposed to. And I know how they're supposed to . . . Once I caught one of the pages with a girl from the village. They were in the gardens early in the morning, and I . . . I watched them from behind a tree. But Gilbert doesn't do that to me. He . . . he does something else.'

'Something else?'

She rolled over onto her side, turning her back to me. 'I'm too embarrassed to say. Please don't make me say.'

I pulled her over gently so she was facing me. 'Mirabel, what is it he does?'

She looked everywhere but at me. 'He . . . pleasures himself. Then he . . . lifts my skirts and puts his hand between my legs. Puts only his wet fingers in, not his . . . I thought he was doing it so that I wouldn't have a child. I thought he didn't want a child.'

I placed my hand over her belly again. I couldn't resist that feeling, the great, sweet promise of it. I wondered what Gilbert was up to, impregnating her in such a fashion. To me it was obvious that impregnation was his object, but why without taking her virginity?

'Promise you won't say anything to him?' she was asking.

I shook my head impatiently. 'What business would I have talking to Gilbert about his bedroom secrets?' But of course I would ask him. Curiosity and I did not get along.

The long road stretched out before us again the next morning. Gilbert roused us early, telling us that to get to London before dinner time we needed to leave immediately. Mirabel was anxious as well as sick now, and her constant protestations of not wishing to travel this early grated on me. Even after we had settled in the dark, cool coach, her girlish voice continued to grumble and gripe. I realised that I was starting to get a headache, a bright flash of pain somewhere over my left eye.

'Please be quiet, Mirabel,' I said softly, reaching across to clasp her wrist. 'There's a dear girl, just be quiet for a while.'

Immediately she became silent, her whole body relaxed into a posture of calm. I looked at Gilbert, surprised, and he laughed at me. 'What's the matter, Elizabeth? Don't know your own strength?'

I squeezed her hand. 'Mirabel?' I said quietly. No response. Once again I glanced up at Gilbert. 'Did I do that to her?'

He shot over to my side of the coach and grabbed me around the waist. 'Clever little witch, aren't you?'

I fought him off and looked back to Mirabel. She was staring straight ahead, looking beautifully serene, her eyes unfocused and a slight smile playing at the corners of her lips. Gilbert was kissing my neck.

'That's incredible,' I said. 'I didn't even mean to . . .'

'Yes you did. That's why it worked, because you really *meant* it. You really wanted her to be quiet for a while. You've done very well. Now come here and kiss me.'

I returned his kiss. He reached across me to let the blind down over the small square window. The carriage rocked along. The sound of the horses' hooves tapping and tapping against the ground drifted through to us. Gilbert had his hands all over me, pushing them up my skirts. I kept glancing back to Mirabel, checking that she couldn't see what was going on. But no, she was beyond comprehending.

'It won't hurt her baby, will it?' I asked softly.

'No, nothing can hurt the child.'

I desperately wanted to ask him about the way he had made Mirabel pregnant, but he had pulled his gloves off and his fingers were busy between my legs, twining in my pubic hair and sliding between the soft folds of my wet flesh. I groaned loudly. He pulled me on top of him and pushed my petticoats up. My knees slipped on the soft leather of the coach seat. He gripped my thighs with strong hands, kneaded the flesh of my buttocks. I hastened to unfasten the points that attached his doublet to his breeches. He squirmed in his seat as I pushed his breeches down and released his erect member. Again I looked over my shoulder at Mirabel. For a creeping moment it felt as though she were looking directly at us, those cornflower blue eyes watching benevolently as I impaled myself on her husband. Gilbert unbuttoned my collar and threw it to the floor of the carriage then unfastened the front of my bodice so that my breasts spilled out into his

202

face. We coupled quickly and violently. The smell of sex mixed with the smell of leather and horse. I came in gigantic circular thumps, then climbed off Gilbert and settled back panting on the seat. My headache was gone. Gilbert re-dressed himself, but I lay motionless for a while, watching Mirabel. She looked positively eerie.

Gilbert threw my collar at me. 'Dress yourself, Elizabeth. We'd better rouse her. She'll realise too much of the journey has passed otherwise.'

I buttoned myself and tidied my clothes and hair. Gilbert returned to his seat next to Mirabel. Once again, I grasped her wrist, but this time my hand was shaking with newly spent passion. 'Mirabel. Rouse yourself, Mirabel.'

Gilbert flicked the blind again and a small square of sunlight fell in her lap.

'Mirabel?' I said.

'Yes, Elizabeth?'

'Are you all right?'

'I'm feeling very sleepy.'

Gilbert put his arm around her back and drew her down into his lap. 'There, dear girl. Have a little sleep. We'll be in London before you know it.' He sat and stroked her hair, looking at me with those intense grey eyes. 'And then we'll really have some fun,' he said.

We had dinner in the well-appointed dining room of the Royal River Inn where we were staying. We ate succulent roast swan, baked chewits, olive pie, fresh peaches and custard. Mirabel only picked at her food, complaining that she was tired and sick. I was tired and sick of her, but I said nothing, only smiled solicitously and asked if there was anything I could do to help. She shook her head weakly and looked back down at her food.

'Well, ladies,' Gilbert said at length, 'we have a whole wonderful afternoon stretching before us. Would you like to wander down Cheapside and buy some pretty things for yourselves?'

I almost jumped out of my seat, but Mirabel protested loudly. 'No. I'm far too sick to go anywhere, and if I stay, Elizabeth has to stay.'

I turned on her, barely concealing my anger. 'Why, Mirabel? I could go with Gilbert and buy you some velvet for a new dress.'

'Because it isn't right for my husband to be out with another woman.'

I was momentarily staggered by this response. I didn't know when she had got this idea into her head. 'But Mirabel, I'm your cousin . . .'

'It's not right. You aren't going with him, Elizabeth. You'll have to stay and take care of me. I don't want to be alone in this horrible big old place.'

I gritted my teeth. I loved London, and I desperately wanted to get out and take deep breaths of it.

'All right then, Mirabel,' Gilbert said. 'It's better that I get my business done so that I can get you back home all the sooner. If you ladies can entertain yourselves this afternoon, I'll be back this evening for supper.' He turned to me and offered me a slight bow of his head. My hands shook with the effort to stay unclenched. He was doing it again, leaving me alone with her. It was fine when he wanted to taste my sex, but when I wanted, no, *needed* him, all I got were conciliatory gestures.

'Fine,' I said. 'Go and do your business. Come, Mirabel, let's go upstairs.'

'Oh, you aren't cross, are you?' she said, trying to sound innocent.

I pushed myself back from the dining table and headed up the stairs, with her scurrying behind me making supplicating noises.

'Only I didn't mean to sound so cruel, it's just not *fitting*, you understand. I'm his wife after all, and you already receive so much of his attention in your painting lessons.' On and on she went, all through the long afternoon, even while I was trying to read, even while I was looking out the window into the deep garden at the back of the inn and rehearsing in my head over and over how I would unleash my anger on Gilbert the instant I had him alone.

After supper, when he still hadn't returned, I began to accept my fate. That familiar feeling of fighting down frustration and anger sat less comfortably on me now than it had in the past because I had been sure that things would be different since I had made my pact. But Gilbert had armed me and not shown me how to use my weapons. We had hardly had any time alone since that evening, and while I felt different, and could now see and hear things not visible or audible to others, I was unaware of the degree of my talent or how to apply it. It seemed, however, that Gilbert had turned his back on me already. I was wretched. Not the least because I was in love with him and expected better treatment than to be confined to Mirabel's chamber while she hounded me for sympathy.

Finally she went to bed, complaining again of sickness and tiredness. I sat in the corner of the room, scribbling away in my journal by lamplight, committing all my bitter feelings to paper. I was just starting to flow with my thoughts, lose myself in the words, when her weak little voice piped up: 'Elizabeth, do put that light out and stop scratching that pen. I can't sleep with that light and that scratching.'

'I'll be finished soon,' I said, making no effort to conceal my impatience.

'Why can't you finish now? I'm with child. I need my sleep. You're supposed to be here to look after me and you're keeping me awake.'

I slammed my book shut and extinguished the flame. Then I strode across to the opposite window looking out into the courtyard of the inn. Men came and went, silently and very far away.

'Are you cross, Elizabeth?'

'Yes.'

'Are you going to come to bed?'

'Just go to sleep.'

'But you're cross.'

I didn't reply. Eventually I heard her shift and make herself comfortable under the covers. I pressed my face against the cold glass of the window and tears sprang to my eyes and began to trickle down my face. I thought over and over to myself, 'But nothing has changed, nothing has changed.' My soul wanted to fly from my body, lift up and out and roam the streets of London, through the arches of Paul's Walk and down Cheapside; to smell the strange bitter smell of the place and see the shadows move and shiver in the dim lamplight, to *taste* the delirious, thrilling tumult of the night. But here I was, trapped again. And that little tingle in my thigh, that witch-mark, reminded me that everything had been lost but nothing had been gained.

I wasn't aware how long I stood like that, watching the faint orange glow of the night-time world flicker below my window. I was thinking about crawling into bed and trying to sleep, when the door opened quietly and Gilbert stepped in. I looked up and his eyes met mine in the dark. I made a deliberate show of turning away from him. He came up to me and put his hand on my shoulder.

'Angry?'

'Furious,' I replied.

He nodded towards Mirabel's bed. 'Is she asleep?'

'Yes.'

'Good.' He tiptoed over to the bed and leaned over Mirabel. I turned to watch him. He put a hand gently across her forehead and leaned close to whisper something in her ear. Then he returned to where I was sitting and offered me his hand.

'Are you ever going to forgive me?'

I brushed his hand away and whispered fiercely: 'I don't see why I should. You left me stuck here all afternoon and went off to enjoy yourself, without any thought for how I might feel. And yet you say you love me.'

He chuckled. 'Of course I love you,' he said, then leaned in and kissed me on the lips.

I broke away and looked towards the bed. 'Mirabel?'

'She's under until I wake her. She'll know nothing.'

'A spell?'

'Yes, if that's what you want to call it. So, are you coming?'

I was confused. 'Coming where?'

'Out. Into the world.'

I raised an eyebrow sceptically. 'The world of men?'

He smiled in the darkness. 'Now there's an idea. Between us we should be able to manage it.'

'I don't understand you.'

He grabbed my wrist and pulled me across the room. 'Come with me to my chamber.'

I followed him to the room next door and watched

as he bent over his case, pulling out his leather-bound book. 'Lie down,' he said. 'Take your clothes off.'

'What are you going to do?'

'*We*'re going to do it, together. We're going to turn you into a man for the evening.'

I stopped unlacing my gown. 'Turn me into a man?'

'Yes, yes. Isn't that what you want?'

'I . . . I don't know. Will it hurt?'

He pushed me onto the bed and began to help me off with my gown. 'Of course not. It's just an illusion, it's not real. You may look like a man, you may even feel like a man. But you'll really still be my beautiful Elizabeth. Trust me.'

I wriggled out of my clothes. It was cold and I shivered a little. He placed a warm mouth over my breast and kissed me gently. 'Close your eyes and think about how much you'd like to be a man.'

I closed my eyes. I thought about all the things I would love to do with my life. I imagined myself striding forth into the world, moving among other interesting people, attending a university, sailing into the East, taking and possessing a woman to rear a family of my own. As I did this, Gilbert whispered lowly over my body. It was strange. I couldn't hear what he was saying, yet I knew what he was saying without the words ever forming in my brain. My body seemed to respond to his words on another level, tingled and hummed with them, dived and fell as his words dived and fell. Soon I had joined him in the mumbling language, without knowing or under-standing fully what the words were. My eyes had rolled back and my breathing had slowed to long, bottomless breaths that pushed deep into my body. Every time I exhaled, the little noises would come out of me, echoing Gilbert's, until somehow it all became one—my words, Gilbert's words, my fantasy of masculinity—one long, low, moving wave of desire that stirred at my feet and began slowly to creep up my body. And I felt muscles tightening and strength growing in my limbs, and I felt a scrambling in my private parts and a sense of hardening up through my chest. I became aware of Gilbert laughing somewhere far away and this roused me from my deep meditation and I opened my eyes.

'Gilbert?' I said woozily.

'Look at you. My God, what a beautiful boy you make.' He helped me up into a sitting position and pointed to the glass across from us. My breath caught in my throat. Staring back at me out of the gloom was a boy of about seventeen, long and graceful, girlish yet unmistakably male. I closed my eyes and let my head drop back, trying to get hold of my fear. I searched deep inside myself and seemed to find the female me, which I clung to desperately. Gilbert tapped my shoulder. 'Don't do that. Concentrate on the masculine, you'll undo the enchantment.'

'I'm sorry. I was scared.' My voice was deeper, more resonant.

'You mean excited. You and I are going to sample the delights of London by night. Here, let me get you some clothes.'

Gilbert dressed me in an ill-fitting but highly fashionable doublet, breeches and mantle of royal blue, creamy silk hose and a feathered hat. None of his shoes would fit me, so I slipped back into my chamber and put on my plainest leather pumps. Gilbert gave me a small purse of money which I tucked away under my mantle, then he and I spilled into the street.

We made our way down to the docks. The river smelled cold and coppery, and it shifted and shadowed its way along until it reached London Bridge, where it roared through the arches as if angry to meet with obstruction. Gilbert paid a penny to the boatman, and we made our way across to the Surrey Bank.

It was too late in the evening to see a play or to watch the bear-baiting. But Gilbert assured me that there was much more going on in Southwark in which to indulge ourselves. We stepped out at the other side and began to walk up a wide, boggy road. It had rained lightly in the afternoon, and the ditches were filled with muddy water. I picked my way around the furrows, staying close to Gilbert the whole time. The dark city was spotted with burning lanterns in doorways and light spilling through latticed windows. Behind closed doors I could hear laughing and shouting. We turned down a narrower alleyway, then into another. Gilbert led me through a bewildering series of twists and turns, along smelly, boggy side streets and dark, quiet alleys, before he stopped outside a neat two storey house with high, narrow windows. Lights blazed inside.

Gilbert turned to me. 'Your name is Edward. Can you remember that?'

'Edward,' I repeated in the unfamiliar voice.

He inclined his head towards the house. 'This is a gambling den. The owners will sell you some potent homemade sack if you ask for it, but they primarily make their money through loaded dice and marked cards. Young men like you come here looking for a good time and wind up fleeced and broke out on the street.' He smiled. 'Of course, that won't happen to us. Tonight, the cony-catchers are going to be caught themselves.'

I shook my head slightly. 'I don't understand.'

'Trust me. Do you still have that little purse of coins?'

210

I felt at my waist. 'Yes, it's here.'

'Good. We'll triple it before the night is over. Come on.'

He rapped hard three times then pushed the door open. We entered a small dark ante-room, but Gilbert seemed to know where he was going and pushed through into another room that was thick with tobacco smoke and the smell of men. A huge fire roared in one corner, making the room far too hot. A group of over a dozen men crowded around a table. One man, with greying hair and a huge nose, sat at one end of the table rattling three dice in a brass cup. Small trickles of sweat shone on his face. His eyes were milky and useless. As he cast the dice onto the table, a young man in a plain green tunic called the numbers. The men around the table alternately moaned or cheered.

Gilbert leaned in towards me. 'I come here periodically. The old man doesn't know it's me of course, he's blind. But he's a wily old fellow. He has three sets of dice and he switches between them without people noticing. One set is fair, one loaded to throw up small numbers, and one set has tiny, stiff hairs glued to the dice so that certain numbers can't come up at all. He lulls the gamblers into a false sense of confidence, then shamelessly fleeces them. It's quite a wonder to see.'

'Then what are we doing here?'

'Don't forget, Elizabeth—I mean, Edward, we have something that the old man doesn't. Come sit down the end with me.' He tugged on my sleeve and we squeezed in down the far end of the table. The boy who was calling the numbers looked towards us expectantly. The dice rattled in their cup.

'The purse,' Gilbert said to me quietly. I fumbled with it and brought out a handful of coins. I could

211

see the boy watching us closely. He leaned in and whispered something to the blind man, who bared his rotting teeth in a smile.

'New to town are you?' he asked kindly. 'Are you in for some dice play, young fellow?'

I looked to Gilbert, who elbowed me, urging me to speak. 'Yes, sir,' I said to the blind man. 'I'm from the country, up Norfolk way.'

'Ah,' he said, nodding happily. 'A farm lad? What are you farming, boy?'

'Sheep, sir,' I replied. 'We're wool growers.'

The crowd around the table began to laugh. A bearded man in a fur-lined cap leaned close. 'Sheep,' he shouted, as if it were the funniest thing he had ever heard.

'Are you in?' the numbers boy said to me.

'Yes, yes, I'm in,' I replied.

'Well, choose your number.' He indicated the badly drawn grid on the table, marking out numbers across the middle, and high and low areas on each side.

I looked to Gilbert, who just smiled at me. 'You choose,' he said.

I took a small stack of coins and placed them on thirteen. I lost.

'Never mind, lad,' said the blind man. 'Have another try, eh?'

Gilbert leaned in and whispered in my ear. 'Be in tune, Elizabeth. You know what number is going to come up. Remember, he's not playing fair, so why should we?'

I looked at Gilbert and nodded. Be in tune. I was feeling hot and slightly sweaty under my shirt and doublet. The dice rattled. A pinch-faced woman had come out with a flask of sack and was filling up people's cups. I watched the blind man carefully,

212

watched his hands, watched the cup. A tiny hum zapped through me, and I knew which number to bet on. I placed a stack of coins on eleven. Two fives and a one came up. I collected.

'Well done,' Gilbert said softly.

'Well done, lad,' the blind man echoed after the numbers boy had related my win to him. 'Are you in again?'

'Certainly,' I replied, and again, as he began to shake the cup, the number came to me. Again, I won.

Five times in a row I won, and the blind man's mouth was getting a little tighter every time. Others at the table were losing their money badly; some left and some sat back to watch me. Perhaps they were realising a lifelong ambition to see the old man beaten at his own game.

After my twelfth win, the blind man pounded the table. 'How are you doing that, lad? What's happening? Carrick?'

The numbers boy leaned in. 'Yes, sir.'

'Get that lad out of here. It's unnatural. Get him out of here.'

The man in the fur-lined cap leaped to my defence. 'What's the matter, don't like to be beaten? You certainly didn't mind beating us all evening. So the lad's having a run of luck, let him go on.'

'No, no. It's unnatural. He's unnatural. And who's with him? I hear someone whispering to him. Carrick, get them out of here. I won't have no unnatural types in here tricking an old blind man.'

Gilbert was up and pulling me to my feet. I scraped my winnings into my purse. The atmosphere had changed from one of jovial warmth to one of venomous intimidation. 'Come on, let's go before it gets out of hand.'

Carrick made his way towards us, but the man in

the fur-lined cap stood in front of him. 'What do you think you're going to do to them, eh? Punish them for winning?'

'Out, out, out,' Gilbert hissed, hurrying me in front of him.

We hastened out of the house and into the street. It was dark and cool in comparison. I heard voices raised, something breaking inside. Gilbert pushed me ahead of him, down the alley and behind a closed shop awning. We turned in time to see people pouring into the street from the gambling house, pushing and shouting at each other.

'Did we start that?' I whispered.

Gilbert was chuckling quietly. The men had started fighting in earnest, and I was amazed by how rough they were with each other, belting each other with fists, and kicking and butting heads.

'Come on,' he said. 'Let's get to our next stop.'

We turned towards the street, and there was a man coming towards us. He was small and thin and limped badly. Gilbert didn't seem to have noticed him. As the man came into the relief of a light shining from a window, I thought I recognised him from the gambling house. He had left shortly after my winning streak began. He tipped his hat and smiled a crooked grin at us. 'Congratulations, young fellow,' he said amiably. 'Good to see old Jack get some of his own medicine.'

'Thank you,' I replied, smiling back.

Just as he was about to pass, he tripped and fell right at my feet. He landed hard on his back and made a sudden groaning noise.

'Elizabeth . . .' Gilbert started, but I was already on my knees, trying to help him up.

'Thank you kindly, lad,' he said, placing one hand on my shoulder. Then he reached up under my cloak

214

for a second, scrambled to his feet and ran away, perfectly able-bodied. It all happened so suddenly I was left kneeling there stunned.

'What was that all about?' I asked Gilbert.

He sighed. 'Check under your mantle. He's cut your purse.'

'He's . . . ?' I felt under my cloak. He was right: the little purse was gone. 'How did he do that?'

'You fell for the oldest trick in town, I'm afraid. I should have warned you.'

I gazed down the street after him. I felt an absolute fool. Gilbert put a hand out to help me up. 'Never mind. We might right the wrong yet this evening. Leave it up to our friends.'

'Which friends?'

He reached between my legs, grabbed my inner thigh where the witch-mark was, and squeezed it sensuously. 'You know which friends I mean.' He laughed. 'Come on, time to sample some pleasures of the flesh.'

CHAPTER
FOURTEEN

Gilbert led me to the dead end of a dusty, smelly alley. Across the way, a plump woman in a garish taffeta gown and a red shawl stood at the front door of a small timber house. She was looking us over. Gilbert turned me to face him.

'You're so beautiful,' he said.

'Even now? Even as a man?'

To prove he meant it, he kissed me, hot and wet on the lips. I drew a breath; something stirred in my private parts, but it felt different. Less of a desire to accommodate and internalise, more of a desire to appropriate and externalise. It felt strange. Strange and wonderful.

We crossed over to where the woman stood watching us expectantly. 'Are you here for business, sirs?' she said.

'Yes. My nephew here would like to sample some of the illicit delights of the city.'

She looked me over appreciatively. 'Certainly. Come in. What's your name, lad?'

'Edward,' I replied as Gilbert pushed me into the house in front of him.

'Well, Edward, why don't you come right upstairs and we'll see what we can do for you.'

The full realisation of what Gilbert intended for

me sank in. I turned to him. 'I don't know if I want to do this,' I hissed between clenched teeth. 'I'm not interested in women.'

He made a dismissive gesture with his hand. I was trapped between him and the plump woman, making my way up a gloomy staircase hung with dusty portraits that loomed out of the darkness as we passed with the lamp. A small glow of orange light seeped out from beneath the doors of two other rooms on the upper landing. In one the sounds of pleasure breathed through the walls. I reached out to grab Gilbert's hand, but he pulled it away. Instead he pushed me gently in the back. 'Be a man,' he whispered. 'It's what you wanted, isn't it?'

The woman brought us to a small, warm room at the end of the corridor. A fire crackled quietly in the corner. She lit a few candles around the place and it filled with a soft orange glow. Gilbert settled in a chair beside the bed, crossed his legs in front of him and watched as the woman led me to the bed and sat me down.

Gilbert leaned forward and stroked my cheek. 'Beautiful, isn't he?'

'Yes, sir,' she replied, lifting my hat off my head and stroking my hair.

'Well, tell him.'

'Edward, you are very beautiful,' she said to me.

'He's never done this before,' Gilbert said, reaching into his purse for a handful of coins and placing them on the table next to the bed. 'Make sure it's memorable for him, would you?'

Her eyes widened when she saw how much Gilbert had left her. 'Of course, of course.'

She slipped out of her shawl and I saw that her dress was embarrassingly low-cut. Her large white breasts almost spilled over the taffeta. She picked up my hands and put them over her breasts. I froze, not knowing what to do. Part of me, the male part, wanted to squeeze and pinch at the soft mounds until she squealed. The female part, buried as deep as it was, protested violently, repulsed by this common whore.

'Go with the moment,' Gilbert said.

He seemed very far away. I looked at him, then back at the woman, who was watching me expectantly, lips pouted provocatively. Something that felt frighteningly like hate zapped through me in the guise of desire. With all my strength, which was considerably more now than it had been, I pushed her back on the bed and tore the front of her dress open. Her nipples were painted dark pink. I rubbed my thumbs over them, feeling the skin tingle beneath me.

She gasped. 'Are you sure you haven't done this before?'

I was all man, just what I wanted being a man to be. 'Just shut your mouth, you stupid trug,' I said. 'Don't speak unless I tell you to.' Again I went at her breasts, kneading and squeezing. I was growing large and hard between my legs—a violent, hot sensation of promise. I put my hand over my crotch and rubbed myself hard. Ah, how it felt. How could I ever explain that feeling, being in possession of an instrument of power? I quickly removed the remainder of her clothes. She lay squirming underneath me on the bed, all soft, white curves. I examined her all over closely, my fingers exploring her flesh and the spaces and hollows of her body. She seemed to have so many holes that required filling, I barely knew what to do.

I glanced over to Gilbert, who was watching impassively, chin resting in his left hand, surrounded by spidery shadows. I flipped the woman over and examined her some more. I slapped her bare backside and watched the ripples of flesh expand out from my hand. I did it again; she squealed. Gilbert laughed.

'Here,' I said, getting off the bed and coming to stand in front of Gilbert. 'Help me out of these ridiculous clothes.'

His hands deftly undressed me, touching my bare torso with lingering fingers. Naked, I fell back on the bed. She scrambled over me and began to cover my body with little kisses. I grabbed a handful of her hair and pushed her head down over my private parts. She opened her mouth to accommodate my prick and I lay back, groaning in pure wonderment. What softer, moister, more perfect place in the world was there than this? She sucked and sucked until I thought I could stand the pleasure no more, then I pulled her head up and pushed her over on her back.

'How does it feel?' Gilbert asked as I positioned myself over her, ready to pierce her softness with years of my rage.

'I feel like a god,' I said, taking her. I cried out and Gilbert clapped his hands together.

'You are a god,' he said. 'You are a god.'

And I was thinking, 'I am a god, I am', as I pounded away at her flesh with this hard, male body that seemed to feel so *right*. I put my hand on her forehead and pinned her to the bed. She writhed and gasped and made little choking noises. I was aware of nothing but my own pleasure. I leaned over and violently sucked one of her round little nipples into my mouth, spat it out. I grabbed her upper arms in my big strong hands, lifted her slightly off the bed and pushed her back down, over and over, shaking her like a rag doll. She was screaming in short bursts, her legs clamped about me and her body pressing back at me. Something hot and fluid gushed up into me and just as suddenly gushed out into her. I slammed my body into her, then fell gasping on her breasts, my face trickling with a light sweat. My eyes locked on Gilbert's, who was still watching closely.

The woman stroked my hair. 'You're a real man, now,' she said. 'Don't you ever forget me, don't you ever forget Amy who did this for you.'

I rolled off her and lay on my back, trying to catch my breath. I became aware that Gilbert was undressing and climbing onto the bed on top of the woman. He coupled with her, right there next to me. I watched them for a little while. The bed covers were dusty and my nose itched slightly. The sight of Gilbert's body made me feel tender inside. I reached out to touch his back, withdrew my hand, threw my arm over my face and lay back with eyes closed. I loved him, I loved him so much. I was becoming slightly queasy, twitchy, feeling weak and spent. I fell back into myself, so dark and lush inside here. I only came back to reality when I heard the woman scream.

But it wasn't a scream of sexual pleasure, because it went on. And then she drew breath and screamed again, and I was opening my eyes and Gilbert was trying to pull the bedspread over me to cover my body. The woman was gagging and pointing at me, and Gilbert turned and slapped her hard. She sat there, nursing her jaw, but quiet.

'Elizabeth,' he said to me, 'cover yourself up. Your true self has upset our Amy.'

I looked down at my body, and that's exactly what it was: my real body. Some time in that small sliver of oblivion I had lapsed into, the enchantment had undone itself. I scurried to my feet and grabbed my clothes. They fitted even worse than before, but at least I got them on. I tucked my hair up under my hat. Gilbert was also getting dressed.

'What are you?' the woman was spitting at me. 'What are you?'

I tried to ignore her, but she got up from the bed and leaned close, pushing a finger into my chest. 'What are you? Are you a devil? Are you a witch?'

I pulled my face away from hers, but she kept advancing. 'What kind of black magic is this? What are you?' Her voice was rising into a shriek again. I drew my hand back and slapped her hard. She began to cry. I pushed her onto the bed and slapped her and punched her around the head. She opened her mouth in a little soundless scream as I continued battering her. The ring I wore on my left hand tore her lip open and she began to bleed. Gilbert pulled me off her, to my feet.

'Come on, that's enough.'

'You're a witch!' the woman screamed. 'You're a devil. Get out, devil; get out, Satan!'

There were noises in other parts of the house, the sounds of people waking and wondering what was going on. Gilbert grabbed my wrist and we raced to the door, out onto the landing and down the dark stairs. I tripped on a rug at the bottom of the stairs, but Gilbert steadied me and we flung the front door open and ran back into the street. Gilbert pulled me into a side alley, then pushed me up against a wall and kissed me. I could feel his pulse pounding in his throat. I gasped for breath. He let me go and took a few paces back.

'You're nothing but trouble this evening,' he said lightly.

I had to laugh. 'I suppose we had better head back now.' I looked down at my body. 'This disguise isn't quite so effective with breasts.'

He reached for me and pulled me into his arms, and just held me. It was surprising. I was unused to

221

just being held. I nestled into his arms and listened for a long time while his heart slowed down and returned to a relaxed rhythm. I tuned to the rhythm, timed my breathing to it. His hands moved slowly over my back, tangled in my hair. He kissed the top of my head through my hat. 'I love you,' he said. 'You are the perfect, perfect woman. What a shame we couldn't have had children, they would have been wonderful.'

I tightened my grip on him. He was so solid and masculine. 'I love you too, Gilbert,' I said. 'But I'm afraid of you sometimes.'

'There's no need to be afraid of me. I'll never hurt you, I swear.'

I relaxed against his chest. We seemed to hold each other for an age, the cold rank air of London stealing around us. Then his voice rumbled in his chest. 'Well, look at that.'

I pulled away from him and looked down the street in the direction he was facing. The figure of a man was emerging around the corner. He hadn't seen us yet.

'Who is it?'

'It's the fellow that cut your purse. Our friends have provided.'

He started towards the cutpurse. I hung back in the shadows. 'Gilbert, what are you going to do?'

He turned to me, gave a smile. 'Don't you want to scare him a little? Didn't you enjoy scaring the whore?'

I had, he was right. And I had enjoyed hitting her, though now it seemed as if somebody else had done that. 'All right, wait for me.'

Gilbert went ahead. The cutpurse looked to him, then averted his eyes and kept walking. Gilbert broke into a run and grabbed the man around one wrist. In that moment, watching Gilbert run the few paces between them, I became terribly aware of the power and the danger of him, as if I were watching a highly intelligent, handsomely built beast narrow in on its prey. The cutpurse cried out as Gilbert caught his arm, then put up a feeble struggle before allowing Gilbert to drag him back into the shadows from which I was emerging.

'What's going on?' the cutpurse said in a whiny, pleading voice. 'What have I ever done to you folks, eh? What's all this about?'

'Here, Elizabeth. Hold him for me.' Gilbert passed the cutpurse to me, and I grabbed him by the elbows while Gilbert searched him. He struggled weakly, but I held him.

The cutpurse craned his neck around and looked at me narrowly. 'We've met, have we? We've met before?'

'Yes,' I said, 'earlier this evening.'

He was examining my clothes, my face. He was obviously very drunk. Gilbert stood up and showed me my purse and the small dagger the man had used to cut it. The cutpurse began to protest loudly. 'Those things are mine. You can't take them, they're mine.'

'Wrong,' I said, taking my purse from Gilbert. 'This is mine. You stole it from me. Don't you remember?'

Gilbert grabbed him around the waist and held him in a bear grip. He handed me the knife. 'Go on, Elizabeth, get some revenge. It's very sweet.'

The cutpurse had his chin resting on his chest, and was mumbling something about it being a lad he'd done over that evening, not a lady. I pressed the point of the knife into his chin and lifted his face to look at me. His eyes widened as he realised how close the tip of the knife was to piercing his flesh.

223

'No, no. I'm sorry. I didn't know you were a lady. Forgive me, ma'am, I wouldn't never have stolen from a lady.'

I looked over his head to Gilbert, who held me steady in his gaze. 'Go on,' he whispered, 'go on, hurt him.'

I caught my bottom lip between my teeth. A feeling of fury was rising in me like a squall. I took the knife away from his chin and slashed him across the chest, lightly, but enough to tear the clothes and draw blood. He let out a hideous scream that chilled me deeply. My hand shook, and I almost dropped the knife. Part of me wanted to reach out and touch his shoulder, apologise, say it would be all right. But again Gilbert caught me in his gaze, and again that feeling of unbearable anger arose, the need to *act* to disperse it. I lifted my knee and punched it hard into the man's groin. He would have doubled over had Gilbert not held him upright. And now Gilbert was laughing, and I was running the knife in lines over his hands. I scraped the point of the blade lightly through the flesh, and in some places it bled, and in some places the skin scraped into white ridges. He made an unbearable keening noise, like an animal.

'Shut up!' I shouted. I took the knife to his cheek, made criss-cross lines of blood. He turned his head this way and that, and I almost took out his eye by accident. He howled, and all I could do was smile. Damn me, all I could do was smile.

'Good girl,' Gilbert said.

I looked at the cutpurse, snivelling and bleeding, and something softened inside me. 'That's enough isn't it, Gilbert?' I asked.

'Enough for you perhaps. Hand me the knife.'

I was glad to relinquish control of the blade. I didn't know what I was capable of doing next. Gilbert still had one arm around the cutpurse's middle. With his free hand he stroked the man's neck, first with his finger, then with the blade of the knife. I could hear the rubbing sound of metal against stubble in the dark secret of the night. All my senses seemed to be heightened. I could see the pulse beating in our victim's neck. I knew what Gilbert was going to do, but before I could scream in protest, it was over and the blood was streaming out over the man's front. He made a desperate choking noise and Gilbert let him go. He slid to his knees and then collapsed on the ground in a growing pool of blood.

'My God, Gilbert! What have you done?' I shouted, falling to my knees, but not knowing what to do with the man's wound. I could see the criss-cross pattern that I had inflicted on his hands and I felt as though I would vomit.

Gilbert bent over next to me and flipped the man onto his back. 'If you didn't like that, don't watch this.' And that was all the warning he gave me before he slipped the blade into the flesh around the dead man's eyes, and began to gouge away unevenly. I turned and stumbled away, throwing up violently in a thistle patch. All I could see was the blade slipping through the flesh; it replayed itself over and over in my mind. I hung my head, spat hard. My body had gone into spasms, and I pressed an arm around my middle to settle myself. I heard Gilbert approaching. He pushed a hand out to help me up, but I turned my head away.

'Come, Elizabeth, don't be like this.'

'You killed him, Gilbert.'

'So? Who was he? Why do you care?'

I turned to him, met his gaze evenly. 'He was a human being, that's why I care.'

'He was a human being, that's why you shouldn't

care. Just another animal. Just another blink in the face of the dark universe.'

'Then aren't we also like that? Aren't we also nothing?'

'No, we are gods. We command the universe.'

I looked down, took a deep breath. Again he offered me his hand. It was streaked with blood. 'He had it coming, Elizabeth.'

I shook my head. 'Now you're trying to justify it to me. Let's at least be honest. He did *not* have it coming. He didn't deserve to die for stealing.'

'He deserved, however, to be mutilated?'

'I didn't . . . mutilate.'

'Elizabeth, let's at least be honest.'

I hated him, I hated him so much. I took his hand and he pulled me to my feet. He was soaked in blood. I cast a sickened glance over my shoulder at the dead man. 'What if we get caught?'

He shook his head. 'We won't get caught. You've underestimated me.'

'You're covered in blood.'

'Am I? Look again.'

Suddenly he was clean. 'How did you . . . ?' Then I peered closer and the blood was visible again.

'Nobody will see what I don't wish them to see. Nobody will ever see what we don't wish them to see. It's our gift.'

He pulled me up against him and tried to kiss me, but I turned my face away. 'Elizabeth, really, you must trust me.'

I didn't answer him. He kissed my cheek lightly. 'You don't understand. You will in time, but for now you don't understand.'

'What is there to understand?'

'Here, let me show you. Turn your face up.'

I did so. His mouth closed over mine. I leaned

into him and closed my eyes. In that moment he somehow transferred his feelings into my body so that I was standing there in the moment of the cutpurse's death, and it was my arms pinning the body to me, and my hand that drew the knife against the flesh, but it wasn't easy and slippery as it had looked. There was resistance, drag, and an almost unbearably gratifying sense of having achieved something when his neck flapped open and the blood began to gush out. Then, as he fell at my feet and the life left him, a swelling of pure pleasure, a warm hot bubble, lifted up through me and burst into my head with bells and lights and the sounds of triumph. It lapped out in rings of joy through my being, and I expanded and expanded with heavenly rapture. I went up, reached up, reached up and up for the face of God . . .

Gilbert broke the kiss. 'We can save the rest for back home.'

'The rest?'

'We must get back.'

'I . . . I . . .' I was speechless, but utterly sure that I had to say something of the utmost consequence, express my soul in a huge shattering cry of ecstasy.

Gilbert caught my face in his bloody hand. 'Do you forgive me, Elizabeth?'

'Yes, Gilbert. I do.' I had no choice.

CHAPTER
FIFTEEN

The desire to know is arguably the riskiest desire of all, though to those who wish for unlimited knowledge, it seems the most noble of pursuits. My need for absolute awareness cancelled out my more worldly need for comfort, solace and peace of mind. As I lay in bed at night, abhorring the tingling, tugging sensation around the numb patch on my thigh, I never once thought of returning to my ordinary old life, which had provided me comfort if nothing else. I had heard that a little knowledge in the hands of fools was dangerous but, for me, a little knowledge in the hands of the thirsty was an infinitely greater threat. I didn't know what I was capable of doing next. Indeed, I was frightened of what I might do next. And Gilbert was always cheerfully willing to lead me into that next step.

Two nights after we returned to Prestonvale, we began our instruction, as Gilbert called it, in earnest.

Mirabel was playing the part of the delicate mother-to-be for all it was worth. She griped and fretted to all unfortunate enough to cross her miserable path. She suffered excessively from pains and aches and flushes and dizzy spells, most of which I assumed were invented for the purpose of garnering sympathy.

We were sitting around the table for supper and Mirabel was complaining about her food when Gilbert spoke to me.

'Elizabeth, *media nocte in tugurium magicum.*'

My head snapped up in shock, then I remembered that we were the only two who understood Latin. I smiled across at him over the flickering candles that illuminated our meals.

Mirabel protested loudly. 'What did you say to her? Don't speak other languages, it isn't fair. What did you say?'

'I asked Elizabeth if she would try to cheer up my little wife. You have been so unhappy lately, my dear.'

But of course he hadn't said that. He had said, 'Midnight at the magic cottage', and I was enchanted both by the sound of him speaking my favourite language and his christening of our workplace as the magic cottage.

'Of course, Gilbert,' I said.

He smiled at me. In the candlelight his pupils were large and black.

'Well nothing could cheer me up,' Mirabel said, pushing her plate away from her. 'I'm wretched.'

Uncle Tom leaned over and stroked her hair. 'You really must try to be happy and to eat well, Mirabel. It's not good for the child, your being thin and morose.'

'What would you know, Father,' she snapped back, her little mouth pinched tightly, 'you're a man.'

She stood up from the table and flounced out of the room. Uncle Tom looked despondently into his supper plate. Mirabel had dealt him an unkind blow. Uncle Tom had lost four other children, the last had also claimed his wife. Mirabel had been the only child to survive. I reached over and grasped his wrist, tears pricking my eyes, the pity in my heart unspeakable.

As my hand closed over his flesh, I was suddenly overcome by a vision so vivid and sharply focused that it took my breath away. My hands were Uncle Tom's hands, and I held in them the bloody wreck of what would have been a child had it stayed in the womb a few more months. The crimson streak of a thing was still attached by its blue and pink cord to the mother, who lay there, pale, flesh in goosebumps and panting the quick breaths of the nearly dead. The child was male, a little boy. I felt a twist of hopeless pain stab me in the gut.

'Elizabeth, are you all right?' Uncle Tom had pulled his wrist free and now grasped my own hands, rubbing them briskly.

The real world lurched back into my perception. I thought enough to say, 'Yes, I just feel a little dizzy.'

'Dizzy? Perhaps you should lie down.'

'It seems dizzy spells are the common malady around Prestonvale,' Gilbert said lightly. I forced a smile.

'I'm fine, Uncle Tom. It seems to have passed already.'

'Still, go and lie down. You can't be too careful. I can't . . . I couldn't bear to lose you.'

I fixed my gaze on his eyes. 'Of course, Uncle Tom. I'm going upstairs now. You aren't to worry.'

I knew I was running on the breathless edge of a terrible chasm. All the time I felt that I was spinning ever so slightly out of control. The only thing that terrified me more was the thought of returning to my life of domestic monotony. I did indeed go to lie down as Uncle Tom had insisted, and found myself dropping into a light sleep. I fell into a fitful dream of myself in the drawing room of our house, embroidering with Mirabel sitting at my knee. My jaws seemed to be glued together, my hands unable to stop the dipping and pulling, dipping and pulling. My youth and beauty seemed to be draining away from me too quickly, running out and forming a pool at my feet, my hands becoming those of a crone with gnarled, and spotted skin. *I want more*, I wanted to scream. *More.*

When I awoke up, I gulped my real world hungrily. No, that wasn't going to happen to me. Never, never, never.

Gilbert had lit a fire in the cottage and it protected us from the cruel icy breeze stalking outside. We huddled close with a thick quilt around us, drinking each other's mouths. To me he was the most perfect creature in the universe, and in his arms I felt as though I were part of a colourful wheel of experience which had until now rolled on without me.

'Elizabeth,' he said, pulling away from me at last, caressing my thigh through my nightdress, 'do you understand the universe?'

'No, of course not. I presume it's far too complex for me to understand.'

He nodded. 'Then you're much closer to understanding it than somebody who presumes the opposite.'

I unwound my arms from around his neck and sat back. 'And you? Do you understand the universe?'

'No. Nobody can understand it. But you can *know* about it.'

'What do you know?'

He clenched one hand in front of me, then slowly uncurled it. Dancing on his palm was a flame. I reached out a finger to touch it. It was hot. I blew gently to extinguish it.

'I know how to do that,' he said.

I laughed lightly. 'And I know that you have a volume of amazing tricks to show off. What I want to know is how it's done.'

He took my hand in his, opened it and stroked it gently. I watched his fingers moving over my upturned palm. He began to talk in that low, enthralling voice. I sank against him, and could hear the tones resonating in his chest. I kept my eyes fixed on my palm.

'Understanding cannot be gained in words. Words are the enemy of understanding. Your energy works only in a state of chaos when words won't form. Remember when you told Mirabel to be quiet in the carriage. And just this evening, when you got that shock from Sir Thomas. The feeling came first, anger or pity, and then before the words came you were residing for a few instants in the chaos—the level between the raw feeling and the logical translation of that feeling. That's the state where you begin to work. That's what you have to capture and perpetuate.' He tapped my palm with his finger. 'So, try it. Feel the fire, but before you allow the thought to form coherently, concentrate it into your palm.'

I clenched my fist. I took a deep breath. I thought of the flame. Gilbert interrupted me.

'No, don't think of anything.'

'How can you know what I'm thinking?'

'You're still in a thoughtful, structured state. Feel, then act. Do not think.'

'I'm confused.'

'You've done it before.'

'Only then I wasn't aware of what I was doing. Now I'm too aware, and I need to be unaware.'

He shook his head. 'The pre-logical level is *completely* aware. When things have names, words, ideas attached to them, they are always limited. We limit them through definition. Before they are named, they are infinite. Everything is knowable in its infinitude. That is true knowing.'

I squirmed and looked at my palm again.

'Relax, Elizabeth,' he said. 'The more you try to control it, the harder it will be.'

'This isn't making any sense.'

'Good.'

I was exasperated. 'Gilbert, I'm not sure I follow you.'

He spoke slowly and patiently. 'Do you slip straight from waking to sleeping instantly?'

I thought about it. 'No, I drift off.'

'And when you're drifting, do you sometimes have thoughts that don't make sense, or seem important although they really mean nothing?'

'Yes. Like not quite dreaming.'

'That's it. The not quite dreaming. That's what I mean. The gap between wakeful knowingness and whatever comes next.'

I curled my fingers over again. Like not quite dreaming. I fought the thoughts off, but gently. Felt something like a flame, the sensation not the word. Not hot, not orange, not flickering. Just the feeling in its infinitude, reeling away from me backwards and forwards and sideways in time. And before the words for it formed completely in my obdurate brain, which had to know by naming, I added a little movement towards my hand. It tingled. I opened my palm. There stood a tiny flame. I nearly choked on something that was almost a laugh, almost a sob. Gilbert put his hand gently over mine, and the flame disappeared.

I sat stunned. I could control the elements. A rush of the purest ecstasy raced through my veins and bubbled out of my mouth in laughter. I fell back onto the ground, flung my arms out and howled. Gilbert fell on top of me and covered my mouth with his. I pushed him off.

'No, I want more.'

He raised his eyebrows, then smiled. 'Oh, God. That's why I love you. You want to devour life. I know people who simply want to get on with the business of dying, but you, you always want more.'

'Only because I've never had anything.'

He stroked my hair. 'Even if you had everything you'd still want more. It's your desire to keep expanding.'

'So I'm doomed always to be dissatisfied?'

'Or blessed always to recognise opportunity.'

'Tell me more.'

'What do you want to know?'

'Why have you made Mirabel pregnant without taking her maidenhead?'

He looked taken aback. 'How did you know that?'

'She told me.'

He shook his head and chuckled. 'I'm having difficulty imagining that. She never speaks a word to me when we're in bed together, it's as if she wants to pretend nothing at all is happening. She actually told you that?'

'Yes, after I drew her out. When I told her she was pregnant, she had difficulty understanding how. So?'

'Just a little experiment. A little joke. Who else was born of a virgin birth, Elizabeth?'

'Jesus.'

'Exactly. The Son of God. It appeals to my sense of the profane to have the Daughter of Gilbert roaming the planet.' He laughed and drew me into his arms.

I wasn't entirely comfortable with this explanation, but I couldn't say exactly why.

234

'Besides,' he continued, 'how could I bring myself to make love to her? She's like a little girl; it would feel perverse.' He was caressing my neck with his lips.

'You said you'd teach me more.'

'Not tonight. Practise what you've learned. There's plenty of time for us, Elizabeth. Everything goes our way.'

And then he was pulling off my clothes and, once naked, his old familiar magic worked and we indulged ourselves in pure carnal pleasure. As always, it was beyond imagining.

I woke just before dawn, surprised to find myself still on the mattress in front of the fire, my naked body entwined with Gilbert's. We were wrapped in the thick quilt. I propped myself up on one elbow and drew the quilt back to reveal Gilbert's maddeningly masculine torso, and softly ran my fingertips over it. He stirred but didn't wake. I placed a kiss on his shoulder, then rested my cheek on his arm. His skin was warm and smooth. I remembered what he had shown me before we slept, and I held my right hand up before my eyes. Clenched my fist, closed my eyes . . . Zap. There, a flame.

I pinched my thumb and forefinger together, rubbed them lightly and, again, a small flame came to my command. I blew it out. I lit another. I made four flames in a row in that manner, blowing each one out gently.

Then, from the corner of my eye, I noticed movement. A face was pressed against the window. I sat up, rigid, and the face saw me and retreated. I quickly pulled the cover off Gilbert, wrapped it around myself and raced to the door. Gilbert was waking and asking me what was going on, but I flung the door open and stepped outside in time to see Nancy hurrying back towards the house.

I raced inside again and pulled my nightdress over my head.

'What's going on?' asked Gilbert, immediately snapped awake and pulling his own clothes on.

'That was Nancy,' I said. 'She saw us. She was watching me through the window.'

'She saw us in bed together?'

'And worse. She saw me flicking flames off the ends of my fingers. We have to catch her before she gets to Uncle Tom. We have to silence her.'

I raced out of the cottage and across the dewy grass to the manor. The sky was still a dull grey and the birds hadn't started singing yet. The house was quiet, with the sounds of sleep lapping the walls. Where was she?

I took the steps two at a time to the upper floor. I caught sight of myself in a huge mirror at the top of the staircase. I looked like a mad woman, with my hair streaming and my eyes wild. I stopped outside Uncle Tom's room and pressed my ear up against the door, but could hear nothing. Gilbert appeared beside me and gave me a quizzical look.

'I don't think she's in there,' I whispered.

Gilbert pushed the door open a crack and peered in, then pulled it shut again. 'No, he's still asleep.'

My heart seemed to be beating hard in my throat, but Gilbert looked cool.

'My God, what are we going to do?' I said.

'You're not to worry. We'll find her. Come on, we'd better get properly dressed before people start waking up. I'll meet you down in the kitchen.' He patted my shoulder briefly, then turned to go to his room.

I went in the other direction to mine, where I pulled on some clothes and tied up my hair neatly.

My hands were shaking and my calves had turned to water. This was it, Uncle Tom would find out what kind of person I really was and what I'd been up to and . . . Did they still hang witches? I felt that all my fragile world was resting in the brutal hands of that disgraceful woman. My stomach twisted. Surely he wouldn't accept her testimony without question. Surely I could lie my way out of this. I was more special to him than his own daughter after all.

I drew a breath and headed back into the corridor and down the stairs. On my way to the kitchen, I saw the door to Master Gale's room open, and Nancy emerged. Her back was turned to me as she tried to close the door behind her quietly. Again my heartbeat picked up, and I ducked into the shadows to wait for her to come past.

I could barely hear her footsteps for the sound of the blood blasting in my ears, but eventually her shadow fell in front of me and I leaped out and grabbed her by the wrist, my other hand quickly stifling her scream. Her eyes rolled madly as she tried to struggle away from me, but I pulled her against my body and held her firm, locking my eyes on hers.

I didn't know what I was doing next, I swear; all I knew was that I wanted to silence her

'*Tace*,' I hissed, shaking her firmly. '*Tace, tace, tace*.' Each time the whisper was more violent, the shake more jarring. The palm that was clamped over her mouth began to tingle, and the word started to lose sense, the sounds merging into one another and becoming scrambled. I knew my lips were still moving, and I could feel my tongue striking my palate, but I did not know what I said. I shook her again and again. And under my palm, the scrambling continued, as if the small piece of the universe I had

trapped under my hand had grown chaotic and senseless too.

Then the feeling passed, and my anger seemed to
have drained out of me. She looked so frightened.
Words returned to me. 'I'll let you go if you promise
to be silent.'

She nodded. I took my hand away.

When I saw what I had done, I screamed.

Somewhere I heard the sounds of people waking.
I practically stuffed my fist in my mouth to stop
myself from screaming again, and I grabbed Nancy
by the wrist and pulled her into the kitchen where
Gilbert was scrambling to his feet, having heard the
commotion.

'Oh, God, look what I've done!' I cried. 'Look
what I've done to her!'

He turned to look, and even Gilbert, even cool
calm Gilbert, made a little choking noise in the back
of his throat, and his eyes bulged. Because it was
horrific.

Nancy no longer had a mouth. The dimple
beneath her nose gave way to a smooth expanse of
flesh with no opening. When she realised what Gilbert
and I were staring at, she made a horrifying muffled
cry in the back of her throat, barely audible. She
pawed her fingers over where her mouth had been
and sweat began to break out on her forehead, her
eyes nearly popping from their sockets.

'My God, Elizabeth, how did you . . . ?'

'I wanted to silence her permanently.'

'You should have killed her.'

'I couldn't kill another human being . . .'

'How long do you think she can live without
eating or drinking?'

'I'll reverse it. I'll undo it.'

238

He sighed in exasperation. 'You can't. You can't. It is done.'

Nancy was now doubled over and groping on the floor for a place to collapse in her horror. People were approaching.

'Collect yourself,' he whispered urgently. 'Nancy has had a strange turn. She screamed and then doubled over as though she were sick. That's all you have to say.'

'But they'll see, they'll see . . .'

'They won't see. They can't. Only we can. Be composed.'

'They'll find us out . . . Oh, God.'

He hissed at me. 'They can't see it. Nancy can't tell them and she's an illiterate fool. By Christ, Elizabeth, pull yourself together.'

Uncle Tom burst into the room and I snapped to attention. He strode over to me. 'Elizabeth, was that you screaming?' He glanced at Nancy, writhing on the floor. 'What's wrong with Nancy?'

'I don't know,' I said, sure that my guilt must be written all over me. 'I think she must be sick. She came in and screamed and collapsed on the floor.'

Uncle Tom bent over Nancy. 'Nancy? What's the matter? Are you ill?'

Nancy made a grunting noise—it was all she could do.

'I can't get any sense out of her,' Gilbert said coolly. 'She's taken some kind of fit.'

Master Gale had entered the room and stood quietly by the door. If Nancy had told him anything incriminating, it didn't show on his face. He looked concerned, but kept well back.

'Master Gale, could you fetch Hugh?' Uncle Tom said. 'Perhaps he can shed some light on what's wrong with Nancy.'

Others were crowding into the kitchen now. Rosemary uttered a little scream when she saw Nancy on the floor, grunting and squeaking like a simple. Somebody fetched a cup of water, which they held up for Nancy to drink, but the water poured down her chin.

'She won't drink,' Rosemary said, and turned to me with urgent eyes. 'Lady Elizabeth, can you do something?'

Nancy began grunting louder and scrambling backwards on her hands away from me.

'No. I can't.'

I stood up and headed towards the door. Hugh was rushing in, still in his nightgown. 'Nancy, Nancy. Oh God, what is it? What's wrong with her? Oh, my love, what is it?' I could feel his anxious energy rush past me, and it was like a knife twisting in my heart. What had I done?

Master Gale stood at the doorway. He reached a hand out for my wrist and grasped it gently. 'Come to see me, Elizabeth,' he said simply.

I met his eyes, terror-struck. He smiled kindly. 'I won't hurt you, I promise. Please, just come to see me. Perhaps today?'

I looked over my shoulder. Gilbert was eyeing us suspiciously. I bent my head close to Master Gale. 'Yes. Today.' I hurried out of the room.

'Jesus offers salvation to all who ask for it, Elizabeth, no matter what they've done.'

I was sitting in the front pew of our empty chapel, Master Gale crouched in front of me holding my hands. He was a man of about forty, with sincere blue eyes and a sensitive mouth.

'I haven't done anything.'

He looked up to the ceiling as if searching for the right words. 'It isn't my place to say whether or not you've "done" something. I just wanted to remind you of the Lord's eternal patience and forgiveness.'

I was struggling to keep my voice even. 'What did Nancy tell you this morning? I saw her coming from your room. Is that what this is all about, because if it is, I want to remind you that Nancy has a grudge against me for evicting her from her cottage.'

'She said very little. All she told me was that she had seen something evil in the cottage, and that she wished to speak to me about it. I was half asleep so I told her to wait in the chapel. As you know, she didn't make it that far.'

'I think she's out of her wits. Why else would she say something ridiculous like that? And you saw her, grunting and squeaking like a mad pig.' I gently pulled my hands away from him, trying not to think about Nancy, trying to blot out that vision of her horrific disfigurement, trying to forget that I did it, trying not to speculate about what would happen to her now. 'I don't know why you've asked me here, and I don't know why you're burbling on about salvation.'

'Because, Elizabeth, you and Mr Lewis are using the cottage. If there were something evil in there, you would know about it.' He smiled gently. 'And, of course, we all know how fond Lady Elizabeth is of healing spells and love potions.'

I squirmed in my seat. 'That's just a rumour.'

'It's one of many rumours about you, Elizabeth.'

'Why? What else is being said?'

'That you and Mr Lewis spend too much time together. That you look at each other like carnal animals.' As I began to protest, he cut me short. 'I'm not making any judgements, I'm not casting any blame. These are just the things I hear in my position. I have as little desire as you to disrupt Sir Thomas's peace of mind.'

Which was, naturally, the most important thing. 'So you aren't going to mention any of this to him?'

'Not a word. I wouldn't dream of it. Especially if they are, as you say, just rumours.'

'Of course. Of course they are.'

'Then neither of us has anything to worry about.' He paused and nodded slowly. 'And you know that if you need me, you can come to me.'

'I know that.'

'No. This isn't a platitude. If you really *need* me. If you get yourself in too deep with something . . .'

'Why do you keep on about that? There's nothing going on.'

'Just know, Jesus offers salvation to all. You only have to ask. You only have to come to me for help.'

I studied his face. I mused on the impenetrability of another person. How could I know if he were being completely honest with me? Did he know more, suspect more, or just expect more? I tried to get into his head, tried the unconscious reaching for meaning: nothing. I softly picked up his hand and held it in mine. This time I got a very strong sense of resistance. I dropped his hand in fright, realising that he understood what I was trying to do.

'Sorry,' I said.

'What for?' He was pretending to be ignorant, that much was clear.

I shook my head quickly. He touched my chin, turned my face to meet his eyes. 'Promise me, Elizabeth, if you need me, you will come to me.'

'All right, I promise. As long as you promise to leave Uncle Tom out of this.'

'I have nothing to gain by talking to your uncle. I save souls, I don't torture them.'

Ah, but I did.

CHAPTER
SIXTEEN

I was missing something . . .

But how the hell did I end up here in bed? I didn't remember coming out of the regression. I didn't remember getting up, showering—my hair was wet—and slipping in between the sheets.

Still, I must have, because here I was with my hands stretched out on the cool cotton covering my body, feeling the fine weave of it under my fingertips. *But think, Lisa, think; you're missing something.*

The cutpurse . . . what Gilbert had done to the cutpurse. His blood let, his eyes hacked out . . .

Just like the killer in the pine forest.

Elizabeth had been reborn. Didn't that mean Gilbert could be back too? If so, then the murders must have something to do with me.

But I was so tired, sleep buzzing in and out of my ears, unable to fight it. I lapsed back into oblivion for a time—I don't know how long—but eventually my sleep became light, dissolved, my thoughts bleeding into it. I turned over, looked at the digital clock. It was just before four a.m., presumably Sunday morning. I stared at the numbers until they blurred and swam in the darkness. My senses were fluttery, my mind dancing around the evidence, desperately trying to resist where my logic was taking me. I threw back the covers, got up, stumbled to my dresser and pulled out shorts and a T-shirt. Climbed into clothes and gym shoes. Put money in my pockets. Locked up my flat and started walking.

I took the pedestrian path that ran alongside the river. The early morning was chill and damp, the river flat and hushed. Along my way, streetlamps threw pools of light on the ground. I kept putting one foot in front of the other, steadily pounding ahead. Occasionally a car sped by on Coronation Drive, or an early rising bird chirped warily in the gloom. My fingers were itchy and my rings were tight with all the sleepy blood lazing in my hands. I took deep breaths. The dark seemed to blur my edges, soak me up. It felt good, almost like not being there at all. What a relief it would be to will myself in and out of existence.

But now I needed to think, to examine, to rationalise.

It seemed too much of a coincidence that I should have a past-life memory of a man who killed people and cut out their organs, while my fans were being picked off in the same way. But was I supposed to believe that Gilbert—like me, in another form—was running around in my world messing with the kind of sorcery he had indulged in four hundred years ago?

If so, was it an accident of fate, or did Gilbert know about me? Was he preying on my fans on purpose? I suddenly felt as though a pack of ants had been let loose in my spleen. How long, then, before he came by to slice me open too? Without realising it, I had picked up my pace. I could see the tall buildings of the city rising dimly around the curve of the river.

I had to keep thinking, but it was driving me crazy. Because now the idea of Karin disappearing at

the same time became too much of a coincidence.
The thought crippled me. I stopped. The muscles in
my thighs twitched. I walked two steps towards the
rock wall that separated me from the river and picked
my way down to sit on a large, flat rock. I put my
head in my hands; this confusion, this mind-
scrambling overload was killing me. I no longer
remembered how it felt not to have something gnawing at my stomach. I no longer remembered how it
felt to stand up without a sense of impending doom
weighing me down.

The rock was cold. I slipped my hands around it.
A light slime came off on my palms. I closed my eyes
and tried to remember what Karin looked like, but it
had been so long and, besides, when you've known
somebody forever you see beyond their physical features. I remembered her hair, pale and fine.
Something about her chin, almost pointy. Fair tips of
her lashes. Not much else.

I opened my eyes. The river was very dark, seemed
to be running thick and sluggish, like oil. I had heard
that drowning was a reasonably stress-free way to die.
The water closes over your head, your body adjusts
to the temperature, you struggle to breathe briefly,
then you're overwhelmed with a lovely sensation of
fulfilment. I don't really think I was close. Maybe the
idea of giving it all in seemed seductive momentarily,
but my fear, or perhaps my survival instinct, stopped
me.

'Please, God . . .' I started. Then felt embarrassed.
I didn't believe in God, I had always sneered at people
who turned to religion when their lives fucked up.
Fat tears screwed their way out of my eyes and
dripped off my chin. Karin could be dead, and before
long I could be too. 'Please, God, please . . .' Futile.

I pulled myself up and kept walking. I was desperately hungry—I had cramps in my stomach. It wasn't too much further to town, then I could buy something at the Night Owl.

My legs were like jelly half an hour later when I stumbled up the stairs of the Night Owl and bought myself a carton of orange juice and some pre-packed egg and lettuce sandwiches. It was five a.m. and cars were parked on the footpath down near the riverside markets as people loaded up their stalls. It made me think of Liam. Small comfort in a scary world. I sat on a bench and ate my breakfast. My thoughts were scattered all around me. I let them go for a while, enjoying the freedom from the responsibility of finding a solution. I swallowed the last of the orange juice and went to find a phone.

It rang about eight times before Liam finally picked it up and groggily said hello.

'Hi. Sorry to wake you.'

'Lisa?'

'Yeah, it's me. Did you still want to go to the markets this morning?'

There was a pause, where I guessed he was gathering his wits. 'Um . . . yes, okay.'

'I'm there already.'

A short, sleepy laugh. 'You're keen.'

'I came out for an early morning walk and ended up here. I need to see you.'

He must have heard the note of desperation. 'Is something wrong?'

Only everything. 'I just want to be with you.' It was the truth. I needed comfort, protection even. I tried not to think about how dangerous it was to know me these days.

'Okay, fine. I'll have a quick shower and come down. Where are you?'

'Meet me outside the McDonald's above the markets.'

'Okay. I'll be there in about half an hour. Maybe a little more.'

I went back into the Night Owl, bought some deodorant and toothpaste, and took a walk down to the twenty-four hour McDonald's. Their toilets had just been cleaned and were heavy with the mock freshness of disinfectant. I squeezed soap from the dispenser, gave myself a cursory wash, loaded myself down with deodorant and cleaned my teeth with my index finger. I left the deodorant and toothpaste for the next all-night reveller and went outside to wait for Liam. The sun coming up made my eyeballs ache.

'Can I ask you something?'

We were sitting at a pastel blue table under the bald lights in McDonald's. Liam was drinking coffee. A muffin covered in sticky strawberry jam sat half eaten and growing cold in front of him.

'What?' I said.

'Why were you out walking this early? You don't strike me as a morning person.'

'Couldn't sleep.'

He looked into his coffee cup, then back at me. 'There's something wrong, isn't there? On the phone you sounded . . .'

'Desperate?'

'Tense. Anxious.'

I sighed and slid forward onto the table. 'I *am* tense. I *am* anxious.'

'Is there anything I can do to help?'

'God, Liam. If I told you, you'd probably . . . I don't know. What if you think I'm a looney?'

'I promise I won't.'

'Ha. Easy to say on that side of my story.'

'Just know, if you want to talk, I'll listen. Okay?'

I shrugged reluctantly. 'Okay.' I didn't feel as though I could tell him anything at the moment. Even if he did believe me, who was I to fuck up his life with my psychodrama?

'So, do you want to go wandering about the markets? It might take your mind off it, whatever it is,' he said.

Fat chance. 'I guess it can't hurt.'

Liam cleaned up his mess and put it in the bin, something I never would have done: corporate giants were there to be exploited. We walked down to the riverfront and joined the early morning shoppers milling between stalls. My legs were tired before we even began. I'm sure Liam had some notion of us wandering about, trying on hats, eating French pastries and laughing together in the sunshine. What followed was actually a sad parody of that, with me dragging my feet while Liam tried in vain to rouse my interest.

He took my hand and gently tugged me along beside him until we came to a stall selling books. New Age books, groaning under the weight of pastel rainbows and waterfalls and stars, lined the front of the stall. Some unimaginative New Age music was playing. I picked up one of the books and flipped it over. A woman with dangly earrings smiled at me from the back cover. 'You can change your destiny,' she told me in friendly, blue letters. I didn't believe her.

'Look, Lisa. They've got some second-hand books around here.'

I walked over to where Liam was squatted on the ground beside the stall, going through a couple of large cardboard boxes of musty-smelling books. I kneeled next to him. 'Anything good?'

'Here's a whole stack of music books.' He pulled

the books out and sat back, dumping them in his lap to sort through them. 'Tchaikovsky. Handel. *The Life of Bach*. Ah, Chopin.' He pulled the book out and handed it to me to hold. 'Piano exercises. Baroque songs. I don't know what this one is, looks like it's in French.'

He showed me a thin book with *La Méthode Pour Chanter* written on the front.

'Singing method,' I said, without thinking.

'Oh, you speak French?'

A tiny thrill licked through me. 'No. No, actually I don't. I must have figured it out from . . .' Then I took the book from him and opened it to the first page.

'*Une personne qui a l'intention de chanter, doit exécuter une modération dans l'usage des produits qui peuvent affecter sa voix.*' I let out a little gasp, almost a laugh.

'What's the matter?'

'This says, "A person who intends to sing must exercise moderation in the usage of certain products that could affect the voice." God, that's amazing. I'm remembering it.' I sat back and flicked through some more pages: I understood it all. This was too, too much.

'So you learned it once?'

'A long time ago. A very long time ago.' Around four hundred years. Somehow, spending so much time reliving my life as Elizabeth had given me her command of French. I could remember every word. This couldn't be happening. Despite the sunshine and the crowd, a dark, creeping feeling stole over me.

He grabbed my hand. 'You're shaking.'

'I'm freaking out. It's all I ever seem to do around you.'

'Just because of the book?'

I leaned forward and kissed him gently on the lips. 'I don't know how to begin explaining. I'm tired, spooked, confused and I smell bad. Can I go home?'

'Of course.'

'Will you come with me?'

'Of course I will.'

I was more than a little embarrassed by my messy flat. I made Liam sit on the couch while I scurried about for a few minutes putting things away.

'Would you like a cup of tea?' I called from the kitchen while I was stuffing newspapers into the bin.

'No. Come here.'

I walked back to where he sat on the couch, and he grabbed my wrist and gently pulled me down next to him. 'Relax,' he said. 'You're making me nervous.'

'Sorry.'

'Don't apologise. Relax. Here, kick your shoes off and put your feet in my lap.'

I untied my shoelaces and pulled my shoes and socks off. He took my feet in his hands and started rubbing them gently. 'Have you ever had a good foot massage?'

I shook my head, sat back and stretched my legs out. He kneaded my toes one by one. I sighed. I let him go for a while, feeling myself unwind. Just his presence made me feel safe, at least for the time being. And watching his warm hands, his strong forearms, was awakening my desire. I pulled my feet away and stood up.

'I really need a shower.'

'Okay. Do you want me to go home?'

I shook my head. 'I want you to join me.'

He looked startled. I grabbed his hands and pulled him to his feet, pulled him into my arms and kissed him. My body melted against his. His hands caressed my lower back and he made a little groaning noise.

'Come on,' I said. 'It'll be nice.'

'Well . . .'

I ground my pelvis into his. 'You want to. I want to. What possible reason could there be not to?'

'No reason, I guess.'

'Come on then.'

I pulled him into the bathroom, closed the door behind us and turned the shower on. It's always hard to be naked in front of somebody else for the first time, and I felt kind of clumsy pulling my T-shirt and shorts off. But Liam caught me in his arms, all warm and smooth against his bare chest, and I forgot everything when he kissed me. I fumbled with the fastening of his jeans and he kicked them off into a corner of the bathroom. We stepped under the warm water and continued our embrace. I explored his bare flesh with my hands. The water ran over our faces as we kissed. It felt like I was drinking him. I pushed his wet hair off his forehead and studied his face. He had a scattering of small, pale freckles across his forehead, and a faint frown line. I pushed myself up on my toes and kissed him just above the eyebrows.

'You're so beautiful,' I said.

'So are you.' His mouth ran over my throat and shoulder, down to my breasts. His hands encircled my waist. I let my head roll back and gave myself up to the pleasure.

We continued acquainting ourselves with each other's bodies for a while, then tried unsuccessfully to make love standing up in the shower. He was too tall. After a couple of aborted attempts, where our embarrassed laughter echoed around the shiny surfaces of the bathroom, I decided to give up. I placed a hand on each of his hips, let my fingers press into his firm buttocks, and slid down to kneel in front of him. He braced himself against the corner of the shower cubicle as I took him in my mouth. I ran my hands over his legs, felt the muscles bunched up in his thighs. The pattern of the tiles was impressing itself on my knees. He groaned and grunted and squirmed for a while, then came with a long, breathless moan. Tenderly, he pulled me to my feet and enclosed me in his arms again. This time he just held me, but tightly, like he was trying to squeeze out all the careless space between us. I wrapped my arms around him and held on. It was like holding onto a rock in the middle of a stormy sea.

Eventually the hot water ran out and we emerged from the bathroom wrapped in towels. A piece of paper lay on the ground directly in front of the bathroom door, and I stooped to pick it up.

'What's that?' Liam asked.

I unfolded it. Brad's handwriting. 'Ah . . . it's from Brad.'

'Brad?'

'Yeah, he has a key.' I read the note to myself.

Lisa, I came by to see if you wanted to go to a BBQ at Dick's today. Sounds like you're getting enough meat anyway. Be at the studio at 9 a.m. tomorrow. Brad.

'He has a key to your flat? You mean he came in while we were . . . ?'

I folded up the note again. 'Don't worry.'

'Don't worry? How embarrassing. I mean, we weren't exactly quiet.'

'I'm sure he wouldn't have heard anything, Liam.'

'Why does he have a key to your flat?'

I turned to face him. 'He just does. I have a key to his flat too.'

'How do you guarantee your privacy?'

I shrugged. 'It's rarely a problem. Don't be cross, I didn't know he'd come over.'

'I know. Sorry. I was just embarrassed.'

'It's okay. Come on, let's go lie down.'

We snuggled up together in my bed. I lay for a while with my eyes closed, and I could hear him breathing deep and slow next to me. Finally, I turned over and pushed him onto his back, propped myself up on an elbow next to him. He gazed at me. He had such beautiful eyes, such a serene expression.

I smiled. 'God. You're beautiful.'

'Don't. You're embarrassing me.'

'What do you see in me? Why would a guy like you be interested in a girl like me?'

'It's not that weird.'

'Yes, it is. Go on, tell me. What attracted you to me?'

He smiled. 'You're fishing for compliments.'

'Absolutely.'

'I don't know. I sit there in my office all day, and people walk in and out of the station and I watch them all, you know. I'm interested in people, that's why I'm a sociologist, I guess. And when you came in, you just seemed so . . . you were really colourful. I think you were wearing a blue shirt and a purple skirt, and your hair . . . What colour is that anyway?'

'The last colour I put in was called Grenada Cherry.'

'You looked like an exotic bird.' He laughed at himself. 'I'm no good at this, I sound like a turkey.'

'So you're a turkey and I'm an exotic bird. We make a good couple.'

'You just seemed—still do seem—to be somehow more *there* than other people. Like you're in sharp focus and the rest of the world is blurry in comparison.'

I realised, embarrassed, that I had a catch in my throat and was on my way to tears. 'God, that's the nicest thing anyone has ever said to me.'

He pushed me over on my back and pinned me down with a kiss. I ran my hands over his smooth flesh.

'I thought you must have been thinking that I'm a basket case,' I said. 'Every time I see you I'm having some kind of hysterical apoplexy.'

He pulled away so he could look at my face. 'You do seem very tense.'

'I'm not usually. Does it turn you off?'

'It makes you kind of interesting.'

'So, do you think that's what's wrong with me? Just that I'm tense? Neurotic? Hysterical?'

He pressed his lips together as if he was choosing words carefully in his head. 'I thought on Friday night that you may have been doing drugs. But then I remembered Brad told me you don't.'

'That's right, I don't.'

'You were talking about bad trips in the forest.'

'Is that why you didn't want to stay the night? Did you think I was off my face?'

'No. As I said, I realised that I was wrong almost as soon as I thought it.'

'Then why . . . ? Oh, sorry, I'm making you embarrassed. Not everybody wants to get intimate on the first date, right?'

'Right.'

'Second date's okay, though?'

'Not usually. You're very persuasive.'

'Third date?'

'Well . . . I don't know. I'm not . . . I mean . . .'

'Are you Catholic?'

255

He laughed. 'AOG.'

'AOG?'

'Assembly of God. Lapsed. Very, very lapsed. My parents, however, are full on. My dad's a pastor.'

'You're kidding. So I blew the pastor's son?'

'You have a wicked sense of humour, Lisa.'

'So how lapsed? Still believe in God?'

He shook his head. 'I don't know. Sometimes. Let's not talk about this. I'm starting to feel like a conservative hick from the country. I'd rather you thought of me as witty and urbane.'

I giggled and pulled him down for another kiss. Twenty minutes later, after an orgasm that made my ears ring, I managed to convince myself for a whole forty seconds that it was all I had needed to blow off my stress. I lay like a jelly doll in Liam's arms, a stupid grin on my face.

'Now,' he said before I slipped off to sleep, 'tell me everything.'

I was suddenly wide awake.

'How about I tell you one thing and, depending on your reaction, we go from there?'

'Fine with me.'

'Okay.' I sat up, rubbed my hands together. 'Okay . . . Ah . . . Well, first things first. I was once involved with a man who was a sorcerer. How are we going so far?'

'What, he thought he was a sorcerer? Like one of those occultists?'

'No. He actually was a sorcerer. Really. I actually saw him do magic. I actually saw evidence that he was sacrificing animals for power. I even saw him kill a man once.'

'Jeez, Lisa. Are you for real? Did you tell the police?'

'Okay, don't freak. It was around four hundred

years ago, in a previous life.' I bit my lip, waited for the reaction.

'Four hundred years ago?'

'Yes. Sixteen hundred and seven to be precise.' I had done my maths—Elizabeth wrote of the queen dying four years before she and Gilbert had made her pact.

He spoke carefully. 'How do you know about this previous life? How do you know this?'

'In January I started having this horrendous recurring dream. I got help from a psychic experience site on the net. I've been having controlled regressions—three so far. It's pretty amazing.'

'And you actually see all this stuff happening?'

'I *experience* it. Lisa Sheehan ceases to exist. I'm only aware of being Lady Elizabeth Moreton, sorcerer's apprentice.' I laughed, but it was a nervous laugh and he could tell. He took my hand and locked his fingers between mine.

'No wonder you're spooked.'

'There's more. Much, much more. Are you sure you want me to continue?'

'You have to. You can't just leave me with half the story.'

I told him everything. Thinking back on it now, it seems as though my voice wound on and on through the soft surfaces of my bedroom forever. That Liam just sat there holding my hand, no readable expression on his face except the deepest concern, and my throat ached with swallowing sobs, and we were eternally trapped in that moment. In reality it only took about half an hour, and when I'd finished I collapsed into him and he held me silently for at least as long, probably weighing up what I had said and deciding which bits to believe and which bits to attribute to my lunacy.

Finally, I pulled myself away and looked at him. 'So?'

'Give me a minute here,' he said. 'You've just told me the most incredible thing I've ever heard in my life.'

'Do you believe me?'

'I've believed in stranger things in my time. Just none of them have ever happened quite so close by.'

'Would a cup of tea make it easier?'

'I don't know. Try me.'

I pulled on my dressing gown and went to the kitchen to boil the kettle. At least he hadn't rejected me out of hand. At least he hadn't given me the 'I believe that *you* believe it's happening' line. I made two cups of rosehip tea and took them back to the bedroom. He was sitting propped up against a pillow, the sheets conservatively pulled up to his waist.

'Lisa, I've been thinking. Your hallucinations. Are you sure that they're all hallucinations?'

'I don't follow you.'

'When Gilbert killed the man, you said he could hide the blood, trick people into not seeing it.'

'Yes, which is why there's no evidence for the police to see.'

'But you saw it. When we were in the forest, you said you saw blood everywhere. I don't think that was a hallucination.'

I nodded slowly. He was right. 'You think that somehow I managed to see through his spell?'

'Maybe. Which would mean you have some protection against him.'

A small wave of relief washed through me. 'Yes, you're right. It's something, isn't it? It's a small defence if nothing else.'

He took the cups from me and placed them carefully on the floor beside the bed, and gathered

258

me into his arms. 'Whatever happens,' he said, close against my hair, 'whatever happens, I'll be there for you.'

I melted into him. Another small defence. If nothing else.

That afternoon, after Liam went home, I drew myself a bath and soaked in it for a long time, my head back and my eyes closed. It drizzled lightly outside. I wondered how the barbecue at Dick's was going. Brad was going to be majorly pissed that I was doing the horizontal folkdance with Liam, but I had more important things to worry about. Like my French, not to mention my Latin which seemed to have returned also. Not bad for a girl with a Year Ten education.

It felt good to know that Liam was with me on this. I hated feeling that I was playing the part of the helpless female, but there was a lot to be said for sharing trauma with somebody bigger and stronger than me.

I was just drifting off to sleep when the phone ringing jarred me awake. I jumped out of the bath, grabbing my towel so I wouldn't drip all over the carpet, and went to answer it.

'Hello?'

'Lisa?'

At first the voice didn't sound familiar. Then I realised it was David. I pulled my towel closer around myself.

'What's up, David?'

'I just needed to talk to someone.'

I settled on the stool next to the phone and reached over to switch on the lamp over my desk.

'Sure, what's the matter?'

'I took the letters to the police station. I don't think they took me terribly seriously.'

'I'm sorry. I think their minds are already made up.'

'I don't know what else to do,' he said shakily. I thought he might be crying. I didn't want this, not now.

'Just hang in there . . . Look, I've got to go. I've got visitors.'

'Oh. I'm so sorry, Lisa. Sorry for disturbing you.'

The guilt walked all over me. 'It's fine, really. Call me back some time.'

'Sure. Bye.'

The phone clicked. The lamplight fell on my legs. I'd had the water in the bath too hot, and my skin was blotchy. Added to that my legs were badly in need of a shave. I couldn't believe I'd taken a tumble with Liam with sandpaper legs.

I peeled my towel off to dry my hair which was dripping down my back. That's when I noticed a small, dark mark on my left, inner thigh.

'Oh my God.' I pulled the skin around to look at it closer, stood directly under the lamp. No, it didn't look the same as it had on Elizabeth—it must be something else. A mole I hadn't noticed before maybe. But I brushed my finger across it and it was numb. I jabbed my thumbnail into it. Nothing.

It seemed it wasn't just the languages that were coming back to me.

CHAPTER
SEVENTEEN

'You look like shit, Lisa.'

Dick stood at the door of the control room. I had been pressing the buzzer for a full fifteen minutes.

'Thanks. Is Brad here yet?'

He showed me in. 'No. Sorry it took so long to hear the buzzer. I was out the back.' He had dyed his hair black, and his skin looked pasty in contrast. The door slammed out the daylight behind us.

'You missed a good barbecue yesterday,' Dick said as I settled in a chair in front of the desk. 'We sank heaps of piss and the steaks were beautiful.'

'Great. I don't drink beer and I don't eat meat. I would have fit right in.'

'Brad said you were doing some guy in the shower.'

I looked up. He was making coffee at the cramped kitchen bench in the corner. 'He told everyone that?'

'Yeah. I think he was bummed that it wasn't him. Am I right?'

'Yes, you're right.'

'So why do you look so tired?'

I palmed my eyes and yawned. 'I didn't sleep much, and not for the reason that you're thinking. He went home around five. I just had trouble dropping off.'

As if anybody could sleep under those circumstances. Before I had slipped into bed to toss and turn all night, I had typed a frantic e-mail message to Whitewitch, telling her that I was regaining more than my memories during the regressions. I guess I just wanted her to tell me that it was normal, though I supposed spontaneously growing a witch-mark on the thigh was not something that happened to everyone. What had Gilbert called it? A nipple for spirits. Well, I knew damn well I didn't want any spirits hanging around between my legs. I had my work cut out just keeping Brad out of there.

Dick came over with a cup of coffee for himself, and a cup of chamomile tea for me. I was touched. 'Thanks, man, that was nice of you.'

'It's okay. You left this stuff here last time. Nobody else has been drinking it.' He took a sip of his coffee. 'My mum's a nurse at a psych hospital. She says if you can't get to sleep you've got to imagine a big blackboard in your head and write on it over and over 'relax, relax'. When it's full, you erase it all and start again. It works.'

'I'll have to try it.' I wondered if it worked against fears of dismemberment, death and eternal damnation. The buzzer sounded and Dick leaped up to answer the door. Brad came in. Then he and Dick discussed equipment for ten minutes. Dick had hired a new compressor rack, which looked like a small highrise, all dark and smooth with rows of LED lights at the ready. They ignored me, speaking as if I couldn't understand their technical talk, which of course I could. It was obviously a testosterone thing, so I let them go. I had too many other things to be concerned about.

Brad finally pulled the broken swivel chair up next

to mine and put his elbows on the desk. 'Lisa, how are you?'

'I'm tired, depressed and on the verge of hysteria.'

'That's how you look. I would have thought the love of a good man would sort all that out, but you actually look worse than when I last saw you. Is hanky boy a disappointment in the sack?'

'I'm not up to this, Brad. Just leave me alone.'

He looked momentarily surprised, then backed off. 'Sorry. Are you okay?'

'I told you I'm not.'

'Anything I can do?'

'Yes. Be nice to me. Stop telling people about my sex life. Treat me like a person, and not like a prize pig that's wandered into some other farmer's paddock.'

He looked suitably chastened. 'Dick, we'd better get started.'

Mixing down was tedious work. We EQed the kick drum then flattened it. We EQed the snare—not good for a delicate head—then EQed the kick and the snare together. It seemed to take forever as, track by track, we adjusted levels and added compression and experimented with effects. By around two that afternoon, we had one song finished, and I swore that if I ever had to hear it again I'd vomit.

'Do you want to keep going?' Dick asked. 'We could do another one this afternoon.'

Brad nodded. 'Yeah, sure. Lisa?'

'Do you mind if I just lie on the couch and try to catch some sleep?'

'Go ahead.'

I dozed fitfully through the noise and cigarette smoke. I thought about Liam, what he would be doing at the moment. Researching his report, typing up notes on his computer, making phone calls. It made me feel warm to think about him, about the ordinary regularity of his life. He had believed me. I don't know why. I wouldn't have believed me. I would have smiled and nodded, then got away from me as quickly as possible. But he had believed me and made me feel safe. I frowned in my doze. How could he make me safe? Sure he was big and strong and male, but what protection was that against a power like Gilbert's? I wasn't safe, I could never be safe until I knew who Gilbert was, until he had been caught and stopped. Sleep dissolved, slipped through my fingers. I sat up. Came back to the desk where they were fiddling with the snare track.

'Too middy.' I said. 'Give it some more top end.'

Brad turned around. 'That was a quick snooze.'

I pulled up a chair and hung my head heavily in my hands. 'Who can sleep?'

'Did you try the blackboard thing?' Dick asked.

'Let's just get on with it.'

At around seven, Dick had popped some kind of speedy pill and was convinced that we should continue until midnight. Brad said no.

'My ears are like cotton wool, Dick. Everything sounds like shit. I think we need a break, come back to it with fresh ears tomorrow.'

'Okay. No problem,' Dick said.

Brad and I walked out to the car park.

'Can you give me a lift?' I asked.

'Sure.' Instead of getting in first and unlocking the car from the inside as he usually did, he opened my side and waited while I got in.

'Thanks,' I said, pulling the seatbelt over my shoulder. I bit my tongue to stop myself from making a sarcastic comment about his chivalry. He came around to his side and started the car.

We drove in silence for a while, then Brad said, 'Are you still mad at me?'

'No.'

'You're so quiet.'

I touched his arm. 'No, it's not because of you. I'm just preoccupied.'

'Thinking about Liam?'

I had to smile. 'Congratulations. That's the first time you've actually used his name.'

'Sorry, I wasn't concentrating. Are you thinking about hanky boy?'

I laughed. 'You're such a cockhead, Brad.'

'Thanks.'

'No, I'm not preoccupied with Liam. I'm preoccupied with other stuff, scary stuff.'

'The murders?'

'Yes. How about you? Do you ever think about them?'

'Sure, I think about them a lot.' He dropped back a gear as a guy on a motorcycle cut close in front of us. 'I think, you know, if we hadn't been playing those nights, then those guys wouldn't have been out and they wouldn't have been killed. But that's dumb. If they hadn't been out seeing us, they would have been out seeing some other band.'

'So you think it's just coincidence that they were both fans of the band?'

'Yep.'

'In a city of a million and a half people?'

'It's only that many if you count the suburbs. The inner city is a small place. How often do you see the same people over and over again? Like the black guy in the green jacket that's always sitting in the Queen Street Mall.'

'I think he lives there. I think he's homeless.'

'Coincidence is always strange. That's why we notice it. That's why we give it a name.'

There was no logic like Brad logic. We pulled up outside my flat.

'Thanks, Brad.'

'Lisa, have you told him about us?'

'What about us? There's nothing to tell, though you almost managed to convince him we were childhood sweethearts.'

'You know. Our past intimate relationship.'

'One fuck is hardly an intimate relationship.' Now I was uncomfortable, as I always was around this topic.

'Have you told him?'

'No, I can't see any reason to. As far as I'm concerned, that's just something you continue to bring up and I continue to deny. I thought we had an understanding.'

'Okay. Whatever. I'm sorry I mentioned it. I'll see you back at the studio in the morning.'

'Can you pick me up? I had to catch the bus this morning. It was full of commuters—they all smelled like hairspray and deodorant.'

'Will you be alone?'

'What do you mean?'

'When I come to get you, will you be alone?'

'Yes, of course.'

'All right then. I'll be here just before nine. But if he's around, I'm not going to pick you up.' He was acting like a prick again.

'Why not?' I asked.

'I don't want him to get jealous.'

Without knowing why, I knew something was wrong

as I stood at my front door fumbling for my key under the dim globe of the stairwell security light. My heartbeat had picked up and seemed to be thumping in my throat, making it difficult to breathe. I almost didn't go in, I almost went to the phone box on the corner and called Liam. But I told myself I was being silly, that Liam had better things to do than run around after his neurotic girlfriend. I took a couple of deep breaths and opened the door.

The light was on in the kitchen. I knew that I hadn't left it on. I didn't close the door behind me. 'Is there somebody here?' I called. There was no answer. I turned the living room light on.

'If there's somebody here, tell me now.'

Nothing.

I walked through the lounge and cautiously peered around the corner into the kitchen. My heart jumped. Dana was sitting at the table, flicking through an old *Time Off* she must have pulled from the pile I kept in the corner of my bookcase. She looked up casually.

'What the fuck are you doing here?' I gasped, placing my hand across my chest. 'You scared the living shit out of me.'

'Yes. How do you like it then? How do you like somebody coming into your house without you knowing? It doesn't feel nice, does it?'

I collapsed into a chair opposite her, dropping my keys on the table. 'So David told you.'

'No, I worked it out myself. I'm not stupid you know.' She spat out the word 'stupid' as if it really bugged her that we might have thought she was. 'That fat little man at the police station called me up and I was interrogated about those letters. Thank you both so much.'

I wanted to tell her she deserved it, but I bit my tongue. 'How did you get in?'

'I told your landlady that I was your mother, that I hadn't seen you for a while and I was worried you might be in some kind of trouble . . . *dead*, even. She let me in.'

I watched her carefully. I didn't like the way she spoke about me lying dead in my flat. Fear prickled lightly at my skin. I told myself to calm down, it was just the shock of finding her here. She was just a sad old bitch with a grudge against me, not a homicidal maniac. She glared at me with flinty eyes.

'You know nothing about me,' she said finally. 'You know nothing about Karin's father. You had no right to take those things. He was a drunk, he was a gambler. He would have bled us dry. Karin was better off without him.'

'Is that why you're here? To give me a tongue-lashing?'

'Do you think those idiots at the police station suspected me of doing away with my daughter? Thought if I couldn't have her, I'd make sure nobody else could? My own daughter! But you think I'm capable of it. That's why you were in my house.'

'I didn't think you'd kill her. I thought . . . you might have had something to do with her disappearance.'

'What, you think I'm crazy or something?' she snapped.

'I always have. You know I always have. You've never given me a reason to think otherwise.'

'And why should I give anything to a cheap, uneducated tramp like you? Why should I put myself out to be nice to a person who only ever put stupid ideas in my daughter's head?'

'Karin was her own person. I didn't put any ideas into her head.' I ran my hand through my hair in exasperation. As always, I wanted to hit her with a

268

blunt object. 'I can't believe we're having this conversation. Get out of my house, you've proved your point.'

'I'm not finished with you. Who's that on your noticeboard?' She pointed to the cork board above my desk, where the news clippings about the two murder victims were pinned.

I shrugged. 'It's the two guys that were murdered.'

'I know that. Why have you got them on your noticeboard? Taken a sudden interest? Going to be a Miss Marple?'

'It's none of your business.'

'Sergeant Pyle told me. You knew them both.'

'When did he tell you that?'

'I was telling him about your band, about the things you do. The drugs and the other things—'

'Dana, I don't do drugs, and all the other stuff is straight out of your imagination.'

'I said, "It's her you should be speaking to, she's the criminal, not me. Her band are criminals, not me", and he said, "By all accounts, it isn't very safe to be at one of her band's performances, now that two of her fans are dead". Ha! Yes, see, the police told me that. And they told me they've been watching you, that they've had detectives at your shows for a few weeks now. It's only a matter of time until they come get you and lock you up in the prison where you belong. Then *I'll* laugh at *you*.' She pointed a finger at me and gave me a brief, toxic smile.

'Oh, you really are nuts.'

She picked herself up and collected her car keys. 'Sure. Make fun of me, but wait till you see what I've got up my sleeve. I can wreck your stupid little band, I can wreck your stupid little dreams. All I have to do is tell people what you do.'

'I don't know what you're talking about. I *never* know what you're talking about.'

'You will soon. Goodbye.' She walked out the front door and slammed it shut behind her. I went straight to the phone.

'I'm sorry, Sergeant Pyle is off duty at the moment,' said the receptionist at the police station. 'Can I take a message?'

'When will he be back in?'

'Tomorrow morning, six a.m.'

'I'll call him then.' I slammed the phone down.

I didn't even shower before I went to bed. I was so exhausted that I just pulled my clothes off and climbed in. I heard the phone ring, but I let the machine pick it up. I slipped into a seamless, dreamless slumber.

Around two a.m. something woke me up. I fought against the rising tide of wakefulness, but there it was again—an itching in my palms. I dug my nails into my hands and scratched, but that seemed to aggravate it. The itching was almost unbearable. I turned my hands palms-down on the bed and rubbed them violently. They burned. I groggily turned on the lamp next to my bed, only half awake. I looked at my hands. On each palm there were three parallel streaks, coloured something like grey or green. I ran a thumb over one of them and was sure I felt a ridge. I pressed down and could feel something moving underneath my finger, as though it was trying to wriggle away from the pressure.

'What the . . . ?' I threw off the bedclothes and stumbled to the bathroom. The light in there was much brighter. I saw myself in the mirror—I was pale with dark shadows punched under my eyes. I looked at my hands, felt them again. The lines seemed to have moved down marginally, towards my wrists. I watched for a moment. I was so tired. My eyes started to close, but as I lost my balance and started pitching forward, I snapped myself up and steadied myself on the sink.

There was something moving under my skin. Slowly squirming forward. I thought about sitting on the rocks down by the river the other morning. Maybe I'd picked up a germ then, maybe some kind of creature had laid its eggs under my skin. I could feel a sweat develop on my forehead. I turned the tap on and ran my hands under the water. The itching continued. The lines kept moving. They were creatures, like thready worms, and they were heading downwards. The idea took me that they were going to get into the veins in my wrists. I panicked. I pressed my thumb on the skin in front of them, but they wormed their way under and kept moving.

Once again my eyes closed and I started to over-balance. Once again I snapped myself awake. Too late to go to the medical centre—the worms would be in my veins before I got there. I staggered to my desk, pulled open a drawer too hard it tipped over onto the floor. I crouched and rifled through it. Not there. Next drawer. My hand closed around the handle of a fine-bladed art knife. I took it back to the bathroom. Why was it so bright in here anyway? I turned the hot tap on, let it run. After five minutes the tap started howling and I realised where I was again. Had I been dozing? Didn't matter. I held the blade under the hot water with my right hand, looked at the things worming under my skin on my left. Thought about having to do the right hand first. This was probably going to hurt. Still, it had to be done.

I screwed off the tap. I steadied myself on the bench. I looked at myself in the mirror again. My eyes looked dull. My hair looked brassy. It was too

271

bright in here. I went to the kitchen, sat at the table. Rested my upturned right hand on the *Time Off* that Dana had been looking at all those years ago. Sleep tried to catch me again, but I fought it off. Got to focus, got to focus. The blade pierced the flesh. Blood bubbled out. Just a little knick across the thing's head. I squeezed, like squeezing a pimple. I caught the thing's head in my good hand and pulled. It wouldn't come. A little more digging with the knife and it slid out. The pain was a big blunt thing in my brain. Three times on the right hand. Then I swapped the blade over. My right hand could barely hold the knife. I bled and bled. I squeezed my breath between my teeth. Three little cuts, a little digging, a little pulling and out they came, long strips of them. They curled up on the *Time Off*. All done.

My hands were stinging. I went back to the bathroom, pulled out a bottle of disinfectant, poured some into my palms. They felt as though they were on fire. I grabbed a towel and wrapped my hands in it. I was so tired. Time to go back to bed. Stumbling towards the darkness in my bedroom.

My radio alarm went off at eight o'clock. I tried to get a hand out from under the covers to hit the snooze button, but it was bound up somehow in the bedclothes. I tried to pull it out, and was greeted with a sharp pain.

I lifted both hands out together, to find they were wrapped in a blood-soaked towel. I gently untangled them. Along each palm were three parallel wounds, still raw and weeping. They ached with a pain that I seemed to feel all the way into my gut. A flicker of memory came back to me—the bright light in the bathroom, looking at myself in the mirror like I didn't know myself. My heartbeat picked up. It felt like remembering a dream. I closed my eyes and concentrated. What had I done?

Worms—that was it, there had been some kind of worms under my skin. But what I could remember of the episode made no sense. It must have been a dream.

No, it wasn't. I had sat at the kitchen table and dug them out. I threw off the covers and went to the kitchen, nearly tripping over the up-ended drawer lying on the floor. The magazine on the table was spattered with blood. Six curled and dry pieces of dead, white skin lay next to my art knife. My stomach turned over. I had pulled off pieces of my own skin, thinking they were some kind of creatures living in my hands.

I collapsed into a chair, staring at my palms. Pieces of white fluff from the towel were stuck to the wounds. My hands were red and shaking. I tried to steady them, but it was as though they belonged to somebody else.

'Jeez, Lisa, you've got to pull yourself together,' I said aloud, trying to gather some strength. I needed to clean and dress these wounds properly, but I was incapable of doing it by myself. I could wait until Brad came by, but then he would want to know what was going on and it would be too difficult to explain. Liam already knew about my hallucinations, so he was obviously the person to call.

I went to the phone, picked up the receiver gingerly between my thumb and forefinger, and carefully pressed Liam's number.

'Hello?'

'Are you busy?'

'Lisa, hi. I tried to call last night but I only got the machine.'

'I went to bed early. Can you come over?'

'Now? I'm just getting ready for work.'

My hands weren't the only part of me shaking now. My whole body had gone into spasms. 'It's urgent. I've hurt myself.'

His voice inflected with concern. 'Hurt yourself? How bad? What happened?'

'I had another hallucination . . . I've cut my hands up pretty bad.' I gulped down a sob.

'Okay, sit tight. I'm on my way over.' The phone clicked.

'How the hell did you do this?'

I had showered, briefly and painfully, and now sat in my dressing gown on a chair pulled between Liam's knees while he bathed my wounds with cotton wool, warm water and disinfectant. He had the bowl of water sitting right next to my computer and I cringed every time he dipped into it, worried that he might tip it over into my keyboard.

'Ouch,' I said as he cleaned the deepest end of the cut. 'I woke up in the middle of the night and I thought there were worms under my skin. I was only half awake, in a kind of trance. I cut them out.'

'With what?'

'With an art knife. One of those real fine blades for cutting stencils. I didn't know what I was doing. I could barely remember it when I woke up. I wouldn't have remembered at all it if it hadn't been for the evidence.'

He pulled his lips into a tight line. I noticed he looked very pale.

'Are you okay?' I said.

'Okay? I'm horrified.' He had brought his first-aid kit over and was rummaging through it for some antiseptic ointment. 'Are you sure you don't want to get a doctor to look at these?' he said as he gently rubbed the cream onto my wounds. I winced.

'Absolutely sure. What would I tell them? How do you explain doing this to yourself?'

He pulled out a bandage and started to wrap it around my left hand. 'Lisa, I'm worried about you. I'm worried about the possibility of permanent damage.'

'These aren't too deep, they'll heal up soon enough.'

He shook his head. 'Not your hands. Your mind. If it's the regressions that are causing these hallucinations, perhaps you should stop taking trips to the past.' He wrapped the bandage twice around my wrist to hold it in place, cut it and stuck it down, then started on the other hand. 'I know I shouldn't be telling you what to do, but I couldn't bear to see you hurt yourself like this again. This isn't that serious, but what else might you be capable of? You've got more than enough to deal with already. I think you know enough about your past life now. I think it's time you started to sort out what's happening in this life, and you can't do that if your brain is addled.'

I sighed and leaned back in my chair. 'You're right. This is too scary, being out of control.' I watched him carefully bandage my hand. When he had finished I leaned forward and gave him a kiss on the cheek. 'Thank you, Liam. Have I made you late for work?'

'I thought I might take the morning off anyway,' he said. 'You know, stay here with you and make sure you're okay.'

'Oh, Christ. You've just reminded me. I'm supposed to be going into the studio today. Brad's coming by to give me a lift.'

He picked up the bowl of water and disinfectant and took it to the kitchen to tip down the sink.

'I think you should have a day off. Can you call him?'

Just then there was a brief knock on the door and the sound of a key turning in the lock.

'Too late,' I said, 'he's here.' I remembered what Brad had said last night about not wanting to pick me up if Liam was here. It was so early in the morning, he would obviously assume Liam had stayed the night.

Brad pushed open the door, saw me sitting there with bandaged hands and hurried over. 'What the fuck happened to you?' Then he looked up and caught sight of Liam in the kitchen. 'Oh, hi,' he said impassively.

'Lisa burnt herself,' Liam said.

'Burnt yourself?' Brad directed the question at me.

'Yeah. I wasn't thinking straight. I pulled a plate out of the oven not realising how hot it would be.'

'This morning?'

'No, last night. Liam came over just now to look at it for me.'

A number of different emotions chased themselves across Brad's face. Anger, concern, jealousy. 'Do you want the day off?'

'If I could.'

He shrugged. 'Fine with me. Do you trust Dick and me to do a good job by ourselves?'

I sighed. 'I don't really have a choice, do I?'

He looked at Liam. 'Are you going to stay here?'

'Just for a while. She won't be able to do much for herself today, not until her hands start to heal.'

He nodded. 'Good. Okay, I'm off. I'll come by on the way home if you like.'

'Yeah, sure,' I said. 'Let me know how much you got done.'

Again he addressed Liam. 'Perhaps you should take her to a doctor. She has to play guitar on Thursday night, so she has to get better quick.'

'We're considering that.'

'Fine.' He looked as though he wanted to say something else, but stopped himself. 'Well, bye,' he said.

I walked Brad to the door and pushed it shut behind him with my foot. I looked at Liam. 'You're a smooth liar. It's not something I would have expected from you.'

He grabbed me around the waist and kissed me. 'You're at my mercy for a whole day and you can't fight me off.' Then he stood back, looking very serious. 'So, no more past-life exploring?'

I held my hands in front of him. 'Of course not,' I said. 'I'm not stupid.'

CHAPTER
EIGHTEEN

Fire Fire had been an unused downstairs room in
the quite ordinary Royal Arms Hotel until the licen-
see's son, Mickey, had reached drinking age and
decided he wanted to set it up as an underground
bar, underground in both senses of the word because
it was twelve stairs below the street entrance. Walking
in was literally a descent into hell, because that's how
Mickey had decorated the room. Two store dummies,
grinning idiotically, had been painted red and fitted
with horns, tails and pitchforks. They flanked either
side of the inside entrance where an unsmiling black-
haired woman with stringy arms took the cover
charge. She was a junkie—I had once caught her
shooting up in the toilets. Inside, the dark, low-
ceilinged room was certainly cavernlike, but the thing
most reminiscent of hell was the smell of the toilets,
which had dodgy plumbing. The tables were red and
yellow; flames had been painted on the black walls,
and 'Fire Fire' was written in flaming neon letters
above the stage.

There was a decent crowd already when Brad and
I walked in. The support band were still on stage, and
we watched them for a while. They played the same
two mournful chords over and over again, while the

singer mumbled some kind of improvised melody over the top.

'Their bass is out of tune,' Brad said.

'Maybe it's an avant-garde thing—we probably just don't understand.'

'Lisa, Lisa, Lisa!' Jeff came screaming up from the mixing desk and grabbed my forearms. He carefully turned my hands over, looking in awe at the bandages. 'God, did you try to kill yourself?'

'Don't be ridiculous,' I said. 'I burned myself accidentally.'

Brad raised his eyebrows sceptically at Jeff. I hadn't realised he didn't believe the story.

'Can you play?' Jeff asked.

'I'll just tune to an open E, then I can fill in with a few bar chords. Brad will have to do most of the tricky stuff for the next couple of nights.'

'Tricky, tricky, tricky,' Jeff repeated, tickling Brad under the chin.

'Jeff, are you tripping?' I asked.

'Yeah, why?'

'Just be careful. The CIB have got detectives at most of our gigs.'

Brad turned to me in horror. 'Detectives? Why? How do you know?'

'The murder victims were both fans, that's all. Nothing to do with collecting drug fines to fund the next policeman's ball. I spoke to Sergeant Pyle yesterday morning. He's the one looking after Karin's case.'

'But how did they know that the two guys were frequent flyers? Did you tell them?'

I nodded. Brad looked as though he wanted to strangle me. 'Jeez, Lisa. We can't have our gigs crawling with cops.'

'Nobody has to know. And I'm warning you, aren't

279

I? Just be careful. And somebody had better warn Mickey too.'

'Are you kidding? He'd never have us back here again. The fewer people we tell the better.' Something caught Brad's eye over my shoulder. 'Hmm, looks like a 747 gig is the place for police staff to be. Your friend just arrived.'

I spun round. Liam was at the counter, about to part with five bucks to get in. I raced up and stopped him handing over any money.

'It's okay, he's with me,' I said to the girl behind the counter. She shrugged and motioned him through.

'Thanks, Lisa.'

'I didn't know you were coming tonight.' I stood on my toes and gave him a peck on the cheek.

'I didn't either. But I was home by myself and . . . I just wanted to see you.'

'Hey, Lisa, is this your boyfriend?' Jeff had approached and was standing uncomfortably close to us.

'Jeff, this is Liam,' I said, taking a step back.

'Are you Lisa's boyfriend?' He ignored Liam's offer of a handshake.

'I guess so.' Liam pulled his hand back, embarrassed.

'Wow. She doesn't have boyfriends very often you know.'

'That's enough, Jeff,' I said.

'And they usually look like criminals.'

I pushed Jeff away gently. 'That girl in the purple top has been watching you, Jeff. You'd better go introduce yourself.'

'Yeah. I'd better.' He wandered off, but took a sharp left turn before he got to the girl and instead joined Brad, who was buying drinks at the bar.

Liam turned to me. 'There's a National Affair van parked outside unloading a camera crew. Do you have any idea what that's about?'

'No. Are you sure they were coming in here?' I felt a small lurch in my stomach. *National Affair*, I knew, was a pseudo current affairs show that specialised in doing hatchet jobs and sensationalist news beat-ups.

'I don't know. Nothing else is open along this street except the hot-dog stand.'

The other band had finished and were packing up their equipment. 'I've got to go set up, do you want to wait down here with Angie?'

'Sure.'

I left him standing there and went up to organise my gear. I tuned my guitar to an open E, which meant I could play some bar chords with one finger. There was never any question of me leaving the guitar off for a couple of nights—it would have felt too weird.

I had my head down plugging in my wah-pedal when somebody said to me, 'Excuse me, are you Lisa Sheehan?'

I looked up and found myself staring straight into a video camera. A man holding a clipboard stood next to it. My very first thought was that I didn't want to be on TV. I thought if I swore a lot they wouldn't get any usable footage.

'Who the fuck are you?' I said.

'I'm Trevor Blake from *National Affair*. We're investigating claims that your band leads a cult of Satan worshippers.'

'I hardly think that qualifies as a national affair,' I said. So this was Dana's revenge. I owed her a grudging admiration for going all the way.

'Can you answer the question, Miss Sheehan? Is your band involved in Satan worship?'

'No, absolutely not. Never has been, never will be.' There was no way they could misconstrue that, twist it out of context.

'Is it true that a number of your fans have been murdered in a Satanic fashion?'

'You'll have to ask the police about that. Now, I'm busy, so would you mind fucking off? And if you value your expensive camera equipment, you'd better get out of the mosh pit.' I put my head down and continued what I was doing. When I looked up again, they were moving around the room, filming the audience milling about.

Brad came over. 'What was that all about?'

'They're from *National Affair*. I think they want to do a hatchet job on us—they're asking if it's true that we're Satan worshippers.'

Brad smiled. 'Yeah? Free publicity. Nationwide. What did you tell them?'

'I told them no, of course, and so will you.'

'Okay, okay. Still, the crowd loves the camera—check that out.' He pointed to where the camera crew stood, filming a stoned girl as she pulled faces and made horns with her fingers.

'Great,' I said.

'Lisa, chill out. It's okay. They can't hurt us, they can only help us.'

'It's my fault they're here. I think Dana called them.'

'Karin's mother?'

'Yeah, she hates my guts. She found out about the murdered guys being our fans. I think that's going to be their angle.'

'Don't worry.' He went to put his arm around me, then seemed to remember that Liam was in the crowd and backed off. He patted my shoulder. 'Let it go. You can't do anything about it now.'

I sat back on the drum riser. Jeff was tuning up his snare, hitting it over and over. Crack, crack, crack. I was sure the level of stress I was living under would have killed anybody else. It seemed like every day something happened to crank it up a notch. The audience began to surge forward, to squash themselves up against the front of the stage. Some of them were already calling out for their favourite songs. One guy called out 'Lisa is beautiful', and I tried a strained smile.

Brad eventually came over and crouched in front of me. 'You ready?'

I nodded. 'Sure.'

'Come on then, get your guitar on.'

We hammered through the first song okay. It was so hot under the lights. The frequent flyers down the front were slamming into each other in joyous abandon. One guy stood motionless with his forehead leaning on the front-of-house speakers. It must have been scrambling his brain.

During the second song, I looked up to search the crowd for Liam. He stood in the dimly lit space next to Angie. The camera crew were filming the band from the side of the crowd near the toilets. A movement by the entrance to the club caught my eye. A tall man had just walked in; at the moment he was nothing more than a silhouette. My ears started ringing faintly, so that the music we were playing seemed separated from me by a short distance. I closed my eyes, willing away that feeling, knowing that it meant a hallucination was on its way.

When I looked again, the man was standing about three metres behind the sound desk. He was still nothing more than a dark shape, and I wondered why because I should have been able to make out some detail by now. Something felt very bad, something felt very wrong. My knees started to shake. The atmosphere seemed too close, too hot. I could feel sweat running into the wounds in my palms, making them sting. I shook my head, tried to clear my brain.

I watched the dark man. I focused on where his face would be. I thought I saw a smile—a close, bitter smile. I watched and watched, my hands mindlessly changing from fret to fret, following the chords of the song. His face started to emerge from the gloom. I felt as though I was choking. He came closer, his appearance, in spite of the darkness, horribly familiar.

Holy fuck, it was the devil.

Not like one of the mannequins standing at the entrance. No, a man with reddish skin, yellowed horns emerging from his forehead, bare torso merging into animal-like legs. I nearly dropped my bundle right there, nearly ran screaming off the stage, but I pulled myself together. I closed my eyes and told myself it was just a hallucination brought on by that stupid camera crew talking about devil worship, that was all. It would go away—they always did. I mustn't believe it was real, I had to pretend that everything was all right. I looked over to Brad. He was singing. The veins in his neck stood out. His hair was in his face, getting stuck in his mouth.

I looked back to the crowd. Now the devil was standing next to Liam, who was completely unaware of his presence. He glanced at Liam, then turned to stare directly at me with eyes like arrows. He made horrendous, theatrical air kisses and grinned suggestively, grabbing his crotch. I shuddered and wondered bitterly whether the camera crew could see him. He'd make a great interview subject. You want to know if we're in league with Satan? Look, I've summoned him up so you can ask him in person.

It was freaking me out that no matter how often

I closed my eyes, each time I opened them he was there again, getting closer, moving between the tables, jostling through the crowd. My heart pounded and my ears rang. This wasn't happening, surely this wasn't happening. But if he wasn't real, how come people moved around him as though he had a physical presence, and how come the people that he brushed against seemed momentarily disturbed, as if they had just thought of their own mortality? But nobody was looking at him, they were looking everywhere but at him; it was only me seeing him. Every instinct told me to get out, run away. I fought it, telling myself over and over that he couldn't be real.

The devil came right to the front of the stage. I looked down at him, forcing myself to remain calm, rational. 'This is nothing. This is a hallucination,' I repeated under my breath. I knew what a hallucination felt like, and I knew that it would go away, and I was *not* going to freak out while *National Affair* was here filming. He reached a hand up—yellowed fingernails like claws and thick black hair growing out of the knuckles—and grabbed me around the upper thigh.

'Elizabeth, you're mine.' He was only whispering, but somehow I could hear him over the music.

I opened my mouth to say that I wasn't Elizabeth, but I couldn't hear myself. His grip tightened, cruelly squeezing my flesh. I was exploding with terror. For an instant, I thought I saw Gilbert's face transposed over the devil's, but the vision escaped before I could properly focus on it. The creature dug his thumbnail into the spot where the witch-mark was. The pain was intense and seemed to set all my nerves on fire. I screamed.

'I own you,' he said.

My legs buckled underneath me and I pitched

forward, landing on my knees, covering my face with my hands and screaming. Moments later, I felt Ailsa's warm, soft hands under my armpits, helping me to my feet. Jeff and Brad kept playing. She pulled my hands away from my face and I realised with overwhelming relief that the devil was gone. Only about half the crowd had noticed what was going on.

'Are you okay?' Ailsa called over the music.

'I think so.'

'Can you keep going?'

'Yeah, yeah, I'll keep going,' I replied shakily. I heard Ailsa's bass join the music again, but I mimed playing until the end of the song. During the break, while the crowd was cheering, Brad strode over.

'What the fuck happened?'

'Nothing, I fell over.'

'You've got to stop lying to me, Lisa.'

'Here, I want to tune up properly. Give me the notes.'

He played his strings one by one and I changed back to the correct tuning. I made a chord. The pain in my hand made me wince, but I liked the way it made reality lurch back into focus.

We started the next song, which was one that I sang. I scanned the crowd nervously, but I couldn't see the devil, or the dark man he had emerged from. My pulse was racing and my thigh ached where his claw had dug into me. A big bubble of feeling, overwhelmingly dark and desperate, welled up inside me. Towards the end of the song, when I was supposed to be singing the last chorus, I couldn't bear it any longer, standing up there singing as though nothing was wrong. I chucked my guitar off and stood at the edge of the stage. Everybody's hands went up— they knew I was going to dive. I put my arms above my head and turned my back to the audience. A cheer went up. I looked at my hands, bandaged and shaking. I bent my knees to give myself a little boost, and threw myself backwards into the crowd.

There was always that split second when I wondered whether the crowd would just clear a spot for me and I would land on my back on the floor and wind up breaking my neck. But they caught me, they always caught me. I lay limp as they passed me along. The bandage on my left hand was coming loose. I remember screaming as their hands fumbled at my body, a primal scream of terror and pain. My hands were bleeding again, small red spots flowering on the bandages. I didn't care. I just wanted to plunge head-first into oblivion.

They threw me back on stage and I dived straight back in. A couple of kids took my lead and started climbing onto the stage then diving back into the mosh pit. The crowd was starting to get aggressive now, sick of being crushed by drunks in Doc Martens. I stayed on stage the second time they threw me back. Brad gave me a look of admiration—he loved nihilism in others. I had such a physical response to that look that it frightened me—big lusty Brad with his hair in his face and his sexy eyes. I felt in that moment that I could drag him backstage and have him on one of the empty kegs we used for seats. Damn it, he was right, I hadn't stopped wanting him.

A fight had broken out down the front; a cluster of people were pushing each other and tearing each other's T-shirts. A bouncer with arms like hams ploughed into the crowd and pulled a couple of the fighters out. I noticed that the camera crew had moved in closer to catch the action and was being jostled by the crowd. Somebody took it as an opportunity to elbow the camera operator in the guts, and he went down like a bag of shit, nearly dropping his camera.

'It's getting out of hand,' I screamed in Brad's ear. 'We should stop playing.'

'No, no way. Keep playing. I live for this shit.' We ploughed into the next song. A kind of euphoria settled over me. Like somehow while I was playing I was exorcising my demons. I could forget everything else.

When we had finally finished and the crowd was cheering over the dying chord of the last song, I walked up to the microphone and said, 'Please, everybody, be careful on the way home.' Somebody called out the name of one of our songs, others cheered mindlessly. I doubt if anyone really took notice.

'What was that all about?' said Brad. 'Are you trying to impress the journalist by delivering community service messages?'

'I've got such a bad feeling, Brad.'

'Is that why you collapsed earlier?'

'It may be.'

'You haven't told me anything. You've known me for nine years; you've known him for twenty seconds.' He indicated Liam, who was talking to Angie. 'Have you told him everything?'

I looked at Liam then back at Brad. He had been chugging beer all through the set, and was starting to look decidedly bleary. 'Yes. I've told him everything.' Of course he was right, I had trusted Liam with my secrets, but only because Brad would never have believed me.

He shook his head. 'I don't get it. I thought we were friends. Something's going on, something that's got you totally spooked, and you can't even tell me.'

I shrugged. 'Maybe I will tell you one day. But not now.'

'Oh, Christ,' said Brad, pointing over my right shoulder. 'Look who's getting his fifteen minutes of fame.'

I turned to see Jeff talking animatedly to the camera crew. 'Go stop him, Brad. He's off his face.'

Brad jumped off the stage and into the crowd, put an arm around Jeff's shoulders and said something to the reporter. Jeff took it as a cue to grab Brad's face in those long fingers of his and give him a dramatic kiss. I had to laugh. *National Affair* would love that— homosexuality and Satan worship all in the same article. What a ratings winner. Fundamentalists all over the country would be praying for our souls before the week was out.

I turned around and saw Liam standing below the stage in front of me.

'Hi,' I said. 'Did you enjoy the show?'

He put his arms up to lift me down from the stage, then closed me in a bear hug. My knees shook and I leaned into him.

'What happened?' he asked. 'Did you see something that freaked you out?' For a moment, something about the way he enclosed me in his arms bugged me, like he was trying to contain me as much as comfort me.

'Only the Prince of Darkness himself,' I said.

Pressed up against his chest like that, I could hear his heart pick up a few beats, feel his body freeze over.

I stood back and looked at him. 'Does that scare you?'

'Satan? You saw . . .?'

'It was a hallucination, Liam. It was horrible but not real.'

'I'm sorry. I was conditioned from an early age, remember.'

289

Brad approached with a pot of beer in each hand. 'Liam, how you doing?'

Liam turned, seemed glad for the interruption. 'Fine, fine. It was a good show.'

'Here,' Brad handed Liam a beer. 'Sit down and have a drink with me.'

Liam looked at me and I shrugged. 'Er . . . why not?' he said at last.

We found an empty table, and Brad dug his cigarettes out of his pocket. He offered one to Liam, who refused. I didn't like Brad being so congenial because I knew it wasn't sincere, but he was half tanked and seemed determined to play-act some kind of mateship ritual. Ailsa and Jeff joined us and we all sat there until three a.m., talking and laughing, fighting off frequent flyers who wanted to breathe bourbon all over us and paw at our shoulders in a display of their admiration. Brad drank and drank. He managed to stay civil the whole time, telling Liam mildly embarrassing stories about stupid things that I had done in the past, in much the same way as a parent might bring out nude baby photos to mortify their kids in front of dates. I didn't mind, I just sat and let the whirl of conversation and cigarette smoke circle around me while Liam stroked my fingers under the table and I tried to forget that horrible clawed hand claiming me as though I was a possession.

When the house lights came up and the nightclub was getting ready to close down, Brad staggered to his feet and pulled his car keys out of his pocket. 'Well, Lisa, if you won't be needing a lift, I guess I'll be off.'

Liam stood up and put a hand on Brad's shoulder. Brad gave him a look that was unmistakably hostile, but quickly hid it.

'You're too drunk to drive, Brad. I'll give you a lift,' Liam said.

'But my car . . .'

'You can come and get it tomorrow. You're way too drunk to drive.'

'He's right, Brad,' said Ailsa. 'You're smashed. And there's cops everywhere.'

'Yeah, thanks to Lisa,' Brad said, only half joking.

'Come on, Brad, come with us,' Liam said.

Brad considered a moment then put his keys back in his pocket. 'Yeah, okay.'

We left the nightclub and I helped Brad into Liam's car. He sprawled across the back seat. 'Jeez, this is a nice car,' he said, and a nasty tone coloured his voice.

'Yes, don't throw up in it,' I said, buckling my seat-belt.

Liam let himself in and started the engine. 'Which way?' he asked.

Brad didn't answer. I turned to see that he had passed out.

'He's out of it. I'll direct you.'

We wound our way through the streets to Brad's place. When we were idling out front, I turned to him and shook him awake. 'Brad, we're home.'

He opened a bleary eye. 'Lisa?' There was such tenderness in his voice that it took me by surprise. He caught my fingers and stroked them, dozing off again.

'You're home, Brad,' Liam said.

Brad snapped to attention. 'Oh, it's you.' Again, the unmasked hostility.

'Come on, get out,' I said. 'I'm tired, I want to get home.'

'Yeah, I'll bet you do,' he replied, leaning forward

and playfully punching Liam's shoulder. 'Hear that? She wants to get home.'

Liam ignored him and faced the windscreen. Brad pushed the door open and moved to get out, then slid back in and leaned forward again, so he was speaking directly into Liam's left ear.

'Has she told you about me?'

I put a hand on his shoulder. 'Brad . . .'

He shrugged it off, almost violently. 'In a seedy hotel room upstairs at a Cairns nightclub where we played. I was her first.'

Liam maintained his focus in front of him, as though he had heard nothing. His face was impassive. His fingers drummed lightly on the steering wheel.

'Get the fuck out of this car now, Bradley Harper,' I hissed.

'I was her first,' he said again, then slipped out of the car and stumbled onto the footpath. I reached over and closed the door behind him. Almost as soon as I had, Liam hit the accelerator and sped off. I looked over my shoulder and caught a glimpse of Brad sitting in his driveway with his head in his hands.

Liam came to a stop sign, slowed down marginally then ploughed through it.

'Hey, get your hormones under control,' I said. 'If you're angry tell me, don't wrap me around a power pole.'

'I'm not angry with you.' He didn't sound terribly convincing.

'I'm sorry I didn't tell you.'

'Why is he such an arsehole?'

It was the first time I had heard Liam swear, and it took me by surprise. 'He's jealous.'

'He's not the only one, but I don't act like that.'

I eyed him curiously. 'What are you jealous about?'

'About him of course. You spend so much time

together, and you're so close. And what he just said
. . . well, that just tops it off. Why didn't you tell
me?'

'Because it's my right not to have to tell you about
my sex life.'

'This is different. You see him all the time. Are
you sure you're not interested in him the same way
he is in you?'

'No, of course not. Look, I'm sorry you had to
find out like that. I was young and I had the biggest
crush on him. He was so gorgeous at nineteen, he
could pull any girl he wanted. He wasn't the least bit
interested in me really; I think he did it as a favour.'

He fell silent for a while, then reached over and
put a hand on my knee. 'I'm sorry. Jealousy doesn't
become me.'

'It's okay. It's nice that you care.'

'You don't know how much.'

For the first time since before our first kiss, I felt
slightly uncomfortable with him. I could sense a
declaration of love coming on, and that was frightening. I felt something so strong and all-encompassing
for him that under any other circumstances I would
call it love. But my brain was so scrambled there was
every chance it was just an outlet for excess emotions.

He must have felt my discomfort because he
squeezed my knee. 'It's okay, we can have this conversation another time.'

It was three-thirty a.m. I settled back in my seat and
leaned into the headrest. Liam hadn't brought up the
dark master's guest appearance at the gig, probably
because it frightened him more than it frightened me.
I didn't want to think about it either. The night outside
the car window seemed very quiet and very serene.

But somewhere, something diabolical was happening.

CHAPTER
NINETEEN

The shrill ringing of the phone pierced through the warm muffle of sleep. I sat up groggily. It was eight o'clock. Liam was stirring beside me. I threw back the covers and raced for the phone, breathing a bleary 'Hello' into the receiver.

'Miss Lisa Sheehan?'

'Yeah, who's this?'

'Inspector Honeywell from City CIB. Could you round up the other members of your band and get them down here this morning for an eleven o'clock appointment?'

'Appointment? I'm sorry, I just woke up, I don't follow you exactly. What's this about?'

'We have two more bodies on our hands this morning, Miss Sheehan. We're hoping that you may be able to help us with our investigations.'

'They were . . . ?'

'Yes, on their way home from a 747 concert at the Royal Arms Hotel. A kid camping in the pine forest found them at seven this morning. They were a young couple: one male, one female.'

'I'll see if I can rouse the others. Eleven o'clock?'

'Yes, fifth floor.' The line went dead. It was all I could do to stop myself collapsing to the ground.

It struck me as we sat in Inspector Honeywell's sparse office in various states of wakefulness that we looked like a group of naughty schoolkids. Jeff was in a crumpled purple shirt; the first three buttons were done up evenly but the bottom three were all one hole out. His face was pallid and his hair stringy. Brad looked sick and hungover, and Ailsa had her hair pulled back in a severe ponytail, revealing a crop of sweat pimples on her forehead. I figured I must have looked terrible too, but at least I fitted in.

Inspector Honeywell talked on the phone while we waited. He had a handle-bar moustache and salt-and-pepper hair. He had been openly unfriendly to us when he had shown us into his office, and the way he was ignoring us while he chatted on the phone for ages was starting to bug me. I made a theatrical gesture of looking at my watch and yawning. He deliberately turned on his swivel chair so he didn't have to look at us. In an instant Jeff had stolen a disposable biro off his desk and pocketed it. I stifled a laugh.

Finally, Inspector Honeywell said: 'All right, Dennis . . . Yep, I'll get back to you as soon as I know. Thank you.' He swung around, put the phone down and looked across at us. We all cringed as if we were in trouble.

'747,' he said. 'So this is what rock stars look like during daylight hours. It's not a pretty sight.' He bared his teeth in something I'm assuming was intended as a smile. Nobody smiled back.

He began to search on his desk for something, and Jeff leaned over and handed him the pen. 'Here, use mine,' Jeff said.

'Thanks,' he replied, taking the pen and pulling

out a thick notebook. 'Now, can each of you relate to me where you were between one-thirty and three-thirty this morning?'

I leaned forward. 'Are we suspects?'

'Standard procedure, sweetie. Just answer the question.'

I was rendered speechless by him calling me 'sweetie', so Brad chipped in. 'We were all together at the venue. Lisa and I left just after three, her boyfriend dropped me home at around three-fifteen.'

'Jeff and I stayed until four, drinking with the bar staff,' Ailsa added. 'We were all accounted for . . . sir.'

Inspector Honeywell didn't hear the sarcasm in her use of 'sir'. 'Good, good. Now, can anybody tell me if they know of or remember any patrons at your shows acting in a strange manner.'

We all looked at each other. Brad smirked.

'Most of them do,' I answered. 'You'll have to be more specific.'

'We suspect you may have a fan who comes to your shows, gets full of drugs and alcohol, then follows somebody home, abducts them and takes them to the pine forest to kill them. Now, such a person may have made himself known to you in the past in a variety of ways—perhaps he acts in a suspicious manner, perhaps he's spoken to you about murder like he was joking, perhaps he stares at other people in the room all night. Does this sound familiar?'

We made a pretence of thinking about it. Jeff shrugged at me.

'No, nobody has stood out for those reasons,' Brad said finally.

'Come on, there must be something.' He sounded desperate. We sat mutely. 'All right, let's try a different tack. Do you know of any reason why somebody would want to kill your fans?'

I held my tongue. A clock ticked loudly in the silence. Inspector Honeywell's face grew darker and darker by the moment.

'Come on, think, people, think,' he said in a bullying voice. He waited a few minutes longer, then said, 'Well, I can't think of anyone I've ever dealt with who's been more uncooperative than you lot.'

'If there's nothing to tell, we can't tell you,' I said. 'Do you want us to make something up? Do you want us to tell you that somebody is stalking our fans because we were bad in a previous life?'

Jeff burst into a loud laugh, then quickly checked himself and looked into his lap.

'There *must* be something,' he said. Again, no answer. He hung his head. 'All right, go home.' We started to leave. 'If you think of something—anything—that you think might help, please call me. And be careful, for Christ's sake. You didn't see what I saw this morning—he had them tied to trees facing each other. For all we know, one of them may have had to watch while the other one had his organs pulled out.'

Brad looked like he was going to puke. I put an arm around him and helped him out. We parted company with Ailsa and Jeff in the hall. I waited outside a male toilet while Brad threw up inside. Inspector Honeywell walked past on his way to the drink machine, his footsteps echoing in the sterile corridor. He bought a Coke then turned back and came to stand in front of me.

'What did you do to your hands?' he asked.

I held them up. Liam had dressed and rebandaged them last night. 'I burned them.'

297

'You're holding something back,' he said casually. 'I can tell.'

I shrugged. 'If that's what you want to believe.'

Brad emerged from the men's room, pale and shaking. Inspector Honeywell watched us go to the lift. He was still watching us when the doors slid closed.

'What a macho fuckwit,' I said as we descended. Brad just nodded, clutching his stomach.

We came out on the ground floor and walked past Liam's office on our way out. He looked up and smiled at me as we stood hanging in his doorway.

'You look great for somebody who's only had four hours of sleep,' I said.

He pointedly ignored Brad. 'Thanks. I think I might knock off early this afternoon.'

'Well, come over if you want.'

'I probably will.'

'See you.'

I led Brad away. When we were outside he finally spoke. 'You must hate me.'

'No, of course not. I'm used to you.'

'*He* hates me.' He indicated the police station.

'Yes, he does. But it took you a full week to alienate him completely. That's got to be some kind of record with one of my boyfriends.'

'I'm going to pick up my car while we're in the city. Do you want a lift?'

'No, thanks. I'll catch the bus.'

My answering machine was blinking at me when I got home. I played the message and was surprised to hear my mother's voice. 'Lisa, it's Mum. I just saw an ad for *National Affair* tonight. What have you got yourself into this time?' Then she left an interstate number for me to call her on, but I erased the message. So they were running with the story tonight. 747 were going to be stars.

'Viewers would have been shocked to hear on this evening's news of a further two victims falling prey to the serial killer who has been nicknamed the Eye Surgeon because of his grisly fondness for removing the hearts and eyes of his victims.'

'Jeez, where do they come up with this stuff?'

'Ssh, Lisa, I'm listening.'

It was Friday evening and Liam and the band were crowded on the couch and on the floor in front of my TV. Jeff had bought a carton of popcorn for the occasion, and was spilling pieces of it onto the carpet.

'So far in their investigations, the police have few leads to go on, and the killings continue. One link that *National Affair* has uncovered, however, is that each victim was a fan of the heavy metal band 747.'

'We're not heavy metal,' Brad protested. 'Who the hell have they got doing their research for them?'

'Trevor Blake filed this report about the disturbing cult that surrounds 747.'

'Oh, this is ridiculous,' I said. 'Surely nobody's going to believe this crap.'

'People believe anything,' Ailsa said, dipping her hand into Jeff's popcorn.

Footage of the venue appeared on the television. They had filmed the weirdest looking punters they could find in various bizarre poses struck for the benefit of the camera. The reporter was rambling on about the underground music scene being a 'breeding ground for occultists'. Suddenly Jeff's face came up on the screen. He hooted wildly and threw popcorn at himself.

'Yeah, man,' he said to the reporter. 'We're in

league with the devil, that's why we're so rich and famous.'

'Oh, Jeff, did you have to say that?' I asked.

'I thought it was obvious I was kidding.'

There was a brief shot of him kissing Brad, and Ailsa nearly fell off the sofa laughing. 'You're out now, Brad. You won't be pulling any more chicks after this.'

We jeered at Brad for a few moments, and he smacked Jeff playfully across the head.

'Christ, it's Dana,' I squealed as Karin's mother appeared on screen. I was so angry with her: surely with her daughter missing she had better things to approach news programs about.

'I've known Lisa Sheehan for many years and there's no doubt in my mind that she's up to evil practices.'

'What kind of evil practices, Mrs Anders?'

'Drugs. Animal sacrifice. Black magic. You only have to look at her to tell she's crazed.' I wondered if she really believed that or if it was just the most slanderous thing she could think of on such short notice.

Then footage of me, kneeling on the stage with my hands over my eyes and my mouth open in a scream inaudible over the music. Then being tossed around on the crowd with the bandages on my hands working loose. Then telling the reporter to fuck off, edited with a strategic beep. Liam slipped an arm around my waist and pulled me close. I could sense how uncomfortable he was with the representation of me on the screen.

But something unexpected was happening with me. Instead of being miserable about the story, I realised guiltily that I found it thrilling to be a celebrity of some kind, thrilling to see myself por-

300

trayed as a damned rock princess with unbrushed hair and a tattoo.

'Looks like you're the head Satanist,' Brad said, with something that approached sneaking respect. We were all out of our minds—we were actually enjoying this.

'We're so cool,' said Jeff, spraying popcorn out of his mouth in all directions.

'But surely nobody will ever turn up to see you again, now that there's the threat of being attended to by "the Eye Surgeon" on their way home.' We all looked at Liam as he said this. He didn't get it.

'That's not going to happen,' I said. 'You don't know our frequent flyers.'

And I was right. That night the Universal was packed: they had to turn two hundred people away.

Dana had just booted us into the stratosphere.

Numb Records called Brad first thing Monday morning to tell him our CD release date had been brought forward nearly a whole month. They flew an engineer up the next day to do the mastering, so Brad and I spent another couple of days holed up in the studio. Over the next few weeks we had photo sessions, interviews and consultations on the cover art, and played an endless succession of sold-out gigs. So this was it, this was what it felt like to be on the verge of breaking really big. I've got to say, despite the rest of my world teetering on the edge of a chasm, it felt really fucking good.

Two days after the release of the CD, we got a call from Musique Noir, the biggest alternative record store in the city. We were their number one seller and they could hardly keep the CD in the shop. Did we want to come down and spend an afternoon signing

CDs for fans? Well, of course we did. We were in love with ourselves.

So, after a week of advertising on the local alternative radio station and in the street rags, we found ourselves sitting at the back of an airconditioned record store, a trestle table in front of us and a steady trickle of people coming in to meet us. At times there was even a queue. Towards the end of the session, Brad was surreptitiously sharing a hip flask of Scotch with Ailsa and Jeff.

'Well, I don't know about you guys, but I won't be tossing off tonight,' Brad said, watching the retreating butt of a particularly nubile female fan. 'My right hand's had it with all this signing.'

'Use your left,' Jeff suggested.

Ailsa dropped her pen on the table and leaned back in her chair. 'We're stars,' she said, only half joking.

'Let's not get ahead of ourselves,' I said soberly. But I had a sneaking suspicion she was right.

'Hey, Lisa, isn't that Karin's husband?' Jeff said, tugging my sleeve.

I looked up. David had just come into the shop and was approaching the table. My heart did a little twist in my chest—please, let it be good news. I stood up and hurried over to greet him.

'David, have you heard something?'

'No. Nothing.' He looked at the ground then back to me. 'Sorry, I didn't mean to get your hopes up. I came to see you, to buy your CD and get you to sign it.'

'Of course. But you don't have to buy it, you can have a free one.' I led him back to the table and put a CD in front of the band to sign. 'I didn't think this was your kind of music.'

'It's not. I just know that Karin would want one when she . . . *if* she comes back.'

I clasped him around the wrist and gave a comforting squeeze.

'Hey, David, remember me?' said Jeff chirpily.

'Yes, of course.' He tried a smile but it failed. No doubt thinking of his last meeting with Jeff had reminded him of happier times. The band passed the CD back and I quickly scribbled my signature on the cover and handed it to David.

'There you go. Keep it in a safe place.'

He turned the CD over in his hands. 'Did you read the paper this morning?'

I shook my head.

'They found the skeleton of a girl who went missing twelve years ago. Twelve years.'

'No, I didn't hear about that.'

'Her parents have been waiting twelve years for her to come home. Now they get to bury her. Now they get to grieve. Lisa, I can't bear this, I can't bear the thought of having to wait twelve years to find out the truth. Or what about never? What if I never find out? What if I die and my whole life is spent waiting like this?' His voice shook. Brad, Jeff and Ailsa were watching him horrified. He was creating a really bad vibe. I took him by the arm and led him out of the store and into the street. I sat him down at a bus shelter and picked up his hand.

'It's okay, David. I feel the same. I just want to know one way or another, good news or bad. I just need to know.'

'I miss her so much. She was so beautiful, so rare and precious.'

'I know. I miss her too.' The City Circle bus roared past, bathing us in toxic exhaust fumes.

'She used to talk about you all the time. She

worshipped you. That's why I can't understand why she hasn't contacted you, that's why I can't—' He broke into a sob, then gathered himself. 'She would have contacted you. I know she would.'

I was sorry for him, so sorry for him. But at the same time I was angry. I was trying to get on with my life, despite everything. I was on the crest of a wave: Liam and I were happening, the band was happening, I hadn't hallucinated for over a month, nobody had been killed in just as long. But here he was, hauling my pain out of the dark place I had buried it and holding it up to the light for me to examine again.

'I'm sorry, David. I can't help you.'

'I know, I know. But you've got friends.' He gestured towards the record store. 'I've got nobody.'

I didn't know what to say. I slipped an arm around him and he put his arms around my waist and leaned into me. I watched people go in and out of the record store. I knew I should be back inside. I realised that David was feeling my back, his hands gently caressing me through my shirt. Surely he didn't mean anything by it. Then his hand slid around and slowly stroked my ribs, his fingertips momentarily brushing the side of my breast. By far the most disturbing thing was the way I responded to it—I almost couldn't bear to pull away.

'David, please.'

'Sorry.' He looked into his lap like a naughty schoolboy. I moved a good distance away from him on the seat.

'Look, I have to get back inside,' I said. My voice was shaky.

'I understand.'

'Feel free to call me.' Phone calls were far more impersonal.

He nodded, and I escaped inside.

'Jeez, he was morbid,' Ailsa said as I took my seat.

'He's got reason to be, don't you think?' Brad said. He gave me a squeeze, but I squirmed away from him. 'Are you okay?'

'No, I'm fucking miserable. He made me think of stuff I didn't want to think about.'

'Karin?'

'Yes. And with that goes the rest of it. Including the fact that we're getting famous because a few people got sliced up by a psycho.'

A guy with short blond hair approached the table and we all smiled and signed his CD. As soon as he was gone, Ailsa turned on me. 'You're such a wet blanket. Just because you feel like shit doesn't mean you have to make the rest of us feel the same.'

'Are you telling me that you've never thought of it? You've never thought about what those four people went through and how we're cashing in on it?'

'No, why should I? We just got an opportunity. There's nothing wrong with grabbing an opportunity.'

'Opportunity? These people are dead, Ailsa. They're not resting before an encore.'

'Calm down,' Brad hissed. I hadn't realised I'd raised my voice.

'You're a hypocrite, Lisa,' Jeff said. 'You're getting off on being the queen of the damned as much as any of us.'

I welled up with anger, most of it directed at myself. I threw my pen at Jeff and violently pushed my chair back. 'Just fucking shut up,' I said, leaning over him. He cowered back in his seat. Brad, who was sitting between us, tried to grab my hand but I wrenched myself away. 'You're all half tanked and full of shit. I'm ashamed to be part of this.'

'Please, Lisa,' Brad said, trying to be reasonable.

But I was storming out of the shop and out into the street. I nearly knocked over a young woman entering the store.

'Hey, aren't you in 747?' she asked.

'No,' I replied. 'I hate 747.' Myself included.

Waking up next to Liam was always wonderful. He had started to stay over more and more, even on work nights. On Tuesday morning the radio burst into life with a Powderfinger song at seven a.m. He turned over and kissed me and nuzzled my neck. I put my arms around him, his skin was so warm.

'Don't go to work today,' I said, like I said every day. 'Stay here with me.'

'Too busy.'

He rolled out of bed and pulled on his jeans. 'Are you going to make up with the band today?'

I groaned. 'I acted like such a bitch yesterday, I can't bear the thought of facing them.'

'Don't you think they had it coming?'

'Not really. They were right. I am enjoying being famous, even if it is on a small scale.'

'Not that small. Everyone at the police station is always asking me about you.'

'I'm sorry. Is that embarrassing for you?'

He turned around and kissed my forehead. 'No. I do have to explain, however, that you don't fry babies' organs for breakfast.'

I laughed. 'Not usually anyway. Only when I need the iron.'

He left me lying there and went to have a shower. When he returned he smelled fresh and clean, and he was buttoning up his shirt.

'You're so gorgeous,' I said.

'Don't. You're embarrassing me.'

'Are you coming back tonight?'

He fell silent for a minute while he finished buttoning his shirt, then came to sit on the bed. 'Actually, I'd better get the house cleaned up. My parents are coming to visit next week.'

'Your parents? Cool. Do I get to meet them?'

'Maybe. It's no big deal if you don't.'

'I want to meet them.'

'Well, like I said, maybe. Anyway, I thought I'd go home tonight. I haven't spent any time there for ages. It's getting a little musty.'

'Fine. Absence makes the heart grow fonder and all that.'

He smiled at me, that smile that melted my joints. 'I couldn't be any fonder of you,' he said.

He kissed my forehead and left. I heard the door close behind him. I sighed and closed my eyes, dozed for a while, thinking about how strongly I felt for him, trying to decide if it was love. I suspected it might be.

I got up around nine and went to check my e-mail. I still hadn't heard back from Whitewitch, and I presumed she must have grown tired of me, or was maybe fearing a lawsuit. It was probably for the best because she might convince me that I needed another regression. My thoughts returned so often to Elizabeth and Gilbert. I wanted to know what happened to them, but I was afraid of the hallucinations that always followed in the days afterwards.

I turned the television on and sat there in my customary morning stupor, sitting through cooking shows and international news programs. I dozed in between, and probably because I was thinking of Elizabeth, I had a small snatch of a dream where I was walking up the stairs of the house at Prestonvale, my hand gliding silently along the banister. I shook myself awake and focused on the television. It seemed very far away. I leaned forward to turn it up. My hand brushed the air a few inches from the volume knob. I collapsed back into the couch. Somewhere through the dozy sensation came a stab of fear. I was going into a regression—I knew the feeling well enough—but it was happening spontaneously, I had no control over it.

With an enormous effort I heaved myself off the sofa and began to pace the room. One foot in front of the other, feeling the floor underneath me. I shook the cotton wool feeling from myself and went to the kitchen. Hard flat surfaces surrounded me, making me feel more stable, more certain. I opened the fridge door, let the blast of cold air revive me. It would be okay. I was going to stay in the twentieth century.

'Elizabeth, where are you going?' A familiar voice behind me. I whirled around. The kitchen kept whirling. I barely had time to utter a cry before the floor dropped out from underneath me and I disappeared into time.

CHAPTER

TWENTY

'Elizabeth, where are you going?'

Gilbert caught my wrist on the stairs as I ascended. 'You're going to see Nancy again, aren't you? You're going to torture yourself some more.'

I pulled myself away from him. 'I'm going to see what I can do to make her comfortable.'

He picked up my hand, lifted it to his mouth and kissed the fingers delicately, longingly. 'There's only one thing that's going to make that woman comfortable, and you're not brave enough to do it.'

I met his eyes. 'I'm not a killer.'

'She's been two days without water. How much longer do you think she can last?'

I leaned into him, rested my head on his shoulder. 'Gilbert, I'm so frightened.'

'Of what? Nobody's going to find out.'

'No, not of being found out. I'm frightened of myself. Frightened of what I'm going to do next.'

'There's nothing to be frightened of. You're in control, Elizabeth.'

I shook my head. 'No. *You* are in control.' I suspected that Gilbert was stopping me from undoing the spell on Nancy. Although he had told me what I had done was irreversible, he couldn't offer me a reasonable explanation why—after all, we had reversed the charm that turned me into a man. So I had sneaked into Nancy's chamber while she slept and attempted to put her to rights. I had sensed an enormously strong blockage, and had failed to overcome it. Gilbert told me it was Nancy, now aware of my power, who was putting up the defence, but I had my doubts. Gilbert clearly had his own reasons for seeing Nancy out of the picture, not the least being the guarantee of her continued silence.

Footsteps approached, and Gilbert and I took a step back from each other. Rosemary came up the stairs behind us, carrying a tea tray.

'Morning, ma'am, sir,' she said as she passed us.

'Are you taking that up for Nancy?' I asked.

She turned. 'No, ma'am. For Hugh. He won't leave her side. It would hardly be any use to give Nancy something. She won't take in a thing.' There was a brief, accusing glance towards me, then she went on her way.

Gilbert raised an eyebrow. 'What was all that about?'

'She can't understand why I won't heal Nancy. She thinks I'm being cruel.'

'So do I.'

I could feel tears well up in my eyes. 'I can't Gilbert. I can't do it.'

'Death is easy, Elizabeth. Meet me at the cottage tonight. We'll discuss it.'

I nodded briefly, then went on my way.

Autumn was well advanced and soon it would be too cold to creep out of my bed at midnight to join Gilbert at the magic cottage. A light shiver of rain misted over me as I ran across the garden, chilling me in my clothes. Gilbert was not waiting for me in the cottage as he usually was, so I kneeled in front of the fireplace and stirred the coals with a poker. I fell back and sat on the feather mattress and rubbed my hands together. I concentrated into my palms then held them open in front of the grate. A flame leaped out and began to burn low and blue on the dead coals. As I moved my hands in front of the fire it grew and grew until it was a healthy blaze that warmed the room. I lit a lamp and waited for Gilbert. The rain had grown heavy outside and the fat drops clattered off the roof. A lazy somnolence settled over me, and I think I was dozing when Gilbert finally pushed open the door and strode in. He was wet and his boots were muddy, and in his right hand he held a hunting sack. Something squirmed inside it. He cast it to one side and pulled his boots off, then came to sit next to me.

'Elizabeth, my beautiful girl,' he murmured, his face buried in my hair.

'Let's talk about death, Gilbert,' I said.

'Death, Elizabeth? Not love, not desire?'

I shook my head. 'Death is far more pressing tonight. I can't stop thinking about Nancy. Are you sure I can't do anything? Are you sure you couldn't reverse the spell?'

'Even if I could, I wouldn't give her her voice back—we'd be right where we started. She would have her filthy secret and we would always be glancing over our shoulders.'

'And why can nobody see what I've done?'

'The limited mind is easily tricked. It thinks in straight lines. The confined sensibility sees what it has always seen.' Gilbert was stroking the back of my neck. 'Elizabeth, we all die. It isn't hard. It's living in spite of death's presence that's the challenge.'

311

'What will happen to her after she dies? Do you know?'

He pulled my head down into his lap. I stared into the fire while Gilbert's fingers played in my hair. I could feel the warmth and power in his hands, in his body.

'Well, what happens to the Nancys of this world when they die depends on a lot of things. How she has lived her life, how she has served the universe. She may go to her grave and stay there forever; she may be reborn later, many years later, and live another life. As may we all.'

'You and I may live again?'

'You and I will almost certainly live again.'

'And we've lived before?'

'Perhaps. I know I have. I can't be sure about you. Do you ever have memories of another time?'

'No.'

'Then perhaps you haven't.'

I lay there silent for a while, the fire making my eyes water. I closed them and snuggled into Gilbert's lap. 'How does one serve the universe well? How does one ensure rebirth?'

'By working with the energy of the universe. People who spend their lives in service of the mundane have no chance. They squander their energy in pot-stirring and baby-raising and petty gossip. We wrench it from the world with our desires and our transgressions. And because we are marked, we are pure channels for that energy. It flows through us, it pours from our hands and our eyes and our mouths. And we will be reborn. Over and over. We will see civilisations rise and fall, we will know more love and more pleasure in our souls than any other beings since time's nativity.'

I sat up. 'Is that why you perform sorcery? To gain energy for rebirth?'

'It's one reason. Like you I started out of curiosity. I keep going because of the pleasure, the worldly rewards, the rush of power, the freedom to do exactly as I please without fear. But I kill for the energy. Always.' He stood and moved towards the squirming sack. 'Here, let me show you. Come with me.'

I followed him into the back room where the warmth of the fire did not reach. I shivered in the gloom. Gilbert lit a candle and it flickered feebly, casting grim shadows. I huddled close to him. He reached for the copper dish at the back of the shelf and placed it in front of us. His fingers rested on the lip of the vessel. 'Blood,' he said, 'is power. The heart is the soul. The eyes are the mind, the memories. Don't be afraid to take these things.' He handed me a pearl-handled dagger with a wickedly sharp blade. I closed my fingers around the handle, trying not to think about last time I had held such a blade in Gilbert's company.

He picked up the sack and opened it, pulling out a squirming weasel. Holding it firmly by its head and its back legs, he positioned it over the copper dish, belly up.

'Go on,' he said. 'Take the energy and dedicate it to our master.'

'Gilbert, I can't do this.'

'Yes, you can. Call it an experiment. See how it feels.'

I reached forward with the knife, but paused when I saw the struggle the animal was making against Gilbert.

'Gilbert, it doesn't want to die.'

'It has to die one day.'

'It's terrified.'

313

'All the more reason to end its misery quickly.'

I froze in that position, my eyes fixed on the creature.

'Your pity tyrannises your good sense, Elizabeth.'

'How do I do it?'

'One long cut across its throat.' He bent the creature's head back slightly, exposing its throat.

'All right. I'm going to do it.'

'Make it quick. And allow the energy to flow through you, don't be frightened. The universe holds its breath in anticipation of your gift.'

One quick movement and the creature stopped struggling. Blood gurgled out and began to collect in the dish. A rush of hot butterfly wings swept through me and made me gasp. One of my hands flailed out to grab the edge of the bench and steady myself. Just as soon as it had come it was gone. It had been like a minor version of what Gilbert felt when he killed the man in London.

Gilbert rested the animal's body in the copper dish. Its fur grew sticky and clogged with blood. He gently took my hand, with the knife still in it, and guided the point towards the weasel's face. I could see every detail, the subtle variations in colour of the fur, the whiskers with their tips stained red. His hand guided mine in removing the creature's eyes. He flicked them out on the end of the knife and put them in my hand.

'Close your eyes, Elizabeth.'

I closed my eyes. Suddenly I was less than a foot high, my snaky, muscular body trailing behind me as I ran through the grass. In and out between towering bushes and running over twigs, scratching my belly. Into the ground, into the ground, dark, then up again, scurrying through the night. A man chasing me, enormous, hands snatching the air behind me. I opened my eyes and dropped the two tiny organs into the copper dish. They left a bloody smear on my palm.

'I had its last memories,' I said.

'You had all its memories if you wanted them. They wouldn't have been much different. By all accounts, weasels live rather dull lives.' Gilbert reached for one of the jars lining the shelves, opened it and dropped the eyes in. Next he took the knife from me and cut out the animal's heart, prying apart its ribcage with his strong thumbs. 'This is difficult with humans,' he said casually. 'You usually require some kind of axe to get through the bones.'

'I won't be doing this to any people, Gilbert.'

'To each his own.' He popped the heart out and placed it in another jar.

'Come on,' he said, 'let's go out in the rain and wash the mess off ourselves.'

He gently pulled me by the crook of the elbow out into the rain. I held my palms up to the heavens and allowed the water to rinse the blood from my hands. I barely noticed that I was getting soaked through my clothes, I was so deep in thought. Perhaps Gilbert was right. Perhaps death wasn't so hard after all.

'Good morning, Hugh. Is there any change?'

Hugh looked up from his doze next to Nancy's bed. Nancy made a grunting noise when she saw me, but I ignored her and perched on the arm of Hugh's chair. He shook his head sadly. 'She's no better. I'm afraid she's going to—' He coughed on a sob.

I took his hand in mine. 'How long have you been married, Hugh?'

'Twenty-four years.'

'I'm very, very sorry,' I said. And I was.

'Thank you, Lady Elizabeth. Thank you for caring.'

'You should rest now, Hugh.' I felt a small charge leave me and worm its way into his hand. Instantly, his head lolled to one side and he drew the deep, regular breaths of sleep.

My skirts rustled as I moved to sit on the edge of Nancy's bed. She thrashed about, but I pinned her arms to her side and leaned close. Her body stank of stale sweat. Her hair was stringy and her skin like dried apple peel. The place where her mouth used to be was flaky and scarred with red streaks where she had tried to pull it open with her jaws. She made a noise in the back of her throat that may have been the beginnings of a plea for mercy. Well, I was doing this out of mercy.

I let go of one of her hands to reach under her for her pillow. She thumped me roundly on the back of my head, but I merely sat up, the pillow in my hands, and whispered 'Sorry' before placing the pillow firmly over her face and holding it down.

She struggled briefly, but I think perhaps she wanted to die then too. I felt it as her life left her, a bolt of passion shuddered through me, something like pain and pleasure, love and hate and desire blended. I cried out. I said, 'Nancy, I commit you to the universe.' Better than lying in the grave, surely. Better than decaying and being forgotten and trapped forever under the ground.

When the thrill no longer tingled in my wrists, I pulled the pillow off her face and placed it back under her head, straightened her hair and walked to the door on shaking legs. I turned at the doorway and looked back to Hugh. 'Wake in one hour,' I said, then left and shut the door behind me.

*

It rained the day of Nancy's funeral, cold sheets of it driving diagonally across the land while we all stood huddled at the outer edges of the family plot. Mirabel shifted impatiently from foot to foot, Gilbert holding a heavy coat around her. Master Gale read a short sermon while Hugh blubbered unremittingly. His grief seemed to reach into my body and rest like a hard nut in my heart. I couldn't look at him. I stared instead at Nancy's body in its winding sheet, dirt crumbling onto the cloth.

We all thankfully left the graveside when Master Gale was finished, except for Hugh, who stayed to help fill it in, mumbling about putting his lovely wife to final rest. Gilbert wore an expression of boredom. I knew he was completely without conscience, but was he completely without compassion also? Surely not. He loved me, and I suspected he was eagerly awaiting the birth of his little daughter. These were signs that he must have feeling in his heart.

Uncle Tom was fussing around Mirabel, making sure she was keeping dry from the rain, so Gilbert slid over to my side as we walked back to the house. 'You should have bled her.'

'That would have been rather more difficult to conceal.'

'You can conceal anything. You should have asked me for help.'

I glanced around to make sure nobody was listening to us. Mirabel was complaining petulantly to Uncle Tom. The rain had eased a little. 'This was a mercy killing, Gilbert. It had nothing to do with sorcery, except, of course, in its origin.'

'Still, it seems a pity to waste the opportunity,

don't you think? It mustn't have felt particularly tremendous.'

'I didn't do it for the feeling.'

Master Gale was approaching. He fell in step beside us. 'Good morning, Lady Elizabeth, Mr Lewis.'

I greeted him. Gilbert didn't look at him, didn't speak to him.

'It seems the sky is mourning along with us,' Master Gale said.

'It's unfortunate for Hugh. I'm sure he'd love to sit by Nancy's grave all afternoon,' I replied.

'I think he probably still will. I just hope he doesn't catch a fever. It would be a tragedy to have two deaths at Prestonvale so close together. I suppose we'll never know what happened to Nancy, why she took that turn.'

Gilbert finally responded. 'A strike to the brain. I've seen it before, people in the prime of their life turned into simples, their faces locked in a horror mask. She probably received a blow to the head when she fell over in the kitchen.'

'She was certainly agitated about something when she came to see me that morning,' Master Gale replied.

I could see a smile creep over Gilbert's face. 'Was she?'

'Yes. I'd love to know what it was she wanted to tell me so urgently.'

'You'll never know. The dead are very silent.'

Master Gale nodded and headed off towards Uncle Tom.

'Why are you smiling, Gilbert?' I asked.

'Because he was trying to frighten me. Stupid man. But he succeeded on you—you've gone white.'

'He knows, Gilbert. He must know. I tried to get

inside his head in the chapel, but he blocked me. I felt it very strongly.'

'Don't fear him.'

'He speaks with God.'

Anger edged into his voice. 'Then he speaks with no-one. A man who speaks with no-one is a madman, is he not?' He brought his emotions under control and smiled at me, that almost animal smile. 'Elizabeth, stop worrying. Everything goes our way, from here to forever after.'

We trudged in silence back to the house.

I sat at Uncle Tom's feet that evening, a roaring fire in the grate, a book open on my knee, and his hand idly smoothing my hair. He stared into the fire, his eyes glazed. Nancy's death had upset him. I wondered if he thought moving her from her cottage had contributed to her illness. Knowing Uncle Tom, it was highly likely. I dropped my book, which I wasn't reading anyway—I could think of nothing but Hugh wailing by Nancy's grave—and patted his knee.

'Uncle Tom, please cheer up.'

He shook himself out of his reverie. 'It's hard to be cheerful, Elizabeth.'

'I know. But life must go on.'

He nodded, gazed at me for a while. 'It's your birthday on Tuesday.'

'Yes.'

'You'll be twenty-eight. Have you given any more thought to remarrying?'

I shook my head. 'I don't wish to be married.'

'You can marry whom you choose, Elizabeth. I don't mind if he has no title. Gilbert has no title, and I was happy for Mirabel to marry him.'

'Because he has money and connections.'

'I don't care if you marry someone without title or money or connections. I want you to be happy.'

'I am happy.'

He sighed and ran a hand through his hair, so that it stuck up at strange angles at the front. 'Think about it, Elizabeth. Your new husband could live here with us. You wouldn't have to move away.'

'Uncle Tom, why the sudden interest in marrying me off?'

'I think it would do you good.'

'You think wrong.' I watched him closely. 'There's something else bothering you, isn't there?'

He was silent for a few moments. 'How are your painting lessons going?' he asked at length.

'Quite well,' I replied. 'I've done nothing that I'd proudly show anybody yet, however.'

'You and Gilbert seem very close.'

'Yes, I enjoy his company, and he mine.'

'I don't know if it's appropriate.'

I nodded slowly. 'So that's what this is all about. You've been listening to village gossip.' I hoped I appeared calm outwardly, for inwardly I was turning to water.

'No. Mirabel spoke to me.' He looked suitably chastened. 'It's not that I don't trust you, Elizabeth . . .'

'Uncle Tom, please. Mirabel is not Gilbert's intellectual equal, he's a very well-read man. I've always craved such company. If Gilbert and I didn't have each other we'd probably both go mad. I know he loves Mirabel. You must trust me, trust *us*. We both have a sense of propriety.' What a twisting shame it was to lie to him.

'I'm sorry, I'm sorry.' He held his hands out and smiled. I grasped his fingers in my own. He squeezed lightly. 'I do love you, Elizabeth.'

'And I love you.'

'But I have seen the way you look at each other.'

'Gilbert and I?'

'Yes. Over dinner. Today at the funeral. I may be getting old now, but I remember what it was like to be young and to have hot blood running through my body.'

I looked into my lap, ashamed.

'Have you acted on your impulses?' he asked.

'I don't know what you're talking about. Gilbert and I are friends. If there is any spark between us, it's the spark of intellect. That is all.'

'Then if that's your final word on this matter, I believe you.'

'Yes, it's my final word.'

'I'll tell Mirabel to stop worrying.'

'Please do.'

'I'm just concerned about the baby. I don't want Mirabel working herself up into a state and losing the child. He's my last hope.'

I smiled at him. 'He?'

'Yes, it must be a little boy. I couldn't be so unlucky. Gilbert comes from a brood of seven brothers, that must have some bearing.'

I had never thought about Gilbert belonging to a family before. It seemed strange, somehow, that such progeny could spring from an ordinary place. 'Don't count too much on it being a boy, Uncle Tom.'

'It has to be, Elizabeth. For the inheritance. I can leave Prestonvale to Mirabel and Gilbert, but I'd rather leave them an annuity and pass on the property to a male child.'

'You're not to worry, Uncle Tom. If this child is a girl, I'm sure the next will be a fit heir.'

I turned back to my book, idly flicking the pages. I was wondering how it would all turn out for Uncle

Tom. Gilbert had told me that some of the future was created in the present, and therefore the future could be partly known. Generally, though, he believed fortune-telling was the domain of the mad spinsters and piss-prophets he scowled upon. I closed my eyes and leaned back into Uncle Tom's legs. He stroked my hair. The fire bathed me in warmth. What was going to happen?

I had a quick flash of vision—Uncle Tom, older, greyer, his mottled hands around the waist of a young girl of about nine or ten. She had blonde hair like Mirabel, yet her face was darker, more striking than Mirabel's. Uncle Tom was helping her fasten her dress. He smiled, but I could sense desolation, emptiness in him. And fear, somehow he was afraid of the little girl. The vision passed just as quickly as it had come and I opened my eyes to find I was still in the warm sitting room. I looked up at Uncle Tom.

'Everything will be all right,' I said. 'You're not to worry.'

CHAPTER
TWENTY-ONE

The foul weather continued for days, right up until the day before my birthday. When the sun came out again, it wasn't the sun it had been before the rain. It was the incipient winter's sun, removed from the earth by a great distance, and glimmering rather than shining in the pale sky. A high breeze had begun the work of stripping the trees, and their branches, like poor bare bones, were exposed to the chill of the early mornings.

I set out early to walk by the river by myself, which I hadn't done for an age. I needed the time and space to consider what I had done, and what I was going to do. Gilbert and I hadn't been together at the cottage since the night we killed the weasel, the weather having been prohibitive.

So I immersed myself in the sounds and smells of the damp bracken beneath my feet, the birds twittering cautiously, the river whispering its secrets to its banks as, pregnant with a week's rain, it curved on its way to some freezing ocean that I would never see. But perhaps I would see it now. Perhaps I was not forever trapped in the life of a woman, perhaps there was still some excitement for me in the world.

I heard a sound behind me and turned to see Gilbert approaching. Something contracted around my heart, and I realised I wanted to be alone, away from everybody, him included. I wanted to feel as if I owned my life, rather than as if I were borrowing it from a man with a stronger claim than mine. I turned away and kept walking as though I hadn't noticed him. He called out but I ignored him. In a few short seconds he had caught me around the wrist and turned me to face him.

'Elizabeth?' His voice betrayed surprise and more than a little annoyance.

'I just want to be alone for a while, that's all,' I said, pulling my wrist away from him.

'Alone, Elizabeth?'

'I need to think.'

He smiled, a wicked smile that betrayed his baser desires. 'You don't need to think, you need to make love.' He tried to pull me into his arms and I resisted weakly.

'Is that your answer to everything, Gilbert?'

'Come, let me make you forget everything. Let me transport you to the seashore.' He closed his lips over mine and the warmth of the tropical sun eased into my bones. I relaxed into it for a moment, then realised that he had won again and made an effort to block his magic from my mind. The warmth retreated, the cool forest trembled on the edge of my perception then solidified around me. He pressed his lips harder into mine, then pulled back momentarily and said, 'You're blocking me.'

Again he tried to force his thoughts into my mind, and I resolutely focused against them. Gilbert grasped me violently around the upper arms and held me away at arm's length. It seemed to require an effort for him to stop himself from shaking me.

'Don't block me,' he hissed, and the anger radiated out of him in frightening waves.

'Why not? Afraid I won't do your bidding any more?' He was scaring me, but I wasn't going to let him see that.

'You know that's not what I want from you.' He smiled a conciliatory smile. 'Come, Elizabeth. Let me kiss you.'

My body relaxed as his anger evaporated. 'I'll let you kiss me, just don't try to get inside my head.'

'I can't any more. Obviously.' Dull acceptance, but still a hint of annoyance.

'You taught me everything I know, Gilbert. Blame yourself if I've learned too much.' I went willingly to his arms and we embraced; he ground his body into mine. His mouth was at my neck, his beard scratching my delicate skin.

'Come to the magic cottage tonight, Elizabeth,' he said between kisses on my earlobe. 'I want to give you a present for your birthday.'

'A present? What is it?'

'Something you need.'

'Will I like it?'

He didn't answer, he was too busy pushing up my petticoats and turning me to face a tree. I put my arms around the rough bark and pressed my face into it. It was slightly damp and smelled of the tang of rain. He ran his hands over my buttocks and between my legs. I looked to the sky glowing dimly beyond the canopy of trees. I still wanted to be alone.

Gilbert pressed his face into my shoulder and entered me from behind. 'You're tiring of me,' he said as he thrust away. I was surprised by the note of sadness that coloured his words.

'Never,' I protested. 'I love you forever, I promise.'

'Be careful what you promise.' He squared himself up against me and hammered at my body. No blinding ecstasy this time, no pulsing spasms. Just two people rutting like animals in the mud.

I huddled close to the fire in the cottage, my knees drawn up to my chest and my cold hands as close to the grate as I dared bring them. I waited for Gilbert one hour, two hours. I read a book, pulled the mattress closer to the fire and kept waiting. When I was finally convinced he wasn't coming and that I should go back to the comfort of my own bed, I heard him at the door. I turned to see him come in, covered in muddy earth from knees to feet, wrists to elbows. Even his hair had clumps of mud in it, and his face was splattered with it.

'What happened?' I asked.

'I've been a busy lad. Hold out your hand and close your eyes, I have your present here.' He had one hand concealed under his mantle.

I eyed him with more than a little suspicion. 'Have you been out chasing weasels again?'

'No, no. Come on, Elizabeth, hold out your hand.'

I held out my hand and he came to kneel next to me, leaving a muddy imprint on the mattress. 'And close your eyes.'

I closed my eyes. I heard his cloak rustle. I felt something cold and wet on my palm, and I honestly thought for a moment that he had filled my hand with a blob of mud, but then I opened my eyes and shrieked. He had dropped a pair of eyeballs into my palm. Before I could throw them away from me, he had closed his hand over mine. 'They're Nancy's,' he said. 'They really belong to you.'

'Gilbert, no. Let me go. It makes me ill even to think—'

'But after all the trouble I went to.'

My mind reeled with trying to comprehend what was happening. He had dug up her grave, torn open her winding sheet, desecrated her remains. Did he honestly think I would appreciate this gesture? I looked at him watching me. Was this was a cruel joke? Was he paying me back for my indifference to him in the forest this afternoon? He had my hand in a vicelike grip and was not letting go.

'Let me go.'

'No. Don't you want to experience her memories?'

I looked down at our interlocked hands. He knew how to tempt me. He had awoken my curiosity.

'Tempted, Elizabeth?'

'No. Just let me go.'

'Think about not thinking, Elizabeth.'

A tingle in my palm. 'No, Gilbert. I don't want to.'

'Yes you do.'

In a new russet dress. Eating a pear on a sunny door step. About four or five years old.

'I don't. Let me go.'

A young and handsome Hugh on top of me, grunting in newly-wed passion.

'Elizabeth, you're already doing it.'

A dark-haired woman, pale skin, beautiful wide-spaced eyes . . . Lady Elizabeth, be afraid of Lady Elizabeth. How awful to realise I was beautiful in the same moment that I discovered I was evil.

'Is it good, Elizabeth?'

I want to scream but I have no mouth. What bedevilment is this? She's going to kill me, and I don't want to die. I'm afraid to die.

I wrenched my hand away from him and threw the eyes into the fire. 'No more!'

'What's the matter, Elizabeth?'

'No more! I'll have an end to it. I don't want to

meet you here any more, Gilbert. I don't want to learn any more of your foul trickery, I don't want to be involved in any more deaths, I don't want to do this any more.' I climbed to my feet.

'Don't be foolish—'

'Just be quiet!' I shouted. 'I know what I want. I'm not an idiot. You've taught me nothing but parlour tricks and haven't warned me of the dangers of my power. I've made a hideous mistake that had to be buried, how long before I accidentally do it again? Where is the magic? Why haven't you taught me alchemy, raising storms, curses and blessings? I'm half damned, half ignorant. I'll have an end to it.' I turned from him and headed towards the door. I managed to pull it open about four inches, but then the handle was wrenched from my hands by some invisible force and the door slammed shut in front of me. I turned back to Gilbert. He sat there with a look like nightfall on his face.

'Open the door,' I hissed.

The fire surged in the grate and began to pop and sizzle eerily.

'Open the door and let me go.'

The door swung inwards violently and slammed into my body. I stumbled back a few paces. Gilbert had turned away from me and was looking into the fire, which had subsided to its original size. I left as quickly as I could.

It was more difficult for Gilbert and me to hide our anger than it had been for us to hide our love. Forcing ourselves to be pleasant in the company of others felt as if we were tossing a bright ball back and forth over a dark abyss. Every word spoken to each other in mock pleasant discourse was heavy with possible meaning. I excused myself early from dinner for a couple of days in a row, pleading weariness, and went to my room to lie down. When in my bed, I would gaze at the pattern in the tapestry above me, unravelling the coloured threads in my mind and trying to forget that I loved the man. Eventually I would drop off into a light afternoon doze and only wake when the shadows of evening were stretching their bony fingers across my room. I would go fitfully about my evening's work, moping between the study and the sitting room until night came and I was once more trapped inside my bed with only my thoughts for company.

Two weeks after our disagreement, a rattling sound woke me from my slumber around midnight. I sat up in my bed and listened. There it was again, a loud rattle against the window. I pulled back the hangings and emerged into the cold night. Somebody was throwing pebbles at the glass. I lit a candle with freezing hands and went to the window to look down.

'Elizabeth,' Gilbert called from below my window. I pushed it open and leaned out.

'Elizabeth, come down.'

'Shh,' I urged him in alarm. I could barely make out his dark figure.

'Don't worry. They're all asleep. I've put them all under an enchantment, except that fool Master Gale, who wouldn't go under. I've locked him in his room. With a bit of luck he won't notice.'

'What are you talking about? What have you done?'

'I want you to come down. I have a surprise for you.'

'If it's anything like the last surprise . . .'

'No, no. This is my apology. I love you, Elizabeth. I love you.'

I peered into the darkness. His pale face shone dimly in the gloom. 'No. I won't come down. I don't trust you any more, Gilbert.'

'Please, Elizabeth.'

'No.'

He fell silent, and I was withdrawing into my room when he called out: 'Wait. Don't go inside. Stay there. I'll give you your surprise anyway, you don't have to come down.'

'Gilbert—'

'No, wait. Stay right there. It will only take a moment.'

I waited. I heard no sounds, and Gilbert was still a dark blur beneath my window. I thought I saw him raise his arms, but perhaps that was a trick of my vision. I eventually became aware that he was making a low moaning noise, like a martyr praying. I leaned further out the window.

'Gilbert, what are you doing?'

He didn't answer. The noise continued. A quick breeze was picking up, stirring the trees and snuffing out my candle. I looked up to the sky as though I might see where it was coming from. It grew in strength until it was a strong wind swooping down from the sky in great gulps. It whipped my hair into my face. I tucked the loose strands behind my ears. A distant rumble sounded. Thunder.

'Gilbert? Is that you? Are you making this?'

Now the wind was howling down the alley between the house and the chapel, and a loose stable door thudded in the distance. I looked up to the sky again and saw that the stars were being blocked out by a fast-moving storm front. Again thunder rumbled, but this time closer. Gilbert made a heavy, guttural sound. I thought I saw him fall to his knees. I raced from the window to my door, then down the stairs and through the kitchen. I hauled open the door and stepped into the storm. The wind pelted icy shards of rain into my thick nightgown. I found Gilbert under my window, on his knees and with his hands spread on the ground in front of him. I went to his side but he looked up like an animal in a trap.

'Stay back!' he shouted. I took a few steps away from him, and he pulled himself to his feet, slowly and fluidly as if he were growing out of the ground in fast motion. I watched him fascinated and terrified. He let out a sudden cry and cast his arms into the air. Instantly, lightning jumped from the sky and thunder cracked overhead. I shrieked in spite of myself. He was magnificent in the instant of blinding light that illuminated him, then he was on his knees again.

'Gilbert, are you hurt?'

'No.' Again he pulled himself up. This time I raced towards him and clasped him around the torso. As he threw his arms into the air and called the lightning down, I felt the charge run through him and fuse me momentarily to his body. I cried out with him.

The lightning flash faded and he kissed my face. 'Come down with me, come down with me,' he said, panting with exhaustion. I moved to the ground with him, touched the earth as he touched the earth, murmured the insensible half language he murmured, pulled myself up and cried out the magic un-word, and lightning forked from the sky like the voice of God.

Gilbert pressed me to him. 'I love you, and I love you, and I love you,' he said over and over. Our bodies were hot in spite of the freezing rain. We tore our clothes from each other and fell to the ground entwined. The storm clattered overhead. Once again, we were one.

*

By mid-December, Hugh was dead and I was a 'grete clerke of necromancye' like Morgan le Fay in Malory's romance. The old man withered and grew pale with a fever he had picked up at Nancy's graveside, and would take no help for a cough that kept us all awake at night. He rattled off one afternoon and we buried him in the dew-drenched morning of the next day. Now I had two deaths on my hands.

But it was hard to feel guilt or sadness when I was locked away most nights with Gilbert in the magic cottage, learning how to make rain, read minds, transform objects, make them disappear, or make them move with thought alone. Gilbert and I had taken to dancing around the room to a symphony of clattering jars and bowls which jumped and jittered on the bench in perfect common time. One evening I made the ornamental legs on the copper dish come to life, and the thing raced around the room with us chasing it like children chasing a reluctant kitten.

I learned astutely and improved with dangerous speed. I could sense that Gilbert's pride in my achievements was mixed with a degree of unease, especially now I had learned to block him out of my thoughts. It was simply a matter of building an imaginary wall of light around my mind. It frustrated him a great deal because it signalled the loosening of his control over me, but he continued teaching me, afraid of another breach in our relationship.

Perhaps the most significant thing I learned was what my limits were. I was drawing much of my power from Gilbert, without him my magic skills were weak and patchy. It finally became clear to me why Gilbert was so obsessed with death—the deaths of others provided him with a seamless, soaring command of magic. The universe, I was beginning to understand, was amoral and chaotic, and rewarded him for such transgressions. And the more excessive the transgression, the more the spirits crowded around him, gasping to do his bidding. Animals, he said, weren't worth much, old people little more; the wise, the young, the pious, the powerful: these were the deaths that mattered. I was afraid to ask him how often he killed. Apart from the cutpurse, I saw no evidence that he was killing during our relationship. I honestly didn't want to know, thinking the truth might nourish my guilt and drown the desires that kept me striving for more knowledge.

But although I still loved Gilbert and was in awe of his power, since our quarrel our physical relationship had lost its intensity. Maybe it was because Gilbert no longer crept into my head with seductive visions. Maybe I was just used to his body and the thrill of novelty had departed. Our love-making was still pleasant, but I no longer desired him with my whole being. I didn't know whether Gilbert felt the same way about me. We didn't discuss it.

By December it was too cold to go to the cottage, so we agreed to a break. The four of us would sit in the winter parlour, a huge fire roaring, enjoying something akin to domestic bliss. Uncle Tom would gaze into the fire; Mirabel, her loose-bodied gown growing tighter every day, would make her ham-fisted attempts at embroidery; Gilbert and I would read, discuss, debate. Sometimes Uncle Tom would join in, and I was surprised to find his propositions thoughtful and analytic. Mirabel piped up in rare moments, telling us that we were all terribly boring, and Gilbert would kiss her face and tell her she was pretty.

One snowy afternoon the week before Christmas, Rosemary came running in, brimming over with the excitement of having news. My Italian was steadily improving, and I was reading Tasso's *Gerusalemme Liberata*, but the light was growing dim and my eyes were straining to see the page in front of me. I was glad of the interruption.

'There's somebody here, Sir Thomas,' Rosemary cried. 'Two young men, they're lost and the snow prevents them from going further.' She turned to face me and said breathlessly, 'They're minstrels.'

'Minstrels?' I stood up. 'Uncle Tom, can they stay? It's been so long since we've had music. Mirabel didn't practise the virginal and now it gathers dust upstairs.'

Mirabel squeaked a protest, but I ignored her.

'Let's see them,' Uncle Tom said to Rosemary. 'Show them through, and tell somebody to prepare Hugh and Nancy's old room for them. You can fix us all an early supper.'

She curtsied and backed out of the room. We heard her footsteps clatter towards the kitchen door. Uncle Tom motioned me to sit down again, and he lit a lamp so that we could all see better. Shortly Rosemary returned with two men following her.

'Sir,' she said, 'this is Mr Ben Archer and Mr Will Finn.' She scurried out and left the two men standing in front of us. Ben was small and thin, with bulging eyes and a scruffy beard. His companion was another thing altogether. Young and soft of face, dark, curly hair, full lips and beautiful hazel eyes which met my own then looked away quickly, as if frightened by the desire they saw there. Uncle Tom introduced us all, and when he turned to me and said, 'And this is my niece, Lady Elizabeth Moreton', Will went down gallantly on one knee and kissed my hand.

'Lady Elizabeth,' he said, 'a pleasure to meet you.' His hot breath on my fingers thrilled me. I knew then where this would go, but nothing could prepare me for how it would end.

Ben played lute, Will was a countertenor. After supper, we returned to the parlour where, for Uncle Tom's kindness in providing a room for the night, they entertained us with their songs. The music was delightful, and Will's voice as angelic as his appearance. I had barely noticed Gilbert all evening, except when he had leaned close at supper and said to me: 'He's smooth, he's beautiful, but he's stupid. Don't be ruled by your loins.' I had merely smiled and ignored him. I presumed he was teasing. Gilbert had once said he had no need for my fidelity, and I believed he meant it.

They played Christmas carols and secular ballads. My eyes pricked with tears over tales of lost love; I squealed with laughter over bawdy ballads that made Mirabel blush, and I clapped after each song until my hands tingled. There was a magic in music that didn't have to do with killing and suckling evil familiars. I was transported by it.

Shortly before midnight, when Mirabel had drooped in her chair and Uncle Tom's yawns were getting closer and closer together, much to my disappointment Ben and Will stopped.

'Oh, just one more,' I pleaded.

'Elizabeth, our guests are tired,' Gilbert replied. 'Be kind to them.'

'Tomorrow evening, Lady Elizabeth,' Ben replied. 'If we can have lodging over Christmas, perhaps we can play for you again tomorrow evening.'

I looked to Uncle Tom who nodded. 'Of course you can stay. I wouldn't be much of a Christian if I turned you out at Christmas time.'

One by one we began to stand and stretch our legs, readying to head upstairs to bed. I wanted to speak further to Will, but couldn't see a chance with everyone around us. He seemed to sense this, and we both dallied as others called their goodnights and left the room. Only Gilbert remained, leaning on the back of a chair watching me.

'Your wife awaits you,' I said.

'I hope you sleep well, Elizabeth. It's a cold night for widows in their beds.' He turned to Will. 'I can show you up to your room if you like. It seems your companion has gone on ahead of you.'

'I know where it is, thank you,' Will replied courteously.

'I insist,' Gilbert said.

Will looked at me helplessly, then back to Gilbert. 'Of course, sir. Thank you.'

They left together, and I collapsed back into my seat to sulk.

The next day I was following my nose to a glorious smell of something rich and cakey cooking in the kitchen, when I found Will and Ben sitting in front of the big wood stove listening to Rosemary's gossip. As I came in, Rosemary shot out of her seat and made as if she were busy.

'Good morning, ma'am,' she said, making a pretence of clattering some pots and pans about.

'Good morning. Sharing gossip, were you, Rosemary?'

'Oh, only a little, ma'am. Just about the villagers.' The way her cheeks flushed told me that perhaps I had been the chief subject of her storytelling.

I stood next to the table and looked down at Will and Ben. 'I trust you were comfortable last night, sirs?'

'Yes, my lady,' Ben replied. 'It's the first good

night's sleep we've had in some time.' He then launched into a detailed narrative of their accommodation arrangements since they had set out two weeks ago, but I wasn't listening. I was trying to think of a way to get Will alone. He sat there at the table, occasionally darting shy glances at me or favouring me with a small smile. Ben continued his tale, Rosemary hanging on his every word. I reminded myself I was the mistress of the house and as such could exercise my will however I desired. I pulled up the chair next to Will and sat down, ignoring Ben.

'Mr Finn?'

'Yes, my lady.'

'Do you read, sir?'

Ben piped up. 'I read, ma'am. Just put me in front of a bookshelf and I can be entertained for hours.'

Will shot me another of those shy glances. 'Yes, my lady. A little.'

'Are you acquainted with the delights of Spenser's *Faerie Queene*?'

'No, ma'am, I don't believe I am.'

Ben was prattling again. I reached across in front of Will and caught Ben's wrist in my hand. 'Perhaps you'd like to help Rosemary in the kitchen this morning,' I said to him. 'You have so much in common.'

Rosemary 'oohed' and giggled like a simple. I felt a tingle leave my palm. Ben looked up at Rosemary. 'Yes, that sounds like a fine way to spend the morning.'

'Mr Finn,' I said to Will, 'please accompany me upstairs. I swear I love that book so much that it would give me great delight to share it with another.'

'Of course, my lady,' he replied, standing and helping me out of my chair.

'Rosemary, if Sir Thomas is looking for me, I'm

in the spinning room. If Mr Lewis is looking for me, you don't know where I am.'

'Yes, ma'am.' She curtsied.

I decided to take Will to the spinning room. I didn't want Gilbert finding us, and he would never happen upon us up there. It was called the spinning room because a spindle and a small loom stood there, but nobody ever used them, so the room had become the dumping ground for extravagant toys that we had tired of.

I quickly dashed into my chamber on the way up to grab my *Faerie Queene*, then took Will's hand and led him to the spinning room. It was on the warm side of the house, and a little weak sunshine struggled through the grimy windows. I looked around. There was nowhere to sit, every available surface was cluttered with junk. I pointed towards an Indian rug rolled up in the corner. 'Will, could you bring that over in front of the fireplace?'

He nodded and turned to fetch the rug. While he wasn't looking I lit a fire with my hands, then began to shove things out of the way to clear a space in front. We unrolled the rug there and sat down together. He seemed uncomfortable at first but I kept conversation light and natural and he began to settle. He flicked through the pages of my book then handed it back to me.

'Go on, Lady Elizabeth,' he said. 'It's your turn to entertain me.'

I began to read, at the start of book three, which was my favourite, and the morning soon slipped away. Every time I looked up from the page, his eyes—those lashes were so dark—would be fixed on my face. When it was time for dinner, I closed the book and rested it in my lap.

'Same time tomorrow, Will?' I asked, stroking his

338

chin gently with my fingers. He caught my fingers in his hand and kissed them individually. My stomach fluttered.

'Of course, my lady.'

Oh, I wanted him. He promised to be as sweet and lush as the first cherries of the season. I leaned in to kiss him, but as I did there was a rap at the door and I drew back swiftly. Mirabel let herself in. She stared goggle-eyed at the two of us sitting on the carpet together, then collected herself.

'Rosemary said you were up here. Are you coming down for dinner? We're waiting for you.'

Will was looking into his lap, a guilty flush creeping over his face.

'We'll be down presently,' I said. Then I waved my hand away. 'Go on.'

When she left, Will looked back up at me. 'I don't want to get you into any trouble.'

'You won't. She's a silly thing. She will have forgotten about us by the time she reaches the bottom of the stairs.'

He nodded slowly. I touched his hair. 'Tomorrow?' I asked.

'Yes, tomorrow.'

That evening they sang for us, and the next morning Will and I met once again in the spinning room. By this time, I was dewy-eyed and besotted with his wistful glances, his shy reverence, and the hot kisses he laid solemnly on my fingertips. I read to him again, his head lying in my lap, my fingers idly twining in his hair. One of his long, pale hands was curled around my knee for most of the day. I had forgotten that Gilbert existed. He appeared a sour old man compared to my sweet young boy.

That evening, as Ben and Will played for us again, Gilbert was sitting next to me stroking his beard. I couldn't stop myself glancing from his profile—dark, dramatic, commanding—to Will's angelic face. Something about it felt like waking up from a long slumber.

Uncle Tom leaned into me during one Christmas ballad and said, 'He's very like Kit, isn't he, that young fellow?'

It gave me a sanctioned chance to gaze at my beloved's face. Yes, he was very like my first husband, the notable difference being that Will adored me, while Christopher had been colder than ice.

I looked back to Uncle Tom, who was favouring me with a knowing smile.

'What?' I asked.

'You admire him, don't you?'

I smiled back. 'Uncle Tom, that's a rather forward question.'

'You've been in high spirits ever since he arrived. And you've been spending a lot of time with him upstairs reading poetry. If I know my Elizabeth, perhaps she's losing her heart.'

'Don't be silly.' He didn't know his Elizabeth. He would die of shock if he knew his Elizabeth. He grasped my hand and held onto it, and fell silent to listen to the music.

The next morning I was too busy with Christmas preparations to sit with Will in the spinning room, and I ached a little inside for want of his presence. We sat across from each other at dinner, stealing glances. Gilbert kept trying to draw me into one debate or another, but I conceded every point to him, all my intellectual energy already occupied constructing the perfect scene for Will's seduction. I wanted to wait no longer. Over dinner I rehearsed in my head what to say to him, and as the others were leaving I grabbed his hand and pulled him into the kitchen.

'Get out,' I said to Rosemary, who gaped at me

before dropping what she was doing and scurrying into the hallway.

I leaned close to Will. 'Tonight,' I said.

'Tonight,' he repeated with a nod.

'My door is the third on the right at the top of the stairs. Wait one hour for everyone else to go to sleep. Do not knock. I'll leave it ajar.'

'Yes, Lady Elizabeth.' He took my hand and turned it over, planted a burning kiss on my palm. My head swam with desire.

After a long afternoon, a late supper and more Christmas music, I went to wait in the dark of my room, every nerve in my body tingling in anticipation. The hour passed slowly, sweetly, torturously, before finally I heard a light step outside my room, then the door closing behind Will as he came in.

'Lady Elizabeth?' he said in the dark.

'Here,' I went to him and he enclosed me in warm arms. He clasped my face in his fingers and he kissed me deeply. I almost fell into a swoon. My body bent immediately to his will—there was not a fibre in me that could resist him.

'Ah, you're beautiful, ma'am,' he murmured.

'Come to my bed,' I said when my powers of speech had returned. I led him towards the warmth under the canopy.

The sounds of our deepening breathing mingled with the rustling of our clothes as we struggled out of them. I melted into his body as he pressed me against his warm, bare chest.

'Lady Elizabeth, I have nothing, I'm not good enough for you.'

'You have everything I want right here in this bed,' I replied.

He was smothering me in kisses. 'If I had the

whole world, it wouldn't be enough to show you how I love you.'

'You love me?'

'Yes, my lady. Yes, I love you.' He pushed me onto my back and was lost in my body, murmuring some sweet, secret language against my flesh. He was so different from Gilbert—gentle, slow, moaning and weeping with delight as we made love. Finally, spent and sleepy, I sent him back to his own room. I lay a while looking up into the darkness.

He loved me. His only failing.

CHAPTER
TWENTY-TWO

The smells of Christmas Eve always reminded me of my childhood. The sweet, smoky smell of roasting nuts, the tang of a pine branch decorated with ribbon in the parlour, wood burning in every grate in the house, and the mingled scents of veal, mutton, spices and sweet pastries drifting from the kitchen.

The servants opened and aired the large dining room, which was used for special occasions, and began to decorate it for the only dinner of the year that we shared with them. I rose full of Christmas cheer, and greeted each of the servants in the kitchen with a 'God be with you' or a 'Merry Christmas' as I poked into all the ovens to see what was cooking. I plucked a hot butternut cake from a cooling tray on the table and headed towards the study, throwing the sweet from hand to hand because it was too hot to hold. I clamped it gingerly between my teeth as I opened the door, only to drop it as Gilbert crept up behind me and grabbed me suddenly around the waist.

'Elizabeth, you're in a very merry mood this morning. I heard you playing quite the magnanimous mistress with the servants.'

'Yes. Well, it's Christmas.'

'Time to be full of goodwill. Or should I say, good Will?'

I was annoyed by what appeared to be an uncharacteristic bout of jealousy on his part. I extricated myself from his grasp and turned to face him. 'Thank you,' I said, 'I did have some goodwill last night.'

'You're loose in the loins.'

'And that's why you love me,' I replied lightly.

'Do I?'

'Yes, you say you do.'

'And did our friend mount you like a slow-witted bull mounts a gatepost? Or was he more like a spotted youth, three quick thrusts and a slap on the bare backside?'

'Why, Gilbert, I believe you're jealous.'

'And you're a whore out of control.'

'Whose control? Yours perhaps?'

He fell silent.

'Gilbert, you encourage me to indulge in these pleasures.'

'But only while I'm there. You can be tumbled by both of them—the bug-eyed one as well—hellfire, every male with hard thighs in the village can climb on top of you, as long as I'm there.'

'That's more than a little perverse, don't you think?'

A servant went past with a broom and we fell silent for a moment. When we were alone again, I said: 'Gilbert, this is my private life. Please allow me that room.' And then when I realised that what I said amounted to asking for permission, I got angry and corrected myself. 'No, I *demand* that room. It's my right. You, of all people, should support me.'

He squeezed my hand once—not tenderly, but violently—and went on his way. I picked my cake off the floor, eyed it carefully and decided to feed it to the dogs.

*

Kit had always said that the ungodly go in danger of judgement by practising sin on Christmas Eve. However, I felt that if judgement were a reality, it was probably too late for me to heed that warning. In contrast to previous evenings, I couldn't wait for Ben and Will to stop making their music and retire, knowing that my young lover would be with me all the sooner. Once again I instructed Will to come to my room in one hour—which would make it midnight, and a very holy hour for unholy deeds—and I let him kiss my hand with the lips that I now knew intimately.

Again I sat in my room and waited. An hour passed, and my heart thudded quickly in my throat. But he didn't come. I waited a further hour, by which time I was growing sleepy and decided to lie in bed to wait, thinking Will must be held up by his companion. The next time I opened my eyes, I could hear morning birds waking outside, and I realised that Will had not come. I worried briefly about my desirability, then thought no more on it until I went downstairs to greet Christmas Day.

Mirabel stood by the window in the winter parlour, hands crossed over her expanding belly, gazing out at the snow which glimmered dimly in the weak morning light.

'Season's greetings, Mirabel,' I said, going to her and kissing her. She smiled in surprise, unused to me being so friendly. I patted her stomach gently. 'How's our little girl today?'

'The one in here? She's craving some of those cakes that Rosemary cooked yesterday, but there are none left. Did you hear the musicians leave?'

'Leave?'

345

'Yes. They're gone this morning, without a word to anyone, without a sound or a thank you. I knew it was a mistake to let vagabonds like that into the house. I wouldn't be surprised to find they'd stolen a few things.'

I felt something sink inside me. Disappointment, but maybe a little fear. To disappear like that in such bad weather seemed odd. Especially as Ben had spoken of staying until after New Year. Especially as Will had proclaimed his love for me just two nights ago.

'Are you sad, Elizabeth?' Mirabel asked. 'I think Will liked you. He didn't take his eyes off you the whole time. You're probably safer without him in the house. People think strange things about widows.'

My ears had begun to ring faintly, and I had a strong sense that something terrible had happened. 'No, I'm not sad. You're probably right.' My voice seemed to come from a long way away.

'It was nice to have the music though, wasn't it? . . . Elizabeth?'

My chest felt constricted. I needed fresh air. 'Excuse me, Mirabel,' I said. 'I've left a book down at the cottage.'

'You have so many books.'

Uncle Tom came in and tried to close me in a Christmas hug, but I slipped past him. 'Sorry, Uncle Tom, I'll be back shortly.'

'Elizabeth?'

I heard Mirabel speak to him as I disappeared down the hallway. 'She's upset about the musicians. I think she liked Will.'

I went to the kitchen, ignoring Rosemary's Christmas greeting, and pulled open the door to the frozen day outside. I could see a dark patch on the snow halfway to the cottage. I began to walk towards it.

'Lady Elizabeth, you'll catch your death. Put something warm on . . . You'll ruin your shoes.'

I ignored her. The dark patch got larger and larger, until I stood in front of it. Blood on the snow. The striking contrast of colours would have been beautiful were it not such a clear sign of evil. Back at the house, I could hear Rosemary calling out, then she dropped her voice and I heard her say: 'Mr Lewis, you'd better go after her. I think she's in a daze.'

I spun around and saw Gilbert advancing from the house. He turned back momentarily and aimed a finger at the kitchen door, which slammed shut, then continued towards me. He was dressed completely in black, even his eyes seemed black. I was terrified of him. My joints had turned to water, and it was all I could do to stand up.

'Gilbert . . .'

'Yes, Elizabeth.'

'There's blood on the snow.'

'I see no blood.'

'It won't work, Gilbert. I see it.'

'Nobody else will.'

My heart contracted with a horrible, twisting pain. I could barely choke my words out. 'You killed them. You killed *him*.'

He didn't reply. He was standing too close for my liking. 'How could you? How could you . . . ? Will you kill me one day?' I asked.

'No.'

'How can I trust you?'

'I promise I will never hurt you. I love you.'

'I don't like your love. It's frightening me.' I fought back sobs, my eyes bulged trying to take in the terrifying twin visions of Gilbert all in black and the garish red splashes on the snow.

'Elizabeth, I had to do it.'

'No, you didn't. You acted out of petty jealousy. Sweet Jesus.' My imagination was reconstructing their murders, Will's murder. I was struck by the enormity of the deed. 'My God, Gilbert. *What have you done?*'

'They were nobody.'

'Will was somebody. Oh, I'm going to be sick.'

'Come back to the house.' He tried to catch my hand in his, but I pulled it away and screamed.

'No! God, no. Never. Never touch me again. I should never have let you back into my life.'

'Elizabeth, calm down.'

'No. You're evil.'

'Then so are you.'

'Not any more. I hate you. I *despise* you. I'll have nothing more to do with you.'

'And return to the life you had before I came along? I hardly think you'll do that, Elizabeth.'

'Just leave me alone.' I began to walk towards the house.

'You'll want me back.'

'Never. I swear.'

'Don't swear, it's dangerous.'

'I *swear*, I will never want you back. You appal me.' My face was contorting with the effort of keeping my passions in check. Something inside me felt empty and tragic, knowing it was over, but I was terrified, furious, sickened. I wanted nothing more to do with him. 'I'm through with your evil magic.'

'You're still marked.'

'I'll starve the spirits that feed there.'

'You can't. It's for eternity.'

'I'm not listening to you any more, you're full of deception.'

'And you're deceiving yourself. You know what you are by now, don't you? You're a witch. You're a witch for always.'

I ignored him and returned to the house. My feet were freezing, and I sat down to thaw them in front of the fire in the kitchen. Rosemary fluttered about making sure I was warm enough. Gilbert came inside and walked through the kitchen without saying a word. Rosemary shrunk from him visibly, taking two steps towards the table as he passed. When he had gone, she said to me: 'There's something unnatural about Mr Lewis, Lady Elizabeth. He frightens me.'

I sat looking at the pots hanging on the chain, the knives arranged in the block. I stood and grabbed a short-bladed knife, and held it in the fire until the blade turned black. 'Have you got a clean cloth, Rosemary?'

She laughed nervously. 'Don't look so serious, Lady Elizabeth, or I'd think you were going up there to cut Mr Lewis's throat. You were arguing about something weren't you?'

'God's teeth, woman, don't be stupid. Of course I'm not going to cut his throat.' Though in my current state of mind, it would have been satisfying.

Rosemary fetched me a cloth. I soaked it in some water boiling in a pan on the stove. 'I'm not feeling well,' I said. 'I'm going to my room and I'm not to be disturbed. Tell Uncle Tom.'

'Yes, ma'am.'

I took the knife and the cloth and slunk upstairs to my room, bolting the door after me.

I pulled a chair in front of the fire, took off my gown and smock and sat naked. I wiped the blade clean and pulled the flesh of my thigh around so I could see the witch-mark. I tapped it with the point of the knife—nothing. I dragged the blade lightly across the skin surrounding it—it tingled with life. I clamped my teeth against each other and pierced the soft skin. The pain sliced into my brain like something made of hot iron. Blood, bright scarlet, ran out and pooled between my legs. I could barely make my hand move to cut the witch-mark out, marking a circle of gore on my smooth flesh, then chipping underneath it. I thought I felt something hammering the skin from within, then was horrified to see a grotesque face push its way out and moan, then disappear. Another one appeared beside it. I grunted and gasped, but wouldn't let myself scream. The faces were stretching and distorting all over my leg, opening their mouths in moans of pain, then dissolving into nothing. One last slice and I had the flimsy piece of flesh with the witch-mark in my hand. I cast it into the fire. My thigh bled as though it wouldn't stop. I pressed the cloth against it and held on. The cold air stung my skin in spite of the roaring fire. I wrapped the wound in the cloth and went to bed, and refused to come out to wish anyone a merry Christmas.

By New Year, the flesh was completely healed, and the witch-mark had grown back. Truly, I was damned.

For this reason alone I took my case to Master Gale. I was determined to be out of my pact with Gilbert and whomever else I had foolishly committed myself to. So I knocked lightly on Master Gale's door early one morning. Shortly after, he opened the door a crack. I could see he was still in his nightgown.

'Master Gale, I need to speak with you.'

His hand stole out from behind the door. It was warm from being tucked up in bed. He grasped my hand and smiled. 'I'm glad you've decided to come to me.'

To my surprise, I began to cry. 'I'm in such trouble.'

'I know, Elizabeth. But everything will be fine now

you've decided to repent. Give me some time to dress, and we'll meet in the chapel to pray.'

'Yes, of course.'

'Meet me in an hour. Keep your resolve firm. There's just as much power in prayer as there is in magic.'

'But is there? The things I've seen . . .'

'God cast Satan from heaven. Don't you believe that God is stronger than Satan?'

'I don't even know if there is a God or a Satan. I'm afraid that there isn't anything but our wishful thinking.'

'Believe me, Elizabeth, there most certainly is. In one hour.' His fingers lingered momentarily on mine.

I nodded and slipped back into the corridor as he closed his door. I went to the winter parlour and sat on the seat in front of the fire, twisting my hands together. My stomach was fluttering and my breath short. What life was there for me when I was absolved of my sins? Gilbert would still be here. I would have to go away. Perhaps I would ask Uncle Tom to find me a husband, an old, feeble one who wouldn't last long. The injustice of my gender burned my skin from within. A noise from the door made me look up. Gilbert, in his house gown, leaned in the door.

'Elizabeth?'

I looked away. He advanced towards me.

'You look tense. What are you up to?'

'Leave me alone, please.'

He came to stand behind me and his big hands rested on my shoulders and began to knead the muscles.

'Don't touch me.'

His hands encircled my neck. 'You don't trust me.'

'No.'

'Your thoughts are scattered all around you. You have to be more careful.'

I pushed his hands away and turned to face him. 'Go away.'

'I saw you coming from Master Gale's room—he can't help you, Elizabeth. It amazes me that you're turning to the oldest and most feeble lie in the world.'

'Just leave me to make my own peace.'

'You won't find it, Elizabeth. You'll only find peace in acceptance of what you are.'

I turned away from him and didn't respond. Mirabel began to call him from upstairs, and he left without a word. I breathed a little easier without him in the room.

The hour passed and I pulled on a cloak and headed out to the chapel. The January wind bit through my clothes as I stood shivering at the chapel door, wondering if I were doing the right thing. I reached out to push the door open, and was surprised to find the wood was hot where I touched it. The door swung inwards. Master Gale was standing at the far end of the room in a long cassock and a thick cloak. He looked up as I stood in the doorway. I nearly ran from him, but he held out his hands for me and said: 'Elizabeth, I've known you many, many years. You've only known Mr Lewis a few months. You must trust me.'

I took a step forward, and again was surprised to feel through my shoes that the wooden floor was hot. I looked down and steam was rising from around my feet.

'Come to me, Elizabeth. The devil knows many tricks.'

Another step and tiny flames shot out from under my feet. Wherever I trod, a blackened footprint was left behind. 'But Master Gale, I . . .'

'I am not afraid, Elizabeth. God will protect us. Come to the altar and we'll pray.'

I stood frozen to the spot. Fire licked out from the souls of my shoes and began to spread along the floor, catching in the rushes. Smoke surrounded me.

'I'm damned!' I cried.

'No, never lose your faith in salvation.'

I looked up. He still held his hands out. I put my hand on one of the pews to steady myself and it burst into flame. I screamed and jumped to one side, overbalanced and fell on the ground. The floor began to smoulder beneath me. Horror wormed into my brain. Master Gale prayed feverishly in a low voice. I climbed to my feet and raced towards him, took his outstretched hands in mine. He screamed in agony, and I realised that his flesh was melting in my hands. I tried to release him, but our hands were locked together. Flames began to lick up his arms.

'I'm not doing this. I swear, I'm not doing this. *He* is doing it.'

'Pray, Elizabeth.' This wasn't Master Gale's voice, but Gilbert's behind me. The chaplain was being engulfed in flames that left my skin untouched. I tried to shake him off, but the blackened skeletal hands were still clamped around mine. I craned around.

'Gilbert, let him go.'

'He's already dead.'

The chapel was burning all around us. Master Gale was shrieking incoherently with pain. I turned my head so I couldn't see his skin bubbling and peeling, couldn't see the flames devour his cassock and cloak, couldn't see his jaw locked open in a scream. The fire was creeping up the walls of the chapel and had caught in the beams of the ceiling. I felt Master Gale release my hands, and turned to see him drop dead on the floor, smouldering and blackened. I howled and fell to my knees.

'Come on, Elizabeth, the roof will fall in shortly,' Gilbert said.

'I want to die. I want to die.' Huge, shuddering sobs tortured my body.

'No you don't.' He put his hands under my arms and pulled me to my feet. I collapsed into his arms, crying uncontrollably, a word of hate caught in my throat but unable to choke its way past my tongue. He picked me up and carried me out of the chapel. I heard part of the roof fall in behind us, then everything went black.

I awoke in my own bed. The hangings were drawn back and Uncle Tom sat next to me, dozing into his chest.

'Uncle Tom?'

He looked up with a start. 'Elizabeth. Thank the dear Lord you're all right.'

'Perhaps you should thank somebody else,' I muttered. I knew who was on my side.

'Yes, of course, thank Gilbert. He saved your life, and he saved this house with his quick action. If he hadn't organised the servants to put out the fire in the chapel so quickly, the flames would have leaped over to the house. Thank God for Gilbert. He has been so good to us all.'

'Master Gale?' Perhaps it had been a nightmare. Perhaps he was still alive.

Uncle Tom shook his head. 'Gilbert wanted to go back for him, but it was too dangerous. I had to stop him.'

'Brave.'

'Yes, very brave.'

I stared at the canopy above me. My heart was empty.

'Perhaps I can tell you something about Master Gale,' Uncle Tom said.

'What's that?'

'Just this morning, just before the fire, he came to ask permission to propose.'

'Propose?'

'To you.'

Tears pricked at my eyes. 'He wanted to marry me?'

'He's always had a soft spot for you. Would you have said yes?'

I shook my head. 'I don't know. It may have solved a lot of problems.'

'In any case, I thought you should know. He was probably planning to ask you in the chapel. He said you'd arranged to meet him there, to ask for advice.'

'Yes, I had.' Just a big hollow bubble where my heart used to be.

'Was it anything that I could help with?'

I shifted in my bed and looked at his face. 'No. Don't concern yourself with my little problems.'

'Do you want to see your saviour?'

'My saviour?'

'Gilbert.'

'Oh. No. I don't want to see Gilbert. We've had a disagreement.'

His face clouded with concern. 'We can't have that. Why don't I fetch him so you can make up.'

'No, not yet. I'll thank him in my own time.'

He patted my head. 'All right. I'll leave you. You need to rest.' He got up and left, closing the door quietly behind him.

I couldn't stay here. Not with Gilbert lurking around every corner. Not with nothing to look forward to but domesticity and death. I could wait out the winter, see the birth of Mirabel's daughter, then run. Dress as a man. Take my small amount of money and book a passage to the Orient. Use my magic. Do *something*. There must be something in the wide world for a woman like me.

For a witch like me.

CHAPTER
TWENTY-THREE

'Lisa? Christ, Lisa.'

'What's wrong with her?'

'She must have fallen over or something. Lisa, can you hear me?'

Swimming up through the layers.

'Ailsa, call an ambulance.'

My hand came up and closed around Brad's wrist. 'Don't call an ambulance. I'm okay.'

My kitchen swung into focus. I was lying in a puddle of water on the floor.

'There are better ways to defrost your fridge,' Ailsa said, helping me into a sitting position.

'What happened?' Brad asked. He squatted in front of me, brushing my hair off my face. My whole body ached from the impact of hitting the floor.

'I blacked out momentarily.'

'Momentarily? Long enough to melt your ice cream is not momentarily,' Ailsa said.

I was still getting used to my new surroundings. The twentieth century was so much brighter, bigger, looser. I rolled my shoulders. They ached. Brad helped me to stand up. My knees were jelly. I hobbled over to the kitchen table and sat down. Brad sat next to me. Ailsa closed the fridge and grabbed a mop to clean up the puddle on the floor.

'Lisa, what the fuck is going on?' Brad asked quietly.

'I blacked out. I don't know why.'

'You need to go see a doctor. Christ, you could have a brain tumour or something.'

I looked up at him. His eyebrows were drawn together, and that line to the side of his mouth had deepened. I reached up and traced a finger along it. I got a tingle. I reached for his hand and squeezed it in my own, reached inside his head.

It worked. He was scared—terrified—of something happening to me. He was scared of losing me. I let his hand go. 'You're very sweet.'

'Sweet? What the fuck are you talking about?'

Ailsa sat down with us. 'Is she okay? We'd better tell her why we came by.'

'I don't know. Lisa, are you okay now? We've got exciting news.'

I wasn't even listening. It had worked. I could reach into people's heads just like Elizabeth could. I got a discomfiting power surge.

'Lisa, hello . . .' Brad waved a hand in front of my eyes.

'Huh? Sorry, what is it?'

'Numb are sending us on tour, right down the coast to Melbourne. It's two gigs a week for six weeks,' Brad said.

Ailsa chipped in. 'They're going to pay for all our accommodation and advance us a wage.'

'And when we come back,' Brad continued, 'Livid.'

'The Livid Festival, Lisa. I can't wait. It's going to be huge!'

'It's going to be so cool, Lisa, we haven't toured for years,' Brad said.

Reality started seeping in. 'Tour? For six weeks?'

Six weeks away from Liam—my heart ached just thinking about it.

Brad and Ailsa were looking at each other.

'I can't help but notice you're less than enthusiastic about this, Lisa,' Brad said slowly.

'Give her some time, Brad; maybe she's still out of it,' Ailsa said.

'No, no. I'm with you,' I said. 'It's just . . . you know, six weeks is a long time.'

Brad fought with his anger for a nanosecond before raising his voice. 'For fuck's sake, what's happened to you? Six months ago you would have jumped at this opportunity. He's got under your skin. You can't even bear to leave him for six lousy weeks. Well, you're not going to let the rest of the band down.'

'Don't yell.'

'He's made you stupid. He's made you weak.'

Ailsa put her arm around Brad. 'Hey, calm down, man.'

'I'm not going to let the rest of the band down.' At least, I didn't think I was. It wasn't just being away from Liam. It was being away from home, from safety. Now it looked as though I couldn't even control the regressions. But I couldn't see my way out of the tour. This was what I'd always wanted to happen after all. And the Livid Festival, it was a dream come true.

'When are we supposed to leave?' I asked.

'Two weeks from Friday.'

'That's pretty close.' I was starting to feel desperate.

'The sooner we go, the sooner we get back,' Ailsa said.

'Yeah, I guess so.' I sat there cradling my head in my hands. I had emotional overload. None of my thoughts was working in a straight line.

'We'd better go, Brad,' Ailsa said.

'Will you be okay?' Brad asked me.

I was suddenly terrified of being alone. What if I had another spontaneous regression? 'Don't go,' I said, my head snapping up. 'What time is it, I'll make you dinner or something. I don't want to be alone.'

Ailsa shrugged. 'I have to go. It's my flatmate's birthday and I promised I'd cook dinner.'

'Where's hanky boy tonight?' Brad said.

'Home preparing for his oldies. It is still Tuesday, isn't it?'

'Jeez, Lisa. Yes, it's still Tuesday. How long did you think you'd been out of it?'

'Brad, you could take me home and come back,' Ailsa said.

He fished in his pocket for his car keys. 'Okay, I'm coming back in half an hour. But only if you promise to go to the doctor tomorrow and get your head looked at.'

'Promise,' I said.

'All right. I'll see you soon.'

Just before they were about to leave, I stopped them. 'Wait. Have you guys forgiven me for being such a bitch at the record store yesterday? I'm really sorry.' Had it only been yesterday? It seemed months had passed.

Ailsa smiled tightly. 'With all due respect, Lisa, we're used to you being a bitch.'

I took it on the chin. She was probably right. They left and I collapsed into my sofa with my arm covering my face. It was too much. I felt like I had finally reached breaking point, like I couldn't keep moving forward. If I was unable to control these regressions, I was in deep shit. I reached under the cushion for the remote control to switch the television on, but I

360

couldn't find it. My fingers tingled. Maybe I didn't need it.

I sat up, looked carefully at the television. The nerves in my stomach twitched. I felt afraid and guilty. I held up my hand and pointed my finger at the television, let my mind drift into the unlogical state. Zap. *The Simpsons*.

'Holy shit.'

Maybe I was imagining it. Maybe I was hallucinating. I concentrated on not concentrating again and it turned off. Suddenly I couldn't bear to sit still.

'Holy shit. Holy shit.' I squirmed, I stood. I looked at the television. What was going on? I tried the lights. I turned them on and off without going near the switch. My stomach had turned to water. I was at once both excited and terrified. I felt a little tingle in my thigh and put my hand over the place where the witch-mark would be.

'God, no. Not that.'

Liam, I had to phone Liam. I sat at my desk—my legs could barely hold me up—and dialled his number. It rang four times, then the answering machine picked up. Where the hell was he? He had said he was staying home this evening. I listened to the message, just to be comforted by the sound of his voice. At the beep, I hung up.

I started pacing. How long before Brad was back? All my nerves were buzzing.

'Okay, calm down, Lisa. Calm down.' I took a deep breath. Perhaps I should assess the extent of this ability. I went to the kitchen and sat at the table. Okay, the taps. No, couldn't move them. Good, good. Perhaps I'd been imagining this. The cupboard doors? They swung open and closed fairly easily the first couple of times, but after that they remained resolutely shut. I looked down at the palm of my hand

and thought of Elizabeth's trick with the flames. I curled my fingers. My hands were shaking. When I opened my hand, a pale flame danced there. I blew it out and slumped forward onto the table.

'Christ, I'm damned in this life too.'

When weird shit is happening, you can hang onto reality for a long time. But not forever. After a while you have to admit that reality was never anything more than a tenuous web of beliefs held together by common experience, which you called truth. Well, there is no 'truth'. There is no 'reality'. There is nothing to hold you up. There is nothing to stop you falling and falling into nowhere. I grew dizzy. I could see that everything was stable and structured around me, but my mind was spinning and diving and disappearing into an infinitude of infinities. Time seemed to have stopped. When I heard Brad opening the door, I realised that I had been staring at the table for twenty minutes. A sickening sense of forever weighed on my shoulders.

'Lisa?' He rounded the corner into the kitchen. 'What's up?'

I blinked and attempted to pull myself together. No need for the rest of the world to know that my mind was no longer under my control. 'I'm scared.'

'Scared? What about?'

I shrugged.

He pulled up a chair and sat down next to me. 'You're pale, you're shaking. What's the matter?'

'I've been thinking about forever.'

'Forever?'

'Yes. Sometimes I can't stand how big it is. Don't you ever think that?'

He nodded slowly. 'Yes, sometimes. Everybody does. Don't sweat it.'

'I can't stop thinking about it. How could anybody want to live forever?'

'I don't know. Stop thinking about it.'

'How?'

'Just stop.'

The definitive way he said it gave me something to hang onto. I began to calm down. 'Okay. I'll just stop.'

We sat quietly for a few moments, then I said, 'Do you believe in anything?'

'Like what?'

'Anything religious or paranormal.'

'Same thing, isn't it?'

'Well, do you?'

He drew his brows together and pondered for a while. Finally he shook his head. 'No.'

'What would it take to prove something like that to you?'

'I don't know. Is this going somewhere? Is that what's been happening with you?'

'Kind of.'

He picked up my hand and squeezed it. I had to fight hard to keep from tuning into his thoughts. 'Lisa, you have to go see a doctor. I think you might have something wrong with your head.'

'Thanks. You really know how to charm a girl.'

'No, really. Blackouts and imagining things and freaking out all the time. That's not normal. I think you've just had too much stress this year. I think you need to get some professional help.'

'Don't be so fucking patronising.'

'I'm not being patronising. I'm trying to help. Jeez, Lisa. I'm *worried* about you. Is that allowed? Or don't nine years together count for anything?'

I hung my head. A big sob got caught in my

throat, and I tried to talk around it. 'Yes, of course it counts.'

'Hey, don't cry. I didn't mean to make you cry.'

'No, it's not you. My life is so fucked up and I don't know what to do.'

He pulled his chair closer and put his arm around me. I rested my head on his shoulder. He had the most wonderful smell about him—shampoo, a light tobacco scent, the smell of male skin. I rubbed my cheek on the sleeve of his shirt. I caught a sense of some overwhelming emotion he felt for me, then quickly blocked up the passage to my brain. I didn't want to know stuff about people that they didn't want me to know.

'You've been so good to me,' I said.

'I've been a prick. You know that.'

'Okay. You've been a prick. Care to sleep on my couch tonight? I'm scared of being alone.'

I knew he would have preferred an invitation to share my bed, but it wasn't forthcoming.

'Yeah, all right. If it would make you feel better.'

'Yes, it would. Much better.'

I slept like the dead. At first going to sleep had been scary because every time I felt that drifting off feeling, I panicked, thinking I might go into a regression. Finally my brain packed it in and I descended into seamless darkness. The next thing I knew it was daylight and I was being woken by male voices outside my bedroom door. I sat up woozily.

'Brad? Are you there?'

The door opened a crack and Liam peered in. 'Hi. How are you feeling?'

'Liam. What are you doing here?' I felt guilty, though I didn't know why.

He came in and sat on my bed. 'I have a surprise for you. But first tell me how you are. Brad said he found you blacked out on the kitchen floor yesterday.'

'Yes. I tried to ring you last night and tell you, but you weren't home.'

'I had to go out. I'll show you why shortly.'

'What time is it?'

'It's one o'clock. I'm having an afternoon off.'

Brad knocked at the door. 'I'll go now, Lisa.'

I looked up. His face was a mask of impassivity. 'Thank you, Brad. I really appreciate you staying.'

'Yes, thanks, Brad,' Liam said. Brad visibly cringed. Liam could sound so patronising.

'I'll call you,' Brad said, and backed out. I heard him shut the front door behind him and I turned my attention back to Liam.

'So? My surprise?'

'You still haven't answered the question. How are you?' He kicked off his shoes and wriggled into bed with me.

'Pretty bad, actually. I had a regression without even trying. I had no control over it, I just went under.'

He grabbed my hand, rubbed my fingers with concern. 'God, Lisa. And how do you feel now? Do you think it'll happen again?'

'I don't know. I'm terrified of it. But that's not all. It seems I got a few hidden extras this time. Watch this.' I pointed towards the door, expecting it to shut. Nothing happened.

'What am I looking at?'

I tried again. Nothing. I was surprisingly angry. 'I have no control over that either.'

Liam looked back at me. 'Control over what?'

'When I first came to yesterday I had some of Elizabeth's magic. Damn it, it's gone.'

365

'I should think that's a blessing.'

I shrugged. 'I don't want to think about that stuff. Where's my surprise?'

He fished in his pocket and pulled something out. 'Hold out your hand.'

'Okay.' I held out my hand.

'Close your eyes.'

'Okay.' I closed my eyes. 'Just don't give me a handful of eyeballs.'

'Eyeballs? What are you talking about? There.' He slipped a ring onto my finger. I opened my eyes in dread. If it was an engagement ring I was in big trouble.

It wasn't. It was a plain silver band with something engraved on it in fancy lettering.

'I went out last night to get you something that would show how much I love you. This is what I found.' He leaned in and kissed me. I pushed him off.

'Don't,' I said. 'Morning breath.'

I held the ring up to my face. My heart was pounding. He had just told me he loved me, and now I guessed I was supposed to respond in kind. The ring said *In aeternum*.

'For eternity,' I said.

'That's what the jeweller said. I knew that you'd be able to read it though.'

I looked up at him. 'Eternity's a long time, Liam.'

'I've never met anyone like you before,' he said. 'I've never been in love like this before. Don't worry, you don't have to say you love me too. I'm prepared for that.'

'It's not that I don't, it's just that everything else in my life is so confusing I'm not sure what I'm feeling half the time.'

'I know, and I don't want to add to your confusion. Just accept the gift, and wear it, and . . . you know, let me know.'

I was touched by his understanding. I threw my arms around his neck. 'You are wonderful. You give me so much comfort. I don't know what I'd do without you.'

He squeezed me hard, then dropped me suddenly. 'Sorry, almost forgot. This was slipped under your door.' He pulled a folded envelope out of his back pocket and handed it to me.

'Under the front door?' I said, examining it.

'Yeah.'

The envelope was unmarked, so I pulled it open. Inside was a stiff sheet of white paper, with 'You must stop' handwritten on it. My brow furrowed.

'Who the hell wrote this?'

'What does it say?' Liam asked.

I showed him the note.

'Stop what?' he said.

I was suddenly covered in goosebumps. '*He* wrote it.'

'You've lost me, Lisa.'

'Oh, God. Gilbert. He wrote it. He must have been able to tell what I was doing. He must *know*. God, what else does he know? How long has he been tuning in to me?'

'You're not making any sense. Calm down.'

I nodded towards the bedroom door and it slammed shut. 'That was what I was doing yesterday. Only it's unreliable. Sometimes I can do it, sometimes I can't.'

Liam looked in horror from the door to me. 'You did that?'

I opened it again. Then closed it. 'Yes, I did that. This is what I was doing yesterday—experimenting.

He must have been able to sense it. I must have been making some kind of psychic noise.'

Liam sat slack-jawed with stupefaction, looking at my bedroom door. 'How did you do that?'

'Liam? You knew some of this was coming back to me.'

He didn't respond. I grabbed his shoulders and turned him to face me. 'You knew that I was getting some of Elizabeth's magic. You know, "seeing" things, and the languages and the witch-mark.'

'But I didn't . . . I didn't think . . .'

'You didn't think what? You didn't think it was true? Are you telling me you haven't believed me all this time?'

'No!' he answered quickly. 'Of course I've believed you.'

I put my hand around his wrist without even thinking, and reached into his mind. He pushed my hand off and recoiled.

'I can feel that, Lisa. Don't.'

'You can feel that?'

'Yes.'

Could everyone feel it? Or was Liam just aware of it because he'd heard Elizabeth's story? 'Sorry,' I said.

'Please, Lisa. I believed you. But I thought maybe some of it was . . . maybe exaggerated.'

I exploded. 'What the fuck do you think I am? Some teenager making myself sound more interesting? Jeez, how can you say you love me when you don't even trust me?'

'I'm sorry, Lisa. My mother always makes every-thing worse than it sounds. I kind of expect these things of people.'

I looked down at the note again. My hands were shaking. Gilbert had been here; he had stood outside my front door while Brad and I were sleeping inside.

What if something had happened to Brad? How could I have coped with that? Panic gripped my heart. My argument with Liam suddenly seemed unimportant.

'I'm not safe, Liam. He knows where I live. And wherever I go, he'll find me. He's got in-built radar.'

'Can't you block him out of your head?'

Maybe I could. Elizabeth had. 'I'll try.' I was scrambling out of bed and pulling a dusty suitcase from my wardrobe.

'What are you doing?'

'Packing. I have to get out. Can I come stay at your place?'

'Well, you certainly can't stay here. I'll book you into a hotel.' He got up and started helping me pack.

'A hotel? Why can't I stay with you?'

He wriggled uncomfortably. 'My parents are arriving on the weekend. It wouldn't be a good scene. My father's a pastor, remember.'

'Well, I'll go stay with Brad.'

'No. Don't do that. I'll pay for a hotel.'

'But I can just go stay with Brad, it's cheaper.'

He opened his mouth to say something then closed it again. Finally, he took a deep breath and continued. 'Please, just let me book you into a hotel in the centre of town. It'll be much more convenient. You know I don't trust Brad.'

I shrugged. 'Okay. Your money.'

'You can stay with me tonight, and I'll put you in the Hilton some time before the weekend.'

'Whatever.'

'Lisa.' He spun me around to face him. 'Are you angry with me?'

I looked up into those sincere eyes and forced a smile. 'I'm angry at life, Liam. Don't take it personally.'

*

We stopped at the police station on our way to Liam's and dropped off the note to Inspector Honeywell, who looked as though he was close to unravelling. No doubt he was under a lot of pressure to solve the case and Gilbert was making things very difficult for him. He accepted the note dubiously.

'Let me ask you something, Miss Sheehan,' he had said, 'what do you think "You must stop" means?'

I shrugged. 'Well, perhaps it's some crazed fundamentalist who wants us to stop polluting the world with our awful noise, an avenging angel sent to purge the city of its underground music scene.' I would have said anything to get him on the trail as quickly as possible, find Gilbert, stop him before he did something hideous to somebody I loved.

'Thank you for coming down. I'll be in touch.' And with that I was dismissed.

Liam and I discussed the note as we drove home.

'Lisa, if it was Gilbert who wrote the note, and if he wants you to stop, then it must be because you've unsettled him. Maybe you've learned too much.'

'But where is the power coming from, Liam?' I said. 'What about the regressions, why are they happening? Especially that last one, without even trying?'

'I don't know.' He shook his head. 'This is all too much for me to deal with.'

I wondered just how little of my story he had believed until he started to see some evidence. Surely he couldn't have been humouring me all this time. Why would he bother? I turned to look out the car window.

'The universe is trying to tell me something,' I said quietly.

'Huh?'

'The universe. You know, some higher power. If I'm in danger from Gilbert, perhaps it's possible that a higher power is giving me the information I need.'

'God?' He seemed to relax.

'Well, no, I don't know about that. What Gilbert told Elizabeth about the universe was that it's amoral. That it rewards those who serve it. Could it be possible that it's looking out for me in some way, for something I did in the past?'

Liam pushed his lips together very hard. We were pulling into his driveway.

'Liam?'

'I'm very confused, Lisa. Let me think for a while. In the meantime, come inside and make yourself at home.'

The domestic normality at Liam's place was as disturbingly seductive as ever. I was very conscious that I had 'moved in', if only until the weekend: I left my shoes near Liam's shoes at the door, I rested my toothbrush next to his toothbrush, I put my cruelty-free shampoo into his shower caddy. And now I stood under his shower, letting the hot water wash over me as I concentrated hard on keeping Gilbert out of my head. Elizabeth had done it by visualising herself building a wall of glowing stones, arranging them around her, higher and higher until they towered above her. I did the same, ignoring the tingle in my thigh—this had to be done for self-preservation, and if that involved summoning up spirits, then I had no real choice.

Elizabeth had said a word, too, but I couldn't remember what it was. I lolled my head back against the tiles and thought about not thinking. A hum of electricity zapped up from my feet and bubbled through my body and out of my mouth in the form of a word which disappeared instantly from my memory. I saw the magic wall in my mind's eye glow once, brilliantly, then fade from my perception so I was once again only looking at the inside of my eyelids.

'Safe,' I said aloud.

Twenty minutes later I emerged in the living room. My skin was red and blotchy from being under the hot water for too long.

'I thought you'd drowned,' Liam said as he passed me on his way to the bathroom.

'Sorry, I don't know how much hot water is left,' I said, heading for the television.

He went to shower while I flicked from channel to channel, looking for a halfway decent show to divert my troubled mind. There was nothing on but the tail-end of a couple of game shows. I solved a few puzzles on *Wheel of Fortune* before anyone had guessed any letters, and decided it must be one of my new gifts. If I could get myself on that show, I could clean up. I heard the pipes creak as Liam turned off the taps in the bathroom. At the same moment, the phone began to ring.

'Liam!' I shouted.

'Can you get it? I'll be out in a tick.'

I rolled over on the couch and scooped up the phone. 'Hello?'

There was a short silence. 'Hello? Who's that?' It was a woman's voice. Sharp, but cautious.

'Um . . . this is Lisa.'

'Sorry, I must have a wrong number. I was after Liam Baker.'

'Yeah, this is his house. He's just in the shower. Can I tell him who's calling?'

Liam had just emerged in the living room wrapped in a thick dressing gown. His hair was still damp.

'Yes, it's his mother.'

'Oh, hello, Mrs Baker.' As I said this, Liam took on an expression of thinly veiled panic, and made a snatching motion towards the phone, but his mother was still talking to me.

'You said your name was Lisa?'

'Yeah, I'm a friend of Liam's.'

'Not a girlfriend?'

I stifled a laugh. 'Well, yeah, I guess that's what you'd call me.'

'It's just that Liam has never mentioned you.'

'We haven't been dating very long.' Liam was almost dancing on the spot, urging me to wind up my conversation with his mother.

'Well, we shall have to meet you. Has Liam told you we're coming to stay for a while?' she asked.

'Yes, he has.'

'Why don't you come by for dinner one night?'

'I'd love to.'

'Fine, organise it with Liam. We'll be staying a few weeks so there's plenty of time.'

'Great. I'll put Liam on now, hang on.' I handed the phone to Liam who took it from me with obvious relief. I moved over on the couch so that he could sit next to me.

'Hi, Mum,' he said timidly. It was clear from the look on his face that she had launched into a tirade about not telling her of this new girlfriend. It amused me. I pressed my hand against one of his hard thighs, walked my fingers into his dressing gown and stroked the bare inside of his leg. He shrugged me off, his eyebrows drawn together tightly. It sparked a tiny flame of anger in me. Jeez, his mother couldn't see what I was doing, what was his problem?

He was explaining calmly to her why he hadn't mentioned me before. I climbed down onto the floor in front of him, parted his dressing gown and pushed my way between his legs. I admit that I was deliberately trying to annoy him, but I certainly didn't expect the reaction I got. Instead of gathering his clothes around himself and offering me a warning glance, he grabbed me hard around the shoulder with his spare hand and pushed me away. I fell onto my backside, grazing my back against the coffee table. I looked up at him with wide eyes, but he just closed his dressing gown and turned away from me. I stood up and kicked the coffee table over in fury. He didn't look at me. I stormed off into his bedroom and slammed the door shut behind me, then lay there in the dim light of dusk, every nerve in my body hot with anger. What the fuck was his problem? I was only mucking around. I could hear his voice vibrating through the door, but not what he was saying. Finally, I heard the phone click and his footsteps approaching the bedroom. When the door opened and the light from the hallway fingered in, I made a pretence of sniffing loudly as if I had been crying.

'Lisa? I'm sorry, did I hurt you?'

'Yes. I grazed my back on the coffee table.'

'You're crying.' He came to sit next to me on the bed. His voice was sick with guilt. 'I didn't mean to hurt you. You just made me so angry.'

'I was only playing around. I didn't mean any harm.' I snuffled a bit more, then realised I sounded like a wimp and sat up. 'Don't ever do that again.'

'I won't. It's just that I get a bit . . . tense around my family. You can understand that, can't you? They are the most heavy-duty Christians you could meet. They think that I'm still a virgin. They'll be expecting you to be a virgin too. If they knew . . . God, Lisa, they'd just make my life misery.'

I strained to see his face in the dark. 'You're feeling guilty about us, aren't you?'

'No.' Obviously lying.

'You weren't feeling guilty before she rang.'

He sighed. 'And I won't be in half an hour or so. But I guess when I'm talking to them I feel kind of weird about how far I've strayed.'

'My little stray sheep.' I ruffled his hair. 'I'm sorry for offering to suck your cock.'

He laughed lightly. 'You're forgiven. Just don't do it again. Do you want me to look at your back, see if the skin's broken?'

'No, it's okay really.'

We sat in silence for a moment, then he said, 'So, do I qualify as a wife basher?' His voice was tense, afraid he'd damaged our relationship irreparably.

'No, you didn't cause nearly enough pain. I must say that I've never seen you so angry, though. It was kind of exciting.' I reached for his leg again, but he didn't respond.

'Lisa, I think I can say this on behalf of most men: talking to my mother can turn me off sex for weeks.'

'Sorry. What was it she wanted anyway?'

He stretched out next to me with a big, unwinding sigh. 'They're arriving early. Tomorrow afternoon.'

'Ah. So I'm being evicted?'

'I guess so. It's up to you whether you want to go tonight or tomorrow morning.'

'Tomorrow morning is cool. I'll help you get the house cleaned up tonight.'

'You're a good sport.' He didn't say anything for a long time. A light breeze fanned the curtain in the window. 'I love you, Lisa.'

'And just right at this moment I love you too. But I might not be sure tomorrow so don't hold me to it.'

'When my folks are gone, you can come back here. Permanently if you like. No more rent—you could quit the job at the Casino.'

It was so devastatingly appealing that I was momentarily speechless. 'I might. But it's a little more complicated than you think. When your parents are gone, I'll probably be on tour.'

'You're touring?'

'Yeah. We're supposed to leave in about two and a half weeks.'

'For how long?'

I took a deep breath. 'Six weeks.'

'Six?' More heavy silence. 'God, Lisa, that's such a long time.'

'It'll go quickly. It's probably going to be good for me.'

'I'll miss you like crazy.'

'Me too. I'll miss you too. I don't really want to go, but I can't let everybody else down. You know, I've been waiting my whole life for this. And now it's happening, all I can do is wish that the timing was better.'

He idly stroked my shoulder. 'Just think, when you come back, everything might be normal again.'

'Oh God, I hope so. I will kiss Inspector Honeywell's fat old arse if he can find the new Gilbert and put him somewhere safe. Preferably six feet underground, because that's the only place I'd trust him not to do me any harm.'

Liam sat up next to me. 'Lisa, do you think you could maybe sense where Gilbert is if you tried?'

I considered the suggestion. 'I suppose I could try. Stranger things have happened since I woke up on the kitchen floor yesterday.'

'Go on, then. See if you can.'

I relaxed the muscles in my shoulders and neck and closed my eyes. I let my mind drift into the pre-conscious state, thought not about Gilbert but the space around him. Just as my mind was homing in on him, I got a barb of pain in my head so sharp that it felt as though my brain had been stabbed. I cried out in pain and fell back onto the bed with my hands around my head.

'Lisa?' Liam was leaning over me panic-stricken.

'He's got that covered, Liam. I think I just ran into his electric fence.'

'You found him?'

'Not quite.' The pain was subsiding, leaving behind a dull, migraine-like ache. My senses were a bit scrambled. 'God that hurt. You've no idea. I'm not going to be able to get close to him that way, but with a bit of luck he's running into a similar defence with me at the moment, so we're even.'

He helped me sit up. 'Can I get you something?'

'An ice pack would be nice.'

'Okay, wait there.' He hurried off into the bright hallway, gently closing the door behind him. The darkness closed over me. I felt strange. I had felt strange ever since I woke up from the last regression, and I was only now beginning to realise what it was that was significantly different. I felt as though my senses were more alive. I no longer had that cotton-wool feeling, like I was on the verge of disappearing into another hallucination. I felt powerful, as though a rod of tempered steel had replaced my spine. Gilbert may have blocked me at the last minute, but I had nearly found him. I wondered if he was scared. Because, like Elizabeth, it seemed I had learned quickly and easily.

'I hope you're scared, you fuck,' I said aloud. 'Because if I find you before you find me . . .' I trailed off, feeling a bit silly. I didn't even know who he was, and he was obviously more powerful than me. What did I honestly think I could do to hurt him?

Still, I had the distinct feeling that I had done it before.

CHAPTER
TWENTY-FOUR

'**M**an, I love hotel rooms.' Jeff took a running start from the door as I pushed it open, and landed on the bed with a loud 'whump'.

'Come on, Jeff. Don't mess it up, I've got to sleep there tonight.'

'Wow, Lisa,' said Ailsa, looking around. 'Do you feel like a kept woman?' She grabbed a tiny bottle of bourbon from the mini-bar. 'Is he going to come visit you for sex?'

'I don't know. He's having a major guilt trip about his parents, I know that much.'

Brad leaned in close. 'Mummy's boy,' he whispered.

I elbowed him playfully in the gut. 'You're just jealous.'

'I sure am. The Hilton no less. I would have thought he'd put you up upstairs at the Royal Arms, in one of those rooms where you have to share a bathroom with a pack of stinky old men.'

'No. No stinky old men here. Check out the bathroom. It's big enough to use as a practice room, and the acoustics are great.'

Jeff was in the bathroom singing loudly, his voice echoing sweetly off the tiles.

I sat on the bed and Brad sat next to me. 'So he must have some money, this guy?' he asked.

'Liam. His name is Liam.'

'Whatever.'

'I don't know if he has money or not. I think I'm here because he was guilty about turfing me out, and I don't feel safe at home since I got that note under my door.' Actually, I didn't feel safe leaving the hotel to go to work, but I was alert to the danger and I figured he couldn't do much to me surrounded by hundreds of frequent flyers. And I couldn't let the rest of the band down.

Brad stretched out, put his hands behind his head. 'You could have come to stay with me, you know.'

'Liam wouldn't hear of it.' I rolled over onto my stomach and looked at him. 'For obvious reasons.'

He gave me one of those sexy smiles, and that familiar thrill licked through me. Jeff jumped down between us. 'Can I stay here with you, Lisa?'

'No.'

Ailsa joined us on the bed. 'How about me? There's room, you know. And who else is going to drink the mini-bar?'

I took the bourbon off her, but she had already opened it, so I handed it back. 'Don't take anything else out of the mini-bar. Liam has to pay for it.'

'Just top it up with cold tea,' Ailsa said, taking another swig. 'Nobody will know the difference.'

'Polly Pureheart alone with a mini-bar,' Jeff said, pinching the bottle off Ailsa and downing a few gulps. 'It makes me want to weep for lost opportunity.' He passed it back to Ailsa.

'Come on, guys. It's three a.m. You've seen the room, now you can go home,' I said sitting up. 'You all smell bad.'

'So do you,' Ailsa said, finishing off the bourbon

379

and tossing the bottle with a loud rattle into the rubbish bin. 'But I'm too polite to say so.'

Jeff pulled himself up. 'Yeah, I got a lady waiting for me in the car park. I'm going to take her home and make her do evil things with me.'

'You made her wait in the car park?' I said, shocked.

'Well, you said I couldn't bring her up here,' he protested.

'What's wrong with the lobby? Jeez, Jeff. Think.' I clipped him around the ear. 'Four fans have been murdered. You'd better go make sure she's okay.'

He shrugged and slouched out casually, Ailsa following him. Brad still lay next to me on the bed.

'What?' I asked as Jeff and Ailsa closed the door.

'I was just thinking.'

Ailsa opened the door again and poked her head in. 'Hey, don't fuck, you two,' she screamed, then backed out and slammed the door again. I could hear her giggles retreating up the corridor. I looked back to Brad.

'What are you thinking?'

'Wouldn't it be cool if we had sex right here in the bed that Liam is paying for?'

'When I'm back from the tour, I'm moving in with him.' I don't know why I said that. I didn't even know if it was true yet.

He raised his eyebrows. 'You are? It's that serious is it?'

I pulled Liam's ring off my finger and showed it to him. 'For eternity,' I said as he tried to decipher the writing.

'When did he give you that?'

'Yesterday.'

Brad nodded slowly. He hadn't shaved for a few days, and the light over the bed glinted on the reddish-yellow hairs on his chin. My fingers itched to touch him.

'Are you saying that it's finished, Lisa?'

'What?'

'Us.'

'There was never anything to finish. I'm just letting you know. Liam and I are a couple. A permanent one.' I tried to ignore the light steel band that tightened over my heart when I said that. I slipped the ring back on my finger.

'Well, I guess if you're that sure . . .'

'Yes, I'm really sure. But you're still my friend.' I felt so bad saying that because I had lied to him about going to see a doctor. He had been pleased to hear that I had an appointment with an imaginary specialist some time next week. 'My best friend,' I added.

He sniffed. 'Great. I'm happy to know it.' His voice was laced heavily with irony. He pulled himself up and stretched. 'Goodnight, Polly.'

'Goodnight.'

He left quietly. I followed him to the door and closed it behind him. I went to the bathroom and turned the shower on, pulling my clothes off while I waited for the water to heat up. The light over the mirror was one of those bright, fluorescent ones. My skin looked blotchy and my hair brassy. I leaned over and flicked the light off. Now the bathroom was dark except for the splash of light from the half-open door. I stepped under the hot water and let it run over me, closed my eyes and leaned my head against the tiles. I heard a door slamming far away. I could hear birds chirping outside my window.

My head suddenly snapped up. It was three a.m. in the middle of the city. There were no birds outside my window. The noise faded down a dark passageway in my mind. Not another regression, please. I stood warily, listening, but all I could hear was the shower running and my own pulse thumping past my ears. I turned the shower off and wrapped myself in a towel. My hotel room seemed very lonely and empty. I wished I wasn't alone.

I was completely disoriented when I woke up. The muted light through the curtains seemed to be in the wrong place—my window was on the other side. Then I remembered where I was and sat up wearily. I fixed an eye on the clock next to my bed. It was exactly midday. I rolled onto my side and picked up the phone to order some breakfast, then got up and drew the curtains. I had an unspoiled view over the grimy rooftops of the city and down to the river and the botanical gardens. I felt like I was a long way away from everything. I watched the traffic grind along below me for a while. It seemed everybody else had somewhere to go, something to do, ordinary lives to lead, without murders and disappearing best friends and eternal damnation to worry them. It didn't seem fair somehow that the lot had fallen to me. I was shaken out of my reverie by a rap on the door.

'Room service.'

I let them in and took my breakfast back to bed with me. I picked up the phone and called my place, dialling in the remote access code to my answering machine. There were a couple of hang-up calls, a reminder from the electricity board that I was behind in my payments, and then a long silence before David's voice cut in.

'Lisa . . . if you're there, pick up. I need to talk to you, Lisa. It's David. Where are you?' Another silence. 'Call me soon. I need to talk to you.'

Two long beeps let me know that I'd heard all the

messages. I rang Karin's place, my heart racing a little. What did David want from me so urgently? The phone rang three or four times before he picked it up.

'David French,' he said in a business voice.

'David, it's Lisa.'

'Lisa, where are you? I tried to phone you all day yesterday.'

'I've moved out temporarily. What's up?'

'Why have you moved out? Where are you?'

My flesh prickled lightly. 'There's a problem with the water at my place. I'm staying at a hotel in town.'

'Which one?'

I didn't speak for a moment, then continued warily, 'David, what did you want?'

'I want to see you. I need to talk to you.'

'About Karin?' I didn't want to see him, I didn't want him to touch me again.

'Yes, but not just that—'

'Have you heard something?'

'No. I just need some company. I'm going crazy without her, Lisa. And you're the only one who understands me.'

I bit my lip, not sure how to word my response. 'David, it's probably best if I don't see you. Let's be honest, last time I saw you, you touched me in an inappropriate way.'

'I didn't mean to. Don't be angry.' A pause. 'Besides, you enjoyed it.'

I couldn't believe I was hearing this. 'David, I'm your wife's best friend. Your missing wife. If you're interested in some kind of—'

'I'm only interested in seeing you, just talking, that's all, I swear. Tell me where you are, and I'll come into town and meet you.'

'I have to go,' I said quickly. 'Goodbye.'

'Wait, Lisa—' I hung up on him mid-sentence, then sat on my bed hugging my body. Sure I felt sorry for him, but he had just got way too creepy. On impulse I picked up the phone again and hit the redial button. He answered halfway through the first ring.

'Lisa?'

'If you hear anything about Karin, leave a message at my house. I'll check the machine regularly,' I said.

'Lisa, come on. Where are you? Meet me in town. I really want to see you.'

'Gotta go,' I said, then hung up once more.

'Have you been crying?'

I let Brad in and closed the door behind me. 'No.' I had just got off the phone from Liam, who had fobbed me off once again, saying his parents were waiting for him at the dinner table. I'd hardly spoken two words to him since he'd moved me into the hotel, and I was going crazy by myself. He had pointedly ignored my teary fit, promising to visit in the morning before work.

Brad shook his head. 'Girl, you lie like a pro. Where did you learn that? Is it something hanky boy taught you, because you used to be a hell of a lot more honest.'

I shrugged. 'Believe what you want. Let's go to work.' I needed to be out in the world, making contact with other human beings. I had cabin fever so bad living in this hotel, and only the scariest thoughts to keep me company.

We struggled through our set at the Casino then headed down to the Universal. We had taken to coming in the backstage door now because the venues were so crowded and everybody wanted to talk to us as we squeezed our way down to the stage. Usually on a Friday night Jeff and Ailsa would be waiting for us, but tonight Ailsa sat alone backstage, smoking.

'Ailsa. Where's Jeff?' Brad asked as he slung his bag in the corner of the room.

'Don't know, I haven't seen him.'

'He went home with that girl last night,' I said. 'Maybe she's holding him up. It's been a while for Jeff I think.'

'Come on, let's get set up.'

Brad and I set up but Jeff still hadn't arrived. Brad spotted the girl that Jeff had gone home with in the crowd, and beckoned her over.

'Hey, seen Jeff?' he asked.

'No. I left his place around midday.' She was stoned, stoned, stoned.

I looked at Brad, then back to the girl. 'You didn't give him anything nasty to take, did you?'

She shrugged and swayed unevenly on her feet. 'Nothing he hasn't taken before. Why?'

I stood up and pulled Brad to his feet. 'We'd better give him a call, make sure he's okay.'

He nodded and followed me backstage, then out into the windy street. We found a phone box and Brad dialled Jeff's number. I waited outside in the yellow splash of light that the phone box cast on the cold bitumen. Nobody answered. Brad hung up the phone with a crash.

'He must be on his way.'

'I hope so.'

'We'll give him twenty minutes.'

Half an hour later, when the crowd was getting restless and the venue manager had been backstage asking us when the hell we were going on, Brad borrowed Angie's mobile phone and we tried calling Jeff again. Still no answer.

'We'll have to go round there,' Brad said.

'Shouldn't we call the police?'

'If he's overdosed, we don't want the police anywhere near his place until we can hide a few things.'

'Brad . . .'

'Are you coming with me?'

I shivered in my overcoat. 'Okay, I'm coming.'

We hurried to Brad's car and headed towards Jeff's place. I could tell that Brad was worried by the way he ran every orange light and drummed his fingers on the steering wheel at every red one.

'Relax, Brad,' I said. 'He's probably just forgotten or something. Or maybe his car broke down. Relax.'

'That girl looked so sleazy. What if she's given him something wicked? Heroin or something?'

'All his girlfriends look sleazy. And I'm sure our Jeffrey is no stranger to opiates.'

He sped through another orange light and took the turnoff to Jeff's place. Jeff lived in one room at a boarding house which was mostly full of alcoholic geriatrics. He didn't seem to mind sharing a bathroom and kitchen with a bunch of toothless old geysers who shat their pants, but I hated going there, it made me so depressed. We parked in the circular drive, which was overhung with weeds and unmowed grass, and made our way through the front door and up the stairs to Jeff's room. The boards of the hallway creaked as we walked over them. One grimy light illuminated our way. Jeff's room was at the far end of the hall, almost in total darkness.

'I can't see a light under the door,' Brad said as we approached. The place stank badly. We stopped outside Jeff's door and Brad rapped hard.

'Jeff, it's Brad. Are you okay, man?' He tried the handle but it was locked. From somewhere inside the room, a low mechanical groaning noise beat over and over. We waited. My eyes were adjusting to the darkness. I turned around to look back up the hallway. An old guy with a scabrous head was peering out from his doorway, I turned back to Brad. My feet stuck in something on the floor.

'Holy shit!' I jumped back and peered at the floor through the darkness. A wet sticky stain was spreading from underneath Jeff's door.

'What?' Brad said in alarm.

'Christ, Brad, it's blood. There's blood every-where.'

Brad looked at the floor in stunned silence for a moment, then began to pound on the door. 'Jeff, Jeff.'

'Break in,' I said.

Brad rammed his shoulder into the door. It creaked. I kicked near the lock and we heard a splintering sound. Between the two of us we kicked and smashed the door until we heard wood breaking and the door swung open a little way. Brad slammed it open and reached for the light switch.

The room lit up. I froze, dizzy with revulsion. 'Brad, oh God, oh God.'

Brad pulled his hand away from the light switch, and his fingers were covered in blood. He turned to me and closed his eyes. 'Tell me I'm not seeing this, Lisa.'

'You can see this?' I was surprised. Gilbert usually hid his tracks.

'Of course I can see it. It's everywhere.'

Jeff, or what was left of him, was tied by his feet to the ceiling fan in the centre of the room. He was just a mess of gore, his guts trailing out, his face obscured by the arterial blood which had poured out of a flapping wound in his neck. His hands, those stupid long skinny fingers, were grey and shrivelled. The fan spun around on low speed, shuddering under the weight of Jeff's body, plaster cracking from the ceiling and electrical wires exposed through the gaps. Blood seemed to be splattered everywhere, long streaks of it along the walls, blotches on the ceiling, soaking into the thin, cigarette-scarred carpet. Bile rose in my throat. Brad was doubled over, his arms clutched around his waist.

'I'm never going to see anything but this again,' he said breathlessly. 'For the rest of my life, this is going to be superimposed on everything I see.'

'Call the police,' I said. 'Call Inspector Honeywell.'

He turned to pick up the phone next to the door. 'Who's Elizabeth?' he said in a tiny voice.

'What?' I turned around in shock. On the wall above the door, written in smudgy bloody fingerpaint, was: 'For you, Elizabeth.'

'Who's Elizabeth?' he asked again.

'I am,' I replied. 'I'm Elizabeth.'

CHAPTER
TWENTY-FIVE

The funeral parlour was freezing. A cruel westerly wind crept through the crack under the doors. People in the cramped room were hugging woollen overcoats around themselves against the chill. Sniffling and snuffling came from every corner, some from tears, some from early morning colds. I sat in the front seat, gripping Liam's hand, looking at the coffin in the alcove in front of me. It seemed far too small to hold Jeff. Jeff's mother and sister sat on the opposite side of the room, and I kept stealing glances at them, trying to figure out how they were feeling. They were stony faced, and I knew that Jeff had parted ways with them a long time in the past. The room was full of frequent flyers. Brad had kicked the media out to make more room for mourners, and now two camera crews and half a dozen reporters waited like vultures outside on the frozen street.

A woman with a nasal voice recited a generic eulogy from a crucifix-heavy corner. Muted lights illuminated the soft surfaces and floral arrangements. I was overwhelmed with grief. I hadn't even realised how fond I was of Jeff until I had fully comprehended what it meant never to see or hear from him again. Liam stroked my fingers with his thumb. I was numb to my core.

The eulogist wrapped up and we all bent our heads in prayer, although I would have been surprised to find more than a handful of believers in the room. When I looked up, four funeral parlour supplied pallbearers were carrying Jeff through the backstage exit to the car that would take him to the cemetery. There would be no graveside ceremony. Thank you and goodnight.

I turned to Brad. It was the first time I had seen him sober since Jeff's death. His eyes were red, and he wore that strange scent of alcoholics trying to cover up their addiction—an excessive soapy smell over pores emitting whiskey fumes. Ailsa, who sat next to him, leaned in. 'I'm going,' she said.

'Going where?' I asked.

'Back home to my parents. I'm not sticking around here to end up like Jeff.' Ailsa was originally from a small country town down near the border.

'Are you for real?' Brad asked. 'What about the band?'

'No life, no band,' she said simply. 'I'm not sticking around.'

Brad looked to me desperately, but I shrugged. What could we do? Ailsa was probably right. Even Brad had temporarily moved back into his parents' house for safety. They were away overseas for a couple of months.

'Is that it, then?' Brad addressed the question to me. 'Is it all over?'

'Brad, we don't have to sort this out right now,' I said.

'How could we have replaced Jeff anyway?' Ailsa asked. 'He was indispensable.'

A small crowd had gathered in front of us. One of them leaned forward and touched my knee. 'Lisa,' she said.

I looked up. 'Yes?'

'Can you sign this for me?' She thrust a CD under my nose.

I was stupefied. Liam saved me from ripping her head off by leaning forward and saying: 'Not now. Please, this has been very disturbing for everybody.'

Something about his firm tone made the group turn away and shuffle out of the funeral parlour. I stared at the space where they had stood. I couldn't imagine a time when I'd ever feel happy again.

'Come on,' Brad said.

We rose and walked out into the creeping wind. My breath made puffs of steam in front of me. A couple of journalists descended on us, barking out questions. 'What is the band going to do now?' 'Have you any idea who did this?' 'Who is Elizabeth?' 'Is it true that most of your fans are Satanists?'

Liam placed his back between my body and the peering television crew. He was as jumpy as a neurotic bomb disposal expert because his parents were in town. What would they think if they saw their son's new girlfriend on television screaming obscenities at news crews? It was difficult enough keeping them in the dark about my part in the latest Eye Surgeon scandal. I was due to have dinner with them on Wednesday night—it had been arranged before Jeff's death—and Liam was desperate for everything to appear normal to them. It had been hard for him, the timing of my latest drama. While he seemed to thrive on my helpless weeping, he couldn't spend too much time with me because he was tyrannised by his mother's opinion. I understood, of course. Or maybe I was too weak and too empty to care.

We passed under the arches of the funeral parlour's front gate and into the car park. Heavy grey clouds scudded overhead. Liam unlocked his car for me. Brad stopped me before I got in.

'What are we going to do about the band?' he asked.

'We don't have to decide that right away,' I said.

Liam came to stand beside us. 'Brad, Lisa has other things to worry about at the moment.'

I threw a warning glance at Liam. Brad glared at him with icy hatred. I reached over and squeezed Brad's shoulder. 'Call me soon,' I said.

'Come on, Lisa.' Liam opened the passenger side door and motioned me in. He turned back to face Brad. Tiny droplets of icy rain began to spit down on us. 'I'm sorry, Brad. I know Jeff's loss has affected you. Lisa tells me he was a very good friend to you.'

I have the utmost admiration for Brad that he didn't spit out the stream of invective that Liam probably deserved at that moment. He quietly swallowed all the offensive words and said simply, through gritted teeth, 'You don't know the half of what I've lost.' Then he nodded curtly and turned away to walk towards his car.

Liam watched him go, then got in next to me. He started the car and the windscreen wipers commenced their lazy beating. I watched Brad get into his beat-up old car, terribly conscious that Liam's was shiny and new, that Brad wouldn't be getting a shiny new car of his own any time soon because this was without a doubt the end of the band. He was already in the process of realising that—no tour, no Livid Festival, no follow-up CD. I couldn't take my eyes off him as we left the car park and merged into the traffic.

Liam took me back to my hotel room and, with profuse apologies and a guilty expression, went back to work. The rain was falling heavily now, and I stood watching rivulets snake over the window. Traffic in the street below moved silently and distantly. This was the first time since Brad and I had made our horrific discovery that I'd had a chance to rest. I didn't have to be at the police station answering questions or organising a funeral or convincing Jeff's mother to part with her meagre savings to pay for it.

The heating was up too high and my skin felt dry and itchy, but I couldn't be bothered walking to the controls which were over by the door. I closed my eyes and tried to organise my mind. A scrap of a vision flashed out of the darkness. I was sitting behind the oak desk at Prestonvale, books spread out in front of me and that musty, cloying smell hanging close about me. A falling sensation accompanied it. I opened my eyes and snapped erect. These flashes were becoming more and more common, instants where a regression tugged at me and only the sheer force of my will could pull me back and keep me in the twentieth century. I focused on the climate control unit and watched as the dial turned down towards the blue section. The dry heat eased a little, making me shiver.

I leaned my head against the window. My breath made misty shapes on the glass. I could see my own reflection—a tatty girl with dark shadows under her eyes, who looked like the world had just got too much for her. It was eleven o'clock in the morning. The day stretched out endless and empty in front of me.

Liam had changed, and although I knew it was only temporary, it had started to bug me. He had been great in a lot of ways—paying for the room and all my meals, going around to my flat to pick up my clothes, bringing me books and magazines—but he rarely stayed for more than twenty minutes, and it was the company I needed, not the consumer goods.

We hadn't had sex once since his parents had arrived, and while I hadn't felt particularly horny myself, it concerned me that he could become so repressed overnight. He was twenty-eight years old, for Christ's sake. Surely he could be himself and let his parents see who that was. Added to that, I was worried about Brad, but I was getting more and more pressure from Liam not to see him. 'I don't trust him' was Liam's standard response. I rang Brad every day—in the morning before he started drinking—to see how he was. He called Numb Records daily, trying to convince them to give us time to get things back together, but their interest was already elsewhere. The whole thing was crumbling, it didn't look as though they were going to offer us another contract. That's how fast dreams can disappear.

And I couldn't stop thinking about death. About subterranean spaces and the decay that consumes us all eventually. It hung over me like a dirty blanket, obsessed me, made me panic when I woke at four in the morning thinking of it, kept me from going back to sleep. It seems I spent a lifetime wandering between the walls of my luxury hotel suite, thinking about the mouldering chill of the grave. Yet somehow, when Liam turned up on Wednesday morning to remind me about dinner with his parents that night, I was supposed to act as though everything was normal.

'Hi,' he said as I opened the door. He closed me in a hug, and I hung onto him, desperate for company and physical contact. He squeezed me once then let me go.

'I'm sick of being alone, Liam,' I said. 'When are your parents going home?'

'This time next week, I hope,' he said, sitting on

394

the bed. 'I'm sorry you've been alone so much. I thought you'd be used to it. You've always lived alone.'

'I need something to stop me thinking. I'm scaring myself.' I lay down on the bed next to him and pulled him down for a deep kiss. He struggled away from me after a few seconds and sat up demurely on the edge of the bed. I traced a finger along the inside seam of his trousers. He grabbed my hand and kissed it, then placed it gently on the bedspread.

'Are you hoping that your virginity will return if you just keep repressing your sexual urges?' I asked, impatience stealing into my voice.

'I'm sorry, Lisa. You have no idea what it's like. My parents are making me pray before every meal, they've given me a long-winded and embarrassing lecture about sex before marriage, and their disapproval . . .' He slumped forward. 'It's really weighing me down.'

'Well I don't want to add to your problems.'

'And I don't want to add to yours. Just bear with me for the next week or so, then you can move in with me. You'll have all the company you want.'

I nodded, but again I got that constricted feeling in my chest just thinking about making such a permanent decision.

'Has Inspector Honeywell called you back?' he asked, deliberately changing the subject.

'No. He's being a bit cagey. I don't mind, I don't have the energy to worry about all that business.'

'Do you feel safe?'

I shrugged. 'I guess so. Gilbert doesn't know where I am.'

'Do you know where he is?'

'I haven't tried again. It hurt so much last time. Please, Liam, I was in a comfortable state of denial. Don't take that away from me.'

395

He patted my leg. 'I'm sorry. I have to get to work. I should be able to get some time off when Mum and Dad are gone, and we'll get away for a weekend. You don't have any band commitments to tie you up now.'

And that made me feel so empty. 'Yeah, maybe,' I said, not feeling anything.

He stood and made his way to the door, then turned. 'Lisa, have you got something warm to wear tonight? It's been getting a bit cold at my place.'

'Yeah, no problem.'

He stood there for a moment, looking as though he wanted to say something.

'What?' I asked.

'Nothing.'

'No, what? What do you want to say? You look like an eight year old with a secret.'

'It's just . . . you know, you're meeting my parents for the first time and I want you to make a good impression.'

I didn't have the energy for this. 'Liam, don't worry. I've got some halfway decent clothes. I won't embarrass you.' This last sentence came out sounding more than a little sarcastic, so I smiled to cover it. 'Don't worry.'

'Thanks. I'll see you at seven. You don't mind catching a cab?'

'Not at all.'

'I'll pay for it.'

'There's no need.'

He nodded. 'I'll see you tonight. Remember, wrap up warm.' He left.

Wrap up warm? Was Liam turning into my grandmother? I slumped back on the bed, preparing for another day of ceiling staring.

Around six-thirty, I pulled my only decent clothes out of the wardrobe. I had bought a navy blue suit once when I'd thought briefly about getting a real job, and I hadn't worn it since. It comprised a pair of tailored slacks, a white silk chiffon shirt, a navy vest and a matching coat. I brushed my hair, put on some lipstick, and dressed, fighting down the suspicion that I looked ridiculous. The coat was too much so I left it off. I couldn't stand padded shoulders, they made me feel like a football player. I shrugged into my overcoat. It was a bit grungy but I planned to take it off before Liam's folks got a proper eyeful of me. I hoped I didn't look as tired and washed out as I felt. I was only going through the motions of this meeting for Liam's sake, but I had the feeling it was a defining moment in his life. Feeling like a girl playing dress-ups with her mother's clothes, I locked my hotel room and went to the foyer to catch a cab.

It was drizzling again, just like the first time I had been to Liam's. I had the most uncanny sense of *déja vu* as the cab driver turned into his pleasant suburban street. Only this time, the idea of domestic bliss was less appealing. I paid the cab driver and started up the path to find Liam waiting at the door. I walked up to him and he gave me a brief hug, then said in a whisper: 'They're in their room. I wanted a quick word with you.'

'What is it?' We entered the house and stood near the doorway.

'I overheard Inspector Honeywell talking to some of the officers on my floor today. They got nothing from Jeff's murder site to help identify the killer.'

'Nothing? He fingerpainted my name on the wall, for fuck's sake. You mean they got nothing from that?'

Liam looked nervously over his shoulder.

'I'm sorry, Lisa. I know you were hoping this would all be over soon . . .'

'Christ! What if they never find him? What if he

finds me first?' My voice cracked and I had to take a deep breath. How could I go through with this sad charade of family bonding now?

He touched my hair, pity in his deep brown eyes. He was so beautiful when he was pitying me. I pushed his hand away and he helped me out of my overcoat. 'I'll think about this later. I'm determined to make a good impression on your folks,' I said, feeling angry that I had to.

'I'm sorry about this timing, Lisa.'

'It's not your fault.' I turned to notice he was holding my coat and staring at my left arm. 'What's the matter?'

'Can you keep your coat on?'

'What? Why?'

'Your shirt's see-through.'

'I've got a vest on. They can't see my tits. Settle down, Liam.'

He made a nervous hand gesture, then continued in a low voice. 'Your tattoo. You can see it through your shirt.'

My fucking tattoo. So this was what 'wrap up warm' was all about. 'Jeez, Liam, I can't believe you're doing this to me.'

He was trying to get my coat back on me. 'It'll just make things easier, please.'

'Fuck. Do you want an easy life or an honest life?'

'Please, keep your voice down.'

I pulled away from him. 'No, I won't keep my voice down, and I won't cover up my arm. They won't notice it.'

'Yes, they will. *She* will. She notices everything. She'll be watching you like a hawk.'

'Liam . . .' I ran a hand through my hair, and Liam reached over to straighten it up again. An angry sob was stuck in my throat. 'Liam, please. You're putting me through hell here.'

'Then just put your coat back on.'

A low rage began to boil in my blood. 'No. I won't.'

A female voice echoed from within the house. 'Liam, where are you? Is she here yet?'

'It's her,' he hissed.

'Good, I'll have her meet me the way I am.'

'Why are you doing this to me?'

'Because Brad's right, you're a fucking mummy's boy. Why don't you grow up and stand up to them?' I realised too late that my voice was too loud. Liam's mother was approaching. She emerged from the hall-way and into the lounge room, peering towards the door disapprovingly.

'Is that Lisa? Is that her?'

Liam spun around to look at her. 'Mum, I—'

'No, I'm at the wrong address,' I said, making a little curtsy. 'I'm actually a whore, but I'm booked for next door, not here.'

Liam turned to give me a look like a black squall. I grabbed my coat. 'Have a nice dinner, hanky boy,' I said. My pulse was thumping in my throat. I expected him to come after me. I walked down the front stairs. Along the front path. Into the street. When I turned, he had shut the door. I was alone. Again.

I walked down to the main road planning to catch a bus back to town. The air was heavy with the scent of wet bitumen, and streetlights reflected weakly in shallow puddles along the road. I sat to wait at a route 67 bus stop which would take me back to within five streets of my hotel. I slumped back into the seat, pulling my overcoat close around me and resting my head on the back of the shelter. The clouds had taken on a pink tinge from the streetlights. Occasionally a car swept past, spraying water up from its back tyres.

'Elizabeth!'

I sat up with a start and looked around. It had been a woman's voice, a cry of pain. I saw nobody, and it took me a full five seconds to remember that I wasn't Elizabeth, that I was Lisa. I jumped to my feet and started pacing. I refused to go under. Hang on, hang on. One foot in front of the other.

'Elizabeth! It hurts, it hurts.'

The voice was coming from nowhere and everywhere at once. I placed my hands over my ears. 'Stop it!' I shouted to nobody. A gust of wind shook the branches of a tree nearby, showering me with cold drops. A taxi went by and I put my hand out to stop it, realising as it spun past that there was already somebody in the back, warm and dry.

'I can't, Elizabeth, I can't.' The voice was fading out now. I clamped my jaws together hard, as if the physical effort could somehow keep Elizabeth's world out of my head. My heartbeat began to slow. Things were returning to normal. Suburban darkness folded around me once more. In the distance a bus rattled out of the dark. I stepped out to the kerb and hailed it down.

My bus pass was too bent to go into the automatic slot, so I fished two dollars out of my pocket and paid the driver. The bus started with a jolt as I made my way up to the back. An unshaven man in overalls ignored me, a middle-aged woman in a green crocheted hat took great interest in my passing, then went back to her magazine. We were the only three on the bus. It smelled of diesel, dirt and old food. Dirty streaks of water from dripping umbrellas crisscrossed the floor. I sat in a torn seat second from the back and rested my head against the window.

The bus driver had the radio tuned to a hits of the sixties and seventies station, and the Byrds segued into the Mamas and the Papas. The tuner was slightly off the station. The music buzzed and faded in and out around corners. I leaned my head on the glass and watched suburbia flicker by me.

'Oh, God, Elizabeth! Father! Elizabeth, get Father, I'm dying!'

I closed my hand tightly around the smooth iron railing next to me. It was Mirabel's voice, emerging and fading out of the darkness. 'Stairway to Heaven' had just started on the radio, dissolving into white noise on every second bar. A slow, dozy feeling settled over me. I felt incapable of fighting it. I felt I should just give in. Something warm and heavy pressed me down, irresistible.

I forced myself to stand up. My foot slipped on the damp floor and I came crashing down on my backside. The bus driver called out, 'Are you okay?'

I got to my feet. The pain had jolted me back into reality. 'Yes, I'm okay. I slipped over.'

I sat down again and looked out the window. We were passing into the city, under a freeway overpass. Tall buildings were lit up against the darkness. People shielded themselves against the rain with umbrellas as they hurried into restaurants and pubs. It seemed as though the whole world was buzzing along without me. I craved company so badly it made my heart ache. The light in the bus seemed particularly bright and cruel.

I reached up and pressed the bell. My hotel was still a few stops away, but I saw a cab rank with five cabs waiting and I couldn't bear to go back to the hotel and sit there alone. The bus driver pulled over and let me out. My body ached from my fall. No voices at the moment, but I wasn't going to chance being alone. I hopped into a warm cab and gave the driver the address of Brad's parents' house. I just hoped he was home.

It had been so long since I had been to see Brad's parents, that I accidentally got the cabbie to drop me off outside number twenty-four instead of number thirty-four. When I realised my mistake, I began to walk up the street. It was raining steadily now, and I pulled the collar of my overcoat up as far as it would go. There were a few cars parked out the front of the house, and lights blazed and music blared inside. At least he was home, but it seemed he had a few visitors.

I stood on the footpath for a few moments, gathering my wits. I didn't know what I was doing; I was just seeking company, physical comfort, trying to keep the voices out of my head. Everything seemed to be swinging inside, and I felt so lonely and excluded from it all, like I was part of the night, part of a dark miasma that the lights and the loud music were attempting to ward off. What right did I have to take my darkness into Brad's party?

But I was getting wet out on the street, so I had no choice. I walked up to the front door and pushed it open. The cloying scent of marijuana hung in the air. I shrugged out of my coat and folded it over a coathook. The house was full of frequent flyers. Some of them called out to me. Brad sat on the couch watching television with the sound turned down while the party went on without him. A girl sat next to him, streaky black make-up around her eyes, her hand firmly jammed between his thighs. I walked up to them and stood in front of the television.

'Lisa?' Brad said with surprise, pushing the girl off and pulling me down next to him. She tottered off unevenly towards the kitchen.

'What are you doing here?' he asked me.

'Are you having a party?'

He gestured around him almost nonchalantly. 'It's been like this every night. I didn't want to be alone, but I'm growing tired of it now. Nice suit.'

I leaned in and sniffed. There was no scent of alcohol or mull over him. 'You're straight,' I said.

'Yeah. I got tired of that too. Somebody's just gone out to get me a bottle of bourbon, but I don't know how much more alcohol I can imbibe without pickling a major internal organ.'

'Anyway, I'm here now. You're not alone any more.'

He gazed at me for a long time. The flickering light from the television reflected in his eyes. 'Where's hanky boy tonight?'

'Dining with the Jesus club.'

He suppressed a smile. 'Sounds like the honeymoon's over.'

I could feel my jaw tremble. 'Liam gets off on my helplessness. If I show a bit of spunk he gets antsy. It's scary.'

He nodded slowly, still gazing at me. Without warning he leaned in and kissed me, full and hard on the lips. My body stiffened momentarily, then melted into his.

'That's what I like,' he said close to my ear as he covered my neck in tiny kisses. 'Give in.'

'Brad . . .' That was the only thing that could make it out of my mouth before he covered it with his again. I wove my fingers into his hair. A helpless groan gasped out of every pore in my body. He wrapped his arm around me, pushed me back on the couch. The music stopped and somebody changed the CD. The Smashing Pumpkins exploded from the speakers, and Brad was still kissing me and I wasn't stopping him. His mouth tasted of the tinny zing of tobacco. From the waist down I was warm, swirling mush. My skin seemed to be turning to liquid. I became aware that we had an audience, and pushed Brad off me. The girl who had been sitting with him was staring at us angrily.

'Brad?' she said.

'Go away.' He stood up and pulled me to my feet. 'All of you go away.' His arm was around my waist and his hand was caressing the side of my breast. I swooned into him. What the fuck was I doing?

He caught my hand and led me to the stairs. 'You coming up?' he said. It was the most unromantic proposal I had ever had, but the most irresistible. A hot flush raced through me.

'Yeah,' I said, 'yeah, let's go upstairs.'

Nobody had taken any notice of Brad's order to leave. The music was still thumping as Brad led me to an upstairs bedroom. He closed the door behind us and pressed me up against it, deftly unbuttoning my vest while he kissed me. I shrugged out of it, and he was pulling up my top, reaching underneath to enclose my breasts in his hands. I was a limp doll in his arms. He took a step back to look at me. 'This is going to be so good,' he said.

He led me over to the bed and we sat down. My eyes were growing accustomed to the gloom. 'This used to be my bedroom when I was a little tyke,' he said conversationally as he kicked his shoes off and started unbuckling his jeans. 'See, *Star Wars* wall-paper.'

I peered at the wall and could just make out a few lightsabres and Tie fighters. I leaned over to unlace my shoes and kicked them under the bed. I could barely imagine Brad as a little boy. At the moment he seemed like the archetypal man.

'So, have you ever had sex in this room before?' I asked playfully.

'No, but I thought about it in this room. I thought about it a lot.' He pulled off his shirt and loosened his hair. The way it caressed the flesh on his back sent a shiver of anticipation through me. He turned to me. 'Do you know what you're doing?' he asked, gently brushing my hair from my face.

'Yes. I know what I'm doing.'

'What about Liam?'

'Just . . . don't even say his name. Let me just pretend he doesn't exist for a while. It'll make it a lot easier to cheat on him.'

'Well, we want it to be easy now, don't we?' He pulled my shirt over my head and unpinned my bra, buried his face between my breasts.

'Do you want the light on?' I said softly, touching the back of his head with my fingertips.

'No. I think we're both a little the worse for wear compared to the last time we did this.'

'I don't even remember the last time really. Do you?'

'I don't remember much. It was a long time ago.' He pushed me down on the bed and went to work on the buttons on my pants. The bedspread smelled old and musty. I wriggled out of the remainder of my clothes. A deep shiver shuddered through me.

'Cold?' he asked.

'No. Nervous. I'm nervous.'

'I remember your skin,' he said, trailing his fingers in long delicate arcs over my belly. 'Really pale and soft. Never seen another girl's skin like that.'

'You were doing me a favour. I was desperate to be rid of my virginity.'

He kissed me once, then stood up and stripped completely. When he lay down next to me, his skin was hot and smooth. I ran my mouth over his neck and shoulders, down to his right arm to find the

405

companion to my tattoo. I licked it slowly. One of his hands dove between my legs. I gasped.

'I can't believe I'm letting you do this,' I said.

'Neither can I.' He rolled over and laid half on top of me, sucking one of my nipples into his mouth. I thought I would explode from the rush of passion. My insides ached for him. He slowly brought me closer and closer to a climax, then backed off at the last minute, leaving me gasping.

'One last time,' he said. 'Are you sure?'

'I'm sure.'

'Then say it.'

'I just did. I'm sure.'

He shook his head in the dark. His hair tickled my face. 'No. Say "Fuck me, Brad".'

I laughed lightly. 'I knew there was a catch.'

'Go on, say it.'

'Fuck me, Brad,' I said in a deadpan voice.

'Mean it.'

I pulled him down on top of me and screamed in my best blue movie voice: 'Fuck me, Brad, fuck me.' We both dissolved into laughter. Eventually his laughter slowed and he just lay there looking into my face. He put a hand delicately on my cheek.

'I love you, Lisa.'

I sighed. 'No, you don't. You just think you do.'

'I know I do.' He pushed my legs apart and I wrapped them around his back, and guided him inside me. He made a noise. A sighing, dying noise.

'I've waited so long,' he said.

I didn't reply. I buried my face in his shoulder and prepared to let the magic happen.

'Elizabeth!'

My body froze. No, not now, not now.

'What's wrong?' Brad asked.

'I . . .'

'*Elizabeth!*' The name echoed around in my head, a light buzzing noise seeped into my mind.

'No!' I called out.

Brad sat back. 'What's wrong? Lisa?'

'Brad . . .' I reached a hand up for him, but he seemed miles away.

'*Elizabeth, it hurts, I can't do it. Elizabeth!*'

'Lisa?'

The room spun around me. Time, again, to descend.

CHAPTER
TWENTY-SIX

Spring outside, hell inside. Mirabel had taken it upon herself to have one of the longest and most difficult labours in history. Since before daylight I had been sitting with her in her chamber, listening to her cries of pain. Outside, the sun had come up on the first warm, clear day of April and I longed to be out roaming by the river, watching the sunshine glance and sparkle off the water, getting some warm, fresh air into my lungs. But I was trapped here beside her. A midwife from the village had come up to help us. Her name was Caroline and she was a hard-faced, taciturn thing with rough hands, dressed like a Puritan. She kept reminding Mirabel that childbirth pangs were a direct result of Eve's first transgression in the Garden of Eden, and that enthusiastic repentance was the only way women could avoid burning in hell. Mirabel was agonised by the pain, horrified by the realisation that there was only one passage through which this baby would emerge, and now terrified of eternal damnation because she knew she had conceived unnaturally. I knew all this from holding her tiny sweating palm all morning. Boredom had led me to tune into her thoughts. I now knew conclusively that Mirabel was a girl of simple notions, and in some ways I was envious of her lack of depth.

Mirabel kept her head steadfastly turned away from Caroline and spoke only to me. Sometimes, during a particularly bad pang, she would tell me that she was dying, order me to fetch her father, but the pain would pass and she would relax again into her bed, her forehead glistening with perspiration and her eyes wide with terror. In her usual fashion, she was attempting to elicit as much sympathy as possible for her pains, and kept up a steady diatribe about her suffering. I believe she thought herself the only woman who had ever been through this, though the population of our country testified otherwise.

The sun was setting, the shadows in the room growing long and spindly, before the child finally made her appearance. I was lighting a lamp when Mirabel let loose an agonised cry and Caroline called out to demand my return. I hurried over and grasped Mirabel's hand. Caroline had pulled up Mirabel's skirt and laid clean linen all around her. A greyish fluid, streaky with blood, gushed out from between Mirabel's legs, and she howled in pain, trying to spread her legs further apart but being hindered by her hip joints. She looked like a child herself, skinny and pale, with sparse, downy pubic hair. She was shouting incoherently now as Caroline leaned over her and said, 'We can see its head,' in an emotionless voice. Obviously the miracle of birth had lost its novelty for her long ago.

It seemed to take forever to get the baby's head out, and Mirabel leaned into me at one point and whispered, 'Can you not give me one of your spells for the pain?' Caroline responded with a glare of mingled fear and malice.

'She's not sensible,' I replied calmly.

Caroline muttered a prayer under her breath and returned her attention to the emerging child. A trickle of blood seeped into the linen, and I knew that Mirabel's soft flesh was tearing and splitting. My own skin seemed to sting in sympathy. With one huge spasm, and a shudder of pain that looked as though it would break her body, Mirabel pushed the child's head into the world, and Amelia Mary Lewis was born.

I was surprised by my excitement and excess of emotion. I was near tears as I raced into the hallway calling for Uncle Tom. I met him halfway down the stairs.

'What? Is everything all right?' he asked. My calls had alarmed him.

'Yes, yes.' I burst into tears and clasped him around the middle. 'Yes, it's a little girl. A beautiful little girl. Uncle Tom, you have a granddaughter.'

He squeezed me tight, but I could tell he was disappointed. It seemed Uncle Tom had some trouble acquiring male heirs.

'There's always next time,' I said softly.

He kissed the top of my head. 'Yes. I'm sure I'll be quite delighted to have a granddaughter. Especially if she's anything like her cousin Elizabeth.'

'Come,' I said, taking his hand, 'let's see if she's ready for visitors yet.'

We ascended the stairs, and I opened the chamber door a crack to see that Caroline was arranging the bed covers over Mirabel's tired little body, and had handed the baby to her, cleaned and swaddled tightly in fresh linen. I pushed the door open and beckoned to Uncle Tom. We approached the bed, and Mirabel looked up weakly.

'Father,' she said.

He leaned over and kissed her cheek. 'Dear girl. How are you feeling?'

'I'm sore and I'm tired,' she said with her customary pout. 'Where is my husband? Why isn't he here? Fetch him, Elizabeth. Fetch him at once.'

Uncle Tom looked to me. 'Would you mind, Elizabeth?' It had become evident to all in the months since Master Gale's death that Gilbert and I no longer got along. We went to great pains to avoid each other. Uncle Tom had been very patient and had asked few questions.

'Of course I'll fetch him,' I said magnanimously, leaning over to kiss the tiny child on its nose. It coughed and began to squall. I backed out of the room and went downstairs to find Gilbert.

I searched in a few of the downstairs rooms before heading with trepidation towards the magic cottage, a place where I no longer liked to be. Gilbert still spent a great deal of time down there, mostly to get away from Mirabel and her constant mewling, which had grown proportionate with her belly.

I hesitantly pushed open the door and called, 'Gilbert?'

'In here.'

I found him in the back room, drawing symbols in blue ink in his leather book. I stood behind him and waited, watching his hand firmly inscribe the intertwining circles and arcs. Eventually, without turning to face me, he said, 'I suppose you are come to tell me that I'm a father?'

'Yes,' I replied. 'A lovely girl. Mirabel has named her Amelia.'

He dropped his pen and turned to face me. 'Mirabel has named her? Have I no rights as a father? Is it not my responsibility to choose a name?'

'She said you had told her you didn't want to be bothered with the child.'

'I might want to name her Beelzebub or Astaroth

or Belial.' His smile curled at the corners of his lips. 'What do you think, Elizabeth?'

'I think you're being foolish and pig-headed.'

He rose and stood very close, seemed to be towering over me. 'Aren't you afraid to be here alone with me?'

'No. Why should I be?'

'Because you, more than anyone, know what I am capable of.'

He was clearly trying to unsettle me. I ignored his remark. 'Are you coming up to the house to see your wife?'

He snorted. 'My wife? She's practically a stranger to me.'

'You have to come. For Uncle Tom's sake.'

'Of course, for Uncle Tom's sake.' His hands encircled my waist. It was all I could do not to swoon into him. He still had some magnetic power and, God help me, I hadn't ever stopped loving him.

'Take your hands away, Gilbert,' I said with some effort.

'Are you sure you want me to?'

'Yes. You're ugly and evil. I despise you.'

A cloud of anger passed over his face. He reached his hand into a bowl of dried plants on the table, then slammed a handful against my belly, saying something low and guttural under his breath. I stepped back in fright, and he swung past me on his way up to the house. I brushed the dirt off my dress and followed him.

Halfway up the stairs a bolt of pain shot through my stomach. I doubled over and lowered myself onto the stair. Again a bolt of pain pierced me. I pressed my hand into my belly in agony. He had put some kind of spell on me, and I was angered more than I was concerned about the pain. He had disappeared into Mirabel's room, so I pulled myself up and went to my own bed to lie down. The pain was constant now and I had to bite my tongue to stop from calling out. Everyone in the house was so excited about the baby that they failed to notice my absence. I lay on my bed for two hours, sweat exploding from my pores, trying to regulate my breathing and my terror. Surely he wouldn't kill me this way. The pain seemed to be moving down and pressing on my lower body. I should never have found myself alone with him. He was dangerous. And although he had always thought himself above crazy spinsters with their low magic, it seemed he had forgotten these elitist notions in his moment of anger.

Finally, after hours of pain, I realised that I had to visit the privy and I agonisingly passed a handful of scratchy twigs, barbed leaves and powdery dirt. With them went the pain, leaving only my bitter anger and a childish desire for revenge. As ever, Gilbert had managed to provoke in me the basest emotions. I padded downstairs to the kitchen and stood at the back door peering out towards the cottage. A faint orange glow flickered in the side window, so I presumed he was in there. I searched in the pantry for a bag of rice and scooped up a handful. I crept over the dewy grass and pushed the front door of the cottage open gently.

Trying to be very quiet, I tiptoed in, over the mattress which still lay in front of the fire, past the canvases that we had never touched, and into the back room.

He wasn't there. He'd left a lamp burning, but he was nowhere to be seen. His *Liber Omnis Scientiae* lay open on the bench.

I looked at the grains of rice in my hand, then back to the book. Not for the eyes of others. And why was that? When he knew everything about me and my sorcery, and I still had no evidence of his making any of the sacrifices I had had to make? I leaned in and looked over the page. It was covered in numbers. I reached out to turn the page, and as I did a horrible screaming sound filled my ears and I started back.

I looked around to discern from whence the noise had come, but could see nothing. Then a sudden rushing of air, almost like a flapping of invisible wings, gathered around my ears and I thought I felt tiny claws in my hair, attacking me. The scream rang out again and I clamped my fists over my ears to block it out. I backed out of the room and the attack stopped. I peered back in at the book and it closed spontaneously with a loud thump. Clearly Gilbert had taken measures to ensure nobody else saw his work.

As I turned around to leave the cottage, Gilbert was striding through the front door.

'What are you doing here?' he demanded. Perhaps he had been warned that somebody was dabbling in his affairs.

My hand holding the rice was clutched in a fist against my chest, and I could feel the rhythm of my heart speed up. Steeling my nerves, I muttered an incantation, flattened my palm and blew on the rice. The grains floated on a warm puff of air over to Gilbert and struck his body. He looked momentarily confused, and I took the opportunity to duck past him and run back to the house.

'Elizabeth!' he bellowed. But I didn't look back.

I went to sit with Mirabel the next morning. Caroline had gone home and I felt I could chat with my cousin a little more freely without the pious midwife present to glower at my every word. Mirabel seemed in good spirits, though she still complained of being very tired. I bounced Amelia gently on my lap.

'You'll have to educate her, Mirabel,' I said. 'If you want her to have a chance in life, she'll have to be properly educated.'

'Of course,' Mirabel replied. 'I'd like her to be clever like you, not a silly fool like me.'

'Mirabel, you're not a silly fool,' I said, surprised that she knew she was.

'Oh yes, I am. We both know that. I'd be delighted if you would take care of educating Amelia. That is, if you don't find a husband and leave us.'

I didn't reply. She had triggered a chain of thought that I had been trying to suppress. Was I going to stay? I loved Uncle Tom, and I loved Amelia, and Mirabel was occasionally pleasant company, but none of these were reasons to stay. Only Gilbert was a reason to stay, and he was also my reason to leave. He was a frightening man, unpredictable and bound by no moral code. And I despised him on my outward breaths and loved him with my inward breaths. Since we had stopped speaking to each other, my life had become an eternal round of tedium. Even those things that had brought me pleasure before his arrival now seemed petty and meaningless. Time was slipping away from me, drawing me closer to death, and nothing meant much any more. I had vowed to stay until the baby was born, and now the time had come to make up my mind.

Uncle Tom knocked lightly on the door and let himself in. He took Amelia from me and cuddled her gently. Mirabel and I smiled at each other, amused by his fondness. He talked some baby language to her then handed her back to me. He sat on the edge of the bed and stroked Mirabel's forehead.

'Feeling any better?' he asked.

'I'm still so tired,' she replied.

As I looked at her, I realised she had taken on an unhealthy shade. The first pang of alarm struck my heart. But then, I reasoned, perhaps she really was just tired.

'Your husband is unwell today,' he replied. Gilbert had taken to sleeping in Master Gale's old chamber as Mirabel's pregnancy had progressed. I found it more than a little perverse.

'Unwell? What's wrong?' I asked, trying to hide my eagerness to know.

He shook his head. 'I'm unsure what caused it, but this morning he woke up covered in tiny white sores. They burst if he brushes up against anything.'

Mirabel wrinkled her nose in distaste. 'Well, he's not to come anywhere near Amelia today.'

'Is he in pain?' I asked.

'Yes, I believe he's in a great deal of pain. He wouldn't hear of me calling out of the village for a physician though. He's lying in his chamber, quite unable to move.'

Good. Now perhaps we were even and there would be no more crone's tricks on each other. According to my spell, the sores would be cleared by supper. Gilbert would know by then that he wasn't the only one who could indulge in petty revenges.

'I'm going to sit with him this morning, see if he needs anything,' Uncle Tom continued. He looked at me slyly. 'He asked me to tell you that he owes you something.'

My heartbeat quickened. 'What does he owe me?'

'He wouldn't say, but I think it might be that long-awaited apology. Perhaps seeing his newborn daughter has softened his heart and he's ready to call a truce with you. You've barely spoken two words to each other since Christmas.'

I knew that Gilbert was not going to repay me in supplications for forgiveness, and I felt weary anticipating what kind of repayment was due me. For somebody who pursued godhead, Gilbert seemed at times to trade in the most primitive of human responses. It made me wonder how much I could believe of what he had taught me. What concerned me most was his notion of good and evil. If the higher power we served was amoral as he said, why did he have to carry out acts that seemed so diabolical? And while he had expected of me the greatest commitment—marking by his dark master—I had not seen evidence that he had made the same commitment. It had crossed my mind since our latest breach that he could be using me experimentally, that maybe I was damned after all, despite what he said. Perhaps it was time I confronted him and worked out some kind of agreement by which we could remain living in this house together, at least until I decided what I was going to do.

I was nervous all day, deciding whether or not to speak with Gilbert. He was right after all, I was afraid of being alone with him. Especially now that I had aroused his anger. I certainly had no illusions that my power could ever be a match for his. Finally, after taking Mirabel's supper up to her and trying not to notice how pale she was growing, I slipped downstairs and into Gilbert's chamber without knocking. I couldn't see him, but the tapestries over the bed were closed so I approached quietly. Just as I was about to part the curtains gently, his hand shot out and clamped around my wrist, and he dragged me down beside him. The hanging closed behind me and I found myself in total darkness.

'Gilbert?' I said fearfully.

'Elizabeth. How nice of you to visit me in my

illness. But you can feel that the sores are gone.' He ran my hand over his body, and I realised he was naked. I shivered in delight.

'I'm sorry. I was angry because you made me very sick.'

'You don't know rage as I do, Elizabeth.'

'Gilbert, have you lied to me?'

'About what?'

'About the pact I made, about the witch-mark. You swear you made the same commitment but I've yet to see . . .'

He was laughing quietly. My eyes were growing used to the darkness and I could make out his face in the gloom. 'Have you ever seen how quickly people turn to God when they know they are close to death?' he said. 'How quickly they reshuffle their beliefs to achieve peace of mind? Is that what's happening with you, Elizabeth? Are you worried about your eternal soul and your entrance to heaven now that you've finished with me?'

'No, it's not that. I was too trusting of you.'

He sat up and pulled back the curtains, reached for a taper on his bedside table and lit it with his hands. The curtain fell and we were enclosed again. He held the taper out to me.

'Examine me, Elizabeth.'

I took the candle from him. 'Examine you?'

He rolled onto his stomach. 'You'll find the same mark on me. If it's damnation, then we're damned together. We can spend eternity in hell in each other's company. Won't that be pleasant?'

I ran my fingers over his strong calves and up along the backs of his legs, the candle lighting my way. Underneath the curve of his left buttock I found it—a mark, almost identical to mine. I touched it lightly. Then I couldn't stop touching him, feeling his hard surfaces and warm crevices.

'Are you convinced now, Elizabeth?'

'Yes. But that wasn't the only reason I came. I want to see if you would call a truce with me. Be friends again, for the sake of peace in the household.'

'What you are doing to me now is not generally encompassed by friendship.'

I pulled my hand away from his body and sat up demurely. 'I'm sorry.'

He rolled over and sat up, then blew out the candle and took it from me and put it down beside the bed. He pinned me down violently and pressed on top of me, his hands pushing up my skirts. With no preparation he forced himself into me, and I gasped quietly from pain. He put his hand over my face, as though he didn't want to see me. I felt violated, insulted. He grunted away as though I weren't there, then rolled off when he was finished and said breathlessly, 'Why should I call a truce with you?'

'Because you love me?' I hadn't meant for it to sound like a question.

'No, I don't. Surely that much was just obvious.'

How could something without physical cause be so painful to my insides? I tried to maintain my composure. 'Well then, because you used to love me.'

'I never loved you.'

'You're lying. You did love me, you told me so often.'

'It wasn't true. You were useful to me, that's all. I needed an apprentice to hone my skills, and what better candidate than a bored widow, desperate for love and foolish enough to believe anything I told her.'

I rearranged my gown and lay quietly next to him.

My heart felt that it might explode. Still, perhaps he was only saying these things to hurt me. I bit my lip to stop a sob escaping.

'I chose you,' he continued. 'At the fair. You don't even know how it came about, do you? My father was meeting with Sir Thomas; we were standing by the exchange stall while you and Mirabel sat watching the puppet show. Sir Thomas pointed out his daughter to us and I saw you. You were perfectly suited to my intentions. Your boredom, your willingness to be leapt by any fellow who looked at you sideways—these things were obvious. And there was something else about you. You reeked of sin. I only found out today what that sin was.'

I could no longer keep my voice even. 'Gilbert, don't say this if it isn't true. At least be honest with me.'

'So I suggested the marriage with Mirabel, suggested it in my own way, that is. My father and Sir Thomas are two of the oldest, stupidest goats in the land so it wasn't very hard to slide into their minds with my wishes. It was all arranged within a week. And then I had my virgin wife and my lovely apprentice.'

'You don't mean it.'

'An apprentice, Elizabeth, that's all you were to me. An apprentice, and a warm, tight place to spill my seed.'

My skin felt hot. All I could do was shake my head mutely in the darkness, push down the wave of desolation before it engulfed me.

'Aren't you curious?' he asked.

'Curious?'

'About your sin, the sin I could smell all over you when I met you.'

'I don't know what you're talking about,' I admitted.

He shifted, made himself more comfortable under a blanket. 'Sir Thomas came to sit with me today. He's disappointed about the girl child.'

'I know that.'

'He let a little too much slip. He bent his head and said he was cursed with girls because of what he had done.'

My heart twisted. Poor Uncle Tom. Of course he would be fond enough to blame himself. What foolish guilt was he nursing in his heart? 'The poor old fellow,' I said, 'after he's been so good to me, I'm sure that he's absolved any sins of his youth.'

'Ah, there's a reason he's been so good to you.'

'Because he loves me, Gilbert. Just because you're incapable of love doesn't mean that others can't feel it and act from it.'

'No, I'm not saying he doesn't love you. He clearly adores you, but there's more to it. I was curious. I, like you, couldn't think what burden he's been carrying, so out of curiosity I took his hand in mine and reached for the answer.'

'And?' No doubt it was something Uncle Tom would rather keep secret, but it seemed Gilbert would tell me anyway.

'Here, let me show you.' I felt him move over me, place his fingertips on my temple. I closed my eyes and he spun the image before my mind's eye.

It was a room at Prestonvale, my room, but different. A different tapestry hung over the bed, my desk wasn't there, nor my bookcase. The bed hangings were pulled back and caught with a ribbon. Lying on the bed was a woman who looked like me, but fuller of figure and younger.

'Mother,' I cried aloud.

'Shh,' Gilbert said.

My mother was dozing with a book on her chest.

It was early afternoon and windy outside, the swinging branches making the sunlight shift and waver in patterns on the floor and over my mother's face. The door creaked and she opened her eyes and looked up, smiling at her visitor. Her voice—exactly as I remembered it—filled my head.

'Thomas,' she said. 'You're home.'

'Yes. I missed you, Eleanor.' He approached and kissed her cheek. It was Uncle Tom, but young and handsome, his beard still richly brown, not streaked with grey. He sat beside her on the bed.

'Everything went well in London?'

He stretched. 'Yes, very well. We left early, that's why I'm back today.'

'I'm glad,' she said. 'I have to talk to you about something important.'

He nodded silently, his eyes fixed on her face, an indulgent smile playing on his lips—the same he gave me so often.

'James Williams has asked for my hand, and as Father is no longer with us, it falls to you to give permission.'

He didn't answer for a long time. My mother watched him carefully. Or was it fearfully?

'You want to go away, Eleanor?'

She laughed quietly, almost nervously. 'You know I wouldn't if I didn't have to. But I have to marry. And James is lovely—you like him, don't you?'

'I don't want to be alone,' he said. I knew that tone so well. Those inflections, that need for love that Uncle Tom still wore so painfully on his sleeve.

'Thomas,' she said, reaching up a hand to stroke his beard. He grasped her hand and kissed it. She closed her eyes and sighed. I was discomfited, I wanted this to stop. I struggled against Gilbert but he held me firm.

422

'Eleanor, you don't love him, you love me,' Uncle Tom said.

'Yes, but you're my dear, dear *brother*,' she replied with significant emphasis. He kept kissing her fingers, turning her hand over, kissing her palm, moving his lips up to her wrist. A guilty groan escaped from his mouth.

'I can't let you marry him,' he said at last, seeming to come to his senses. 'I need you here with me. I can't manage without your help.' He let her hand go and looked into his lap.

She set her jaw, as if she had been expecting this. 'If you don't let me, I'll elope. He has money, we don't need my dowry.' She paused for effect. 'He loves me.'

'*I* love you,' Uncle Tom said to her.

She sighed. 'Yes, as a brother should.'

'I can be more than a brother.'

'Thomas, don't start that—'

He leaned over and silenced her sentence with a kiss. I felt a worm of shock wriggle through me. She let him kiss her for a few moments, then pushed him off.

'No, Thomas. I think it's clear that we need to be apart from each other.'

Uncle Tom made a little cry of pain, and angry tears began to spill from his eyes. 'You won't go.'

'I will go. I have to go.'

He clasped both her hands in his, bent his head onto them. Lowly, slyly, he whispered: 'You'll stay. I'll ruin you for any other man.'

'Thomas, listen to what you're saying.'

His grasp on her hands tightened. She tried to pull away but he held her firm, his knuckles turning white. With a kind of violent reverence, he pushed her arms over her head and pinned them down with one hand. The other hand he drew in circles over the bodice of her dress. I didn't want to see this, I could hear my own whimpering from miles away.

My mother struggled against him, fear—but no surprise—in her eyes.

'Thomas, you mustn't do this.'

'You have asked for this with your eyes, and your hands, and your body,' he said, though it seemed to be directed at himself rather than at her—a necessary justification. He was shaking with passion. He pushed up her petticoats and plunged his hand between her legs. She squealed, shook her head from side to side. Then I saw her spread her legs voluntarily. No matter that she was crying out, struggling against him with her upper body, I saw her do it.

I fought against Gilbert and broke free. The dark under the canopy rushed back into my senses and the vision of my mother and my uncle disappeared. I gasped for air, my jaw was trembling.

'Who was your father, Elizabeth?' Gilbert asked.

'James Williams. He was a spice merchant. He died at sea before I was born.'

He shook his head. 'No. He died at sea before he could marry your mother. Before he knew she was already pregnant with her brother's child. Sir Thomas is your father. He raped your mother. Although she didn't seem to mind too much, wouldn't you agree?'

'Don't, Gilbert,' I cried in anguish.

'You see, you can't blame me for ending up where you are. You were conceived of evil, I have merely returned you to it.'

I felt soiled. Gilbert's bitter seed was sticky between my legs. I was suddenly desperate to clean myself.

'I was afraid,' I said. 'When I came here tonight I was afraid that you would hurt me. And you did.

Nothing you could inflict on me physically could be as bad as . . .' My sentence dissolved into weeping.

'Go away, Elizabeth,' Gilbert said. 'I am tired of you.'

I gathered myself up and made to leave. My world was crumbling, but I had too much dignity to let him see that. I took a deep, trembling breath and merely said, 'You are a cruel and heartless man.'

'Go and be alone with your thoughts,' he said.

'I will,' I replied.

He waited until I was almost out the door before adding, 'May they torture you ever after.'

CHAPTER
TWENTY-SEVEN

By the following day, it was clear to me that Mirabel would not live. Her skin had taken on a greyish tinge, and her 'tiredness' had evolved into long periods of deep sleep, which she only roused herself out of to feed the baby, whom she quite clearly adored. I sat with her early in the morning while she slept, and put my hands on her belly to see if I could discern the cause. Something was poisoning her from within, a bloody mass still clung to the walls of her womb and sat putrefying. More than that, the weight of death was upon her so heavily that I despaired of helping her with magic. Even Gilbert had not yet learned to cheat death. Still, I tried an incantation and I tended to her well. Periodically she would wake and chatter to me as though nothing were wrong, play weakly with Amelia's tiny hands and feet, feed her lovingly, then drop back into a slumber bordering on unconsciousness. I felt very lonely sitting next to her, my chin resting on my hands, watching and waiting for her death.

Even Uncle Tom, in the moments that I could bear to look at him, seemed to have realised that there wasn't much hope for Mirabel. Every time he entered the room to sit with her and hold her hand, I made an excuse to leave. I no longer saw in him my loving uncle, I saw only my incestuous, raping, lying father. And I couldn't get the idea out of my head that because I looked so much like my mother, he must surely have a similar fascination with me. I replayed our entire history over and over in my head, looking for moments of inappropriate touching, but I found nothing conclusive, only shameful suspicions of sickening motives. I could not love him any more. I could not think of myself the same way any more. My barrenness, long thought to be a random chance of fate and a blessing, became the result of unnatural conception and a curse. My similarity to my mother was not the result of an unknown father's weak features, but the result of undiluted hereditary. Uncle Tom's intense desire to keep me happy not borne of love, but borne of guilt and duty. I hated my life intensely. But I hated Gilbert more.

That afternoon, Uncle Tom came in quietly and stood behind me. I didn't know he was there until I felt his warm hand caressing my hair. I couldn't stop myself—I jumped away and turned back to stare coldly at him.

'What? What's the matter, Elizabeth?'

I headed to the door. 'Excuse me, I have something to do.'

'Elizabeth, please. What's wrong? Have I done something?'

I was almost drawn in again by those pleading eyes, but I steeled myself against it. Awful, awful man. I turned my back to him and left the room.

Gilbert was waiting outside in the corridor.

'Your wife is going to die,' I said.

'I know,' he replied impassively.

'Are you concerned?'

'No. Are you?'

'I'll miss her sorely.'

He shrugged. 'Have you made your peace with her?'

'Me, make my peace?'

'Yes. You seduced her husband.'

I shook my head. 'I think it is you who should be making peace with her. Despite everything, I did love her. You were colder than ice towards her.'

'You loved her? That makes what you did worse. I never professed to love her. She will die knowing that at least I was honest. But when I tell her about you and I—'

'Don't dare to do such a thing,' I hissed.

'Perhaps I won't then. If you think it would be a bad idea.' He smiled. 'Sir Thomas is very concerned about you. He spoke to me this morning. You've been avoiding him since yesterday at supper. What's the matter?'

I clenched my fists at my sides. 'You know what the matter is.'

'He asked me to find out what's wrong. What shall I tell him? That you're afraid he'll force his wizened old prick on you? That you don't think you'd be able to resist, just like your whore of a mother?'

I shuddered and turned away from him. He put a hand on my shoulder. I shrugged it off violently. 'Don't you touch me!' I screamed, not caring who heard. 'Don't you ever lay a hand on me, you sick, evil man.'

Uncle Tom emerged from Mirabel's room and stood looking uncertainly at Gilbert and I.

'Elizabeth? What's wrong?'

I ignored him and ran to my chamber, bolting the door behind me. I threw myself on my bed and wept.

It must have been in the early hours of the morning

that a faint knock on my door awoke me. At first I thought I must be dreaming, it seemed so distant, but then it came again. Behind it a weak voice. 'Elizabeth?'

Mirabel. What on earth was she doing out of her bed? I jumped up and opened the door. She nearly collapsed into my arms. She stank of approaching death, her breathing was shallow and her body burning up with fever.

'What is it?' I asked, taking her to my bed and sitting her down.

'Gilbert. He's taken Amelia.'

My sleep-addled brain couldn't quite grasp what she was saying. 'Taken her where?'

'He came in just before, he thought I was asleep. He took her and he's gone down to the cottage. I'm scared. He scares me.'

Terror froze me. Gilbert had taken Amelia to the magic cottage. My whole world was crashing in. He could have only one purpose in taking his newborn daughter to the cottage, and the horrible realisation temporarily stupefied me.

'Elizabeth? What is he doing with her? I don't know why he would take her there, but I watched him go from my window and that's certainly where he went.'

I touched her hand. It was freezing. 'Here, put this on,' I said, handing her my robe. 'You must keep warm. Stay here, I'll go and see what he's up to.'

'Elizabeth, you sound afraid.'

I picked up a gown and skirts that were hung over my chair and fastened them on quickly. I gave her a brief smile. 'Just be a good girl and wait here.'

I slipped on a pair of shoes and raced from my room, down the stairs and out to the cottage. I could hear Amelia crying, which was a good sign. Perhaps

I was judging Gilbert wrongly, perhaps he had some other, more benevolent motive. I pushed open the door and made my way into the back room. Gilbert looked up. He had Amelia lying naked in his copper dish. She was crying from the cold and discomfort.

I rushed in, meaning to grab her, but he blocked my way. 'Don't you stop me, Elizabeth.'

'She's a tiny, defenceless baby.'

'She's a virgin child of a virgin birth. She's going to make me a god.'

'You can't be serious. How do you think Uncle Tom is going to react?'

'What do I care? I'll be gone. After this, I won't need you, or him, or this house. Have you any idea how strong this will make me? I'll be so powerful, I'll be able to command anybody to do my bidding. Now let me be.'

I struggled with him, but he was far stronger than me and overpowered me easily. He pinned my arms painfully behind my back. I cried out.

'Elizabeth? Gilbert?' A weak voice near the door. Mirabel stood gaping at us. Dark shadows ringed her eyes. She looked like a wraith, and I was momentarily convinced that she had already died and this was her ghost come to haunt us. But when her eyes lit on Amelia and she moved forward with outstretched hands, she stumbled like a dying woman, not a dead one.

'My little girl,' she said. 'Why have you got her in there? She must be so cold.'

Horrified, I watched as Gilbert pounced on Mirabel and knocked her down. She sat, bewildered, on the floor. Gilbert turned his attention to me, pushed his face very close to mine. 'If a sick child is the only reinforcement you can call on, you're in

430

serious trouble. It would seem little Amelia had better accept her fate.'

'Don't kill her, Gilbert, I beg you,' I said, fat tears spilling out of my eyes. 'Kill me instead. Surely I must be worth something to you.'

'You? Bastard child of incest. Whore of grand proportions. Tumbled your cousin's—no, your *sister*'s husband in her own house. You are worthless.' Suddenly his face contorted in a grimace and he twisted away from me with a loud cry of pain. I hadn't seen Mirabel approach with the short-bladed knife she must have found next to the copper dish, and plunge it hard into Gilbert's back. Its handle protruded from just between his shoulder blades. He performed a spasmodic jig, trying to reach the handle, but the wound had hindered his movement. A trickle of blood stained his shirt.

Mirabel scurried out of the way, howling like a child. 'What are you talking about? What are you going to do to Amelia? You can't kill her, you can't kill her.' Her face was twisted with rage and anguish. I moved to grab her, get her out of Gilbert's way. The wound was not enough to finish him off, only enough to rouse deadly anger.

'Elizabeth,' he cried in pain. 'Help me for God's sake, get this thing out of my back and help me to the house.'

I looked up in shock. Did he honestly think I would help him?

'Elizabeth, please. It hurts. God. Elizabeth, *help me*.'

'Help you? Are you mad?'

'I won't hurt the baby. Get me upstairs. Don't let me bleed to death.'

My heart was pounding. I looked from Mirabel, to Amelia, to Gilbert. I loved and hated them all, bound as I was to them. I approached Gilbert, turned him around and gripped the handle of the knife in my right hand.

'Hold still,' I said breathlessly.

'Thank you, Elizabeth. Thank you.'

'Mirabel,' I called, 'take Amelia.' But Mirabel had collapsed on the floor, breathing raggedly. I turned my attention back to Gilbert, put my left arm around his middle to get some leverage, and pulled the knife from his back. A stream of blood followed it.

Not enough to kill him. I would have to take care of that.

'Thank you. I love you, Elizabeth,' he said.

'I love you too,' I said.

Then I reached around, the bloody knife clutched in my right hand and, with one swift movement, cut his throat.

He made a horrible noise. A gurgling noise, surprise, fear, anger. I saw Mirabel stare up at me wide-eyed. He slipped from my arms to the floor, holding his throat. Mirabel crawled towards him and placed her hands over his. 'Gilbert, Gilbert,' she cried. Blood pumped out of his neck and covered her up to her wrists.

I felt a slow shaking start in my ankles and my knees. At first I thought that it was my nerves going to pieces, but then I realised with horror what it really was. I had killed him. His life was leaving his body and all his power was about to be transferred to me.

I cast the knife aside and reached for the bench, trying to steady myself. A rush of silver washed through me, deafening me as it swirled around in my head. The whole universe spun around me, my centre disappeared and I exploded into a billion drops of liquid gold. When they regrouped, I found myself standing, my hands on my knees, bent over Gilbert's body. I stood up, and it was as if my spine ran with the lava of the gods. I raised my hands and uttered a cry, a word I did not know and would never be able to recall. A howling wind rose from my fingers, blowing Gilbert's books around, shattering the jars on the shelves. Even the walls of the cottage seemed temporarily to bulge outwards. Mirabel screamed. Amelia cried. It seemed to go on for eternity, then the power of the wind sucked back into my fingers and into my body and the cottage suddenly fell deathly quiet. Mirabel had fallen into quiet awe; Amelia hiccoughed softly.

I had his power. I had his magic. I did not have him.

I fell on the floor next to his body and wept, trying vainly to massage life back into the fingers, trying to stem the blood flow with my hands. 'What have I done? What have I done?' I said over and over. There were no answers: the dead are very silent.

After a time, I turned back to Mirabel, whose hands and robe were stained with blood. She looked back at me in shock.

'We have to bury him,' I said.

She nodded.

'You can wait here.'

'No, I'll come. He was my husband.'

I could tell she was going to take her last gasp at any moment.

'Amelia?' she said, looking up towards the bench, where her baby struggled against the cold copper.

'I'll take care of her.' I stood and picked up the baby in my bloody hands, took her to the front of the cottage and wrapped her loosely in blankets on the same mattress upon which Gilbert and I had so often made love. I started a fire with a blink. As effortlessly as exhaling. My hands shook. Everything

I had always wanted tingled in my palms and now I wanted only to expel it, to have ordinary, human hands. An ordinary, human life.

I went back to Mirabel and helped her up. She slumped against the door frame. I pulled Gilbert's *Liber Omnis Scientiae* from the shelf and handed it to her. 'Carry this,' I said. She pressed it against her chest as though it could prop her up. I grabbed Gilbert's limp arms and dragged him through the cottage to the front door. He left a bloody smear on the floor. My arms were aching from the effort.

'Wait here,' I said to Mirabel. I went around to the back of the cottage where Hugh's old gardening equipment was kept. I grabbed a spade, disentangled the gardening cart from the weeds growing through its axle, and wheeled it around to the front of the cottage.

'Can you help me lift him in?' I said to Mirabel.

She shook her head. 'I'm so tired, Elizabeth.'

I handed Mirabel the spade and heaved Gilbert up by the chest, covering myself in his blood. I pulled his upper body into the cart, which began to tip over. I steadied it with my thigh and folded Gilbert's legs into it. I had to stop for breath.

'We'll hang for this, Elizabeth,' Mirabel said.

'No, we won't.'

'Yes, we will. We killed him.'

'We won't hang. We're going to tie rocks in our skirts, and we're going into the river.'

She burst into tears. 'I don't want to die,' she cried. 'I don't want to die.'

She hadn't even realised how close she already was to death.

'What's our alternative?' I asked. 'Hanging? Do you want your father to have that over his head forever? Two murderesses in his family. This way,

434

nobody will ever know what happened.' Though I don't know why I cared so much about what would happen to Uncle Tom in light of what I now knew.

I picked up the handles of the cart and wheeled it into the early morning. Far away, the sun was coming up, and the sky was an unearthly grey–blue. Mirabel shuffled along beside me, cradling Gilbert's book in one arm, dragging the spade unevenly in the other, her crying never for an instant easing. We rounded the corner of the magic cottage and plunged into the forest.

Death. Where Gilbert now resided. Somewhere black, or not black, just a void. Our lives stretched bright and too thin across the top of it, and one small breach would undo us. I was horrified. Mirabel would not stop crying. The stench of Gilbert's blood hung over me. The smell of the blood of the man I loved. I inhaled it purposely, torturing myself. My arms ached. With the powers I had, I could have pushed the cart to the river without ever touching it, but I was disgusted by those powers, disgusted by the unnatural tingling just under my skin. Were there spirits all around me now, waiting for me to command them to push the cart so that they would have permission to suckle from my thigh? I would not let them, I would starve them at the source. I did not want to feel their greedy mouths caressing me.

On and on we went, Mirabel wailing, periodically screaming at me that she didn't want to die. The wheels on the cart squeaked under the weight of Gilbert's body. I found myself crying silently, wanting to say a word that had forever passed from my life, never to return. A word that I had forsaken the instant I had separated Gilbert from his breath. The forest crowded close around us, whispering its arcane secrets to the dewy dawn. The trees formed ragged lines and

435

pathways, their branches reached out to caress us lasciviously, scratching our faces and tangling our hair. We finally came to the river. Mirabel collapsed next to a tree. I noticed that the red stain on the lower half of her robe had spread, and was still fresh and wet. I realised it wasn't Gilbert's blood but her own. I took the spade from her and drove it into the ground beside a tree.

Over and over I drove the spade in, removing wedges of earth. I know not from where I got the strength, but it was purely my own, not that of unnatural beings. I glanced over to Mirabel frequently. She lolled semiconscious against the tree trunk.

It was a shallow grave, but it was all I could manage. I took Gilbert's book from Mirabel and threw it in, then upended the gardening cart, watching his body slide into the grave and fold unevenly on the ground. I straightened his torso and limbs with my foot, then began to cover him. Sobs twisted my body as I threw the first spadeful of dirt over his face. When I had at last finished, I went along the river's edge, collecting large rocks which I brought back to cover his grave. The sun was up when I finally approached Mirabel with an armful of stones.

'Mirabel?'

She didn't rouse. I put my hand in front of her mouth. She was still breathing. I tied the stones one by one into the hem of her robe. I straightened up and walked down to the river to wash my hands. Mud and blood flowed off them, staining the water. Early morning, normally so full of promise, sat heavily on me with its expectations.

I loved him and I had killed him. There was nothing more for me.

I turned and walked back to Mirabel. She was

conscious and gazed up at me weakly. 'Elizabeth, what about Amelia? What will happen to her? Who will educate her? Who will make sure she has a chance in life?'

I shook my head. 'I don't know.'

She began to blubber again. 'My little girl, Elizabeth. I'll never hold her again.' She picked up the hem of her skirt and indicated the stones I had tied in it. Obviously she had accepted her death.

I grieved, too, for the lost opportunity. No doubt Uncle Tom would soon come looking for us all, and find only Amelia squalling in the magic cottage. My heart ached for his pain. Nobody left. Always so afraid of being alone, and then finding himself with only a newborn child for company. And what of Amelia? Gilbert's child.

'Wait here,' I said, standing up.

'Don't go, Elizabeth. Don't leave me here alone.'

'I'll be back soon. Wait here and rest. I want to make sure Amelia is taken care of.'

'You're going to leave me here alone. I'm *scared*.'

'Hush. I'll be straight back. Don't be scared. I promise I won't leave you here. I promise I'll be back for you.'

She nodded, then said weakly. 'Is it true what Gilbert said? Did you lie with him?'

'Yes,' I said. 'I'm sorry.'

'How can I trust you to come back then?'

'I'll be back, I promise.'

She closed her eyes and leaned her head against the tree. I raced off through the forest, along the path we had taken—I could tell by the drops of blood that signalled my way—and back to the magic cottage. Prestonvale was still asleep in the distance. The child was a girl—what hope did she have if I weren't around to educate her? Uncle Tom would be dead before she

437

was in her teens, and she would be farmed out to some distantly related family who would marry her off just to be rid of her. I couldn't let that happen.

I found Amelia lying quite peacefully in front of the fire. She gazed at me as I kneeled over her and placed my mouth next to her tiny, pink ear. Knowledge was armour. Whatever else it could lead to was Amelia's decision. I only hoped that she wouldn't be seduced into her ruin the way I had been. I closed my eyes and concentrated, felt something warm bubbling up from my feet. I opened my mouth, and a long whispering sound came out as I poured all my knowledge into her. It hissed and sparkled off the walls. She lay passively, not frightened by the unnatural sound of those words that weren't words. Amelia Mary Lewis, I gave her the start in life that I hoped would lead her on to greatness.

I climbed to my feet, drained, aching, tasting my own mortality like a bitter kernel on my tongue. I entered the woods once more.

Mirabel was not where I left her. I found her body about three-quarters of the way back, face down in the dirt. Her hand had grappled at the ground, maybe trying to help herself up, maybe trying desperately to hold onto life. She had been afraid to die alone and had come to find me, but hadn't made it. I was beyond tears, my very soul was numb with pain and pity. I lifted her light body and carried her down to the river, cast her on the water and watched her sink.

And now. What of me? To go abroad, university, have my own business, mansion, family, find another love or have many lovers. All were ashes of dreams. I collected stones from the shallows, tied them in my hem as I found them. I wandered further and further up the river, feeling the stones in my hands, enjoying their smoothness against my fingertips. I felt as though I were watching myself from a great distance. My gift to the universe—my own life.

When I was certain that my body wouldn't be floating back to the surface to haunt Uncle Tom, I stepped into the water and waded in. Further and further, the water tickling my throat, then my nose, then my forehead. Still further, putting as much water as I could between myself and the world.

Still further, and my lungs were bursting. My body wanted to breathe, but I stayed under, I did not swim to the surface for that last breath of the morning, the beautiful, glorious morning that would go on without me, turn to afternoon, to night and so on forever whether I was here or not. I could see the world moving green and blue somewhere far above me, through a distorted glass. My head was filled with stars and black dots. The stars grew smaller, the black dots larger, making patterns in my head. Blackness engulfed me and I was not afraid. Death crept into my toes, up my legs, through my body like a tingling black worm, took my fingers, took my chest, rushed past my ears with a horrible, gushing, gusting cry.

It was dark for a very long time.

CHAPTER
TWENTY-EIGHT

There is an absolute darkness breathing along with us. It counts down our breaths. When the breaths run out, it claims us. We are all afraid of it. But it's familiar, it's comfortable. And while we are there we want to stay, because Nothing is so undemanding, and to go through childhood, puberty, adulthood again is too exhausting to contemplate.

I resided in that Nothing briefly. I was completely happy there, because I had no consciousness, no knowledge of either Elizabeth Moreton or Lisa Sheehan, or anyone before or in between. I didn't know Brad or Liam or Karin, I didn't have friends and acolytes that could be killed, I didn't know what the sun looked like or what an early summer afternoon breeze smelled like, laden with frangipani and barbecue.

But it passed in a flash, so that now when I think back on it, it's just a small black dot in the shiny fabric of my life. A spot I can't account for, that terrifies me when I contemplate it too closely. Because now I know what it's like to be dead, I *remember*. And while death is peaceful, it is not living. Living is a gorgeous swamp of colour; death is the absence of everything. And death pre-exists life, not the other way around, so that all our lives are bright, brief parentheses. All else is black.

The first thing I became aware of was somebody breathing. Deep, slow breaths. I listened to it for some time before I realised it was me. Then the smell, like something sterile laid over sickness. I was in a hospital. Sounds—something far away clattering to a tile floor; lifts ringing and footsteps in corridors. Then someone else's breathing, nearby. I opened my eyes. It was Brad. He sat in a plastic chair beside me, reading.

'How did I get here?' I wanted to ask. But the words wouldn't form. Instead a strange, weak croak came out of my mouth. Brad looked up in surprise. I put my hand to my throat and he stood hurriedly and poured me a glass of water from the jug on the stand next to my bed. As he did so, I looked around. I had an intravenous drip attached to my left arm. Two other beds in the room stood empty. A third was occupied by a wrinkled woman with yellowy hair in a pink nightie, flicking through a magazine. 'God, I could do with a smoke,' she was thinking, though I don't know how I knew.

Brad held the glass to my lips and the water was cool as it slid down my throat.

'Thanks,' I said.

'I should get the doctor.'

'Don't get the doctor. There's nothing wrong with me. How did I get here?'

'Nothing wrong with you? You've only been unconscious for three days.'

Three days. 'I was dead,' I said.

Brad looked at me dubiously. 'You were unconscious. The doctors couldn't find anything wrong with you. It was like you were just sleeping and nobody could wake you up.'

'I was dead. I died,' I said. 'I'm sorry, I should have told you everything from the start.'

'Too late. Liam told me everything.'

'You've spoken to Liam?' Guilt, guilt, guilt.

'Of course I have. I had to let him know what was going on. But I told him nothing about . . . you know.'

'Thanks,' I murmured. Who had the energy for guilt and self-flagellation? 'So where am I? Who brought me in?'

'You're at the RBH. I called an ambulance. I freaked out, didn't know what was wrong with you. I raced downstairs naked and called an ambulance, kicked everybody out then came upstairs to dress you. You were like a doll, all limp and pliable. I lost it; I was screaming and shaking you, trying to wake you up, but you were gone.'

'Yeah, gone. Back about four hundred years.'

'I'm sure that must have been what it seemed like to you. You did the right thing not telling me, I would never have believed you.' He paused for effect—obviously he still didn't believe me. 'So anyway, I came down here to the hospital to wait, and I sat out in that stupid waiting room all night, just staring at the walls and waiting to find out what was wrong with you. I could still smell you on my fingers, and I didn't want to wash my hands in case . . . I don't know, in case that was all I had left of you.' He looked into his lap. 'I didn't call Liam until about midnight. He's out of his mind.'

'Where is he now?'

'At work. Unlike me, he has gainful employment to divert him.'

'I'm perfectly all right, you know.'

'I think I should call a doctor.'

I waved him away with my hand. 'Go on then.'

He leaned over and gave me a chaste kiss on the forehead. I settled in under the stiff white sheets as he left the room.

So Elizabeth had killed Gilbert and drowned herself, leaving me with all the bad karma. Finally knowing what this was all about didn't make it any easier to take; in fact, it made it worse because clearly revenge was on Gilbert's agenda, and I supposed eventually my life would be forfeit as payment. I wanted to hide under the blankets of my hospital bed, only come out when somebody else had sorted out the problem. Which, of course, wouldn't happen. It was clearly *my* problem.

Brad returned with a hard-faced doctor. She took my temperature, looked in my eyes, asked me questions, made ticks and crosses on her clipboard.

Finally she said: 'I'll contact Dr Lindsay about coming to see you tomorrow morning. He might want to do some more tests. In the meantime, you're to rest.'

'Can you take this out?' I asked, indicating the drip. 'And can I have a shower?'

She eyed me carefully. 'Okay. I'll send a nurse up to help you.'

'I can manage.'

'Miss Sheehan, you have been unaccountably unconscious for three days. Excuse my caution.'

I nodded, and the doctor left.

'I called Liam,' Brad said. 'He's on his way down.'

'I'm scared to see him.'

He shrugged. 'If it's any consolation, we may have started having sex, but we didn't finish. Perhaps you can justify it that way.'

I laughed weakly.

By the time Liam got there, I'd been released from my drip and had had a warm shower and washed my hair. My knees felt a little weak and shaky, but I was mentally very clear. I wore a pair of cotton pyjamas that Liam had bought for me and left in the stand next to my bed. They were a little too small and the button over my tits kept popping open. Brad was searching for a safety pin for me when Liam raced in, throwing his jacket and his car keys down carelessly.

'Lisa!' It came out like a gasp. He enclosed me in an inescapable embrace. I took deep breaths of him, his smell, which was just a mixture of his soap and his shampoo. His hair was messy and he looked a bit rumpled.

'You're a little windswept, babe,' I said, laughing softly.

'Sorry, it's just the car park was full and I had to park on the roof. It's so windy outside today, my skin's all dried up like a crocodile's . . .' He realised he was rambling and checked himself. 'Sorry,' he said. 'Sorry for talking too much about nothing.' He released me and sat back to look at me.

'It's okay,' I said.

'Sorry for—' He coughed and I realised he was about to start crying. Brad looked politely in the other direction. 'Sorry for kicking you out that night, I'm . . . I'll never . . .'

I touched his face. 'It's okay. Really, don't torture yourself.' Not like I was torturing myself.

He kissed my hand and pressed it to his cheek. 'God Lisa, if anything had happened to you . . .'

'It did. I died. I drowned myself. I killed Gilbert and drowned myself—I couldn't bear to live without him. That's what this is all about.'

He nodded slowly. 'Don't worry about all that business right now,' he said. 'Just concentrate on getting better.' Perhaps when he had filled Brad in,

Brad's relentless scepticism had rubbed off on him. It was obvious he was viewing me very differently now.

'I'm all right,' I said, my voice one notch off anger. 'Liam, there's only one way Gilbert will finish this—he's going to kill me. All the other stuff is revenge, designed to make my world a misery. But in the end it's about me—I'll have to pay with my life.'

He looked concerned, but still tried to calm me down. 'Nothing's going to happen to you while you're in here,' he said. 'There are people everywhere.'

'There were people everywhere when he came into Fire Fire that night disguised as Satan. Nobody saw him but me.' Taking a small step outside myself, I began to realise how insane what I was saying sounded. I looked at the wrinkled, yellow woman in the other bed. She was trying hard not to stare, pretending to look at the ceiling above my bed. I shut my mouth. 'Yeah, perhaps I just need a rest,' I murmured.

Brad stood and stretched. 'I'd better go.' He leaned forward and pecked me on the cheek. I turned my head away, my heart thudding hard in my throat. I felt so guilty, it must have been written all over me, but Liam didn't seem to notice. He and Brad exchanged glances. They obviously didn't like each other, but were being polite for my sake.

'Bye, Lisa,' Brad said. I watched him go then turned to Liam.

'Don't you believe me any more?'

'Lisa, I just want you to relax, to recover. You've been out of it for three days. Just give yourself some time before you start worrying about all that stuff again.'

I nodded. 'Have your parents gone home?'

'Yes, they left shortly after . . . after our argument.

I told them everything.' He laughed lightly. 'I'm not the favoured son any more, to put it mildly.'

'How does that make you feel?' I reached up to stroke his cheek. He had shaved that morning, and his skin was dry from the cold weather.

'It's a bit hard to get used to. They're talking about me having to find my own place—you know, "no fornication in the house that your mother and I are paying for".'

'Fornication? What a great word, it makes it sound so dirty.'

He smiled.

'So,' I continued, 'I've been nothing but trouble for you, haven't I?'

'Well . . . maybe. But it's been worth it.'

I didn't believe him for one minute. Unless my suspicions were right and he was addicted to psychodrama. I had certainly provided plenty of that.

'By the way, Karin's husband called,' he said.

'David? He called you at home?'

'Yeah. He heard you were in hospital and he wanted me to phone him when you regained consciousness—he wants to visit. Still no news about Karin, though, but it sounds like he's starting to accept that she may have run away.'

'How could he have heard I was in . . .' My words suddenly became stuck in my throat. 'Oh my God, Liam.'

'What's the matter?' Again that odd, patronising tone of voice.

'Nothing, nothing.'

He caught my hand in his and squeezed it. 'Just relax, Lisa. Let it go for a day or two.'

I fell silent. Rolled onto my back and closed my eyes. I don't know how thought processes link up and suddenly make things clear that until a few heartbeats ago were perfectly obscure, but my addled brain had just managed to throw up a whole bunch of related facts that hadn't seemed related before, and it scared me to death. *David.* David always wanting to know where I was. David and my best friend, now missing. But most importantly, David and that mark on the back of his leg in exactly the same place as Gilbert's witch-mark. What more clever place for Gilbert to hide than right under my nose, pretending to be the most ordinary person in the universe?

And there was more . . . of course, of course. Karin was pregnant, and what about her ambivalence about their sex life, and that vision I'd had in Dana's attic of Karin with her hands covered in blood like Mirabel? She was caught up in it too; she was Mirabel just as I was Elizabeth and David was Gilbert. And Gilbert—David—was doing it all again: Karin was his breeder for another virgin child of a virgin birth. All my muscles froze, I had to bite my lip to stop from crying out, because the last thing I wanted was a whole lot of people who didn't believe me keeping me in here and sedating me. I needed to get out and I needed to find her. Every other time I had come out of a regression, I had more of Elizabeth's power. Perhaps I could home in on Karin or David now; perhaps he couldn't put up a fence to keep me out.

'Are you tired, Lisa?' Liam was saying.

'Yeah, real tired,' I replied, somehow managing to keep my voice even.

'I'll be right here if you need me.'

Karin, Karin, where are you? I had an indistinct impression, a sense of her presence, then a barbed jolt to the brain so painful that I gasped loudly.

'Lisa?' Liam was on his feet again, by my side.

'Headache,' I replied. A continuous throbbing pulsed in my brain.

'Do you want me to get a nurse?'

'No. I'll be fine.' It had felt so familiar, right up until the pain. I'd had that sense of Karin before, like the nerves in my body had hummed with her energy. But where was it? I concentrated, remembered fresh air smells, the feeling of warm wood beneath my hands. *Think, Lisa, think.*

Of course, in the sawmill. When I was in the middle of my hallucinations, when I had thought it was just another trick that my brain was playing on me. Was she there? Of course, she must be. My new-found intuition was strong and reliable.

'Liam,' I said, sitting up.

'Yes?' I wished that I could tell him, wished I could have him on my side again. But it was clear he would not take me seriously until six doctors, four specialists and an act of Parliament had declared me of sound health. It twisted in my heart, made me terribly sad. Like a gap had just opened up between us.

'I could really do with a cup of herb tea.'

'A cup of tea?'

'Yeah. Chamomile or lemon. They probably don't make it here, but I'm pretty sure there'd be a cafeteria downstairs that sells it.'

He smiled gently. 'If it's your heart's desire, I'll try to find it for you.'

'Thanks, darling.' I was eyeing his car keys, cast carelessly on the table next to my bed.

'Back in five minutes,' he said, checking for his wallet and heading outside.

As soon as he was out of sight, I threw back my covers and climbed out of bed. I went through the drawers of the dresser, finding the clothes I had worn to Brad's house folded neatly in the bottom drawer. They smelled faintly of stale cigarette smoke. I pulled my pyjama bottoms off and struggled into the blue pants. The woman in the other bed watched intently.

'You won't say a word,' I said, and felt a charge leave my body. She nodded obediently.

I unbuttoned my pyjama top and changed into the white chiffon blouse, leaving it untucked. I couldn't find the vest so I grabbed Liam's corduroy jacket off the back of the chair and zipped myself into it. My shoes weren't there and I imagined they were still under the bed in Brad's childhood bedroom. I picked up Liam's keys and quickly checked the corridor. It was lined with nurses and doctors going about their business. An old man shuffled along in ridiculous fluffy slippers, rolling his drip along with him.

'Nobody will see me,' I said to myself, and I don't know if my uninterrupted trip to the lifts was due to that minor incantation, or just due to luck. From a dining cart standing mutely in the hall I lifted a steak knife encrusted with dried mashed pumpkin. The lift bell rang and I stepped in, got out on the first floor, took the pedestrian overpass to the car park and headed up to the top level where Liam had said he'd parked his car. There it was, not quite straight between the yellow lines, as though he had parked in a big hurry. Which of course he had. He'd been far more eager to see me than I to see him. But I couldn't think about stuff like that now, because I was going out to the sawmill to find my best friend.

I hoped that was all I would find out there.

CHAPTER
TWENTY-NINE

I didn't drive very often, so I was glad Liam's car was automatic. I pulled into the street then onto the arterial road that would take me out to the highway. I turned the radio on and switched on the heating. My feet were frozen. I thought about going home to get a pair of shoes, but that would slow me down. Surely that would also be the first place that Liam would look. The clock in the car said it was ten past four. The sun sat low. A westerly wind set leaves in the gutters dancing, made the trees throw shifting shadows. I was humming along with a Cousin Em tune on the radio.

My mind was a jumble of half-formed ideas and thoughts that didn't make sense, like the thoughts you have drifting off to sleep. But I was wide awake. My nerves sang with some kind of high, fine energy. I realised I was jiggling the muscles in my left leg. I realised I was ravenously hungry. Then I was aware only of the road in front of me, the white line disappearing beside me. I hummed along with songs I didn't know, made up words for them. Somewhere shortly after the turnoff onto the freeway, the radio spat out a 747 song. I barely noticed it.

I know it wasn't luck or memory that brought me to the exact lot where Liam and I had wandered that night. I know it was something else, something with a name like destiny, or instinct. The shock of the cold ground on my feet jolted me. I took two steps into the forest, then went back to the car for Liam's torch and the pumpkin-encrusted knife, tucked them in various pockets of Liam's jacket. I felt odd, disoriented. I kept my fingernails pressed into my palm. Be here, Lisa. Be here.

The low sun gleaming through the trees was glorious. Long shadows ran beside me, dots and dazzles of sunlight flickered over me. I was small, so small. Watching the sun set is watching the world turn. I could feel it turning, rolling backwards. I steadied myself on a tree. I looked down at my feet. It seemed I had stubbed my toe on a stone. Caked blood, dirty feet. They were so cold. I hugged Liam's jacket around me and kept walking.

'Maybe I'm not well,' I said out loud. Nobody replied. 'Maybe I should have stayed in hospital.'

My feet beat a rhythm on the ground. I started reciting a poem I had learned in high school. '*Tyger, Tyger, burning bright, in the forests of the night, what immortal hand or eye dare frame thy fearful symmetry.*' These were the only lines I knew. I said it over and over. 'It doesn't even *rhyme*,' I told the trees.

I almost thought I heard them answer. Something bigger than me sat heavily on my body, amorphous and invisible. 'What do I do?' I said aloud. Then I shrieked. '*What do I do?*'

I focused ahead of me. I could see the clearing, the old sawmill shed.

Karin.

I sat down in the dirt. 'I'm very, very confused.' I put my fingers in the ground. Grit got stuck under my nails. I lay down, looked at the sky wheeling above me, the tall trees pointing in the same direction. An unbearable sense of helplessness washed over me. I began to weep. The clouds moved on above. I sat up, hung my head between my knees and sobbed. The air seemed very thin, almost delicate, as though my sobs were tearing it in places.

I needed to be lucid. I needed to be together. I knew what I needed to do, though it made my skin crawl.

I closed my eyes and breathed. 'After I made the ultimate sacrifice . . .' I said, but it only left my mouth as a sad, hissing noise. I choked back a sob, then turned my eyes skyward. The awful magic word tripped off my tongue and at once there were tiny invisible hands helping me up. I looked around me, but I could see nothing except an occasional transparent spot that shivered like water in the air around me. My thigh swarmed with warm, greedy mouths. I walked towards the old shed, my attendant spirits tangling invisible bony fingers in my hair, whispering unintelligible secrets on the wind.

I pushed open the door. The shed was empty.

'Where then? Where if not here?' I walked in further. A sticky cobweb attached itself to me. I sat on the edge of one of the enclosed wooden platforms, where I had sat that night with Liam. It was growing dark. Shafts of light burst through cracks in the wood. I placed my hands on the wood beside me. It felt warm, as it had last time. I turned over and crawled on my hands and knees along the platform. I pulled out Liam's torch and shone it along the planks. Nothing, nothing, nothing, then . . . at the far end of the platform, a perfectly neat trapdoor.

'Invisible to the untrained eye,' I said in a B-grade movie voice as I crawled down and scrabbled at the corners of it trying to get it open. But of course I didn't need to do it myself. An unspoken, unarticulated command and it swung open. More sucking from the witch-mark. I shone my torch into the hole. The light reflected on cobwebs and steel girders.

Look again.

Okay, I thought, I'll look again. And there it was, a clear path through the cobwebs to a door. The distance from the wood platform to the cement floor in the shed was about one metre. The distance underneath the platform was about two and a half metres. That meant that the door led underground. It also meant I was going to hurt myself getting down there. I shimmied through the hatch and my legs dangled into nothing. I let myself go and, rather than falling hard, some willing little hands caught me, helped me up, chattered almost inaudibly among themselves.

'Thanks,' I said aloud. I picked my way to the door, ducking under the girders. I jammed the torch under my right arm and I used both hands to haul the door open.

I found myself standing in a room that looked suspiciously familiar. Shelves lining the walls, jars, copper vessels, books. I shone the torch around. It was laid out exactly like the room in the magic cottage. The torch beam lit on the spine of an unspeakably old volume. I picked it up and looked at it in awe. *Liber Omnis Scientiae.* The very same book that Gilbert had been writing, its leather pages worn and faded but still largely intact. No doubt some sinister spell had been employed to preserve it this way.

I suddenly realised he must have dug himself up to get this. I paused in horror for a moment, wondering when he had done it, what he had found—brown and mossy bones, rotted pieces of his own skull from a previous incarnation.

But I had to focus. Karin, where was Karin? I placed the book back on the shelf and swung the torch beam around the walls. I had to fight back a rising tide of bile as I identified various body organs preserved in jars on shelves around the room. What looked like a complete human skin hung limp and sad from a hook in a dim corner. My torch lit on another door. I looked behind me. The faintest glimmer of daylight reflected from the trapdoor down to here, but the further in I moved, the darker it would become. I took a deep breath and opened the door.

I stood in a long passageway carved into the ground. I ran my hands along the walls—smooth earth. No doubt David had been setting busy spirits to this task for quite some time. There was a damp, though not unpleasant, smell. I walked along. My feet were freezing. The passage took a sharp left turn then descended down stairs carved into the ground. I was scared to death, but there was no way I was turning back.

'David, is that you?' A voice. Karin's voice.

I hurried down the stairs into a tiny dark room. The torchlight picked up a flash of brilliance that was Karin's blonde hair. She lay on a mattress in the corner of the room, covering her eyes from the beam. Her stomach was hugely swollen, which it shouldn't have been because she was less than five months pregnant. A foul stench of human waste came from the corner, and I nearly tripped over a plate with some fresh food scraps by the door.

'Karin?'

'Who is it?' She was frightened.

'It's me. It's Lisa.' I took two quick steps towards her and sat with her on the mattress.

'Lisa?'

In a blink, I knew David had just found me. She

had said my name aloud, and wherever he was, he was listening. I could almost see his eyes flicker with realisation. I hoped he was far enough away for us to get out.

She clung to me. 'Is this a dream? Is this a dream?'

I stroked her hair. 'Come on, we have to get out.'

'He's a monster, Lisa. He's a demon.'

'I know.'

'A monster . . . A demon.'

I realised that she wasn't entirely coherent. I guess five months living in an underground chamber will do that to a girl.

'Come on, just be quiet and let's go.'

'I'm scared to go. He'll know and then he'll hurt me.'

'He's not here. We have to go before he gets here. I'm not going to let you die here alone.' Again. Like Mirabel.

She gathered herself up and I helped her to her feet. We laboured up the stairs and back along the passage. Just as we were approaching the door to the magic room, it slammed shut in our faces. Karin screamed.

'Shit!' I cried.

'He's going to kill us, he's going to kill us!' she yelled hysterically.

'Be calm. Be calm.' I hummed in my head for my spirits to come, and the door swung open again. We moved into the magic room. The door to the outside was closed there too. Again I summoned my attendants, but there seemed to be a problem this time. David knew what I was doing. The door wouldn't budge. I sat Karin down on the floor and kneeled in front of her, checking her limbs.

'Has he hurt you?' I asked.

She shook her head, then indicated her stomach. 'Look what he's done.'

'How did he do that?'

'A potion . . . smells awful Once a day he rubs it in. He hasn't been today, but he'll be here, he'll come, he always does. I thought he was trying to kill us . . . me and the baby . . . but he's made it grow faster. Look, look.' Without warning she hoisted her skirt above her swollen belly to show me the skin. It was streaked with painful red welts, shiny with being stretched so quickly. She put her hands on her bare belly and let out a sob.

'Karin, please, hold yourself together. It's important. Tell me, did you and David ever have sex naturally?'

She looked over my shoulder. 'He'll come soon. He'll kill us both.'

'Karin? Did you and David ever fuck?'

She turned her eyes back to me. They were haunted and empty. She shook her head. 'No. I didn't want to tell anyone, let anyone know I'd made a mistake.'

So it was as I thought. He was trying again. And if he'd suddenly started accelerating the growth of the child, it was because he'd got nervous that I'd find him before the child was born. He *was* scared of me.

'He told me strange things. I saw strange things,' Karin was saying. 'I was somebody else . . . I don't know what to believe.'

'Believe it all.'

She began to hum softly, absently under her breath. Her whole body was shaking and shivering. I pulled Liam's coat off and wrapped her in it. Now I was freezing. I stood and went to the shelves. I found a candle and lit it with my hands, just like Elizabeth used to do. It cast a dim glow in the dark. I switched

456

the torch off and handed it to Karin. I stood in front of the door, tried hauling it open with my hands but it wouldn't budge. I tried to open it with magic again, but nothing would move. I knew he was close. I searched on the shelves for anything that might help. I found a sharp knife, which I knew would be his sacrificial blade, and picked it up.

As I hefted the handle, I had to fight off memories of horrendous murders. Images of terror and pain, screaming faces, Jeff's among them. Oh God, poor Jeff. How he had struggled, how he had tried to hang onto the life he normally treated with such careless abandon. The pain drilled all the way into my soul, inscribed my hatred for David in huge flaming letters. I pushed off the thoughts and took the knife to the door, jammed it in the crack and used it for leverage. It was useless. I shoved the knife in my waistband.

Karin was watching me narrowly. 'Are you with him? Are you with him?' she said over and over. At first I couldn't make out what she was saying but, when I realised, I came to squat in front of her.

'What's the matter? What are you saying?' I reached over to touch her hair, but she flinched away from me.

'Are you with him? Did he send you?'

'No. No, Karin. I'm here to help you. I'm your best friend, I *love* you.'

'You left me in the woods to die. You went back and you took my baby. Oh God, oh God, my baby.' She started howling and streaky tears ran down her face.

'No, you're getting confused, Karin. I'm not Elizabeth. I'm Lisa.'

She turned those awful haunted eyes on me again, her mouth open and gasping sobs like a baby. Snot trickled out of her nose and gathered on her upper lip.

'I'm Lisa,' I repeated.

'Lisa.'

'And I'm going to get us out of here. Just try to be calm.'

She nodded, seemed a little more lucid. 'Okay, okay. Be calm.' Then she fell silent.

I turned my attention back to the shelf, knocked over a few items looking for something that would help. My fingers brushed across the spine of the magic book again, tingled slightly. He had told Elizabeth it was not for the eyes of others. I pulled it from the shelf and laid it on the table.

'What are you doing? When are we getting out?' Karin said in a breathy voice.

'I'm looking for some way to undo the spell.' But that wasn't the whole truth. I was satisfying my curiosity. Just what was in this book anyway? I opened it warily.

I flicked through the pages, arcane symbols etched on them, all preserved perfectly by some dark magic. I remembered Gilbert as clearly as if he were Brad or Liam. I had an achingly sad longing to touch his face, kiss his lips. I had to shake my head to fight off the sudden flush of desire.

The old stuff was mostly symbols and inscriptions in a hand I could barely decipher. Quite a lot in Latin, but some looked like an ancient Eastern language, and some was in English. I flicked through and found the start of the modern section. More diagrams and weird circles, long spikes flowing from them, numbers, upsidedown, backwards, in fading maroon in places as though they were written in blood.

But among the spells and incantations there were coherent scribblings in the margins, and short diary entries interrupted pages and pages of unintelligible secrets. I looked over my shoulder at Karin, who was staring into her lap humming again. It was eerie, hearing that childish tone warming the cold dankness in the underground room. I could sense my spirit attendants still trying to open the door. Every now and then my nerves would buzz as though a crack of liberty had just lighted the darkness, but just as quickly it was gone and David was pushing back, trapping us in here to wait for him. I turned back to the book, began to read the half-finished diary entries.

> *The lad didn't squeal much. Like he expected it. Bad family life—not as innocent as I thought. Only moderate charge—perhaps his sister.*
>
> *Sometimes the blood is hard to wash off—the smell lingers.*
>
> *Poor hysterical girl. Body like an overripe pear. Surely she didn't really think I wanted her for sex.*

I skimmed over these entries, which were obviously written some time ago. I was looking for my name somewhere amongst the mysterious inscriptions.

> *I've found Elizabeth. Sweet. I'll be there within a month.*

Then a few pages on.

> *She has a band. I've seen them twice, managed to get a fix on her. Watching her in my mind. Lisa is her name. The promise is unbearable.*
>
> *Too, too perfect. She has a friend—the same silly girl again. This conquest will be easy.*

'Lisa, hurry,' Karin said from her corner. 'Lisa, please, I don't want to die, I don't want to die.'

'I'm still looking.'

The chamber is almost finished. I'm exhausted. I'll need to kill again very soon.

A horrific diagram of a human body, showing locations for incisions. A bloody thumbprint smudged into the ink

Got her on the web. Sent her a spell to mess her head up a little. She's got an idea about Elizabeth. I want her to remember, I want her to sense her doom, I want her terrified out of her wits when I finally split her open. It will be bliss.

My body turned cold. *He* was Whitewitch—she wasn't some benevolent fairy godmother as I'd so foolishly assumed. He had sent me the spell that I'd used so willingly, the one that had sent the horrible hallucinations, the regressions. But why would he do that if he knew it would return my powers to me? I flicked forward, nearly missed an entry and turned back a few pages.

The stupid girl is remembering too. I don't know where this is coming from. I'm getting her away before the two of them get together and figure it out.

And one small, unsure scribble in the margin:

Sometimes I don't know who is in control.

'Have you found anything yet?'

The stupid girl never stops crying. I'm tired of her. Sometimes not sure what to do.

I didn't answer her, moved forward. There were three sickening pages of a detailed description of his murder of the young couple. I shuddered.

Not good—Elizabeth is learning again. Why, why, why? This should not be happening.

460

So it wasn't all going his way after all. I took comfort from the fact. Clearly it was as I had thought—something was looking out for me.

'*Lisa!*' Karin screamed and I looked around. She was pulling herself up and heading towards the door. 'We have to get out—I'm going mad, I'm going mad!'

I stopped her, moved her back to her corner. 'Okay, okay. I'm sorry. I'll do what I can.'

'But what can you do? What can any of us do?'

What could I do? I pulled out the knife and stood in front of the book laid open on the table. When Elizabeth had tried to look at it, she had found it protected by spirits, spirits who were clearly occupied elsewhere at this moment—holding back the door most likely. I plunged the knife into the cover of the book. It screamed. Unearthly. I opened the first page and slit it with the blade, then the second. A greasy, reddish fluid flowed out of the cut like pale blood. Suddenly I was kicked back by a painfully powerful force, and at the same moment the door swung open. I dropped the book, noticing that the page was beginning to repair itself, and gathered up Karin to half guide, half push her out the door. It began to swing shut on me as soon as Gilbert's attendants realised they had been unfairly diverted from their task, but I squeezed out just in time, tucking the knife into my waistband. The back of my blouse was caught in the door and ripped loudly. I pushed Karin in front of me and we ran down to the hatch. I made a step for her with my hand but she was too afraid to climb up.

'Come on, Karin. He's on his way here.'

'You go up first and pull me up. Here . . .' She turned her back to me and bent over slightly, inviting me to climb over her. I hesitated momentarily—surely this wasn't good for a pregnant woman—but I had no choice. I carefully lifted myself up on her back and grasped the edges of the wood just as the trapdoor slammed shut, mashing the fingers on my left hand. I screamed out and Karin and I both fell to the floor.

'It's okay, it's okay,' I said as Karin started howling. My hand throbbed. I was sure at least two of my fingers were broken. I fought my way through decades worth of cobwebs and pushed the wall of the platform. It gave a little at the top, but at the bottom it was firmly cemented. With one useless hand, I wasn't going to have much luck. I hauled myself up by the girders surrounding me and aimed a kick at the wall. Something splintered. I let myself back down, wincing as my ruined fingers brushed the girder. I focused all my energy on the planks, but no matter how hard I pushed, David was pushing back just as hard. He wanted me here, without a doubt. If I'd had time to think about it, I would have brought the magic book with me. I didn't know what to do next and I was scared to death.

I went back to Karin, who was sitting on the floor, her legs spread out in front of her, sobbing like a child. 'You've got to remain calm,' I told her. But she was out of it, completely spooked. After what she'd been through, her brain was probably mush.

I looked around for something to beat at the wall with, then gave up and went to kneel by Karin, nursing my left hand in my right.

'What are we going to do?' she asked in a small voice.

'I don't know. Let me rest a minute and I'll try again.' A sharp, continual throbbing shot up from my fingers into my hand and arm. I wanted to examine my fingers, see how badly damaged they were, but I was afraid the sight of them bent at strange angles would make me ill. I regrouped my attendant spirits for a rest and a rethink.

'He's coming,' Karin said.

'I know.'

'I'm frightened . . . I saw things, I heard things.'

'Do you know what he's been doing here?'

'Yes. I heard them screaming for help. He's a monster, Lisa. Why couldn't I tell? Why did I marry him?'

I didn't know how to answer her, so I went back to the wall and rammed my shoulder into it a couple of times. Nothing would budge and my whole body was singing with the pain in my left hand. Panic was rising in me and I was starting to lose my concentration. That's when I noticed the smell.

Smoke. Acrid and close by.

I looked over to Karin, who looked back at me in horror. 'Oh no,' she whispered. 'He's going to burn us alive.'

'He's not going to burn us alive. He needs you— you still have the baby.'

'He's going to kill us.' She was not with me. I knew that David would not kill Karin, but perhaps he would kill me. Perhaps he'd finished having fun with me and now it was time to pay off my debt to him. My joints went weak. My fingers throbbed. It seemed I couldn't get enough air into my lungs. I had seen him do it before. The flames would consume me, leaving Karin unscathed. I would burn like Master Gale. I could already imagine it, the fire biting into my soft flesh. I fought down a rising hysteria. I did not want to die, not like that. Not at all.

Suddenly the hatch shot open. I warily looked up. I could see nothing but the late afternoon gloom in the shed. The smell of smoke still hung on the air.

'Okay, help me up,' I said to Karin. Once again

she helped me up to reach the hatch, and I clambered out. I lay on my stomach on the floor and reached my good hand out to pull her up. I hadn't the strength to do it by myself, but my attendants were back, and we hauled her out easily. Smoke was lightly drifting through the shed, but it wasn't the shed that was on fire.

We ran out into the fading daylight. Then stopped.

The forest was on fire in a perfect circle around us. There was one clear space, about five metres across, directly in front of me. And standing in that space, looking like the devil himself, was David.

CHAPTER
THIRTY

Gone was the benign, uninteresting face. I wondered how I had ever thought he looked boring. Behind the round glasses were intense, hate-filled eyes, utterly compelling as I looked across at him, spellbound. I became aware that I was facing down my doom.

I judged the distance between us to be around twenty metres. If I made a run for it, he would catch me in his arms, then what? If I went back to the sawmill he would trap me there—same outcome. I wanted to break down and cry, give in, collapse on the ground and let him take me, hold me in his arms and separate me from the world, return me to the abyss. I was so tired of it all. Then out of the weariness came a bolt of clarity—*he's in your head*. I tore my eyes away from his, and the desire to give in dissolved. I refocused, and because I didn't know what else to say, I said: 'I'm not Elizabeth. This isn't fair.'

He shrugged. 'Life's not fair.'

Karin was drawing short little gasps. I turned to her. 'Sit down and rest,' I said. 'He's not going to hurt you, you have the baby.'

She looked at me with wide, wild eyes. 'The baby? Why does he want the baby?'

I didn't answer; instead I returned my attention to

David, watching the space just below his eyes, not daring to let myself be drawn in again. From the corner of my vision I could see Karin's legs buckle under her as she lowered herself to the ground.

'Now would be a good time for you to tell me what you're going to do to me,' I said to David, keeping my voice even to efface the terror that was consuming me.

'You ruined the fun, Lisa. I had so much more planned. Next thing, I was going to do those two stupid but pretty boys you've been fucking. You always were too easily beguiled by pretty male flesh. And the baby—I was going to send you her little hands in a package.'

Karin let out a shriek and buried her face helplessly in her hands. My heart twisted in my chest. David took a few steps towards me, stopped a couple of metres away.

'I've been looking for you for centuries,' he said.

'David, please. Please don't kill me . . . I . . .' My voice cracked and I had to draw a deep breath. 'This is stupid. *I* didn't do anything, *I'm* not responsible.'

On the ground between Karin and my left foot was a thick branch. I pressed my toes into it.

'Make no mistake, Lisa. You *are* responsible. We all appear innocent on the outside, but the soul is always a very dark place. It's privy to all your prejudices, all your jealousies—from every life. It's not a ray of light, Lisa. It's a cankerous pall.'

I had to lock my knees to stop them from shaking. 'How did you know about us?' I asked, stalling. 'I didn't know.'

'I made it my business to remember—something Gilbert didn't teach Elizabeth. I set up a trigger, a few words that would remind me. I recalled it all as a ten year old at a fair with my mother. She took me to one of those gypsy fortune-tellers. The woman took one look at me and broke into a sweat, told my mother I was an evil child. That triggered the memories. Then my mother—afraid of me, the superstitious old whore—sent me to boarding school. All that time alone, with bored and willing live subjects, was the best thing she could have given for me. I've been thinking about finding you ever since. When *she* was with you,' he indicated Karin with a sweep of his hand, 'it was just an added bonus. A chance to finish some other unfinished business.'

I felt the whispering of icy voices near my ear, but all I could think about was getting my hands on the branch at Karin's side. It seemed a very long way away. I was frozen, didn't know what to do.

'I did nothing to you.'

'You betrayed me.'

'No, *Elizabeth* betrayed *Gilbert*, then she drowned herself because she loved you, loved him. If it was me—'

'*It is you!*' he screamed, taking a few steps closer. 'It is you, you're one and the same person. You say she drowned herself?'

'You didn't know?'

He shook his head. 'I assumed she—' He broke off, shook his head. 'That's why you . . . why she . . .'

'Why what?'

'Why you're being looked after so well. You committed your own life to our master, you've given the universe something I haven't.' He set his jaw hard. 'But don't think that it gives you the upper hand, I'm still more powerful than you'll ever be.'

'I know that, I know. Please, let Karin and me go. You're too powerful to do this . . . This is just petty revenge.'

'Petty? You have underestimated the depth of my

467

hatred. Today, Lisa, you will kiss hell. Perhaps in a few hundred years you can tell me what it tastes like.'

In the instant before he sprang, I ducked and reached for the branch. Because my left hand was ruined, I had to reach across my body with my right and I nearly tipped over. It gave David time to see what I was doing, and he kicked me so that I tumbled backwards, landing hard on my butt. But I still had the branch in my hand and, with one mighty sweep, I smashed it up into his balls. He screamed and doubled over. I scrambled to my feet, took the branch in both hands, gingerly keeping my broken fingers out of the way, and whacked it into his face. I heard his glasses smash. He was making an effort to get to his feet, but not managing. Blood trickled over his face, and a shard of glass had driven into his eye. It sickened me to look at it.

I helped Karin to her feet and we began to run for the gap in the fire, but as we approached the flames leapt across. The fire gained intensity, licked further into the forest: David was furious now. I turned to see him struggling to his feet. I saw him pick the shard of glass out of his eye with shaking hands, then begin walking towards us. There was a gap between trees about two feet across. I summoned my spirits around me, held Karin tightly in my arms. She twisted and shrieked as I began to walk towards the fire.

'Just hold still. You're not going to be hurt. It's me he's trying to hurt.'

We squeezed through the trees, Karin wriggling and screaming in my arms. The flames were close enough to kiss me, but my spirit attendants were doing their best to protect me. David was right behind us. I could smell my hair burning, and a few sizzling plates of pain pressed on my arms and shoulders. The woods started to open up, but David lit the way in front of us. I didn't know how much longer my spirits could help me.

'You *are* with him!' Karin cried. 'Let me go. I don't want to die.'

'Karin, just hold on. You have to trust me. He's not trying to hurt you, he's trying to hurt me.'

Then I stepped on a burning lump of something with my bare feet and screamed in pain. I released Karin and yelled at her to run. She hesitated, but I urged her away.

'He won't hurt you. He wants the child. Get away! Run!'

She nodded and backed away from me, then turned and raced off through the trees. I stumbled forward, watching the ground, cursing my lack of shoes. I could hear David approaching but dared not look around. His fingers brushed my shoulder and I screamed, summoned up a last desperate burst of energy. But the uneven ground was my enemy, and David caught me easily, cleared a little spot in the flames and pulled me to the ground.

His left eye and his nose were bleeding and he was breathing raggedly, but he sat me in his lap and clasped his arm around the front of me so there was no way to escape. I felt him pulling at my clothes and realised he was searching for his knife. He let out a little gasp of pleasure as his hand closed over it. I realised with absolute certainty that I was about to die. I couldn't breathe properly, and golden stars spangled on the periphery of my vision.

'Please,' I said, 'please . . .'

'Help you? The way you helped me?' He had his chin resting on my shoulder, and blood drizzled onto the front of my blouse.

'David, please.' I was watching the hand that

pinned me to him. His fingers moved against my belly, rubbing gently through the thin cloth. All my senses were magnified; his fingertips were hot and stung with his desire. I knew I was going to cry. A huge sob shuddered its way out of my body. It seemed very loud. Other noises in the forest were dying down, and I realised that he hadn't the energy to keep the fire going. We sat among the blackened, smouldering tree trunks. The sky seemed a long way away.

He was kissing my neck, bloody kisses on my skin. I couldn't move. 'Elizabeth,' he said. 'How does this feel?'

I didn't reply.

'How does it feel?' His hand slid up my shirt and cupped my breast. I groaned; it could have been a groan of pleasure. His thumb brushed over my nipple. It felt as though sparks were jumping from his skin to mine.

'How does it feel?' he said again, nipping and sucking at the skin on my shoulder. 'Do you still want me? Do you still love me?'

My body burned, but my nerve endings were so overloaded I didn't know if it was fear or desire. 'No. Please, just let me go.'

His fingers were pressing harder and harder into my flesh, his gentle kisses were turning into savage bites. 'You do, you do still love me.'

I stiffened my body against him, summoned up my iciest tone. 'David, I hate you.'

Then I felt the blade, cold and sharp, scraping against my skin. 'No matter if you love or hate me, as long as you feel it with your whole being.'

'I'm going to die, aren't I?' I said, and my voice came from a great distance.

'Your skin is so soft. It will be like cutting through butter. And then . . .' He drew a deep, shuddering

470

sigh. 'Godhead, Elizabeth. To murder my murderer, to murder my lover, to murder the woman who willingly dedicated her magic to the universe. You, Elizabeth, will bring me godhead.'

I could do nothing but wait for my destiny, his warm breath on my cheek. I took one last look at the sky, and it seemed to me tragic that I wouldn't enjoy today's sunset, today's twilight, today's evening breeze and stars, that I would never see Brad or Liam again. My heart twisted inside me, and a huge lump of grief blocked my throat beneath the freezing steel of his blade.

'Are you afraid?' he asked, rearranging me so I was in the most advantageous position for the kill, squaring himself up against me.

Tears squeezed out of the corners of my eyes. My terror was unspeakable, a towering, sickening oppression. I waited for the final few seconds of life, the hot blood and the growing dimness.

When he screamed it nearly deafened me, and when his arms released me I was confounded. I scrambled away on my knees and turned to look. Karin stood over him with the knife I had stolen from the hospital clutched in her right hand. She must have found it in the pocket of Liam's jacket. David turned and I saw a bloody wound across the back of his neck. He reached up to her and she cut him across the hand, then plunged the knife into his chest. It didn't go in very far before the blade broke, and she took two quick steps backwards.

He turned back to me and in his face I could see the horror of shame. He had allowed it to happen again. He crawled towards me, but didn't get very far before he curled up on the ground and groaned, his hand clutching at the soil.

I looked at Karin. 'We've got to help him,' I said.

471

She shook her head. 'Let him die.'

'Trust me, you don't want that hanging over you for the next few centuries. Get the knife.'

She withdrew back into herself, sat heavily on the ground and put her face in her hands. I picked up David's sacrificial blade from the ground where he had dropped it, and cut off an uneven strip from the bottom of my blouse. I crawled back to David, pulled his hands behind his back—he gasped in pain—and tied them together securely, tucking the knife back into my waistband.

'Can you walk?' I asked, close to his ear.

He shook his head.

'What if I help you?'

No answer. I pulled him up, he was heavy. Karin looked up at me, scared out of her mind.

'Karin, he's going to bleed to death if we don't get help.'

'Why are you helping him?' she said. 'What the hell are you doing? Let the monster die!'

What the hell was I doing? Avoiding a repeat performance in another four hundred years? Or was it something else? What was that overwhelming feeling that threatened to undo me? Was I acting out of feelings I hadn't had since 1608? Surely not, surely pity takes on many guises. I swiftly pulled the broken knife blade out of his chest, releasing a spurt of blood.

My attendant spirits came to help. David staggered along, I held him. I put my hand over the wound on the back of his neck, and the blood pulsed through my fingers, slowing down now. I walked him through the forest as quickly as I could, with him dragging his feet, near to collapse. His skin was pale like alabaster.

'Please don't die,' I said. He didn't respond.

Karin shuffled along behind me, begging me to

let him go, asking me over and over what I was doing. I blocked her out and concentrated on the ground in front of me.

Suddenly she stopped. 'Hear that?' she asked sharply.

'Hear what?'

'Somebody's calling you.'

I shook my head. Strained my ears. Maybe Karin was hearing my spirits, their strange hisses and arcane whispers. Then I heard it too. Far away, someone calling, 'Lisa!'

'It's Brad,' I said, shocked. David stumbled and nearly fell. I steadied him, my heart beating fast.

Then again, 'Lisa, if you're here, call out.'

'And Liam.' I tried to pick which direction their voices were coming from. 'Over here!' I yelled.

I heard nothing for a while, then their voices were closer. 'Lisa! Lisa!'

'Here!' I called again, moving towards their voices. I could feel David's life ebbing out of him with each passing second. 'Hang on,' I whispered to him. 'Please, hang on.'

I could hear more clearly as Liam and Brad approached now, feet in the bracken, talking lowly and urgently to each other about the smell of smoke, the possibility of fire. They crossed our path about a hundred metres ahead, stopped in twin astonishment as they saw me supporting David's bloody body.

'Help me get him to the car,' I said.

'What happened?'

'Just help him—he's going to die otherwise. Don't let him die again.' I realised my voice sounded hysterical. Brad grabbed David's feet and Liam got him under the arms. I walked along beside. David rarely opened his good eye, but when he did it fixed on me, sometimes with daggers of hatred, sometimes with helpless fear.

'What's going on?' Liam said, gasping under David's weight.

'It's him, Liam, it's Gilbert.'

His eyes bulged and he sped up, hurrying Brad along. We emerged onto the roadside and I grabbed Liam's jacket from Karin to find Liam's car keys. Brad's car was parked on the strip too. I took David from Liam and jammed the keys in Liam's hand.

'Quick,' I said, 'to the hospital. Quickly.'

Liam unlocked the car and Brad and I carefully sat David on the back seat. I sat beside him and beckoned for Karin to get in beside me.

'No,' she said with a trembling lip. 'No, not in there with him.'

'Please, Karin, please. We have to hurry. I'll explain it all later.'

Brad pushed Karin into the front seat and climbed in beside me. Liam started the car and in an instant we were merging into traffic. A thick sense of urgency twitched under my skin. I had my arm around David and his head lolled on my shoulder.

'How did this happen?' Liam asked.

'He was going to kill her,' Karin said. 'I stopped him, but now she wants to keep him alive. He was going to kill us all. He would have killed us all.' I could barely hear her as she descended into her rambling again. I was only half aware of Brad sitting next to me, his eyes flicking from the road ahead to me and to David, wondering what the hell was going on. I leaned into David. Our faces were almost touching.

'Elizabeth?' he said weakly.

'Do you forgive me?' I asked.

'No, never.'

'Forgive me. We can't do all this again. Forgive me, let me go.'

'No. You betrayed me. You deserve no forgiveness.'

'*Forgive me, fuck you!*' I screamed.

'Lisa?' Brad said. 'What's the matter?'

Liam glanced into his rear-view mirror, then turned his attention back to the road. 'What's going on back there, Brad?' he asked anxiously.

'I don't know. She's not listening to me.'

'Forgive me, forgive me. I'm sorry.' I wept into David's shoulder. 'Let me go. I can't do this again, I can't.' The months of stress, the years until my inevitable death, the centuries between now and the last time, now and the next time, weighed on me like the ocean. I couldn't move for a sense of unbearable oppression.

'No,' he hissed through gritted teeth. 'I will finish this business.'

So. I fumbled in my waistband for his knife, hefted it in my left hand and, between aching fingers, transferred it to my right hand over the back of his head. He was going to die anyway, anyone could see that. I would not be so foolish as Elizabeth, I would not waste it all.

Brad called out, 'No!' just as the blade slid across David's throat. And it was like cutting through butter. There were screams and cries all around me—some, I'm sure, my own—then the universe turned upside down and I was at its centre.

I drank him in one gulp.

EPILOGUE

I love to watch the world wake up.

When I have trouble sleeping I get up and watch the sky brighten behind my flat, count the lights coming on in the highrises all around me, imagine myself amidst the ordered comfort of ordinary people's lives. Sometimes it's cold on the balcony and I have to nurse my teacup between stiff fingers, breathe dragon's breaths into the morning air. It's nice to have a habit, it's nice to have structure in my life. It makes me feel better about the chaos that I feed off, the chaos that feeds off me.

My life is not ordinary. Sometimes I pretend to be ordinary, but I don't convince myself. I seem to exist at one remove from everybody else, like there's an empty silence where my aura used to be. And with a blink I can perform miracles, with a hum I can tune into anybody's thoughts, except Liam's because he can feel it. He's more than he appears, a little intuition gone wild. That's how he knew to look for me in the forest. That's why he found it easier to believe me than the others did. That's probably even why he was attracted to me in the first place. I don't think he knows that about himself. I think if he knew he'd be horrified. Yesterday I told him that Brad and I fucked. He took it badly.

I can know anyone, but I can trust no-one. Liam, Karin and Brad all saw me kill David, but they covered for me. Self-defence, they said. Never mind that the guy's arms were tied behind his back and he was bleeding to death. They stood up for me. But now they're all wary of me. Brad no longer makes lingering eye contact—he's afraid of what he might see in there. He hasn't picked up the guitar in weeks and he drinks like there's no tomorrow. Well, perhaps for him there isn't.

Karin's kid was born a week ago. She's back living with Dana, and I visit when I can. She still isn't completely with it, and I wonder if she ever will be. Her eyes are so empty, her hands are always ice cold. The child is a little girl. She called her Amelia.

Liam and I, well, there's a lot for him to get his head around. He didn't call for a week, then when he did it was to make excuses. 'Give me time, Lisa,' he kept saying. Finally he came by last night. We sat in my kitchen and he told me he wanted to try to keep our relationship together, but that he was afraid of me.

'Afraid of what? I'm the same person, I just have a few added extras.'

'Lisa, I grew up in a God-fearing household. The stuff you've told me, it's Satanic.'

'You think I'm evil? Is that it?'

His silence, his downcast eyes confirmed the suspicion. How could I tell him? How could I tell him that a belief in evil comes with a complementary belief in good, leaving room for hope? Evil was not something to be frightened of.

But there is no evil, there is no good. There is only infinite random variables, chaotic energy that flows every which way at once, a universe that stretches on beyond the limits of its own imagination, crawling into frozen places as it searches, endlessly and endlessly, for an outer limit. I own a small piece of that, nothing else. All the answers are as far from my grasp as they ever were. Despite what Gilbert told Elizabeth, I have no evidence that those who hold power and command spirits are any more important in the scheme of things than others. In the confusion that followed David's death, I managed to salvage his magic book from the underground chamber. Some of the spells and scribblings confirmed that he had been coming to the same conclusion himself, that through my death he hoped to transcend that boundary and find something more beyond it. To believe in anything was to have hope.

For Liam, to believe in evil must be very comforting and I wasn't going to take it away from him. I watched him leave and I didn't cry. There are few tears left inside me.

I'm going down to the river today.

I'm going to pull this stupid ring off my finger. *In aeternum*. I'm going to hold it between my forefinger and my thumb, roll it between my fingertips, and I'm going to drop it into the water.

The fewer people I'm bound to for eternity, the better.

If you enjoyed this book,
Why don't you read some more
ORIEL novels?

THE BONDMAID by Catherine Lim
£5.99 * 0 75280 851 6

Set in Singapore in the fifties, *The Bondmaid* captures the special ethos of a wealthy and powerful Chinese household. Full of passion, darkness and mystery, it chronicles the transforming power of one woman's love.

OUT OF LOVE by Victoria Clayton
£5.99 * 0 75280 901 6

The last time Min saw Daisy they quarrelled bitterly. Fifteen years later, they run into each other unexpectedly and Min invites Daisy to stay . . . An outstanding first novel about the value of love versus that of friendship, and what happens when one must be sacrificed for the other.

HEARTLAND by Jann Turner ·
£5.99 * 0 75280 902 4

Elise and Sandile come from opposite sides of the tracks. But when Sandile comes back after a long exile, a tender, passionate love grows between them which threatens to destroy the foundations of their lives. This powerful and deeply romantic first novel set in the new South Africa explores the blossoming of new opportunities and the prejudice that remains after apartheid.

IT COULD BE YOU by Josie Lloyd
£5.99 * 0 75280 913 X

Charlie finds herself coping with a series of disasters as backstabbing colleagues, best-friend crises and a boss who just can't keep his hands off her, threaten to overwhelm her. You'll adore this deliciously funny, romantic first novel about the trials and tribulations of being single – and female.

THE SECRET DIARY OF ANNE BOLEYN by Robin Maxwell
£5.99 * 0 75281 550 4

The newly crowned Queen Elizabeth I is given a diary written by her mother Anne Boleyn – and makes a resolution that will change the course of history. In her timeless story of love, power, politics and treachery, Robin Maxwell not only brings the two queens to life, but all of bloody Tudor England as well.

ALL SHE WAS WORTH by Miyuki Miyabe
£5.99 * 0 7528I 555 5

An engrossing, clever mystery set in contemporary Japan involving a search for two women caught in a nightmare labyrinth of debt.

RUNNING THE RISK by Christina Jones
£5.99 * 0 75280 928 8

When tall, fair and hunky Rory Faulkner walks into Georgia Drummond's life, she begins to ask herself whether there is a connection between Rory and the much larger haulage firm which seems intent on stealing their business. A sizzling story of sex, suspense and intrigue from the bestselling Christina Jones.

STEALING THE SHOW by Christina Jones
£5.99 * 0 7528I 605 5

When Nell buys a dilapidated merry-go-round with carved horses and an organ she takes on a lot more than she bargained for. Her brothers, who run the family fairground business, are horrified and her fiancé furious – especially when he realises that the gallopers come complete with a handsome restorer . . . A warm, funny, romantic novel by the author of *Running the Risk* and *Going the Distance*.

ROCK N ROLL BABES FROM OUTER SPACE
by Linda Jaivin
£5.99 * 0 7528I 426 5

When Baby, Doll and Lati, three spunky alien babes, abduct Jake, a minor rock star and dread-headed charmer, and toss him in their saucer's sexual experimentation chamber, the global warming begins. A hilarious erotic romp by the author of *Eat Me*. The big bang was never so much fun.

WHO'S BEEN SLEEPING IN MY BED?
by Emma Davison
£5.99 * 0 7528I 44I 9

If you lived in Kensal Rise and worked for a posh estate agent in Notting Hill, might you not occasionally use the properties you were selling as though they were your own? This is what Martin does. Until one day a body turns up that has Martin's prints all over it . . . A sexy, sassy thriller from the author of *Catwalk*.

SOHO BLUES by Neil Blackmore
£6.99 * 0 75281 425 7

A haunting first novel of love found and lost - and found again in a different form. The austere fifties are ending when Betty breezes through the door of the Hudson Café in London's Soho, smack into the life of Harry Hudson who falls for her hook, line and sinker. Betty is the object of Harry's dreams, yet if he'd only known what had happened before he met her . . .

SPLIT MY HEART by Neil Blackmore
£6.99 * 0 75282 134 2

Damascus, 1945. When Marina discovers that her husband is having an affair with his Arab researcher Sulayman, three lives spiral into emotional crisis, jealousy and betrayal. Moving away from the grainy, jazz-drenched London of *Soho Blues*, Neil Blackmore focuses on the vast, sparse grandeur of the sun-baked desert fringe and three people in turmoil.

WHO KILLED MARILYN MONROE? by Liz Evans
£5.99 * 0 75280 914 8

Introducing PI Grace Smith. Set in a down-at-heel English seaside town, this bracing, funny crime novel begins with the murder of Marilyn Monroe, a beach donkey found with its throat slit in a deserted outhouse. PI Grace Smith, too broke to be selective when it comes to work, is called in by the donkey's owner to investigate this bizarre crime – and finds herself drawn into the investigation of another murder . . .

JFK IS MISSING! by Liz Evans
£6.99 * 0 75281 436 2

PI Grace Smith is asked to find a missing person. But her blind client Henry Summerstone has no idea of the name of the young jogger who used to talk to him on his solitary walks, or what she looks like; in fact, he's not even sure that she is missing. But he's offering cash – an offer Grace finds hard to turn down. . .